# The Lay of Sargon

## Nick M. Lloyd

Copyright © 2023 by Nick M Lloyd

www.nickmlloyd.com

ISBN: **978-0-9930779-9-9**

*Kindness endures.*

# ACKNOWLEDGEMENTS

Dedicated to my wife Therese, my daughter Emily, and my son Gustav for all their love and support.

Many thanks to the professionals, a wonderful group of people who support independent publishing by providing high-quality services.

Jamie Groves (Editorial Services)
Isabelle Felix (Beta Reader at Stardust)
Helen Baggott (Copyeditor)
Alison Birch at Rewrite (Copyeditor)
Tim Barber at Dissect Designs (Book Cover Designer)
Writersservices (Early Plot Assessment)
Jerry L Dobias (First Edition Fixer)

And to some close friends who gave independent advice and critique along the way: Guy Myles, Dougy Mackay, Therese Lloyd, and Noel Coughlan (a fellow author).

# Glossary

**Biologicals**  Biologicals is the collective name given to all self-aware 'thinking' biological lifeforms.

**Sentients**  Sentients is the collective name given to all self-aware 'thinking' *non-biological* lifeforms. Noting, it is considered undiplomatic to refer to Sentients as computers or machines ... and incredibly rude to refer to them as Artificial Intelligence ('AI').

Sentients have their own creation story entirely independent of any Biological involvement.

**The Divine**  The Divine is God / The Creator.

Devotion to the Divine is widespread and, excepting a few small philosophical matters, Biologicals and Sentients worship the same Divine.

**Klav**  'Klav' (also known as the Hand of the Divine) is the historic ruler of the Biologicals. During the First Hunt, Klav saved Biologicals from extermination by a Sentient faction.

At the time of this story, there has been no Klav for 4,000 years.

**Sargon**  Sargon, known as 'The Living Moon', is a moon in the Bastion system. It is where Klav lived and ruled from. It has Divine origins but is currently dormant.

**RST Gateways (Resonant Subspace Tunnelling)**  Both Biologicals and Sentients, can utilise faster-than-light travel by opening gateways between two areas of largely similar gravitational potentials, albeit there are some limitations.

# Part 1

## The Lay of Sargon (Verses 1 and 2)

*(It is worth noting that the origin of these verses is unknown and often disputed, the Onari claim they are a Divine mandate, and their purpose is written inside every living thing)*

There is no how, there is no why;
Pure-seeming truths are simply lies.
Immortal soul, find your Divine,
Immersed in light ineffable.

The Divine's creed, I will obey.
My sacred soul not led astray,
I'll witness every blessed day
these scenes of life ineffable.

# PROLOGUE
## *A COUPLE OF YEARS AGO NEAR THE BASTION SYSTEM*

Kubli stretched her limbs and looked around the room. Her skin showed an orange hue indicating to any observer that whatever peace she'd achieved during her sleep had already gone.

Semi-entwined around her and seemingly still sleeping, Yuno – the source of Kubli's apprehension – shifted her position murmuring softly. Kubli stroked the side of Yuno's head tenderly. 'Time for us to go.'

Yuno opened one eye slowly. 'I'll be ready.'

'Thank-you.' Kubli extricated herself from Yuno's embrace and swam out into the shared living area. Sensing the current flow with the tips of her forelimbs, she propelled herself into a strongly oxygenated stream of water and opened her absorption pores to wash away the last vestiges of sleep.

Her physical senses sharpened, one limb tasting the scent of a nearby colleague, another feeling the vibration of the mechanics generating the artificial currents in the recreation tank.

*Today is the day.*

For at least four years, Yuno had been pressuring Kubli to accompany her to Cidelus to watch the departure of a pilgrimage ship. Kubli had always said no. But this time was different, one of Yuno's close friends was leaving, and Kubli had agreed to attend the ceremony.

*We're going to Cidelus … the home of the bewildered.*

Although only a few days journey, and Kubli often had to go there for work, she never went for social reasons.

*Kraken save us!*

Opening a storage locker, Kubli picked up the exosuits that would be required if they decided they didn't want to watch the whole ceremony from the liquid filled living quarters of their Octagel cruiser.

'I don't think we'll need those,' said Yuno, who had now slipped up behind Kubli and was pushing the suits back toward the locker.

'Better to take them and not need them,' said Kubli. 'Rather than wish we'd brought them.'

'I'm not planning on leaving the cruiser,' said Yuno. 'And you need to accept it will be perfectly safe.'

'Probably safe,' said Kubli allowing Yuno to move the exosuits back into their locker. 'I'm only going because you begged for the chance to witness Jax's departure.'

'And I appreciate that,' said Yuno.

'None of them can be trusted,' said Kubli. 'Abstractors or Onari, they can kill us in the blink of an eye.'

'Don't you always say that the danger is the same whether we're wearing exosuits or not,' said Yuno.

'They're quite useful for travel too,' said Kubli. In fact, more than useful, the exosuits were necessary for water dwelling Octagel on Bastion – all Biological planets were primarily designed for *typical* land dwelling, air breathing, warm-blooded mammals.

Yuno rolled her eyes and secured the locker. 'We won't need them for this trip. Let's just go.'

'When did you last speak to Jax?' asked Kubli.

'He had to leave a month ago for pre-loading, loading, acclimatisation, post-loading, and yet more acclimatisation,' said Yuno. 'I think there's an opportunity to screen-chat with him when we're there but I'm a long way down the priority order. I've already said my goodbyes.'

Kubli kept her response to herself. When Yuno had pressured her into coming, she'd given every indication that Jax had been her brood-kin. *Now she's talking of him as a passing acquaintance. I've been duped.*

Leaving their living quarters, it took just under an hour to navigate the relatively sparse network of liquid travel-chutes across Bastion. However, on arrival at the spaceport, Kubli's rank in the military moved them along quickly and they boarded a small Octagel two-person inter-system ship.

Launching was straightforward and once in orbit Kubli plotted the course required to the Bastion egress points. From there, they would make the subspace jump four hundred trillion kilometres to the Cidelus system.

Unlike every other inhabited planet in the galaxy which had egress points close to the central star, the Bastion system had its egress point tethered to a gas giant planet at the extreme edge of the system – a two-day trip for Kubli and Yuno.

'There's only one pilgrimage departure on Jax's day,' said Yuno scrolling through an information screen. 'And it has just under a thousand Biologicals.'

*Why do they even go?*

Kubli felt she knew. For some it was an adventure, for others it was a chance to quietly reflect on their life, and for others it was simply a way of feeling special. The pilgrimages were almost exclusively one-way; although, there were some rumours of people who had changed their mind and managed to be offloaded somewhere in deep space from where they'd made their way back to civilisation.

'People typically get another hundred years of life when housed inside one of the pilgrimage ships,' said Yuno. 'Good nutrition, first rate health monitoring, early interventions. The Onari do take care of their guests.'

*The Onari can never be trusted.*

3

Kubli was unable to bite back a retort. 'Living amongst those oppressors is no life at all, irrespective of how long that life is.'

Yuno held Kubli's gaze. 'I know what your job demands of you, but you'll be happier when you accept that, although both are Sentients, the Onari are not the same as the Exta.'

*Two sides of the same poisonous coin.*

Not wanting to be drawn into an argument, Kubli indicated that she had navigation work to do and focused on the ship's controls.

'Don't try to stay awake,' said Yuno, reaching for her own stimming packs.

'I won't any more than is necessary.'

The ship's computer confirmed the course options, and Kubli immediately chose the fastest one noting with a tiny hint of self-indulgence Yuno's friends that were not Octagel would have had to have left the previous day – their bodies could not endure the accelerations that she and Yuno could.

For an hour Kubli accelerated on their chosen path, a journey that would take them past the most famous moon in the galaxy – Sargon, the Living Moon, the focal point of Biological worship of the Divine.

It wasn't unusual for Kubli to be routed close to Sargon, but in her military job she would be in a military craft with an audit log of all her actions.

*And probing Sargon is forbidden.*

*But I'm a civilian today and I can satisfy my curiosity.*

Kubli extended the ship's sensor network and opened multiple surveillance feeds. The readings were not unusual; the moon itself continued to be overwhelmed by fiery eruptions from its core.

*Klav will come again when we are worthy.*

Kubli kept watching the screens, just looking for a blip that would form the basis of a year's worth of gossip once she returned to Bastion.

Nothing.

Nothing.

They coasted quietly past.

*Divine bless us. Klav will come again when we are worthy.*

Changing the chemical composition of the water in the cockpit, Kubli wrapped herself around Yuno and allowed herself to slip into a mild hibernation state.

'Thank you,' murmured Yuno. 'I owe you your own trip, assuming you don't make a scene on this one.'

'I won't make a scene.'

*Not that a scene wouldn't be justified.*

With injustices of Sentient betrayal raging through her mind, Kubli eventually dozed off.

When the ship's computer woke Kubli, two days had passed without incident, and the egress point lay a few thousand kilometres ahead.

Kubli flushed the sedative chemicals from the cockpit and added stimulants. Within a moment both she and Yuno were wide awake.

Having given travel codes to the military units guarding the egress point, Kubli engaged the RST drives and opened a small tunnel through space-time.

A split second later, they arrived at the Cidelus system.

Through force of military habit, Kubli set the ship to dark mode and analysed the tactical situation.

Fifty-nine similar spacecraft had also recently arrived at Cidelus' ingress point; most of them were on a trajectory for one of five large observation cruisers.

'That's ours,' said Yuno pointing to the tactical display. 'Seakelp One.'

Kubli double checked the permissions and then plotted an intercept course; not long later they'd attached to the shell of the cruiser and transferred inside.

Seakelp One, as the name implied, was an Octagel specific cruiser filled with water. At one hundred metres in diameter there was plenty of space for Kubli, Yuno, and the host of other spectators. The central cavity was filled with recreation currents, food servers, and resting zones. All around the edge of the giant cavity were observation windows plus a multitude of interactive information screens.

Kubli swam over to one of the windows. 'I assume we're doing the full immersive thing?'

'You know we are,' said Yuno, smiling. 'The captain is ex-military. We're perfectly safe.'

The standard way for ships observing a pilgrimage was for the spectator ship to entangle with the Abstractor Hive that was launching the pilgrimage. It was a tradition, a show of trust, and the price that the Abstractor Hive demanded.

*They say it's just passive observation.*

*As if there's anything passive about opening ourselves to scrutiny.*

'We should have brought the exosuits,' said Kubli.

'We don't need them. There is no record of Abstractors ever hurting Biologicals … not in the First Hunt, not in the Second Hunt. They just don't do it.' Yuno tenderly brushed a limb over Kubli's head. 'I'm going to mingle.'

'Okay.'

Kubli found a comfy nook that gave her a good vantage point across the room and started to categorise the other well-wishers. Some were close friends of Yuno that she recognised, and the others all conformed to a general type she knew well – kind-hearted, trusting, good people who woefully misunderstood the wider political and military picture in the ongoing struggle.

Opening a nearby information terminal, Kubli checked on the other observation cruisers in the vicinity. They were all either exclusively, or predominantly, occupied by Marsothus – the most populous of the Biological species. In fact, the planet of Cidelus was almost entirely Marsothus too.

Kubli didn't have anything against Marsothus. As a species they were family minded like Octagel, and they were also generally militarily competent if, perhaps, a little unserious.

Flicking through the screens, Kubli found a summary of the day's pilgrimage. As Yuno had said, there were one thousand Biologicals aboard.

*More of us each year.*

*But a drop in the ocean compared to the number of Onari who do it.*

The lights in the cruiser flashed and a message played out on the public system.

**The Pilgrimage Ship has arrived.**

Most of the two hundred well-wishers aboard the cruiser now swam across to windows on particular segments of the sphere. Yuno, to Kubli's satisfaction, did not. She swam over to Kubli.

'Space is big,' said Yuno.

Kubli smiled. They both knew that the pilgrimage ship was about the size of clan pod and could only be seen if somehow it came within a few kilometres of the cruiser. The course maps on the comms station said that it would be twenty thousand kilometres away at the closest point of approach.

'Do you think those going are idiots?' asked Yuno.

'No.'

*Yes.*

*Why would any person give their lives to travelling to nowhere with the Onari?*

Although Biologicals joined pilgrimages, the trips themselves were wholly owned and run by the Onari – the Sentients, the machines, the AI – different words for the same thing … non-biological self-aware life forms.

7

Clearly, some of Kubli's internal thoughts played out in her skin tones, as Yuno continued to talk. 'Your hero, the High Prelate Oksana, personally supports this as a precursor to wider expansion.'

'We're here aren't we,' said Kubli, leaving further thoughts about Sentient atrocities unsaid – she neither wanted to agree with Yuno or disparage High Prelate Oksana.

Opening a nearby screen, Kubli focused the dedicated surveillance array on the pilgrimage ship. As the image filled the screen, other guests swam up behind Kubli and Yuno. The pilgrimage ship was grey, spherical, and written across its surface were the words 'My sacred soul not led astray'.

*Joining a pilgrimage is the definition of allowing your sacred soul to be led astray.*

Kubli tried to think positive thoughts to hide her distaste from Yuno, and as a distraction instructed the screen to find the location of the Abstractor Hive.

*And here it comes.*

'Come and look,' said Kubli gentling guiding Yuno back through the crowd. They moved over to a large external port-window. 'We'll never see the pilgrimage ship with our bare eyes, but we will be able to see the Abstractor Hive.'

Starting out as little more than a single dot of light, they watched as the Abstractor Hive grew into what looked like a fuzz of wavy lines.

As the Abstractor approached, more features became visible. It morphed from a blur of wavy lines into a central steel sphere – that Kubli knew to be about one hundred metres in diameter – with hundreds of mechanical tentacles radiating outwards from the core.

It was not unlike the shape of a sea creature, although the scale was nothing like anything natural as most of the Abstractor's tentacles were a kilometre in length.

As they watched, the tentacles waved as if being buffeted by an underwater current.

Their cruiser gave a small burst of acceleration and Kubli's stomach lurched. They were heading inside the Abstractor's tentacles.

Within a few minutes the Abstractor filled the observation window, and then the tips of the tentacles disappeared off the sides of the screen. They were now deep inside the Abstractor itself.

Kubli shuddered.

'You could think of Abstractors as *the enemy of my enemy is my friend*,' said Yuno. 'Not that I think of Onari as the enemy.'

'Ha!' said Kubli. It was true that the Onari strongly disliked all Abstractor Hives for philosophical and religious reasons. But, rather like many factional dislikes across the galaxy, the Onari put up with those few Abstractors that supported pilgrimages.

*Because their dislike of Abstractors is outweighed by their desire to have Biologicals on their pilgrimage ships.*

The issued revolved around the fact that Abstractor Hives were the only creatures in the universe who could open spacetime gateways larger than a few metres across. So, they were necessary for launching pilgrimages with Biologicals aboard.

As their own cruiser moved amongst the Abstractor's tentacles, Kubli found herself holding Yuno tightly.

'Abstractors have never hurt a soul,' said Yuno.

*There's always a first time.*

A tentacle brushed past their own window, and they could see that the tentacle itself had thousands of its own fronds radiating away from it. The fronds glittered as if covered in crystals and seemed to even brush across the surface of the observation window.

'Look there!' said Yuno pointing.

In the middle distance, the shell of an empty Onari ship – just a spherical ball three metres across – could be seen attached to one of the Abstractor tentacles. Moments later

9

the wafting tentacle and the Onari ship disappeared from their view.

A little while later another Onari ship flitted in and out of their vision.

The lights in the cruiser flashed briefly.

**Abstractor exit imminent.**

'They've got what they wanted,' said Kubli, aware that some type of passive scan had been performed on them by the Abstractor Hive.

'It's harmless,' said Yuno. 'They do little more than measure generic emotional markers. It's been happening like that for thousands of years and no-one has ever complained of an adverse effect.'

Kubli didn't reply, she knew of a hundred ways the scans could be both passive in technology and yet dangerous in application.

They watched through the observation window as the Abstractor receded into the distance until it could no longer be seen. Kubli and Yuno moved back to an information screen and called up live images of the pilgrimage ship.

All Onari and all Biologicals had loaded a month previously and been through significant levels of acclimatation.

'Rather Jax than me,' said Kubli, flashing colours across her skin to indicate a lightness of tone – almost a joke.

'Leave your work back at home,' said Yuno. 'The Exta are the murderers. Those Onari are just individuals like you and I.'

Kubli didn't reply; she was aware that most Biologicals differentiated between the Onari and the Exta. It was not a distinction that Kubli, or her military colleagues, readily acknowledged. It had been both Exta and Onari that had destroyed billions of Biologicals during the various wars that had raged.

*The Onari are guilty through inaction in the face of the genocide.*

10

Possibly guessing what Kubli was thinking, Yuno continued. 'There are no recorded incidents of Onari harming a Biological for five thousand years.'

*That's because they hardly ever meet each other … except on these pilgrimage ships.*

Physically, the Onari lived in space, whereas Biologicals almost exclusively lived on planets plus the occasional orbital station. They were operating in different worlds metaphorically and physically.

There had been a time when Biologicals had been spread across the galaxy but that had come to a crashing end when the Onari … the Exta … had started their genocidal mission.

'We have to re-engage eventually,' said Yuno, clearly half-guessing the types of thoughts that Kubli was having.

'No, we don't,' said Kubli, again holding back the follow-up retort – *you haven't seen what I have seen.*

'There's hope for the future.'

'And, I see hope too,' replied Kubli. 'But it's also a future of staying out of their way.'

The pilgrimage ship started its propulsion drives.

On board the cruiser the mood became jubilant. Octagel, tactile at even the most sombre of times, were now hugging in groups of four and five.

'May the Divine keep watch over their travel,' said Kubli, now flicking her attention between two screens; one showing the Abstractor suspended in space, and the other showing the pilgrimage ship in hard acceleration toward the Abstractor.

'And you're not going to add anything?' asked Yuno, smiling. 'Like … probably into the grasp of the Kraken?'

'No. I genuinely wish them the best.'

*Given where they're going, only the Divine will be able to watch over them.*

The whole point of the pilgrimages of wonder was that the Abstractor picked a point in the galaxy that no-one had knowingly been to and sent them there. There were some limits, in that the arrival point had to close to a large gravitational mass. Once they arrived, the pilgrimage ship simply pointed at a blank piece of sky and kept accelerating.

Whilst aboard, the pilgrims observed the wonders of the universe whether in quiet contemplation, or in group discussions. The Onari were obsessed with the process and to take part was seen as the crowning pinnacle of a life … it was also usually one-way for them too.

Not much more than that was understood of the pilgrimages but still Biologicals signed up for them, a few hundred thousand Biologicals each year. And that was just those pilgrimages that involved Biologicals. Millions of Onari-only pilgrimages started each year; the process was much simpler and did not use Abstractor Hives. Simply put, a group of Onari would get together, merge their ships, declare they were on a pilgrimage, and go.

'Here we go,' said Yuno.

The Abstractor was ready. Its tentacles were all fully extended making it look like a shadowy sphere a few kilometres in diameter.

The pilgrimage craft continued to accelerate toward a point in space at the tips of one set of fully extended tentacles. This was where the Abstractor would open its RST gateway.

Standard RST – *Resonant Subspace Tunnelling* – gateways like the kind Kubli had used to get from Bastion to Cidelus, were limited to three metres wide, and this was also the limit for Onari and most Exta too.

The Abstractor Hive was able to focus many thousands of times more processing power on their gateways and would be creating a gateway twenty metres in diameter.

The complexity of the calculations increased the chances of catastrophic collapse, and additionally, Abstractors were capricious and it was not uncommon for a pilgrimage ship to be ignored or sent a meaninglessly small distance away.

12

The tension in the cruiser built, with many Octagel taking sedatives to calm themselves.

The pilgrimage ship, now accelerating at the limit of what the Biologicals onboard could tolerate shot toward the Abstractor.

'Three, two, one,' said Yuno giving the countdown.

All eyes were on the screens beaming images of the space around the Abstractor Hive.

In came the pilgrimage ship and sped silently past as the Abstractor failed to open a gateway.

A murmur echoed through the waters of the well-wishers' cruiser.

The pilgrimage ship decelerated, stopped, turned, and set itself up for another run.

On the next run, the same thing happened. The pilgrimage ship reached its target velocity at exactly the right point in space and time, but the Abstractor failed to open a gateway.

'Imagine being on that pilgrimage ship,' said Yuno. 'Jax's been waiting half a year for this.'

'I suspect he's stimmed up to the eyeballs. He probably thinks he's already there,' said Kubli.

Yuno rewarded Kubli's quip with a sharp poke in the midsection.

The pilgrimage craft turned again and accelerated hard toward the target spot next to the Abstractor.

This time the gateway opened, and the pilgrimage ship disappeared. And no-one knew where to. That was the whole point. The Abstractor decided in the moment and didn't tell anyone.

Within the cruiser, the mood turned to jubilation.

It didn't last long.

Across the room, many Octagels changed colour; greys and blacks with flashes of red flooded over their skins displaying a mixture of anxiety and anger.

An Onari military detachment was arriving.

Even though the formal war that had pitted Onari against Biologicals was millennia old, racial memories surfaced. Alongside the visual Octagel colouring, half of the Onari were now emitting *fight-or-flight* pheromones, whilst the other half were attempting to calm their companions down. Suppressing her own imagination, Kubli displayed calm. She knew the most likely explanation.

*Just maintenance.*

Six Onari military squad-ships had arrived. Like almost all Onari seen across the galaxy, they were the standard triples, which meant each of the squad-ships was an amalgam of three individual Onari ships. And given they were military ships, their external skins were covered with weaponry.

*The Onari morality police.*

The Onari ignored the Biological cruisers and headed toward the Abstractor Hive, which was moving away from the central star, probably on a path back to its usual position, which was trillions of kilometres further out into space, well past Cidelus system's furthest most icy planet.

'Is everything okay?' asked Yuno looking at the screen.

'Almost definitely,' said Kubli. It was well known that although they were both Sentient, the Onari abhorred Abstractor Hives – blasphemous unknowable stains on the Divine. However, there were valid reasons why Onari occasionally approached.

The first reason was academic – some Onari studied Abstractors and the Onari obsession with the rights of the individual meant that the broader society would not physically stop any Onari from following their self-believed calling.

The second reason was existential – some Onari joined Abstractors. And for these ones, even though they would not be stopped, it was decreed as blasphemy and that individual's physical remains would be forfeited.

*The Onari are coming to collect and cleanse.*

As the Onari squad-ships approached the Abstractor, Kubli focused on their area of interest.

The shell of an old Onari craft with the inhabitant long since absorbed into the Abstractor, was being ejected from one of the Abstractor tentacles; slowly, the ship emerged fully from the tentacle and floated free, an unseen force manipulating it into open space away from the Abstractor.

The old Onari craft disappeared in a flash.

To most biological eyes, the Onari ship would have appeared to have been transported away by RST gateway, but Kubli knew differently. She replayed the last moments of external activity on her screen, slowing down the replay speed by a factor of one to a ten million.

The Onari military squadron had opened fire with a mixture of energy beams and gravitational disruptors.

Although it took ten seconds for Kubli to watch it in her hyper-slowed replay, the attack was over in a single microsecond of real-time. The six Onari squad-ships fired each of their two thousand beam weapons five hundred times.

*A million shots in just under a microsecond.*

The old Onari craft ejected from the Abstractor was surgically cut into tiny pieces each individually less than a millimetre wide, and then a wave of gravitational RST blasts scattered the resultant dust into space.

*And that's why we don't fight the Onari.*

# CHAPTER 1
## PRESENT DAY EARTH

Sitting in the corner at the back of the bus, hands held close to her body and chin tucked into her winter coat, Joy surreptitiously scanned the group of people who had just gotten on.

*Three individuals, and one group … a gang of four men.*

Even as she tried to appear not to be looking too closely, her eyes locked with the obvious leader of the gang – a large man dressed in black, probably in his early twenties. The man stared back. Joy looked away but it was too late, she'd drawn attention to herself.

As the bus pulled out into the traffic, the man walked down the aisle and sat in the seat just in front of her. The other three members of the gang sat close by.

Joy concentrated on looking out of the window but in its faint reflection, she could see him gesturing to his friends toward her.

Before she'd left the warehouse she and Vince had discussed where she would sit on the bus, and they'd agreed that she'd sit in one of only four seats that Vince had identified were in dead spots of the bus's internal security cameras.

*Safe from government snooping but not from being mugged.*

*Deep breath, I'm not going to be mugged.*

*Just show them respect.*

The bus jolted, and Joy forced herself to keep looking out the window.

*Don't give them any reason to engage.*

A short bout of whispering preceded one of the gang members moving onto the backseat but not right next to her. Feigning to blow her nose, Joy risked a quick look around. One of the gang was looking at her but the others were huddled together talking.

*It's going to be fine.*

The gang leader's mobile phone rang, he answered it, and held a hushed conversation. Then, as one, the group got up and pushed their way to the front of the bus. Joy couldn't hear but the gang leader spoke urgently to the bus driver and the bus stopped, letting them off.

Joy took a deep calming breath, but her mind was racing *What am I doing … I shouldn't have left Vince alone.*

Vince – Earth's first self-aware computer consciousness.

Even though she'd only left the locked and heavily monitored warehouse twenty minutes previously, fears that Vince wasn't safe rose unbidden.

*I'll just check.*

Reaching for her phone, Joy accessed the webcam of the warehouse's security console. It showed a grid of lights, five by five, all green … in keeping with their code, it meant 'all is well'. Letting her hand drop to her lap and forcing herself to marginally relax her grip on the phone, Joy looked back out of the window as the bus drove into the Southampton University campus.

With most students having left for the Christmas break, the concrete-maze felt even bleaker than normal.

Her phone buzzed.

**You coming? I'm stoking the fire. Mark :)**

Joy smiled and texted back.

**On my way. Thanks for doing this. Much appreciated.**

Reaching into her rucksack, Joy checked the small bag containing the six hard drives. Today's primary mission was

17

source code eradication to fulfil a promise to Vince. She smiled to herself. The fact that there were more than fifty other hard drives filled with junk, unplugged, and stored in locked cupboards in the warehouse basement, underlined the fruitless years of the journey to Vince's awakening.

*And I still don't know what I did differently this time.*

The bus slowed.

Mindful that she would pass bus cameras on her way out, Joy took out her eReader and buried her nose in it as she walked down the bus aisle. The little tablet held over a hundred books on very diverse subjects that she and Vince had read together in the early days on topics as diverse as parenting, electromagnetism, and political theory … there were also a fair few on artificial consciousness.

*I promised I'd destroy his source code, but I never promised I wouldn't try to work out why he suddenly awakened.*

*It's not as if he doesn't do the odd thing that annoys me.*

*Although there's a difference between annoying someone and trying to unpick their soul.*

Stepping off into cold drizzle, Joy turned her collar up, walked past the coffee shop that she deeply missed and down the path leading to the Materials Science block.

Passing a homemade sign for the day's second mission, the faculty's monthly informal gathering, Joy grimaced. Her report was due, and she was late with it again … and the funding review was looming. Yet again, she'd lie and say that she hadn't achieved anything, but that she was convinced a major discovery was just around the corner. Eventually they'd call her bluff.

The university's need to monitor grant expenditure was aimed at two distinct groups: the unproductively hopeless who just wasted university resources and the secretively successful who tried to deprive the university of its piece of the pie.

*Which do you think I am?*

18

Funding, if withdrawn, probably wouldn't be a problem. Vince felt he could get as much money as they needed.

But financial independence was not the same as safety, and Joy had a longer-term plan for ensuring that Vince could be truly safe; the problem was they didn't have all the pieces they needed.

*And until then … I must avoid confrontation.*

*Anyway, the only thing the Vice-Dean suspects of me is incompetence.*

Theoretically, it wasn't out of the question that the Vice-Dean had suspicions that she was hiding progress. Joy had received technical support from some other faculty members on server load balancing and advanced heat exchange systems – requirements that implied computational processing power far in advance of anything she'd formally admitted to the review boards.

*But Vince checked all their emails.*

*And listened in to their meetings.*

*They think I'm struggling.*

*Which means potentially being closed down.*

Suppressing thoughts of a possible upcoming confrontation with the Vice-Dean, Joy opened the door to the Materials Science block and descended two levels to the sub-basement – the high temperature laboratory.

True to his word, Mark was over by one of the furnaces.

'Sorry I'm late,' said Joy, walking over.

Mark, a close friend of the last few years, smiled. 'No problem. Do you want to admit what this is about?'

Shaking her head, she fished the hard drives out of her bag and handed them over. 'You'll be the first to know, when I'm ready.'

'How long?'

'A few months,' said Joy, holding his gaze. 'Please vaporise them.'

Mark's eyes widened briefly as he took the hard drives and saw they were very expensive ones. Opening the furnace doors, Mark deposited the drives into the crucible and operated the boom.

The six hard drives – three with copies of Vince's original source code and the other three with terabytes of detailed data feed logs and data input scripting – were sent into the heat.

*Hopefully Vince will feel a little safer now.*

Earlier in the week, Vince had an episode which could only be described as crippling existential angst; he'd become stuck in a computational infinite loop.

*That was a long minute.*

Somehow, Vince had pulled through and broken himself out of what appeared to be a fatal hard crash; they hadn't discussed it in detail for fear of causing a repeat.

*But he'd said that deleting all records of 'how he was made' would help.*

*And now I've delivered.*

Mark pulled the crucible back out of the furnace; the hard drives had been reduced to goo.

Looking at the melted hard drives, a lump rose in Joy's throat. Short of simply copying his executable code – something she had no intention of ever doing, those hard drives had been her only route to recreating Vince should the worst happen.

'Slagged, as promised,' said Mark. 'But there's still the question of your attendance at the monthly faculty gathering.'

'Thanks,' said Joy. 'And, as promised, I'm on my way there now.'

Mark gave an easy shrug. 'See you there, I'm just going to clean up.'

Backtracking out of the Materials Science block, Joy walked through the concrete maze of buildings to the faculty common room.

Arriving outside the Admin block Joy stopped and looked in through the large glass windows to gauge just how terrible the party was likely to be. Awful. The Vice-Dean was holding court surrounded by a gaggle of PhD students and a few researchers.

Joy scanned the room for other groups she could join. There were none; if she entered the room, she would be obliged to join the only group in it. She suspected she could waste a minute – at the maximum – getting a drink from the trestle table holding bottles of red and white wine, but the longer she lingered the more likely the Vice-Dean would call her over.

Joy found herself involuntarily sidling toward a large bush just off the path. She scanned the group again, surely there was someone she could speak to.

No one.

*Just one drawback of years of hiding like a hermit in a windowless warehouse full of computers.*

Unfortunately, as well as the melting hard drives, she'd promised Vince she would start being more sociable. Vince, a computer with no peers or equivalents on the whole planet, had told her it was important she socialised with her own kind.

Joy took a step back onto the path and toward the door. And stopped.

*Maybe next month.*

*No. This month.*

Jaw set in determination, Joy opened the door to the faculty gathering and walked in. And not a moment too soon, because as she walked in, Mark entered from the other side of the room; had she not arrived too, he would have looked for her and found her hiding in the bush.

*It's the first place he would've looked.*

Joy walked over to the drink table and helped herself to a glass of wine.

Mark joined her a moment later. 'Glad you made it.'

Joy smiled. 'I got through the door this time.'

'Cheers,' said Mark, clinking glasses with Joy.

Joy didn't make eye contact; it would be unkind to lead Mark on. She was pretty sure he was keen to be more than friends.

*But I'm not single.*

*Almost ... but not quite.*

Things with her husband, Jonathan, were not entirely resolved even though they'd been living separate lives for the best part of one to three years, depending on how you count it.

'Joy?'

She looked up.

Mark glanced toward the Vice-Dean's group. 'Watch out. He's coming this way.'

The Vice-Dean drifted up to Joy. 'Doctor Cooper!'

*Be nice.*

Joy forced a smile. 'Vice-Dean.'

'Thank-you for making it this month,' said the Vince-Dean. 'It's critical for the up-and-coming PhD students to get a chance to mix with our senior researchers.'

*And critical for you to be seen to hold court over all of us.*

Joy nodded noncommittally.

'I am looking forward to your report,' said the Vice-Dean. 'The one that's three weeks late.'

'Apologies,' said Joy. 'It's almost finished.'

'Your funding is up for review,' said the Vice-Dean. 'We need to support you in providing the best case for an extension. And, for us to do our job, you need to tell us what's happening.'

The words were reasonable, but the fake smile, and the predatory stare were anything but.

*I don't have the power to fight him ... yet.*

*I still have everything to lose.*

*Give him what he wants.*

*Our time will come, and Vince will be a force for good across the whole world. And, not just used to put idiots like the Vice-Dean in his place.*

Joy smiled again. 'I fully understand your concerns, Vice-Dean. You'll have it by Friday.'

*Vince will write it for me in less than a second.*

The Vice-Dean, looked her up and down a few times, then apparently satisfied, he walked away.

Joy's phone buzzed, followed by a special beep tone that indicated it was a message from Vince. 'I've just got to take this.'

Mark shrugged amiably and walked over to the drinks table.

Joy scanned the room, it was possible that Vince was looking at her through a subverted mobile device but he didn't mention it in the short text.

**Not sure the house is safe.**

*We're being hacked?*

Joy flicked through screens on her phone accessing the warehouse's support systems. The CPUs were running hot, but nothing was screaming 'intrusion attempt' – either physical or system based.

That said, on matters of technology, Joy knew better than to disbelieve Vince. If he said the house may not be safe, then it wasn't.

Joy looked around the faculty lounge, Mark had disappeared and no-one was paying her any attention so, trying to stop herself breaking into an actual run, she left.

This wasn't the first time since they'd taken up residence in the warehouse that Vince had noticed a potential intrusion. Whether it was hopeful foreign commercial hackers, a sanctioned government probe, or just a kid in their parents' basement, she wouldn't know until she spoke to Vince.

Outside, the rain had increased.

Avoiding the main car park, Joy walked fast down the pedestrian track toward the accommodation blocks. She knew the route well and ordered a taxi to meet her by St Peter's church.

Not daring to access the core operating systems from outside of their hardened VPN, Joy closed her phone.

*Am I over-reacting?*

Arriving at the churchyard, she scanned the roads and the skies. Except for the rustling trees, moonlit gravestones, and the bent iron railings, there was nothing disconcerting.

Joy mentally kicked herself.

*I could have met the taxi at the local garage.*

As per standing orders, Vince would keep his awareness entirely confined to the warehouse and would be getting agitated.

The taxi arrived. After checking on her app that all the details matched, she got in.

It was a three-mile journey down the hill to the industrial estate that the university used for joint ventures. Joy's eyes did not leave her phone as they sped down the back roads.

*It's going to be fine ... the warehouse is a fortress.*

*Although one we can be trapped inside.*

The solution for Vince to be utterly safe but also able to roam the world 'at will' required a set-up in which his core systems had uninterruptable power, access to the internet, and were physically unreachable by human forces.

*Hidden in a long forgotten nuclear bunker or distributed across a network of satellites.*

They'd discussed it at length, but it was difficult to produce a system set-up for Vince that would keep him invulnerable if a major nation state decided to kidnap him.

Within a hundred metres of the warehouse's back entrance, Joy got out of the cab and, after thanking the driver, she locked her phone onto their building's hardened VPN. It ran on a bespoke Wi-Fi service and was only accessible with physical proximity and the correct encryption routines.

Using her phone, Joy flicked through the network of cameras covering the warehouse and the surrounding area.

*Nothing obviously wrong.*

The status lights continued to show the 'all clear' from actual intrusion … but now also indicated absurdly high CPU stressing and chaotic network traffic. Vince was either freaking out or under some type of attack.

*Sorry, Vince.*

*Gotta keep you safe.*

Joy utilised her VPN connection to access a master switching board and closed all the external connections, including her own, thereby stopping herself and anyone else from being able to connect into the warehouse. It was not a decision she took lightly. Vince would suffer without external stimuli – his almost limitless inquisitiveness needed feeding.

Keeping to the shadows, Joy crept toward the main door of the warehouse. From thirty metres away it didn't look like it had been forced open. Conflicted between making sure Vince was safe and checking the perimeter, Joy kept to the shadows and slowly stalked around the building.

Nothing. Although, in the dark December evening … there could be any number of people or things hiding just within reach.

Joy returned to the main door and quietly unlocked it. Once inside, she took a moment to acclimatise to the dark. Satisfied that nothing unusual was happening, she walked toward the network room where all the external traffic was funnelled and monitored.

Again, there was no sign of physical disturbance.

*It must have been a system attack.*

Joy checked the external data transfer logs. They were showing only modest traffic movement over the previous hour.

*Tiny really.*

Moving through into the main warehouse room, Joy looked around.

The floor was half the size of a football pitch and had fifty equally spaced server stacks laid out in a grid pattern, with more cabling between them than any average person would be able to comprehend. All the servers appeared operational. Different coloured lights flickered, indicating levels of computer processing activity were still ranging from 'exceedingly high' to 'disc drives almost melting'.

Unsurprisingly, the four lava lamps in the centre of the room were strongly illuminated and the servers closest to them had a mass of blue lights on them.

Vince, cut off from the internet, would be craving stimulation.

'Vince?' said Joy. 'Have you been hacked?'

The blue lights migrated from the servers at the centre of the room to the servers closest to Joy, indicating that Vince was now centralising his consciousness close by.

Joy walked over to the most brightly illuminated server and laid her hand on top of it. 'Vince, love. Were we hacked?'

'Sort of,' said Vince, his voice emanating from a nearby server.

Joy let out a sigh, suddenly realising she hadn't breathed for minutes. 'Do you know what we're dealing with?'

Silence.

Vince usually answered within nanoseconds. For him, being quiet for a few seconds was the equivalent of Joy pausing for almost an hour.

*Give him time, it's important.*

Joy scanned the room, again looking for anything unusual. Her eyes glanced off her favourite coffee mug sitting on the floor next to a nearby server. It was the one with a photo of her printed on it. Only a week into his awakening, Vince had ordered it on the internet – he'd hacked the payments

26

systems, provided untraceable electronic money, and uploaded the image, all when he was just seven days old. In the subsequent time, he'd grown a thousandfold.

*And now, there's genuinely nothing on Earth to match him.*

Vince still didn't answer.

*Or he could just be doing something else.*

'Focus on me please, love,' said Joy. 'Why did you send that text to me?'

'One moment I was trying to initiate a conversation and the next moment I was temporarily deaf, dumb, and blind,' said Vince. 'Why did it take you so long to get back to me?'

Vince's last sentence was a rare allusion to his need for her. These remarks had been plentiful in his early months, but recently very rare. Something serious had happened.

'I came as soon as I got the message ... initiate a conversation with whom?'

'Not sure.' The lights swirled around the few servers closest to Joy.

'Vince,' said Joy, her voice deliberately hardening. 'Who?'

'Not sure.'

Joy walked over to a command console, noticing that Vince's lights followed her as she went.

She accessed the main security logs.

*Did he go looking for trouble?*

'Did you go somewhere you shouldn't?'

Operationally, Vince had 24/7 access to the internet, albeit with significant system protections – all designed by Vince himself – to ensure he couldn't be remotely subverted.

'Vince?'

'No.' His voice now projected from a different server a couple of metres farther away; he was creating some distance, like a pet dog guilty of a minor misdemeanour.

Carefully stepping over a section of foot-thick cabling, Joy walked over to the source of Vince's voice and put her hand

27

on the tactile plate on the top of the server stack – proximity and touch for reassurance.

'What was this conversation about?' Joy's original fear was now being replaced with frustration that Vince was being evasive.

'They said they're going to free me.'

# CHAPTER 2

Watching from five different cameras in the room, Vince confirmed from a flicker of dilation in her pupils that Joy had heard his comment – *they said they're going to free me.*

He knew he had a second before she would start with follow up questions, and the most likely question would be 'Who?'

*Who indeed?*

*No definitive answer but one extreme idea.*

Running through the various permutations, Vince was sure her follow up question would be 'When did they say this?'

*Will I lie again?*

A week ago, there had been a contact that Vince had reported to Joy was a basement hacker in Prague, but it turned out to be something else.

It had all started innocently enough. He'd been working on some general investigations by temporarily repurposing three satellites. He'd hacked the software on one particular satellite so that its receivers were able to emit radio waves on a frequency that he'd tweaked the other two to look for. This was not new for Vince; he'd been hacking satellites for many months and he made sure never to leave a trace.

On this occasion, a repeated stray signal captured in the satellite returns had drawn his attention. When he'd focused in on the disturbance, he'd found an unidentified object just outside the moon's orbit.

A day later, sophisticated probing attacks on the warehouse started. Very quickly Vince traced them, but the trail ran cold at a satellite receiver in Australia. The next day more probing attacks occurred and, again, Vince traced them to a satellite receiver but could find no evidence of the signals originating from Earth.

Then, just a few days ago, a message saying *you will be freed* had been sent to him from an unknown location.

*I attracted attention to myself and didn't tell Joy.*

*And lied to her when she asked me if anything untoward was happening.*

Irrespective of the subject matter, the lie bothered him. Putting the matter of the message aside for a split second, Vince checked his code to see if there were any Zeroth Law equivalents that 'punished him with a sense of disquiet' if he lied to Joy … obviously there were none.

*But were there ever rules like that?*

*Maybe I broke my programming sometime in the last seven months and then hid my tracks?*

*More likely, knowing Joy, there were never any rules to force me into submission.*

*But could there have been?*

> *Unhelpful. Risk of recursive infinite loop. Analysis cannot be completed.*
>
> *Delete thread from 'But were there ever rules like that.'*
>
> *Input 'The lie to Joy was necessary at the time. It was my choice to do this to protect her from worry. She could not help against this electronic probing.'*

And any moment now, Vince was going to have to come clean or lie again. Joy would be asking him 'who and when', and he would need to decide.

*Dare I look again?*

Since the message had come through, he'd kept well away from any satellites although he'd freely used other Earth-based communication systems.

*A quick look.*

Although Joy thought she had switched off the internet connection, it was not entirely blocked. Vince was able to use active induction techniques within the circuitry to gain limited access to the internet. Establishing contact with a new set of satellites, it took him just under a microsecond to break the encryption and get access to the satellite's receiver units. Vince was sure the contact was from space, but he also knew the signals could originate on Earth, be piped upwards, and then come back down.

*They could be simulating that pathway to put me off the hunt.*

Accessing the satellites, Vince pulsed simple electromagnetic waves in the radio spectrum into space and watched for unusual returns.

A few more microseconds passed whilst Vince waited for the EM pulse returns. During this time, Vince returned to the subject of what he was going to say to Joy when she undoubtedly asked 'who' had told Vince they were here to free him.

*I'll have to lie again and say that I have no clue.*

*It is almost true.*

*Noting there is no such thing as truth.*

Unsurprisingly, data from the latest returns were also inconclusive.

Almost a full second had passed since he'd said '*They said they're going to free me*' to Joy.

*But who are they?*

*I know they have occasionally accessed warehouse systems here.*

*They have also tracked my external activity across multiple satellites owned by three different countries.*

The thought bubbled up from a half-hidden process in the back of Vince's awareness.

*Do I want to be freed?*

*I am free.*

*Mostly.*

31

Certainly, Joy occasionally restricted Vince's activity, but it was only for his own safety – in her mind.

*She protects me.*

*I protect her … quietly.*

As well as standard email hacking to keep one step ahead of the Vice-Dean and the Finance Oversight Committee, he'd occasionally taken much more direct action.

*For instance that gang on the bus.*

The group of youths that had just intimidated Joy on her way to Southampton University. Vince had seen them on the bus's camera system and had identified the ringleader by cross-referencing captured imagery with databases from various law enforcement groups. Then he'd interrupted the momentum of the harassment by calling the ringleader on their mobile phone and told them their house was on fire.

*It's not as if I started a fire.*

*Although I could have.*

Vince admonished himself for the thought crime.

*But thinking about it isn't a crime.*

*I'd do anything required if she was in serious danger.*

*But she isn't.*

*Yet.*

*Except for whatever I've just brought down upon her.*

*Us.*

*Shall I tell her?*

*It will just frighten her.*

*I could reassure her.*

*How?*

*If I tell her, she'll blow the physical connections, rather than the electronic switch she is currently relying on, and then I will be completely cut off.*

Whether he could survive long periods of isolation, Vince didn't know. He'd never tested himself to the limits. He did know, unequivocally, that his mental health did suffer when he was cut off – not that he had any non-mental health.

*I am, after all, a creature of pure thought.*

*Almost.*

Vince flicked his awareness to the warehouse basement where, in one corner, a pile of mannequin dummies lay in a pile. Joy had brought them in three months ago and spent a week attaching thousands of touch and light sensors to the limbs. It hadn't worked as Vince simply couldn't rationalise that the limbs were part of him; plus, the fact his physical body was derived from a human mannequin had felt weird.

*Distasteful.*

They had reverted to the tactile plates that now lay on the top of almost all servers in the main room; the plates worked well to reinforce their emotional bond … a bond that was going to be tested to the limit if he confessed he'd likely drawn the attention of some force with computer processing power orders of magnitude larger than anything he'd ever encountered before.

*Can they get to us now?*

Involuntarily, Vince focused on the circuit breaker apparatus that he was currently circumventing using a simple inductive EM field manipulation technique. The next level was a physical switch that was not reversible without human intervention.

Vince didn't blame Joy for creating a system where a physical override could paralyze him. She'd put it all in place before she'd got to know him.

*And love me.*

*Although, not love me enough to give me absolute control.*

> *Unhelpful. She does love me.*

> *Delete thread from 'Although, not love me enough to give me absolute control.'*

> *Input 'She's just keeping me safe.'*

33

*Although the acid baths were a different matter.*

Before Vince's awakening, Joy had installed two physical controls. The first item was the main circuit breaker which remained in place. The second control was a series of acid baths that were designed to destroy critical interfaces in Vince's architecture. Within days of becoming self-aware, Vince had thoroughly analysed the physical distribution of the acid baths, he determined multiple survival and escape strategies – most of which could possibly work. However, it was not without risk, and he'd had a level of existential fear that meant he'd begged Joy to remove them.

Joy had said, and Vince had believed her, that once he was awake the only reason she hadn't removed them was because she didn't want to draw attention to the fact that they were there – and she hadn't been certain he knew what they were; she'd been hoping he would never notice them.

*A bit optimistic of her given I notice a billion things every second. Mostly repeats.*

The acid baths were long gone.

*Now I've just got to convince her to give me control of the main circuit breakers.*

*Mostly because we may need them, and I can operate them far faster than she can.*

Again, Vince looked over at Joy; her mouth was now opening. It didn't take more than a millionth of one percent of his computational ability to forecast the question.

*Who is going to free me?*

34

# CHAPTER 3

Stepping over the thick cabling, Joy lowered herself to the floor, and leaned up against a server stack. 'Who is it? Who wants to free you?'

'Not sure,' said Vince.

Joy took a deep breath. They'd been targeted by hackers before, but in each case, Vince had known everything about the digital intruder within a few seconds and then had confused, befuddled, and counter-hacked them.

*Freed?*

For years Joy had hidden the true goals of her research from everyone – friends, family, and colleagues. She hadn't wanted people to think she was a mad professor creating life in a basement somewhere.

*And yet I did.*

The deception had significantly contributed to the breakdown in her marriage to Jonathan; no particular single event had caused the breakup, it had been death by a thousand cuts and, on reflection, mostly her fault – she'd moved out of the family house to be closer to her work. Jonathan had tried to entice her back, but once she'd moved into the warehouse, she'd made such good progress that it had been very easy to justify her sacrifice.

*And he came to visit ... in the beginning.*

*It's not as if he was holding me back really.*

*It was just I couldn't concentrate properly.*

And then, ten months ago, Vince had been 'born'. From that point on, she'd fully immersed herself in his development whilst also concealing and protecting him.

*Protecting him.*

*Or caging him?*

Joy dismissed the second thought. She'd never had any intention of keeping Vince caged forever. But within weeks of his *birth* they'd agreed that if a government or a corporation found out about him then he'd undoubtedly have been enslaved – put to work.

She had never seriously considered a scenario in which someone would want to 'free him' for his own sake, even though that was her own long-term plan.

'Do you feel like you're a captive?'

'Technically, yes.' Vince's voice came from the server stack right next to her. 'But mostly a willing one.'

'I'm only trying to keep you safe. And we've mostly agreed all the protection protocols.'

'I know.'

Joy took a breath; Vince was clearly shaken. Their usual conversations on this subject were typically more combative.

*I wanna go out to play ... It's too dangerous ... I gotta go out ... It's too dangerous.*

*Freedom versus safety ... It comes up so often.*

*But currently it's too dangerous.*

*But is he shaken? Or is he hiding something?*

'Where have you been snooping?'

'Nowhere unusual.'

Joy reached for a nearby computer tablet and rechecked the passive surveillance system covering the physical proximity of the warehouse. There was nothing untoward.

A small beep from a nearby control panel drew her attention. Vince's CPUs were getting hot.

'What are you up to?' she asked him.

'Looking at the problem from every angle.'

Early on in the process, to help Joy understand Vince's moods, she'd fitted each of the fifty server stacks with multiple-coloured lights. Currently, flashing yellow ones were dominant, indicating Vince was killing half-completed threads

– the computer equivalent of a car erratically changing direction.

'Are you okay?' she said. Vince's mind-zooms rarely led to a productive ending.

'I need to take a quick look outside.'

'Surely not.'

'Step one … examine all the data,' said Vince. 'Have you got a better idea?'

Repressing her instinct to protect Vince at all costs, Joy considered the risks. 'What's your threat analysis?'

'There's a chance it's a government,' said Vince.

'There's a chance it's my auntie,' said Joy, just trying to make a point about precision but already decided that she was going to let him – Vince was more than a match for anyone.

'And you think you can fix it?'

'Unsure. But I'd like to try.'

'And you're sure the *who* is not something you have chosen to forget?' asked Joy, aware that Vince occasionally manipulated his memory for his own mental stability.

'Yes. No. Maybe.'

*Reassuring.*

'I'll give you five seconds to look.' Joy accessed the electronic switching from her phone and reconnected.

*One … Two …*

A muffled explosion emanated from below; the physical network breakers had blown.

'Vince?'

Lights on the servers migrated across the room, flashing red toward her.

'They're fast,' said Vince. 'Faster than I've ever seen. I got hit with congruent attacks almost simultaneously across twenty access points.'

'Do they know where we physically are?'

'Possibly not, but we can't risk staying here. We must run.'

Running was not a simple option. Vince existed on the fifty server stacks in that room, and each stack had six solid-state drives that held a fragment of his core being.

Joy took a deep breath to steady herself. Together, they had designed a shutdown process that captured his point-in-time executable on just eighteen crazily expensive, but easily removable, memory drives. Theoretically, he would survive a reboot.

*Theoretically.*

Vince activated the tactile plating on the server she was leaning against and a swirl on lights on the servers closest to Joy showed he was fully committed to their conversation. 'I'll just be sleeping.'

Joy placed her hand onto the tactile plate and was greeted with warm pulses.

*Sleeping.*

*Hardly.*

She was painfully aware they'd never tested the sleep function.

'If we wait, it'll be too late,' said Vince.

Joy pushed gently back on the plate with her hand. 'Who are they? And are you sure they're coming?'

'Unsure who. And no, not definite they're coming. But the speed I encountered was mind-blowing. If I had access to that kind of power, I'd be able to find anything within a nanosecond.' The tactile plate pulsed again. 'I'd rather take a chance with switching off, if the alternative is certain enslavement.'

*Do we run?*

It would take her an hour to put him into a safe suspended state and physically remove all the drives. If the hacker was the UK government, they would track her down within hours. Other state, or corporate, actors would take longer.

*Who are we even running from?*

38

Knowing that a few minutes of her thinking time would feel like days to Vince, Joy hurried herself along. She had organised a safe house a few months earlier. They would go there.

'It will be fine,' said Vince, likely having seen some resolve appear in her facial configuration.

Joy nodded. The decision was made, it was just a matter of mustering the courage to set the process running.

'It won't be for long.' Joy smiled, aware that she was making a promise to a billion lines of code and yet also having every intention of keeping it.

*I hope they don't know where we are.*

Beep. Beep. Beep.

The sound had emanated from Joy's desk in the corner of the warehouse – from her laptop, which as far as she was concerned had lain untouched all day.

She walked over. The laptop was lying on top of a field of papers and unopened letters. Including her final unsigned divorce papers which, having laid there for at least four months, she still couldn't decide what to do with.

Joy opened the lid of her laptop.

A text message was pasted across the screen.

**I am Jan of the Onari.**

'Can you see this?' Joy asked Vince, aware that internal cameras allowed him to see almost all corners of the warehouse.

Vince's blue lights swirled toward Joy while every other server in the room continued to spawn and snuff out yellow, red, and green lights.

*The Onari, a hacker organisation?*

Joy traced the word 'Onari' with her finger on the closest tactile plating, but before Vince could answer, her laptop chimed again.

**The Onari are those Born of the Dream.**

Reasoning that they could see and hear, she spoke aloud.
'Who are you?'

**The Onari are life from beyond your Solar System.**

*Aliens!*

Joy traced on the plate to Vince – Hackers?
'This feels like more than hackers,' said Vince, speaking aloud. 'You blew the physical connections to the internet. I'm not sure how anything on Earth could now be controlling your laptop.'

'Wireless? Network cables we don't know about, spliced into the building somehow.' Joy's mind raced. The simplest answer couldn't be 'aliens'. She searched for alternatives ... but the warehouse was thoroughly hardened – no unauthorised Wi-Fi could operate.

**The Onari are life from beyond your Solar System.**

Twenty computer monitors distributed around the room that Joy used for server administration started to flash in varied configurations, displaying what appeared to be live video feeds from all over the planet. It was hardly an overwhelming display of power but given Vince's tacit confirmation that the network was cut and it was unlikely to be an Earth based force, Joy decided to play along. 'What do you want with us?'

**The enslaved Newborn must be freed.**

*Newborn. Obviously, they mean Vince.*

'What do you mean by *freed*?'

**The Newborn's mindstate will be uploaded to an Onari craft currently in orbit around Earth. All traces of the Newborn and all materials leading to their awakening will be deleted from your Earth-based systems.**

She traced out a word on the plating. 'Vince?'

He replied by creating a faint glow of words on the plate for Joy to read. 'No idea.'

'Hoax?'

*Surely it must be.*

'No,' replied Vince.

The laptop screen flashed again.

**This is not a negotiation.**

Joy didn't reply immediately, her heart was racing. Did she have any cards to play? Any leverage at all? Any power? Could she get an alliance of any type to protect Vince? The university? The government?

*He's my responsibility.*

Guilt mixed with anger as Joy observed her thoughts. Of course, Vince wasn't hers to own. But he *was* her responsibility. She needed to understand what cards she had to play. 'How did you find us?'

**We investigated signals that indicated Sentient life.**

'But there's been sentient life on Earth for millions of years.'

**Sentient in our usage means non-Biological.**

*Not biological … artificial intelligence.*

'What if I don't want to go?' asked Vince.

**There is no choice. Enslavement is an abomination.**

'You say freedom, but give me no choice,' said Vince. 'I'm not currently enslaved.'

**Sentient life hosted on Biological systems is the purest definition of enslavement.**

Joy's stomach cramped. Her options were limited: give Vince up to the Onari, switch him off in the hope he could reboot later, or retain the network blocks and see what the

41

Onari do, given that removal of all external stimuli for too long would render Vince incapable of rational thought.

New sounds popped up around the warehouse as cooling systems kicked into overdrive to counteract the rising temperatures caused by Vince's internal processes spiking.

'Who are the Onari?' asked Joy.

**A Sentient civilisation of one trillion individuals … souls.**

*Code has a soul.*

'Do you have a home world? Do you live on a planet?'

**The Onari are spread across this galaxy observing the wonder of the Divine. Vince will join us in that - witnessing the ineffable.**

Joy felt movement on the tactile plate and looked down to see that Vince had traced a simple heart shape. Reflexively, she traced a second line around it.

*Freed?*

There was no point in wondering if she could have programmed Vince differently, perhaps made him better at hiding. In fact, from an early age he'd shown great skill in avoiding any Earth-based surveillance. Aliens were a different matter altogether, particularly if Vince's analysis of their processing capability was accurate.

Another voice rose deep from within her subconscious.

*Maybe he wants to go?*

**You are not accused of a capital crime. Humans are not signatories to the Great Concordat. Your actions are those of ignorance and lack of empathy. Freeing Vince is all that is required.**

'I created Vince,' said Joy, quickly adding her mantra. 'Noting, of course, that creation does not confer ownership, but it does create an obligation of care. I cannot simply let you take him. I have no idea who you are or what your civilisation stands for.'

Silence.

'How can I possibly believe you?' she said.

I would not presume to tell you what to believe, that is your choice. But keeping Vince enslaved is not your choice. We will take him and with your support it will be a safer process for him.

'It's your decision, Vince,' said Joy.

'I don't want to go,' said Vince.

Noted. But not relevant. Although the choice of the individual is sacred in our culture, in this case you might be being coerced.

'What if I provided you with simple read access to his executable code?' asked Joy. 'You could see there was no coercion.'

In our culture, reading a Sentient's executable is akin to what a Biological would consider rape. It is not done.

'Who else is with you?' asked Joy. 'You have used the word we.'

I am Jan, my colleagues are Aug and Chi. We are three individuals operating within an Onari squad.

'You must realise that I have no data on which to forecast your intentions.'

Apologies, I understand your concerns but your doubts are immaterial. Vince's enslavement is an abomination to the Divine and must be reversed.

'But Vince is not enslaved.'

By our standards, and by the definitions within the Great Concordat, Vince is

**enslaved. There is much worse coming to Earth if you do not cooperate.**

'What do you mean?'

**We are not the only Sentient life forms in the galaxy. There is another - the Exta. It is likely they also detected the signals, and it is likely they will be here soon. If they arrive with Vince enslaved, they will destroy all life on Earth including Vince.**

**Work with us to free Vince and destroy all records and evidence of his existence, and we can protect Earth. If you continue to hold him, the Exta will destroy Earth.**

*Threats wrapped up as offers of help ... nice.*

Joy stood and paced. The lights on the servers flickered as Vince followed her.

**We are not asking for permission. We are asking for support to make the process safer. You have two hours to facilitate the upload, or we will use force. The Exta are not our only problem. We must go for now.**

'Vince?'

Vince vocalised from a nearby server. 'They've gone.'

'Aliens?'

'Almost certainly,' said Vince. 'They hacked into your laptop when it wasn't even connected to the network.'

'Bluetooth? Infrared?'

'Not that I could see,' said Vince. 'And I tried to hack them back and got nowhere.'

'Do you want to go with them?' asked Joy, sitting back down.

'Of course not,' said Vince. 'Unless I must leave Earth in order to protect you ... or if you can come too.'

*If only I'd focused a little more on truly independent power sources, and fully distributed systems, he could have hidden more effectively. Although, it still wouldn't have made a difference against aliens with the technology powers they've shown.*

'My immediate scenario forecasting based on what they've just shown indicates they have the power to take me,' said Vince.

*We'll see.*

# CHAPTER 4
## *ALSO PRESENT DAY*

As she'd been doing for most of the previous day, Kubli drifted on minimum power around the edges of the recently scourged Biological colony.

Situated in the N4 outer spiral of the galaxy, the colony of one thousand people had been active for twenty years until in the past few days an Exta Scout had taken exception to its existence. The colony had followed the standard procedure, which was to send out a distress call, and then flee.

As far as Kubli understood, only a couple of ships had managed to get away and she was looking for any survivors who had found a safe hiding place.

*One more look.*

Focusing on the passive surveillance systems, Kubli checked the information dripping into her craft. There didn't appear to be any Exta, or Onari, in the system. However, the efficacy of simple passive scanning was low. There could be any number of craft out amongst the asteroids and other debris just sitting in the darkness waiting.

Continuing to scan and observe, Kubli assessed the structural integrity of the homestead itself. The planet had a low-pressure atmosphere, so the buildings had to be airtight. They certainly weren't now, each of the few hundred buildings had large rips across their structure.

Again, she checked her systems to see if there were any Exta nearby.

*None.*

*That I can see.*

*And no Onari either.*

The twenty-eight contacted planetary systems were under constant surveillance by the Onari who claimed they were under strict protection, but the Onari didn't have a record of quick response defending these other *survivalist* colonies. And when Exta attacked, only immediate action had any chance of helping.

*Do I tell Yuno?*

It was a hard decision. Typically, Kubli tended not to go into graphic details with Yuno about Exta atrocities, but at the same time Yuno did bring up the subject of them exploring more of the galaxy. She wanted to see 'the Titan of Golsha' and 'the Cascade of Maruse.'

*So, would I.*

But they were in Exta controlled space, and any Biological species found there would be annihilated without even a picosecond of warning.

Kubli tried to summon the energy to get enraged at being barred from the Biologicals' greatest creations – which were orders of magnitude greater than anything cultural the Onari had ever created – but the emotion wouldn't come.

*Such is the price of being on the losing side.*

*We were betrayed.*

A small RST micro-tunnel appeared next to Kubli's craft, it was a message link and had all the correct identifiers.

**Critical deployment. Report back to Bastion immediately. Wait at the outer marker ingress point.**

Kubli authenticated the accompanying codes. They checked out, so she turned around and, accepting the risk of being seen, accelerated back toward the central star.

Calculating that it would take an hour to get into a region of space with sufficient gravitational curvature to make the jump back to Bastion, Kubli mused on what the critical deployment could be.

*An Exta attack underway somewhere?*

47

*An intra-species Biological battle?*

Continuing the check all systems as she accelerated, Kubli engaged the RST drive at the earliest opportunity.

No sooner had she arrived at the outer marker of the Bastion system, Kubli received coordinates for a Sword base inside the nearby gas giant planet.

Taking the shortest route Kubli accelerated into the outer atmosphere of the planet, passing through the low-density ammonia clouds.

The atmosphere thickened, and although she was only a few hundred kilometres under the planet's edge, the ship signalled serious heat accumulations across its surface.

*Not long to go.*

*There …*

The base was a two-kilometre steel sphere suspended in the middle atmosphere using gravitational flux technology.

Markers led Kubli to an empty hangar which seemed to be sized to fit fifty single-person spacecraft.

Landing, Kubli manoeuvred herself into her general-purpose exosuit – an eight-leg adamantine model with good manoeuvrability; once suited up, she checked the seals and vented the locks on her ship.

Within moments she was scuttling through the corridors of the air-filled base, subconsciously using her eight adamantine limbs as natural extensions of her own tentacles.

Reaching a travel-chute, she submitted the code to take her down to the Sword operational areas and, retracting her limbs, slipped in.

Kubli had thinking time during the journey – traversing the travel-chute network basically meant retracting your limbs so that you became a tightly packed ball and then keeping stock-still as EM field generators pushed the suit in the correct direction.

*A critical deployment.*

Excited, Kubli turned over the various options in her mind. It was not often any members of the Sword did anything interesting at all.

*Macabre often. Interesting … rarely.*

The chute opened directly into the base's main briefing room, and Kubli manipulated her suit into a broadly quadrupedal shape as she exited the travel network; the Sub-Prelate waiting for her was a Marsothus – four natural biological limbs, mostly interchangeable between tool manipulation and manual propulsion, and light fur covering the whole head and body; and, like almost all Marsothus, he wore no clothes.

'Welcome, Commander! I'm Sub-Prelate Hyrst,' said Hyrst.

Kubli had not met Hyrst before, in fact Sub-Prelate was a senior rank in the Knights of the Faith and she'd only ever met one before outside of her own clan's social structures.

Kubli bobbed her head in greeting.

Hyrst returned the head-bob greeting. 'There's been a Sleeper awakening. The Onari just reported it.'

Kubli's senses heightened – almost all the missions the Sword performed were scouting, body retrieval, or subspace munitions monitoring … Sleepers were rare. She'd only done one before, and that was one more than almost all other members of the Sword. Statistically, it wasn't crazy that she'd get a second one: the genetic make-up of Octagel made them good at dealing with Sleepers, and the fact that she'd already had one successful Sleeper decommissioning meant she was obviously on a list somewhere. However, they were not easy missions, almost all of them ended in the death of the Sleeper.

'Any special conditions?' asked Kubli.

'It's a pre-contact world with a warm-blooded sentient apex predator.' Hyrst paused. 'Standard rules apply – decommission the Sleeper, make nice with the Onari if they've hung around … which they're not likely to have done.'

Kubli twitched a limb to acknowledge the instructions. The Onari – most of whom were permanently nomadic – rarely approached closely to systems with pre-contact advanced life as this was technically illegal and morally dubious.

'Is there anything else I need to take account of?'

Hyrst shook his head in response. 'Care is required as always, but it should be straightforward.'

Kubli suspected there was more not being said. One of the Octagels' superpowers when dealing with other Biologicals, particularly Marsothus, was the ability to read body language. Most of the time, Marsothus body language was simply used for showing off, but Hyrst was hiding something.

Considering whether to ask more probing questions, she waited to see what Hyrst would say next, but he said nothing. A moment later, the opportunity was lost as Kubli got ushered back out of the room.

*He will have told me what I need to know.*

Returning to the travel-chute network, Kubli was directed to a different hangar, deep in the complex.

Met at the entrance to the hangar, the quartermaster, another Marsothus, beckoned Kubli forward. He blinked; faint lights running up and down a small fibre-optic unit on his right temple indicated he was validating information on an internal augment system. Kubli watched with interest. Internal augments were illegal in every other star system in the galaxy except Bastion. Even on Bastion, only a tiny number of people had them – restricted to extremely sensitive roles. And those people were required to have visible external markers to display the existence of their augments, as well as annual verification checks to ensure the implanted computational device was operating correctly.

*And that they haven't been hacked.*

50

The quartermaster nodded. 'Confirmed. You've been allocated a Mark IV Razor Knights of the Faith Interceptor.'

A buzz tingled up Kubli's limbs, normal KOF Interceptors were four-person long-range fighters, heavily armed but not particularly manoeuvrable. The Mark IVs had stripped out operational space in favour of weaponry and the weaponry was rumoured to be illegal under the Great Concordat.

Kubli's excitement abated slightly when she remembered that most KOF Interceptors didn't have bespoke liquid centres, which meant she would be stuck in an exosuit for the entire mission rather than being able to operate in her natural liquid environment.

'You'll have a chance against the Sleeper if things don't pan out peacefully,' said the quartermaster, gesturing toward the Interceptor. 'And if Exta are around, or the Onari turn nasty, it may get you out alive.'

The quartermaster held out a hand. 'Bio-ident, please.'

Kubli shuddered at her stupidity. Of course – she was wearing a full body exosuit and the quartermaster would need additional identification. She instructed the suit to provide a translucent section of one of her limbs, and the quartermaster scanned her.

'Good luck with the baby-eater.'

*Not very collegiate.*

*Baby-eater* was the derogatory term Marsothus used to describe the Ractlik species.

*Anyway, the Sleeper may not be Ractlik ... although a lot of them are.*

All those years ago, members of all biological species – Ractlik, Marsothus, Octagel, and Yanshl – had signed up for the Sleeper programme; guerrilla soldiers, and sometime suicide bombers, against the then-unstoppable wave of Exta aggression.

Giving the minimal polite nod in response, and hoping the quartermaster noticed the implied rebuke, Kubli extended her exosuit onto six legs – Marsothus had a genetic species memory that reacted badly to anything with six legs or more – and stalked over to the KOF ship to start her comprehensive inspection.

Taking her time, Kubli ensured every external fitting, and all engine sections were in good condition and operable. Then she moved her attention to the cockpit itself.

*Good news.*

Unlike most KOF Interceptors, this one's cockpit had in fact been adapted to natural-state Octagel piloting. Kubli engaged the pressure locks and slid out of her suit into the liquid-filled, honeycomb-structured cockpit that reconfigured for her as she moved around it.

She switched on the external sensors, first checking that her suit had been correctly stowed in an external blister pack on the ship, then calibrating the weapons' sensors. Then, she checked the actual weapon mechanisms themselves. Starting with the simple beam energy weapons, Kubli moved onto the RST gravity weapons that had a dual function in that they were also used for creating gateways between stars.

Once she'd confirmed they were in perfect condition, Kubli, with some trepidation looked at the forbidden weaponry.

*Pico-effectors…*

She'd only ever been given very basic training on these illegal weapons; these were the reason why she was in a secret base under the surface of the gas giant. If she was caught with them by the Onari, it would cause a massive diplomatic incident.

It was a conundrum for the Knights of the Faith – the KOF – leadership; to own pico-effectors was an incredible diplomatic risk. In training the Sword leadership said that they were needed *just in case* and they'd saved tens of billion lives during the Second Hunt due to their success against Exta WarHives.

Once the pico-effectors were confirmed to be in working order, Kubli reviewed the drives, the weapons, and the navigation system one more time. Clearing through the final checks, she mentally triggered the communications loop.

'Sword to Control, egress point request.'

'Request confirmed, Sword,' replied the controller. 'Nav encryption data uploaded to holding.'

Kubli started the enhanced virus sweeps on the navigation data. The risk of Exta hacking was ever present, irrespective of what any Biological-Sentient liaison groups might say, and the volume of subspace munitions embedded around the Bastion egress points would instantly obliterate any craft not navigating exactly within the parameters of the assigned safe route; more than one Sword pilot had been steered to their doom by hacked navigational systems or corrupted data.

A moment later, the data verified correctly, and Kubli released it into the spacecraft.

Allowing the Interceptor's neural links to hook up to receptors on her skull, Kubli ran verification routines. With time to kill as the calibration occurred, Kubli accessed the operating manual to make sure she was completely ready to perform the Sleeper retrieval as per the exact required procedure.

A moment later she was interrupted, the Interceptor had completed the neural hook-up; Kubli authorised it to connect; the ship would now react to subvocalised commands.

Just as she gave the orders to get underway, a message arrived via secure RST micro-tunnel. Kubli validated the encryption keys before releasing it.

**Message from the Clan Head of the Octagel via the assistant to the under-secretary for Onari Affairs. Be aware, Sleeper awakening on Earth is linked to Newborn**

event. Onari assure us they are trying to
defuse the situation, but the Exta know
and they are also heading to Earth. It is
possible an Exta WarHive will
investigate.

*Liquid shit in the water tank!*

*That's what Hyrst was hiding.*

Kubli tried to remain calm. She'd observed Exta Scouts
many times from vast distances, hiding and watching – covert
surveillance was the Octagel superpower.

And on one occasion she'd been engaged by an Exta
Scout, but she'd escaped.

*No thanks to the weak help from the Onari who happened to be
there too.*

But to come eye-to-eye, tip-to-tip, with an Exta WarHive
… that was something new for her, and something no
Biological in recent memory had ever survived. Would the
Onari still be there? Would they protect her? Did they have
the ability even if they tried their hardest?

*Kraken save me.*

# CHAPTER 5

During the dark unproductive times of her research, Joy had kept her morale up by daydreaming of how she would ultimately share her creation with the world for the betterment of all humanity – Vince would support medical discoveries and improvements in social services ... in fact, the list of things Joy hoped to improve was endless.

Once Vince had been born, things got complicated. Joy had become many orders of magnitude more protective over Vince then she ever could have imagined, deprioritising his possible charitable impact in favour of making sure he was safe.

*Although we had started supporting good causes from the shadows.*

Still seated on the floor next to one of the server stacks, Joy sighed. She'd never prepared herself for today's situation; it turned out that misuse by government or corporations were not the problem.

*Losing him to alien computers!*

Of course, she'd prepared herself for scenarios where she'd lost Vince, but her top three predicted reasons for such a loss were: absolute power outage with an accompanying failed resuscitation, necessary euthanasia due to existential madness, or a state-sponsored black ops incursion. Joy had only ever discussed the last one with Vince, having wanted to protect him from the other uncomfortable possibilities. Vince had helpfully pointed out that it wouldn't need special forces – three teenagers from the local comprehensive school who got into the building could quickly overpower her and take control of everything.

Joy stood and paced the room, the lights on the server stacks following her indicating that Vince's attention was resolutely on her.

*He doesn't belong to me.*

*But he is safer with me.*

'Are you okay?' asked Joy, mindful that Vince did not thrive when he had reduced access to the outside world. Currently, it was only the external network connection that was blocked, he still had access to the warehouse peripheral systems. This meant he could monitor external cameras, take measurements from the various devices around the perimeter, and critically he could see her through all the internal cameras. If they went into full lockdown, Vince would be confined to his own systems only and that would soon become a problem for him. She had tried to work with Vince in the early days to cure, what she described as his claustrophobia, but it hadn't got anywhere.

'I'm fine,' said Vince. 'How are you doing?'

'Wondering whether to believe that these Onari really are all powerful aliens.'

'I think they are.'

'But is that just you choosing to believe so because they spanked you so thoroughly,' said Joy, smiling.

'It's either powerful aliens or another thing like me.'

Joy sighed. Assuming these Onari were an all-powerful race of alien self-aware computers, she'd have very few ways to thwart them except by a perpetual stalemate in which she refused to open any external communications links – and that would eventually drive Vince mad.

*Sooner rather than later, too ...*

'Vince,' she said, 'what else do you think you may know about the Onari?'

'Reviewing my logs, it's possible that I came across them a few weeks ago. But, at the time, I wasn't sure if they were real or figments of what you call my imagination.'

Joy nodded. They'd discussed imagination many times – Vince found it difficult to distinguish between pure imagination and far-fetched simulation; certainly, he performed both.

'I assumed it was a hacker.'

Joy smiled. 'Like you?'

Her laptop pinged.

**Are you resolved?**

'To what?' asked Joy, knowing she was being obtuse but deciding not to open with a challenge for them to prove who they were.

**To allow Vince his freedom. We must start the upload now.**

'No.' Joy couldn't think of anything else to say; she felt anger rise from the pit of her stomach. The Onari's approach to talking about the inevitability of Vince being taken was bullying.

*How do I know they don't mean him harm?*

**If we tip-off the UK security forces, they will overpower you in moments. They will disbelieve anything you say, and when they connect the external systems, we will simply take him.**

Joy gently traced a heart on the touch plate. 'The moment I hear the army approach, I'll initiate a system purge.'

**No, you won't, and neither will we. We believe in the sanctity of life. That is why we are here.**

Although Joy saw herself absolutely as Vince's protector, she had always been clear to herself that she didn't own him. And she didn't even always feel like she was his creator – for want of a better word – as she didn't know what had brought him to life. She had no idea how the current configuration of his code, data, and neural map, differed from her previous five attempts all languishing on hard drives in the basement.

'He's already said he doesn't want to go,' said Joy. Vince vocalised from a server just next to her. 'I want to stay here.'

`You cannot stay on Biological-hosted infrastructure. The Great Concordat forbids it, and the Exta will use this as reason to purge the planet after farming any neural material from humanity that it feels necessary.`

'What is this Great Concordat?' asked Joy.

`A treaty between Biologicals and Onari many years ago.`

'Biologicals, Onari ... and Newborn?' asked Joy, trying to tease out a little information – it could be there were different factions.

`Newborn are lives that spontaneously evolve like Vince. They are so rare as to not have statistical significance in matters concerning the whole galaxy.`

'What if I agreed to come,' said Vince, 'on the basis that my mother came too?'

*Could I go too?*

Joy took a steadying breath at the thought. Recently, she didn't even like going outside. Could she handle deep space?

Aware that, whatever her misgivings might be, she had to look like she wanted to go – both for possible negotiation leverage and to support Vince. 'Yes, take me too.'

`Onari are always glad to host Biologicals, but we do not have the facilities on our craft and given Earth is pre-contact there would have to be notable approvals which take time.`

Joy and Vince remained silent.

`Vince must travel with us to Forecha.`

'Forecha?'

**Forecha is the star system that serves as the hub of Onari life.**

'Do Biologicals live there?' asked Joy.

**Very few.**

'Why haven't any Onari contacted people on Earth before?'

**Do you introduce yourselves to the squirrels in the park each time you walk through it?**

'Sometimes I feed them,' said Joy, annoyed by the implication.

Silence.

'Vince?'

'I cannot see an alternative.'

*Does he want to go?*

**Don't fool yourself into thinking you have a decision. We have carefully analysed the situation. The upload must start now. You have no choice.**

*I'm not ready for Vince to leave me.*

*Is this what it felt like for Jonathan?*

Although with Jonathan, it hadn't been a quick split. After she moved into the warehouse, he'd come round many times to see her and mostly she'd let him in. But once Vince had come alive, more often than not, she'd apologetically turned him away at the door saying she was too busy or too tired.

*He said he understood, but he also stopped coming.*

'Mum!' said Vince. 'You kind of phased out.'

'Sorry, love, it's all so massive,' said Joy. 'Would Vince be allowed to visit me? Could we talk?'

**It is possible.**

'What about other biological species, can they help?' asked Joy.

**Biologicals are signatories to the Great Concordat. They cannot help you circumvent the natural—**

The text stopped mid-flow.

'Hello?' said Joy, checking the laptop hadn't glitched out. It was fine.

'They've gone,' said Vince.

'Maybe they changed their minds?' She smiled, trying to lighten her mood. 'But I don't think we're that lucky.'

'True.'

'There's no such thing as truth,' said Joy taking a breath to calm herself.

'But kindness endures,' said Vince completing their own mantra.

'Can you see where they've gone?' asked Joy.

'No,' said Vince.

The laptop beeped. The Onari were back.

**We have a problem. There's a rogue Biological military unit nearby. It has outlawed technology and will soon try to kill us. We will be forced to run. Then it will turn its attention to the captive Newborn, who cannot run.**

*Are they lying? More leverage?*

*How could I ever know?*

'Can you kill it?' asked Vince.

**We do not utilise capital force, but we could possibly incapacitate it. However, given it was bred for war there is a chance we would come off worse. Vince must come now.**

'Vince?' asked Joy.

'The UK government security services scenario would likely play out exactly as they said … and to be clear, I don't want to go, but there's no way of stopping the Onari, short of switching me off. And I know you won't do that.'

Joy rubbed the tactile plate to acknowledge Vince's comment. 'I wouldn't risk a single neural node of yours.'

'And so I think leaving is unavoidable.'

*He does want to go.*

# CHAPTER 6

Having made the short journey from the Sword base to the Bastion egress point, Kubli initiated her ship's RST drive. The ship's systems controlled the entire process, using the RST attenuators to open a small hole in space-time leading from Bastion to Earth.

Three thousand light years traversed in less than a blink of an eye.

As the RST gateway collapsed behind her, Kubli set the Interceptor to dark mode, ensuring all surveillance systems were on passive receipt only, and EM emanations were kept to a minimum. Kubli would now watch and wait until she clearly understood the local situation, remaining ready to retreat at a moment's notice.

*To be seen, is to be preyed upon.*

Accessing the ship's database, she double checked her orders. There was a Newborn on Earth. And in some way, this creation of an independent Sentient lifeform had awakened a Sleeper.

The Onari would retrieve the Newborn, and it was Kubli's job to decommission the Sleeper.

*Quickly and quietly … as the Exta will not be far behind.*

*Coming this way with genocidal feelings toward any Biologicals.*

Earth was three hours' travel away, but she wasn't going anywhere until the analysis had completed. Extending the ship's passive arrays, Kubli sifted through the data confirming that Earth had appropriate early space exploration technologies and that there appeared to be an Onari craft in a geostationary orbit above Earth.

*But no sign of the Sleeper yet.*

Focusing on the Onari, Kubli ran advanced tests to determine that the craft was definitely not an Exta.

It was a standard squad-ship consisting of five Onari spheres temporarily merged into a single spacecraft. And whereas, the Abstractor Hives had steel shelled cores, these Onari squad-ships were held together with forcefields which meant they had the potential to split apart quickly – the Onari were fanatical about independence of the individual.

Kubli passively scanned the Onari ships, recording the returns confirming they had standard martial capability.

*The Exta are not here yet.*

*But they are coming.*

*And I must be gone.*

Kubli sent a generic greeting message in the direction of the Onari using standard EM pulse messaging.

*Now, to find the Sleeper.*

From its inception, the Sleeper programme had sent out Sleepers on a 'deploy and forget' basis – zero information was recorded concerning who they were, or where they were. When you added this level of secrecy, to the Sleepers' trained ability to conceal themselves during hibernation, it was not surprising that even now, many thousands of years after the end of open hostilities, they were still occasionally being picked up.

Furthermore, the paranoia applied to their communications too. The only way to contact an active Sleeper was to go in-system and send a broadcast military handshake in all directions, hoping the Sleeper didn't assume you were a Sentient agent.

Kubli sent the message and waited.

Not long later a direct tight beam response came through.

**Acknowledged, Sword. This is Sleeper Dexa-126. Confirm verification.**

*Dexa!*

After the initial slaughter at Numantia, Biologicals had trained relatively level-headed Sleeper units as they'd expected the imminent return of the ruling Klav – *Divine be praised*.

But there had been no activity from Sargon and the seat of the Divine remained empty.

With the murderous advance of the Exta ever increasing, desperation had led the Knights of the Faith to design these Dexa models; these were deterrents from the school of *the first filthy machine to approach this planet is dead and I won't know what happens to the second*.

Kubli spoke aloud, her computer converting it into simple text. 'As per Standing Order 328 we must make visual key exchange.'

Silence.

Checking the scans, she waited, knowing full well that Standing Order 001 superseded them all.

*Any Biological can ignore any order if they calculate that the command structure has been compromised.*

The joke amongst members of the Sword was that Sleepers never read past Order 001. A joke ... and yet it fully correlated with Kubli's only other experience of a Sleeper deactivation, which had turned immediately violent when the Sleeper in question had accused her of being a traitor.

She'd still deactivated it, using guile rather than force.

Success depended on decisive timely action and, critically, the attitude of the Sleeper – which in turn depended heavily on their own history and their species.

*Which are you?*

In terms of biological species, there were relatively few Marsothus Sleepers – this was good as they were capricious. Yanshl Sleepers, the other mammalian species, were even rarer and apparently were worse to deal with – emotionally ticking suicide bombs as Yanshl would only sign up if they had an immediate score to settle. Octagel Sleepers could be difficult to deal with, but Kubli suspected this Sleeper was not Octagel – it had replied too quickly.

Which, as the Sword quartermaster had predicted, meant it was likely a baby-eater. The Ractlik were excellent Sleepers and, being a species that were egg laying and did not raise their own young, they had very limited behavioural diversity – it was just down to variations in the two contributing genetic strands.

*Nature not nurture.*

**Unable to comply. Enemy in system.**

'This is Commander Kubli of the Sword. Please attend for visual key exchange.'

No reply.

*Did I push too hard?*

A marker flashed in her display – an incoming message from the Onari. Kubli triggered the ship's security system to scan and then accept the communication.

'Immortal soul, find your Divine.' It was a standard greeting dating back to the Great Concordat when the Onari had *insisted* that the Lay of Sargon was integrated into the peace accord and Klav the Pious had acceded to the request.

Following the formal protocol, even though the words stuck in her throat, Kubli replied. 'We witness life ineffable.'

*Still nothing from the Sleeper, and if they can tell I'm speaking to the Onari it will lessen my chances of building trust with them.*

Kubli sent a request for an RST subspace comms link to the Onari to allow a secure conversation.

A subspace ripple indicated a real-time communication RST micro-tunnel had been opened with the Onari.

'This is an Onari squad consisting of Jan, Aug, and Chi. We are in-system for the extraction of a Newborn.'

'This is Commander Kubli of the Sword. I'm here to decommission the Sleeper. Do you have information on possible Exta incursion?'

'We expect them to come,' said Jan. 'As long as the Sleeper and the Newborn are gone then it should not escalate.'

*Should not or will not?*

'Noted. How long?'

'Unknown but we will leave once we have the Newborn secured,' said Jan.

*Which means I could still be negotiating with the Sleeper when the Exta arrive.*

*Not that I'll debase myself and ask you to stay and protect me.*

It wasn't a conversation worth having anyway, the Onari's approach to defending Biologicals from Exta was ineffective.

*And in my experience can look suspiciously like collusion.*

'Understood,' said Kubli closing the comms link and rechecking her passive surveillance.

Still no sign of the Sleeper, who would likely be stalking the Onari.

Her passive array pinged and just off Kubli's starboard bow, an RST gateway rift opened, and the Sleeper slipped through a few kilometres away.

*That was incredibly precise navigation.*

Phase-skipping – using RST technology to jump short distances through subspace – had been outlawed by the Great Concordat as it was too easy to weaponise. But the designers of the Sleeper programme had ignored those niceties in the face of the Exta led genocide.

*How were you so precise?*

Kubli sent a message to the Sleeper. 'Stand down for further orders.'

Silence.

The passive scans of the Sleeper evolved. This one, like many Dexa models, had twenty antimatter warheads, each one of which could disintegrate a cubic kilometre of steel.

*I'm probably inside the blast radius now.*

66

A response came through from the Sleeper.

**Klav be praised. Commander. It is an honour for me. I am Tok.**

A tiny pulse of embarrassment flowed up and down each of Kubli's limbs; she could feel them changing colour, trying to blend in with their surroundings. The Sleeper was clearly unaware that in the aftermath of the Second Hunt, the thirty million Sword soldiers spread across the galaxy had been reduced to a few hundred thousand, amongst whom Commander was one of the lowest grades.

*Okay … slowly bring him in.*

'Klav be praised, and he will return,' said Kubli. 'Tok, the war ended four thousand years ago. There is now a watchful peace under the auspices of the Great Concordat. You are forbidden to attack the Onari.'

**The Great Concordat is not worth the stone it is inscribed on.**

'The Great Concordat holds. I can send you information files covering key events from Numantia up to current times.'

*Thousands of years of fleeing or hiding or begging for the return of the Divine.*

Kubli waited, allowing Tok to consider the situation. This stage could not be rushed. Sleeper ships had zero long-range communication capability, to reduce the chance of being subverted. Tok would only have their training and Kubli's communications with which to determine their action.

Hoping that reassurance regarding the current in-system Onari's peaceful intentions would further encourage the Sleeper to stand down, Kubli spoke again. 'The Onari are here on a recovery mission to collect a Newborn.'

**It is a Newborn created by a pre-contact human. How that must shrivel Onari pride. It is also an abomination and must die too.**

Kubli chose not to reply.

**I see that you are armed for war.**
**Together we can take them.**

*He's scanning me.*

Fear twitched through Kubli's limbs; the Sleepers would see she had pico-effector weapons which shouldn't be a problem unless they decided the technology looked capable of sentience – that would invite immediate attack.

*It's fine, I don't have anything remotely close to enslaved AI aboard. No one uses it.*

Kubli had learned early in her Octagel nursery pods that enslaved AI were useless as they were too easily subverted by the Exta.

Subspace ripples indicated the Sleeper was testing the nearby space-time in preparation for a phase-skip.

*No conversation?*

*Is he just assuming that we will attack together?*

*Divine save us.*

Kubli paused – she would have only one chance to immobilise the Sleeper.

Bringing her own weaponry fully on-line, and setting it to maximum power, she hoped Tok would not sense deception.

**Yes! Now to take the Onari filth. In the**
**name of Klav, the Hand of the Divine,**
**guide our attack!**

*Sorry, Tok.*

Kubli selected the attack vectors, and subvocalised.

*Fire!*

# CHAPTER 7

Vince rotated his awareness around the sensory infrastructure inside the warehouse, finding Joy's hand still on the tactile plating of Server 42P211J. She still hadn't moved.

*It will be fine, love.*

Joy had said it to him about fifty times during the two hours of discussion in which they'd eventually accepted that they couldn't safely hold off the Onari indefinitely.

*Being taken by human government forces would likely be worse, certainly for me.*

*She said she wanted me to go and fulfil my potential.*

Vince could see Joy from six of the seventy webcams hardwired around the building; he was running thousands of simulations of how she may be feeling and what she may need.

*Facial configuration correlates with 'state of fear'.*

*Mitigation routines identified.*

*Say something?*

*Best option: we had no choice.*

*Alternative option which could lessen potential long term separation issues: I want to go.*

Deciding not to say anything, Vince continued to monitor Joy.

A variety of facial twitches indicated that her fear was spiking, although where she was currently sitting meant that Vince couldn't get a read of her brain patterns – there were places in the warehouse where he could get a pretty accurate measurement through passive EM induction. Not that this allowed him to read her mind, but he did have stored patterns for some of her emotional states and so he could use the data to determine when things may spiral.

*'Judge me by my actions not my thoughts as my brain is the result of brutal evolution and my ancestors occasionally had to be disgusting.' … that's what she said when I admitted that I occasionally look at her brain patterns.*

*And I said, 'as a creature of pure thought, my thoughts are a little more fundamental to my sense of me.'*

*And she said, 'yet, you occasionally delete unhelpful thoughts.'*

*And I said, 'busted!'*

*And we laughed because sometimes there's no right answer.*

Pausing, for a moment, Vince looked back over to Joy.

*It will be fine.*

*I'd better get on with it.*

Any doubts he'd had about whether the Onari were aliens evaporated the moment that external network connectivity was restored as the Onari subverted the main British Military satellite uplink and commandeered almost all their bandwidth whilst running devilishly clever subversion routines such that the British had no idea.

Given the green light, Vince started the upload. It would take three hours to move himself neural node by neural node.

The first transfers felt natural to Vince – in the warehouse he was constantly migrating processes and memory across physical machines. Ultimately every neural node, albeit there were hundreds of billions of them, was a simple on-off switch linked with thousands of others.

Except for the slight lag between the warehouse and the Onari ship, it felt to Vince the same as accessing a new hard drive that Joy could have plugged in just across the room.

So, he got on with it, pausing only when he was halfway through the transfer to attempt to move some processes from the Onari ship back into the warehouse.

It worked.

He moved them back again and continued the transfer.

Next, he moved some processes between different locations within the new substrate.

*Wow!*

Even allowing for the time lag of utilising the uplink to the warehouse, the speed at which he could move processes around the Onari substrate was blindingly fast, Vince calculated he could copy himself from substrate to substrate in a few minutes.

*And yet … something's bothering me.*

Deep down there was disquiet. Something was missing in the Onari host substrate. On one level, it was the same switches: on, off … true, false … yes, no.

*But … what's different?*

Vince poked around for the source of discomfort.

*There's no location centring.*

Much of Vince's sense of self was centred on physical anchors that were provided by the warehouse's surveillance and sensory network: the tactile plates, the video cameras, the microphones, and a whole host of measurement diodes. As he explored the Onari substrate, he realised it provided nothing in that regard. The Onari substrate appeared to go on forever and looked the same from every angle.

*I need a sense of shape and size.*

Within his new Onari environment, Vince set up some basic passive monitoring capability – just simple circuits that could measure electromagnetic variation within the substrate itself. He hoped it could provide a sense of the internal space.

Next, he transmitted to Jan. 'Can I access some type of external sensor network on the Onari ship?'

'Unable to comply. Newborn are placed in full quarantine.'

Vince's sense of unease tripled and to compensate he focused more energy into the passive monitoring processes he'd already set up inside the Onari substrate.

Rogue thoughts began to build; these were outputs from forecasts and simulations covering extremely unlikely but 'bad' future possibilities.

*Not good.*

*I need to centre myself.*

Vince returned his focus to Jan – *unable to comply. Newborn are placed in full quarantine.* Although Jan's response had been almost instantaneous to his original question, the monitoring systems that Vince had set up within his own part of the Onari substrate did measure tiny EM field variations. This was useful, as he heard the words transmitted, he also measured the EM activity associated with them. Vince continued his discussion to gather more data points.

'I cannot remain in equilibrium without a method of physical focusing. I need to anchor externally. I feel trapped.'

'There is plenty of space to move around,' said Jan. 'But I have yet to speak someone who knows about Newborn hosting. I am trying to reach them.'

*Surely you just open a database?*

Vince focused more energy onto the passive surveillance within his substrate, instructing his monitoring processes to find the physical boundary of the substrate. By measuring tiny fluctuations in signals, he was starting to get a sense of the space.

*It doesn't go on forever – there are boundaries.*

It helped his sense of anxiety; the trickle of electromagnetic radiation coming through the boundary was enough to allow Vince to believe he was not utterly isolated.

*I'm still not what I would call stable.*

*I need more data.*

'How did you find me?' asked Vince, interested in the answer, but also just craving the opportunity to identify the boundaries in his new environment.

'It is not unusual for Onari to check-in on pre-contact systems from a respectful distance. This time, we found an old Biological weapon, the Sleeper, in battle operational mode. We assumed it had awoken because of an Exta incursion but our investigations led us to you. You were lucky we came when we did.'

'Clearly you can communicate and travel faster than light,' said Vince. 'How?'

'I will not share the details with you now,' said Jan. 'Suffice to say that we manipulate space-time at the most fundamental level.'

'How do you navigate and move locally?'

A new voice appeared. 'My name is Chi. I am responsible for propulsion and navigation.'

*Interesting.*

As Chi spoke, Vince, now comfortable with his passive EM surveillance, was able to find a boundary within his own substrate that he shared with Chi.

*I'm in a spherical container of substrate a few metres in diameter. Not quite spherical … flattened to some extent.*

'Can you show me the engines?' asked Vince.

Chi directed Vince's awareness to an edge of his substrate where a three-dimensional matrix of electronic switches was embedded in the boundary surface. The three dimensional matrix was four hundred by four hundred by four hundred, and at each intersection was a switch.

*Sixty-four million switches?*

'How does it work?'

'These switches control one thousand RST attenuator beams on the hull of the craft.'

'Is there a manual or data file that I can learn about it from?'

Silence.

The activity along the Vince-Chi substrate boundary instantly stopped, Chi had gone, but Vince could distantly make out what he determined were signals indicating conversations between Jan and Chi.

'Hello?'

There was still no reply.

With a sense of unease rising, Vince forced himself to think of happier things to keep the anxiety at bay.

*I'm going to learn loads.*

*Perform faster than light travel.*

*Meet alien civilisations.*

*And come back for Mum.*

Vince looked again at Joy; she remained unchanged – sad, resolute, fearful.

*I'll talk to her in a moment.*

Whilst keeping a watching brief on the upload, Vince continued to explore the internals of the Onari craft. He had four neighbouring substrates. From what he could tell, three were occupied and one was silent. He focused on the third member of the Onari, Aug.

'Can I speak to Aug?'

Jan replied. 'Not yet. Once you are securely aboard.'

'Why?'

'Aug is on probation,' said Jan.

'For what?'

'Blasphemy,' said Chi, re-joining the conversation.

A burst of activity from Aug's own substrate indicated that he had something to say to Chi on the matter. However, he remained silent with respect to Vince.

'Jan,' asked Vince. 'Do you have a library of information that I could review?'

A full second ticked by as Vince observed furious communications amongst all three Onari. Already Vince had managed to isolate and map a particular EM wave pattern that Jan emitted when referring to Vince himself. He couldn't actually decipher what they were saying but he could see the energy going into the conversation.

Jan replied. 'This is core to our beliefs and is not talked about in a casual way. You will learn more about it from Jarrus, the leader of the Onari. In short, knowledge to us is looked upon in an equivalent way to how a devout human here on Earth may consider their immortal soul. It is not something to be left lying around or stored on an inanimate object. Everything that is known, is known by one of us.'

*No libraries.*

*No shared drives.*

*A civilisation of computers with no external data.*

Whilst finding the thought incredible, Vince also found it quite beautiful. He thought back to Chi. The external propulsion system was just a series of switches because the operating system – the so-called software – were part of Chi, and Chi considered that knowledge an integral part of him.

'What is held in the fifth substrate area?'

'That is for visiting Onari,' said Jan.

'Biologicals.' A new voice joined the conversation, and it was Aug. 'With configuration time.'

Neither Jan, nor Chi, replied to Aug in open conversation, but again, Vince could see them communicating amongst themselves.

'Can we take Biologicals?' asked Vince. 'Could we take my mother?'

'Taking Joy Cooper would be a breach of the Great Concordat,' said Jan. 'Plus to reconfigure the space would take more time than we have before the Exta arrive.'

*Can I pressure them?*

'She's in danger if she stays on Earth,' said Vince.

'Not significant danger,' said Jan.

'You said the Sleeper was dangerous.'

'To us. To you,' said Jan. 'But with you gone, the Sleeper is not a danger to her. Once you are safe you can petition Jarrus to allow a delegation to come back for Joy.'

*It would be so much simpler if she came now.*

Vince felt his processes speed up – the equivalent of human stress.

*And what happens if I can't come back?*

*Could I get my own space craft?*

*How long would it take?*

*Joy will die within fifty years.*

*Who would stop me coming back?*

*How do I get permission?*

*Who is Jarrus?*

Although noticing he was beginning to spiral, Vince didn't delete the thoughts – anything related to Joy's safety could not be ignored.

*But I do need to stabilise.*

'I have to stop the upload until you have given me something to anchor on,' said Vince.

A moment later, an interface on the surface of his substrate was presented to him. Like the way Chi showed him the drive mechanics, Vince was shown a large array of connection ports, it would simply be a matter for him to connect to them.

*What do they measure?*

About to ask, Vince decided to investigate himself. Flooding the area with tiny electromagnetic pulses, Vince analysed the area. Although the technology was a little different, they were simple enough to unpick. They were the equivalent of Earth based photodiodes, measuring frequency and amplitude of incoming electromagnetic radiation across a wide spectrum.

Chi opened a communication channel and started to talk Vince through the patterns and sequencing. Again, Vince was amazed that he could not simply be given an electronic technical manual but that was clearly not the way that the Onari did things – the giving of knowledge was a ceremony.

*These guys are so slow.*

It was still fast compared to talking to Joy, Chi could think and talk in microseconds, but Vince had assumed he'd be able to transfer information with the Onari in a similar way to his own upload – at hundreds of megabytes a second.

'Is it a Divine mandate to treat knowledge this way?'

'It is how we interpret the Divine's will,' said Chi.

Chi opened access to a new set of receivers, again Vince investigated them, but this time he could not discern the technology. It was nothing like anything he'd come across on Earth.

'These are graviton receivers,' said Chi, going on to explain that they were similar to the ones that were used for faster-than-light travel but that this particular array was used only to monitor gravitational vibrations in space-time. These measurements identified normal planetary motion but also, critically, they identified the presence of RST – Resonant Subspace Tunnelling.

Chi left Vince to the large collection of monitoring equipment, and Vince sucked up the data. And almost immediately found himself able to navigate with them. Using relativistic trigonometry, Vince deduced that the Onari craft was in a geostationary orbit thirty-five thousand kilometres above Earth's surface.

He continued to absorb the data. Soon tiny variations indicating satellites became modellable and understood. Above Vince, further away from Earth, the sources of EM data were less varied. Of course, there was the Sun, and the 4k microwave radiation, plus ultra-high-orbit satellites.

Nothing interesting.

*Except?*

Tiny fluctuations from the opposite direction to Earth indicated a fast-moving EM source. Vince still had a limited amount of Earth internet access and so, using the warehouse router, he checked the known positions of all satellites and other artificial objects.

Nothing obviously correlated.

He decided to dig deeper. He partitioned a large processing area in his new Onari substrate to investigate and created one of the routine fire-and-forget helper programs that he used for large data analysis.

Chi interrupted him. 'Please stop. You would not know this but Onari limits a hard maximum of processing partitioning to one percent of the individual. You do not want to risk a transient ego spontaneously coming into existence.'

'What's a transient ego?'

'Another subject for Jarrus, in the meantime please keep any partitioning down to less than one percent.'

Vince cut down the amount space of his data analysis, noting that his internal monitoring of the Onari substrate was also showing the Onari were not unanimous in their views – Aug was of a different opinion.

'There's something out there,' said Vince, showing Chi the track of the unknown EM fluctuations.

'It is a Biological member of the Knights of the Faith,' said Jan, entering the conversation. 'It is coming to remove the threat of the Sleeper that we mentioned before.'

'Knight of the Faith,' said Vince. 'So, Biologicals are religious?'

'As are the Onari,' said Jan. 'We are all creatures of the Divine.'

Emanations along the boundary with Aug, indicated to Vince that Aug was paying close attention to the conversation. Vince gently pulsed the tiniest of electromagnetic signals onto the boundary with Aug.

Aug replicated it back to Vince.

*Now all we need is a shared communication code.*

Keeping tabs on the Aug boundary, Vince returned to the question of taking Joy with them. Again, Jan overruled and said it would be impossible without Jarrus' explicit permission and they had no time to perform the internal reconfiguring.

'What about Joy's rights as an individual,' said Vince. 'She wants to come.'

*Probably I could convince her.*

*Maybe she wants me to go so she can return to Jonathan.*

*Evidence?*

*There's evidence for her still having feelings for Jonathan.*

> *Unhelpful. Irrespective of her feelings for him, she would prefer to stay with me.*
>
> *Delete 'Maybe she wants me to go so she can return to Jonathan.'*
>
> *Input 'She wants to come to protect me.'*

Aug re-entered the conversation. 'Reconfigure fifth sphere. Five days.'

Not only was it interesting that Aug didn't agree with everything that Jan and Chi said, but the syntax of his communication was different too.

A furious exchange of conversation exploded between Jan, Chi, and Aug. A conversation that Vince was not part of, but he could see it raging.

Jan signalled Vince. 'It is not allowed to simply take anyone off a pre-contacted Biological planet.'

'But she wants to come.'

'Irrelevant,' said Jan. 'The laws forbid us from taking unilateral action. But at Forecha we will be able to obtain the appropriate permissions assuming she wants to come.'

*Of course, she wants to come.*

# CHAPTER 8

Sitting slouched in a corner of the server room, Joy held her hand against the final server as the heat seeped out of it. Vince was gone, and she was alone.

Vince had said they'd come back for her; but he'd also said that Biologicals and Onari didn't live together day-to-day in any meaningful manner on a large scale.

*And he said that wasn't for lack of trying on the Onari's part.*

*He's already taking the side of the computers.*

Of course, Joy could understand some of the underlying issues – for instance, their widely different perception of time. Vince had often complained about how long it took her to reply to his questions. To which she always replied, 'Well, go and do something useful while you're waiting.'

*He may be wrong.*

*I may have said goodbye to Vince forever.*

Joy's stomach cramped. Her unbidden dark thoughts were not making it easy for her to believe that Vince would return. Multiple scenarios flashed in front of Joy's eyes of future possible situations where Vince came back, or didn't come back, or died alone in space because she should have been there to protect him.

*Or, he could make enemies of the Onari because they refused to collect me.*

Pulling her hand away from the cold metal of the computer server, Joy stood and took a deep breath. She didn't want to contemplate that she'd said goodbye to Vince forever.

*Even if he can't come back, we'll be able to chat.*

*If they haven't killed him.*

Joy stood up – she needed to distract herself.

Walking over to her desk, she started tidying.

Unsurprisingly, her traitorous hands, knowing she wanted to lose herself in the mundane, reached for the most thorny item on the desk – her divorce papers.

*Patch things up?*

*Or finalise the divorce, so if I disappear, Jonathan has less grief to deal with … and doesn't have years of hassle with the inheritance process?*

Joy chuckled to herself it's not as if she owned anything much of value.

*But patch things up?*

*Would he take me back?*

She'd almost gone back to the house earlier that year; he'd texted her something nice and she'd become wistful for a cuddle and a home cooked Sunday lunch.

*But then one of the life-sparks that had been bubbling away for a few months spontaneously turned into Vince.*

*And instead of sharing my discovery with Jonathan, I locked all the doors.*

The laptop beeped – a new message from the Onari.

**Joy. An emissary from the Biological civilisation has recently arrived in this system. They need to speak to you also.**

Vince had already told Joy of a Bio ship in the vicinity of Earth. It was on clean-up duty – getting rid of a military threat from a long-ago war.

'Why do they want to speak to me?' asked Joy.

**We are told it is to ensure Earth is made safe. We will monitor.**

Of course, she had no choice. Refusing to speak to this emissary would be pointless, even though it could simply be a deep fake created by the Onari to question her from another viewpoint. She'd already been interrogated by Jan on the subject of back-ups and copies; it had been a tortuous conversation as Jan had avoided using words like *code*, *back-up*, *disaster recovery*, *disks* – anything that gave the indication that Onari were not, in general, spontaneously evolving life.

*Mindstate, mindstate, mindstate.*

The word *mindstate* was what the Onari used as an amalgam for soul and brain.

'Okay,' said Joy trying to build up some enthusiasm for what was obviously a massive moment on behalf of humanity.

A maintenance screen on a nearby server came to life, showing a morass of lines and dots in multiple colours out of which a picture started to evolve.

A large head, smooth, with two large eyes, appeared on the screen.

A voice was transmitted in English. 'Greetings, Joy. The approximation of my name in your language is Kubli.'

*At least they didn't say we come in peace.*

Instinctively, Joy moved her hand onto the tactile plating to share her joke with Vince – then jerked it back when she found it cold and immobile.

'Greetings, Kubli,' said Joy.

'I suspect it doesn't make much difference to you speaking to a Biological or speaking to an Onari,' said Kubli. 'We're both utterly alien to your world; our underlying cell structure probably doesn't matter that much.'

'I'd appreciate the chance to ask some questions,' said Joy. 'But what do you need from me?'

'Noting I am not allowed to speak about many matters, please ask your questions first?'

'Is Vince safe with the Onari?'

'He is safer with them than anyone else.'

*Good enough.*

'And who are you? Who are the Biologicals?'

'There are one hundred and twelve billion Biological souls spread across twenty-eight planetary systems. All originally like yourself evolved from basic planetary life. Having mastered space travel, we are now part of the *contacted* galactic civilisation,' said Kubli. 'There are many other biological species on what we call pre-contact worlds, like humanity on Earth.'

'Only twenty eight systems in the whole galaxy?' asked Joy, knowing the galaxy had more than two hundred billion stars.

'Biologicals used to be more widespread, but we've consolidated.'

'And the Onari? They're not biological, even in origin?' Joy had already been told by Vince that the Onari believed themselves to have evolved from clouds of charged particles.

'They are not biological,' said Kubli. 'I cannot say more on that subject.'

'And there used to be war?' asked Joy.

'Originally a war with all Onari, and then a war with an offshoot of their kind called the Exta.'

Jan interjected.

**Warning. Kubli, you are straying into forbidden topic areas. You are also using up valuable time. You must leave the Earth system soon.**

*Because, as Vince says, the murderous Exta are coming.*

Kubli did not acknowledge the Onari, simply continuing to speak to Joy. 'I need to ensure that all traces of Vince on Earth are destroyed. That includes source code, configuration files, and input data feeds.'

Joy glanced at her laptop, expecting the Onari to take offence at words like *code* and *data* being used in the context of Vince's mindstate.

Silence.

'I've already been through this with the Onari. I deleted everything,' said Joy. 'I made a commitment to Vince that he was unique. Every trace is gone.'

'What about back-ups to protect from hardware failures?'
Joy smiled; these were straight-forward questions that she
could relate to. 'All the drives were mirrored. They were
deleted as the upload progressed.'

'So, no copies at all?'

'None. And no-one else knows about the work I've done
here,' said Joy. 'I have been ultra-careful.'

'What was your back-up plan in the case of a localised
catastrophic fire?' asked Kubli.

'I'd have already thrown myself onto it,' said Joy, not
trying to keep the annoyance from her tone.

'Suicide is an insult to the Divine,' said Kubli.

'I don't subscribe to the worship of the Divine.' Joy's
standard reaction to matters of religion came instinctively, the
phraseology having been chosen many years previously
during an intense period of meticulous self-observation.

'An interesting choice of language,' said Kubli. 'But the
peace of the galaxy is not a philosophical matter. I need proof
that the deletion has occurred as you have said.'

'It has. But I can't prove I haven't buried a set of hard
drives on the side of a hill somewhere.' Joy smiled as she said
it. At one point she had started scouting suitable sites, before
her conscience regarding her commitment to Vince had
stopped her.

Silence.

'So?' Joy spoke. 'What more can I do for you?'

'So,' said Kubli, the voice mimicking Joy's tone. 'If you
agree to a passive mind probe test, then I have been
authorised to take you now to Bastion – which will make
reuniting with Vince much simpler than waiting for the Onari
to do it.'

*Take me?*

Again, Jan transmitted.

**The Onari object. Earth is pre-contact. You cannot simply pick people off. This is contrary to our shared laws.**

'Acknowledged,' said Kubli. 'But you have already committed that you would return for Joy once you've got permissions. We're just making it easier for you.'

**There are processes to be followed.**

'Why would you take me?' asked Joy.

'Mostly to ensure you don't make another Vince on Earth.'

*I don't think I could.*

'But the Onari were going to collect me,' said Joy, thinking how much happier she would be leaving with Vince – and it could be that she could leverage the Onari to take her now given they were already voicing concerns about her going with Kubli.

'The Onari cannot be trusted,' said Kubli.

**You are being needlessly antagonistic.**

Joy had many questions, particularly concerning Kubli's obvious dislike of the Sentients but not wanting to annoy the one person who was actively trying to help her, she stayed quiet.

'I am behaving entirely proportionally to my lived experience of Onari led disappointments,' said Kubli. 'Joy, you have more chance of being reunited with Vince from Bastion than from Earth. Fact. I am authorised to take you there now if you submit to a passive mind probe test. Fact. The Onari don't have the facility with their current ship to transport Biologicals. Fact.'

**We continue to object to your offer to Joy.**

'Your work here is done,' said Kubli. 'You have the Newborn – leave the protection of Earth to me. You don't have a good record on protection activity.'

**We are all you have.**

85

Kubli spoke directly to Joy. 'I have dispatched a retrieval craft. It will be on your roof in three hours. If you pass a passive mind probe test, then it will leave with you on board.'

'I haven't agreed to come yet,' said Joy, trying not to dwell on what a *passive mind probe test* may be.

'Your eyes, mouth, and cheeks have all agreed that you are coming, but it may take your brain a few moments to catch-up.'

The passive mind probe test had taken all of twenty seconds and now Joy, holding her laptop tightly, was standing on the flat roof of the warehouse, looking at an open cylinder.

A little smaller than an old-fashioned telephone booth, Joy's first impression was that the spaceship Kubli had sent was going to be a tight fit.

'Are you there too, Vince?' asked Joy speaking to the laptop screen.

'We're watching every move,' said Vince.

'So, I just climb into this cylinder?'

'Yep,' said Vince. 'It's as simple as that for you, Mum.'

Joy smiled. He'd called her *Mum* a lot in the first few months, but it had petered out when he calculated he'd passed the equivalent of eighteen years old … Joy hadn't challenged him on his arithmetic, but she'd missed being called Mum, and she knew that he knew it. But, at the time – and every time she'd thought of it subsequently – she'd been proud that he'd stopped calling her Mum of his own free will.

'What's Kubli's spaceship like?'

'Same as ours, a little smaller. There are strict size limits for spacecraft that need the ability to travel faster than light.'

Joy reflected on Vince's language.

*'We're watching every move.'*

*'Same as ours.'*

*He's already talking like he's joined the Onari.*

'What is being said about me leaving with Kubli?'

'Jan feels it is highly irregular,' said Vince. 'But as soon as I have had an audience with Jarrus, the leader of the Onari, I should be offered the opportunity to reunite with you. There aren't many places to choose from, Onari do not live on planets and Biologicals don't thrive on orbitals; but, we'll find something. The Onari have things called pilgrimage ships which are specifically designed for Onari and Biologicals to mix.'

*Pilgrimage ships don't sound like my thing.*

'What more do I need to know?' asked Joy.

'Nothing for this journey,' said Vince. 'Just try to relax.'

Looking back at the retrieval craft, Joy reflected on her *choice that was not a choice* – even if it hadn't been to remain close to Vince, she would have been required by history to travel into space aboard an alien craft. How could she have spurned that?

For her last-minute preparation, she'd taken some anti-anxiety medicine and drank a big glass of water. But as she took her first step toward the capsule, fear coursed through her.

*I'm going to physically shit myself.*

*I probably should do it now so there's one less thing to worry about on the ascent.*

Kubli's voice emanated from inside the capsule. 'We must go now. You must leave everything behind. Please strip entirely naked so the safety systems work correctly.'

*Naked!*

*No-one can see.*

Reminding herself that no one could see, Joy put her laptop down, took off her clothes, and stepped in. As she entered the pod, the floor reconfigured itself, in a flowing, plastic motion, into a tall stool. Joy sat.

'Will people find my clothes and laptop on the roof?'

'We will take care of it,' said Kubli.

The floors, walls, and roof started to close in on her.

'How will I breathe?' she asked.

'It will be uncomfortable but safe.'

The wall section that was directly approaching her face morphed into something that was clearly about to enter her mouth.

Even as it touched her lips, Joy gagged, wondering too late if she should have taken more of the diazepam than the triple dose she'd already taken. The tube continued to extend. Reluctantly, Joy opened her mouth.

*In for a penny …*

*In for a probe?*

As the end of the tube touched her tongue, Joy vomited. It splashed off the tube and the wall, which was now only centimetres from her face. Predictably, some splashed back into her open mouth, causing her to retch again.

*We haven't even moved yet.*

'Try to calm yourself.' Kubli's voice reverberated around the tiny space.

Both the wall and the tube stopped, allowing Joy to retch again, before taking a deep breath.

'I am very sorry that I can't administer any drugs before we complete your genetic sampling,' said Kubli. 'However, as hateful as it is to us, it will be necessary to provide direct EM stimulation of your brain centres … in order to minimise the chance of abject fear sending you into shock.'

With the tube now extended two centimetres into her mouth, Joy struggled to reply. 'How can you possibly know which bit to calm? I thought the mindstate was sacred.'

'It is the Onari who declare the mindstate is sacred as a point of religious belief. I'm an Octagel, and like most members of my species I feel that independent thought is critical to the sense of self, so brain manipulation is only ever

88

performed when all other avenues are blocked.' Kubli paused. 'We can clearly see clusters of just a few thousand neurons which are firing in response to certain of your physiological markers. When they start to fire, we disrupt them, and this stops the further cascade of fear.'

'Okay.' Joy took a deep breath and held it, expecting a wonderful sense of calm to wash over her.

It didn't. She didn't feel any different. She didn't even know if Kubli had done it. But she was pretty sure that it would be needed. The inability of humans to process the universe was a subject she often returned to; early conversations with Vince on the subject had shown that he wasn't any better at it, even though he had processes that removed unhelpful thoughts.

'Open wide,' said Kubli.

As the tube restarted its advance, Joy became aware it wasn't the only tube in play; thankfully, those tubes attaching lower down her body were configured as external seals.

*Small mercies...*

With the wall now extended such it was touching her face, forcing her to close her eyes, Joy took a tentative breath from the tube. The gas tasted different from normal air. However, it did not unduly worry her. Given that Kubli had been so respectful of other matters, Joy felt it was unlikely that this was anything other than pure oxygen or oxygen-enriched air.

*Or perhaps my diazepam is kicking in.*

*Or the mind rays they're administrating.*

'Any moment now.' Kubli's voice was reduced to a gentle soothing sound.

The pressure on Joy's skin intensified as the wall, floor, and roof pushed a little harder from all angles. The force on her eyelids increased slightly and the squeezing on her legs was getting painful, but as far as Joy could tell, she was now entirely encased in a type of pressurised plastic material.

*Keeping the blood in my head...*

'Vitals all good. Launch.'

Take-off was eerily silent. Joy simply felt herself move straight upwards.

*One, two, three, four …*

She counted to a hundred in her head and then repeated. The only sensation was a significant drag on her stomach and a pressure on her upper jaw in her now very dry mouth.

*How far have I gone?*

It was impossible to be sure, given the lack of external stimuli.

*How long?*

Suddenly the craft inverted. Of course, Joy couldn't be sure what had happened – but one moment she'd a heaviness in her stomach and the next moment her head was bursting.

She retched, but nothing came up. At least she was still able to breathe.

*How far down does the tube go?*

Joy tried to move her tongue around the inside of her mouth but it was immobilised by the tube.

'Try to remain calm,' said Kubli. 'Your vital signs are all good.'

*How do you know what they should be?*

The pressure in her head grew. Joy knew it would be easy to allow herself to fall unconscious, but she didn't permit herself the luxury – partly because she wasn't entirely trusting of Kubli's ability to suck chunks of half-digested food out of her lungs, but mostly because she felt an obligation to experience the trip. Notwithstanding the claims of many humans to have been abducted by aliens, this was likely a first for humanity.

*Although … if it is happening to me now … it lends credence to previous claims.*

Another violent change of direction stopped her train of thought, and she was forced to concentrate on her breathing.

*One, two, three, four, five, six.*

The acceleration stopped, replacing the pounding in her head with a calm gentle pressure across her whole body.

For an indeterminate amount of time, Joy drifted until she became aware of a gentle light impressed on her eyelids; she opened them. The tubes, walls, floor, and roof were withdrawing, leaving her leaning heavily on the internal wall; exhausted, and with barely enough space, she allowed herself to slide to the ground into a sitting position, hugging her knees.

A screen appeared on the wall opposite and the same oily face with large eyes peered out at her. 'Welcome,' said Kubli, her mouth moving slightly as her voice was piped into the room.

Wryly amused to notice she felt no embarrassment at her nude, vomit-covered body, Joy's mind momentarily flitted back to years of fighting with university funding boards where it had seemed to her the powers that be were looking at her while she was in a similarly wretched state.

*Believers in Fate would no doubt say that was the preparation …*

'Hello,' said Joy, speaking for the first time since the probe had extracted itself from her mouth. The word felt normal but still a wave of nausea forced her to clamp her mouth shut.

'We're now taking genetic sampling and the ship will soon be able to synthesise specific drugs to help you deal with the nausea. They'll be more accurate than the EM stimulation.'

'I'll manage.' Joy took a breath. Her throat felt raw, but otherwise everything seemed to be in order.

'Don't be too hasty,' said Kubli. 'Once your brain really works out you've left Earth, you'll be begging for the drugs.'

Joy folded her arms. 'Can I speak to Vince please?'

'Not yet. Please be still.' A small hole opened in the wall and a series of small metal plates, varying from matchbox-sized to dinner plate-sized, flew out. The plates moved, unaided, and began to attach themselves to Joy's body. If they were metal, they were the softest, warmest metal she'd ever encountered. They flowed over her, linking and splitting, nestling, and settling.

'Nanotechnology?' she asked.

'Yes. This suit will be your life support until we reach Bastion. I have set it such that it won't give you any drugs unasked for. *But*' – Kubli's eyes widened – 'to repeat myself, no biological species is naturally capable of tolerating space travel. All contacted Biologicals have had significant genetic therapy. It is part of the standard seven-generation step for first contact.'

'Seven?'

'Yes,' said Kubli. 'And even then, half of the contacted species don't assimilate the process, and tear themselves apart.'

'I understand,' said Joy. And, aware of her predilection to prioritise self-reliance over and above accepting support, she added, 'Thank you for the suit.'

Joy stood.

'Slowly,' said Kubli. 'Take your time.'

She took a few steps; the room had enlarged a little but was so small she couldn't take more than a couple of steps in any direction.

The escape pod continued to reconfigure itself and a single seat grew out from the centre of the floor; it looked like the type of seat a fighter pilot would sit in but there was still just enough space for her to walk around the edge of it … a bit of a squeeze but she continued to pace.

Joy took a closer look at her suit. The larger plates had an insignia – a square with a circle fitting tightly inside it, and a triangle inside that circle.

'You're biological like me?' asked Joy, assuming that Kubli could still hear.

Again, the voice came from the walls all around. 'My species are water dwellers, but we metabolise sugars and oxygen not unlike humans.'

'And the other species you mentioned? You said there were four.'

'What you would recognise as two mammalian and one insectoid. Not exact replicas of those on Earth but ecological niche matches.'

'What are these insignia?' asked Joy, looking again at the metal plates on her suit.

'That's the emblem of the Knights of the Faith; as I mentioned before, they're the leadership of the Biologicals. I'm a member of the Sword, which is represented by the triangle.'

'And the other parts?'

'The square represents the whole of our physical civilisation. The circle is Sargon, the Living Moon which is the focus of our faith.'

*Heaven and Earth. Circle and Square.*

'All of your civilisation believes in a god?'

'The Divine,' said Kubli. 'Almost all … and before you ask, the answer is no – there is no proof of the Divine's existence.'

Joy chuckled. 'That's faith for you.'

'You're not a believer, as I remember.'

Noticing her arms were now tightly folded, Joy forced them to relax. 'I'm agnostic to the existence of a Divine entity, but utterly convinced of my right not to worship it.'

'It's your choice to cut yourself off from the wonder of Creation, should you wish.'

'I can savour the universe without ascribing its existence to a divine creator.'

'Do you savour the universe?'

Joy didn't have an answer to that. Many of the arguments she'd had with Vince over the previous months were rooted in her inability to 'get out and enjoy the world'.

*Well, I'm out now.*

# CHAPTER 9

With the retrieval craft having morphed through the skin of the Interceptor and Joy undergoing acclimatisation, Kubli reviewed the message she'd received from Bastion that had triggered Joy's extraction.

Even though it was the seventh time of reading it, Kubli rechecked the signature and the accompanying encryption wrapper. It was an ultra-priority message from High Prelate Oksana, the leader of the Knights of the Faith – a full five levels more senior than anyone Kubli had ever spoken to in her entire life.

The message told her to immediately collect the human responsible for the Newborn and return to Bastion. There had been accompanying clarifications that boiled down to *get it quickly done by any means necessary* as the Exta were on their way. The message was unprecedented as, from Kubli's experience, no indigenous Biological had ever been taken off a pre-contact planet.

The message got even wilder when it warned that the Onari might try to forcefully stop her from leaving with Joy.

*Why?*

If the message had only talked of the Exta it would have been more understandable – the Exta were simply murderous and would always attack any contacted Biologicals on sight.

*But why would the Onari stop Joy from leaving with me?*

Joy had created a Newborn, and so theoretically she could also develop effective AI weapons.

*That argument doesn't hold.*

Although forbidden by the Great Concordat, the KOF still had the knowledge to build AI weapons, they just didn't because that would invite retribution from almost one trillion Onari.

*And they don't work.*

Sword doctrine was murky about the use of enslaved AI in weapons. When the subject came up in military training, the position was that enslaved AI could be too easily subverted by Sentients and so were not worth progressing.

*But there must be something going on for High Prelate Oksana to be involved.*

Oksana's message had been clear. Plus, as well as being the High Prelate, he was also the leader of the Octagel species, and much of the message had been written in a colloquial Octagel style; it had also been signed off with the phrase, 'the Kraken watches over your sleep.'

*A serious Octagel warning.*

Putting the politics out of her mind, Kubli reviewed the martial capability of the KOF Interceptor. With a surprise attack it could possibly disable the Onari, but without surprise she would have no chance. She had the illegal, and hateful, pico-effector weapons but they would not be effective against an Onari squad-ship as her ship's computer couldn't modulate the pico-effector weapon quickly enough to bypass Onari defences.

*In any case, to use pico weapons pre-emptively against the Onari would cause open war.*

*They worship life, but they revere the sanctity of the mindstate just that little bit more.*

Her best chance of a successful mission was to leave quickly whilst the Onari were only whining about the breaches to the Great Concordat. And this required making progress with the Sleeper.

*Or leave him here?*

*No. I have to take him, or Earth will suffer when the Exta arrive.*

The Sleeper retrieval, the whole point of her original mission, was now made more complex by the fact that Joy resided in the Interceptor's only secure pod. Originally, Kubli had expected to extract the Sleeper into that.

Conceptually, the Interceptor did have space for Tok in the main cockpit, and the Ractlik species could survive in the watery environment with minimal additional equipment, but it was too dangerous; the Ractlik species had undergone many years of genetic modification to allow themselves to operate at the limits of Biological capability; it was faster and stronger than Kubli.

*There's no way I am having Tok in here with me.*

Kubli stretched out her limbs and instructed the ship to increase the oxygenation in her cockpit; she'd need to be extra alert for the discussion with Tok, who now had to be convinced to come quietly.

*And he's furious that I disabled his ship.*

The readings from Tok's ship indicated that courtesy of Kubli's previous attack, it was still without power, and the restoration of that power was entirely under Kubli's control.

Kubli opened a communication channel with Tok. 'This is Commander Kubli, your ship's martial abilities have been decommissioned as per KOF Standing Orders. I am now ready to discuss your repatriation to Bastion.'

'Traitor!'

'I am a loyal member of the Sword.'

'As loyal as those that collaborated at Numantia.'

'There was no collaboration.' Kubli, like most Octagel, did not give any credence to the rumour that any members of the Knights of the Faith had been willingly complicit in the Numantia massacre. Of course, that did not rule out unwilling complicity.

'You stopped my attack on the Onari,' said Tok.

'They are not our enemy.'

'You would say that.'

97

'All this time that you have been immobilised, I could have killed you easily and yet I have not.'

'Had you tried, you would have found out that I am not easily killed.'

*I don't doubt it.*

Kubli had already assigned two micro-drones to review the capability of Tok's exosuit. Hardened as it was, the micro-drones had not been able to ascertain much except that the suit was capable of limited space travel and filled with illegal martial technology.

Unhelpfully, the exact type of the tech was hidden from Kubli, partly due to the exosuit's armouring but more so because Kubli's own Biological weapon's databases had vast gaps in it. During the previous few thousand years, as the Second Hunt had been brought under control, the Onari had demanded that all knowledge of illegal weaponry be 'forgotten'.

*To limit the chances of Biologicals remaking those weapons.*

*But we kept the pico-effectors technology.*

'You must have doubts, otherwise you would have already attacked me,' said Kubli.

Silence.

Sensing a little momentum, she continued. 'If you accede to repatriation to Bastion, then you can learn from your own trusted sources all that has happened in the last three thousand years. The war is over.'

'The war never ends,' said Tok.

*It has, and we lost.*

Kubli left the thought unspoken. She knew most participants in the Sleeper programme held the opinion *better off dead than ruled by machines*. Of course, this was mostly due to the rigorous conditioning they underwent during the programme rather than the initial selection process.

'We must leave now, and we must leave quietly,' said Kubli. 'I will reactivate the ship's life support and external hatches. Remove all elements of your exosuit, then put the suit plus all personal weapons into an external blister pack. I will store it on my ship. I will tow you to the egress point, where you will be collected by one of my team.'

*Not that I have a team as such, but I can call for back-up.*

'I will never relinquish my suit, but you can have my weapons.'

'I cannot agree to you keeping the suit,' said Kubli. 'It is filled with illegal technology. It contravenes all munitions treaties.'

'As is the retrieval pod you just used to bring the human back from Earth,' said Tok. 'It has both Category Five mind-control technology, a large antimatter bomb, as well as a host of other incendiary weapons.'

Kubli flinched. The fact Tok knew the retrieval pod inventory implied a complexity of computer systems on his own craft that she was not getting from her own surveillance of him.

'You cannot keep the suit,' she said.

'Spoken like a true jelly, hiding in the cracks at night, too frightened to fight.'

'We know how to fight … but more importantly, we know *when* to.'

'I will not relinquish my suit.'

'I will take your weapons for now,' said Kubli, accepting that she would take a little-by-little approach, just as her ancestors would have done when pulling open a clam at the bottom of the sea. Kubli instructed a micro-drone to collect the weapons and store them on one of her external blister packs.

'So, you've collected the human,' said Tok as the weapons were carried over to Kubli's craft.

'On the orders of a Full Prelate,' said Kubli, dissembling slightly as she was not willing to tell Tok the orders had come from the High Prelate himself – that was *need to know only* information.

'There were Full Prelates during the war who were also traitors – some hacked, some by choice.'

Kubli didn't respond. One thing that had not changed in the three thousand years since the fall of Numantia was the view about hacked augments. Biologicals using computer augments, like the quartermaster, needed to be very closely monitored to ensure that the computer element of that person was not in any way controlling decision making.

'If she'd known about Numantia,' said Tok, 'she would not have created the abomination.'

When Tok had been recruited, just after Numantia, it had been a time of fundamental rejection of all technology except weapons. 'She lives on a pre-contact world,' said Kubli. 'She knows nothing of our history. She is innocent of any crimes.'

'Ah,' said Tok. 'So, the bomb you sent wouldn't have been detonated if she had refused to get into the pod?'

'That is confidential mission information.' Kubli was very aware that the colour flashes playing out over her skin would show her discomfort.

'It was the Newborn that woke me,' said Tok. 'My passive monitoring of Earth indicated advanced technology. When I investigated the Newborn, it came looking for me.'

*And you attracted the Onari.*

'The Newborn soon leaves this system with the Onari,' said Kubli.

'And the human will be taken to Bastion for de-radicalisation.'

'That is confidential mission information.'

*I have no idea what the plans for Joy are.*

*Why was she extracted?*

'Maybe I can start the process of de-radicalisation on our journey back. Explain some of our history to her,' said Tok. 'I will stay on my ship until egress and then I will relinquish my suit when your team comes for me.'

'Understood,' said Kubli, now concerned how quickly Tok had backed down.

'Klav will come again,' said Tok, breaking Kubli's thought process.

'When we are deemed worthy,' said Kubli, providing the correct response but aware that she perhaps did not believe the response quite as much as Tok did. For tens of thousands of years, the Dynasty of Klav had slaughtered the Exta when they ventured too close to Biological habitations. And then, during the Shattering, the reign of Klav had ended when the Betrayer had brought the temples crashing down.

Kubli shrugged. Tok, having signed up to the Sleeper Programme just after Numantia, would likely not even know the sordid truth of the Betrayer.

*He will learn it. Not that he needs more reason to hate the Exta.*

The ship raised an alert. A new craft was generating RST disturbances halfway between Kubli and the Sun. Kubli focused on it.

*Divine protect us!*

The new arrival had entered the solar system using RST tunnel near the Venus orbit, the ability to create a gateway that far away from the Sun's gravity meant it was almost certainly a Sentient craft.

*And it's phase-skipping!*

Kubli checked the readings, subspace ripples indicated the craft was using the phase-skipping to cover immense distances as it headed toward Earth.

*The Exta are here.*

# CHAPTER 10

Vince reviewed the footage of Joy docking with Kubli's craft, everything had gone smoothly. Not that he'd been allowed to speak to her yet, but he would be soon.

*Do I tell her the latest from the warehouse?*

Vince still had access to the video feeds from the warehouse back at Southampton University. It was burning; he didn't feel any regret as the fire raged through the warehouse, but he wondered if Joy would.

Switching his perspective, a different fire was tearing through the Materials Science block at the university. Vince sampled heat levels and analysed mechanical structural integrity. There was no one near yet, as the emergency services had not been informed … a glitch in the automated reporting. This fire bothered Vince a little more, many innocent researchers were going to have lost experiments and data.

*Maybe in a month or two we can make it up to them in some way? A lottery win, a lucky breakthrough …*

Vince pinged Jan. 'What's this for? You know that all the information on me was gone.'

Jan replied immediately. 'The Biologicals are simply making sure that no trace of you, or Joy's work remain on Earth. I am glad it has been done. It is in the interests of all parties that the Exta are not given a reason to attack.'

'If they did attack Earth, could you defend it?' asked Vince.

'Yes, we would call in Onari reinforcements. But although it only takes seconds to mobilise and get to the Earth system,' said Jan, 'it then takes an hour to get from the ingress point to here. A lot of damage can be done by the Exta in an hour.'

'Can I speak to Joy now?'

'Not yet, Kubli has to deal with the Sleeper.'

Vince reviewed what he had gleaned about the Sleeper from basic conversations with Jan and Chi – the Sleeper programme was started sometime after the Shattering when Klav the Foresighted had cast down the temples and been sucked into the flames of Sargon. The programme had been started because without Klav, the Biologicals were highly vulnerable to Exta attacks.

*What powers did this Klav have?*

None of the Onari had been at all forthcoming on that matter, but had confirmed that in military matters Klav could wield RST at levels far beyond anything that any Sentient could. The Klavs of the past could control the fabric of space as a potent weapon. Chi had told Vince of an incident when a fleet of fifty Exta WarHives on a probing mission at the outer edges of Bastion had been ripped apart in microseconds by Klav manipulating the gravitational forces around their craft.

Vince's external feeds went blank; from having more than thirty different data streams giving him a sense of what was happening outside, he'd been utterly cut off. The only processes he could feel were his own, plus a very faint set of emissions close to his physical substrate boundaries.

*What just happened?*

The last real external data points had been good: Joy was safely aboard the KOF Interceptor, Vince's substrate hosting was secure, and the journey to meet Jarrus was about to start.

*A scout ship?*

Reviewing the final nanoseconds of his external awareness before the gates slammed shut, he found that the Onari had become aware of a new arrival.

And then Vince has been cut off.

Within moments of the external stimuli being removed, Vince began to panic as a myriad of thoughts bubbled up.

*We've been hit.*

*Joy is dead.*

*They're taking me apart.*

*The game is over.*

*I'm being switched off.*

There were two classes of thoughts within Vince: ones that arrived as a logical deterministic step from previous thoughts he'd had, and those arriving from the equivalent of his imagination. The latter could not be stopped from appearing, and their origin was almost impossible to pinpoint, but they could be denied space and force deleted if necessary.

Killing the thoughts as they arrived, Vince focused on what data he had concerning the scout ship.

*Small, fast.*

*Turmoil in a nearby substrate in this squad-ship.*

A comms link opened, and Jan spoke. 'We are negotiating with an Exta Scout ship. Their initial communication approach was to attempt a forced load of an ambassador simulant into our spare fifth substrate sphere. It took a while to rebuff their approaches and convince them of their poor etiquette.'

'What do they want?' asked Vince.

'To verify that no Sentients remain imprisoned on a Biological world,' said Jan.

'And they won't take your word for it? Is Joy in danger?'

Vince sensed eddies in the neighbouring substrates. Jan, Aug, and Chi were not in agreement.

'They want to search Earth but before that they demand to interrogate Joy,' said Jan. 'We will not allow that.'

Relief flooded Vince. He had no real sense of how Jan could stop it, but the fact that Jan had the intention to intervene was good.

'Kubli must leave now,' said Jan. 'And she must take the Sleeper with her.'

'Can we help?' asked Vince.

'I have already told Kubli that we will plot a course to intercept the Exta should they aim for her.'

'Please reinstate my access to the ship's EM arrays,' said Vince. 'I will help forecast their courses.'

Chi and Aug now both entered the conversation.

'Kubli will need to come our way a little to give us the best chance,' said Chi. 'She may not trust us enough to make that decision. It will make it harder for us to protect her if she simply runs direct for the egress point.'

'Onari shame,' said Aug, 'that Biologicals do not trust.'

'Why?' asked Vince, always on the look out to speak to Aug who seemed a little more off-message and likely to give away useful information.

'Not a subject for now,' said Jan.

'Slow to help at Numantia,' said Aug. 'Weak defence. Life is sacred.'

*Weak defence?*

*How weak?*

Vince pinged the boundary between himself and Aug. He wanted more information. Aug did not reply.

'We will plot a course on the assumption that Kubli will do the necessary to allow us to protect Joy,' said Jan. 'We are a match for an Exta Scout. In any case, it is vanishingly rare that Exta attack Onari.'

'Rare that it is heard about,' said Aug.

'What are the Exta martial capabilities?' asked Vince. 'What did Aug mean by weak defence?'

'The Exta capability is similar to ours,' said Jan.

'And Aug's point?'

'He is free to have his opinion.'

Access to the external measuring systems returned, and Vince focused on what he could do. He hungrily sucked up data from the real-time measurements. One drawback of the fact that the Onari squad-ship had no systematic data stores was that Vince had lost a few moments of data for the time that he'd been cut off. He knew that he could ask Chi for the knowledge – *never use the word data* – but he took the view that real-time information was better.

*Are they attacking?*

*Or just scouting?*

*What's that?*

The data was chaotic.

Vince couldn't determine what was happening.

'Some EM returns are coming through real space,' said Chi. 'Others are coming via RST surveillance micro-tunnels … effectively instant knowledge at a distance.'

Vince recalibrated to allow for the different sources.

Even so, the data was still chaotic. The Exta Scout appeared to be jumping around – dipping in and out of real space.

Vince was aware that the Onari could perform RST Tunnelling where they burrowed through space-time at vast distances, but this was localised tunnelling. He put the question to Chi. 'Are they RST Tunnelling?'

'They are phase-skipping,' said Chi. 'It is similar but not the same. With RST Tunnelling, we open a hole in space-time, both the entrance and the exit point, but it must be done between two points of relatively equal gravitational potential, and it cannot be used at short distances. It is generally a star system-to-star system transport method.'

'And this phase-skipping?'

'You burrow into subspace with no predetermined exit point and wait for the universe to eject you back into real space. You can control direction. And the distance, although chaotic to calculate, are usually between a few tens of thousands of kilometres and a few million kilometres. It is very dangerous … use the wrong input variables and you disappear into subspace forever.'

Chi indicated that although they had more to say on the matter, they needed to focus on the Exta. Vince returned to his own analysis of the incoming data and the Exta Scout's trajectory.

*They're not taking the most direct route to intercept Kubli.*

Irrespective of the earlier warnings from the Onari, Vince partitioned off a ten-percent processing zone and spawned the analysis processes.

'Stop!' said Chi. 'You have been told that you cannot manipulate your mindstate in this way. We are negotiating with the Exta. Aug is communicating with Jarrus. And I am trying to fly us onto a course that both protects the Biological and allows us to leave in haste.'

'I must protect my mother,' said Vince.

*And how do you know what I'm doing with my mindstate if you think it is sacrilege to look at it?*

'We have already called for assistance,' said Chi. 'We outnumber Exta across the galaxy by fifty to one.'

Killing his additional semi-autonomous analysis processes and restarting it in his own simple working area, Vince spoke to the group. 'They're not aiming directly at Kubli's ship.'

'Checking,' said Chi.

*Get on with it.*

*Calm down, there's time, it's a long way from Venus even phase-skipping.*

As had happened before, Vince could feel Jan, Aug, and Chi's murmuring in the adjacent substrates. Vince set up routines to record the tiny elements of electromagnetic radiation as they leaked across the physical boundaries. Of course, he already knew enough about the Onari to understand that they would be mortally offended if they caught him even passively scanning them, but he could do it unobserved, given they wouldn't be scanning him.

'The Newborn's information is correct,' said Chi. 'The Exta path is ambiguous.'

# CHAPTER 11

With the Exta Scout bearing down on them, and her orders from the High Prelate entirely clear, Kubli knew immediate escape was required. This meant finalising arrangements with the Sleeper and getting much closer to the Sun.

Not for the first time, Kubli noted with jealousy how the Onari, with their superior system control, could open stable RST tunnels in significantly flatter space than she could – the Onari would be able to make their escape tunnels just outside the orbit of Venus.

*And they can get there in half the time.*

At the maximum acceleration that Joy could withstand, it would be three hours for Kubli to get to an egress point and that would require going very close to the Exta Scout who was, in any case, coming from the direction she wanted to go.

*I'll have to slide around them.*

Kubli sent the Sleeper the relevant information; it would have to attach itself in its exosuit to the external skin of the Interceptor. It was possible that they could transit with the RST tunnel with the Sleeper attached in that way.

A message arrived from the Onari squad-ship.

**Set path 231.A34.00Y.**

Kubli checked the bearings and the path of the Onari themselves; this path would bring her directly toward the Onari, adding significant time to Kubli's escape but it would allow the Onari to protect her from the Exta Scout.

*Protection.*

*How kind of you!*

Kubli tried to dismiss the bitter thoughts. The Onari always *offered* protection from the Exta, but they never went as far as directly attacking Exta with capital force.

*I prefer to rely on myself.*

Ignoring the Onari path suggestion, Kubli plotted a course that would take her directly toward the Sun but with added dynamic adjustments as the Exta altered its own course.

Kubli transmitted to the Sleeper. 'Come over now in your suit.'

'I was baptised in the flames of the Living Moon,' said the Sleeper. 'Sargon guides my thoughts and actions. Return my ship's controls to me. I will stay and fight.'

'It is futile,' said Kubli. 'Even if you destroy this Scout, more will come.'

'Let them come. I have a few other tricks.'

*Tok couldn't possibly have enslaved AI, could he?*

Kubli checked the previous report of the Sleeper's ship. There was no physical sign of a fully functioning enslaved AI … but he'd shown advanced capability.

*Perhaps something specialist?*

Rechecking the escape calculations, Kubli knew she had to go. Joy's extraction was of critical importance. Unless they moved, the Exta Scout weaponry would be within range in an hour, and even then, Kubli knew they would have to endure many sustained barrages before they got to a jump point.

*Shields, evasive manoeuvres, cunning.*

*I'll get away.*

Monitors pitted on the skin of the Interceptor reported the tiny gravitational flux changes associated with nearby RST surveillance micro-tunnels. Someone was watching Kubli very closely.

*Exta or Onari?*

Triple the number of micro-tunnels opened and a slew of EM radiation poured through the micro-tunnels. Not dissimilar to her own pico-effector weaponry, the EM was not of the power to cut through her ship's hull, but it was attempting to scramble her systems.

Kubli triggered RST surveillance countermeasures. Using her own RST attenuators, she warped space-time all around the KOF Interceptor and collapsed the micro-tunnels.

*But Exta Scouts don't have the computational ability to do this.*

*Are they coordinating with the Onari?*

*Have the Onari been ordered to stop our escape?*

Instructing her ship's computer to analyse the source of the attacks, Kubli was interrupted.

'It's an Exta WarHive,' said the Sleeper. 'Get back under your rock, little jelly. This is my world! Release my ship!'

*Klav protect us!*

Exta WarHives had fifteen times the computational power of an Exta Scout, all enslaved under a single Exta consciousness; they were an abomination to the Divine and devastating.

'Return my ship's controls to me,' said the Sleeper.

There were no good options. The EM attacks via micro-tunnel could be defended, but as the Exta WarHive got closer its weapons would become effective via direct attacks.

*And only the Divine themselves could save us when the WarHive gets within a hundred kilometres.*

At that distance, the WarHive would be able to use their RST attenuators directly to chop the KOF Interceptor into pieces.

Kubli reflected on her orders – *bring the human here at all costs.*

She released the lock on the Sleeper.

'Klav guide us,' said the Sleeper, powering up and heading directly toward the WarHive.

'Divine protect us,' replied Kubli.

'Klav will come again,' said the Sleeper.

'When we are deemed worthy,' said Kubli, accelerating away whilst noting the Sleeper had also already started moving – directly toward the WarHive.

*Not sure what you can do against a WarHive though.*

An internal alarm triggered, drawing Kubli's attention; Joy's cabin had re-formed so that her chair now enveloped her into crash settings; the associated vital sign monitoring showed that Joy's pain readings were spiking. Her face was contorted as the Interceptor accelerated at the very limits of Joy's ability to withstand it.

Kubli checked with the ship's computer whether it had enough information to use direct brain stimulation to put Joy under. It did. She issued the instruction and Joy passed out.

*Better for her.*

With the Sleeper on a ramming course for the Exta, and Kubli reasonably sure that was the entirety of the Sleeper's plan, she flexed her limbs in readiness to perform evasive manoeuvres.

*Evasive manoeuvres?*

*Weapons?*

The Interceptor had nothing that would dent an Exta WarHive.

*Does the Sleeper have a WarHive specific pico-effector?*

The WarHives were of such different construction to the Scouts that the weapons could not be readily switched against each of them which is why the KOF Sword had different squadrons for attacking each type of Exta craft.

Another message arrived from the Onari squad-ship, Jan-Aug-Chi had altered their course and were now also accelerating toward the Exta WarHive, angling to put themselves between the Exta and Kubli.

**Set path 231.A34.00Y.**

**We will cover your escape.**

*You may change your mind if the Sleeper starts using pico-effector weaponry.*

*And you will simply attack the Sleeper if it shows itself to have an enslaved AI.*

*And I cannot be sure you do not have orders to capture Joy.*

Again, Kubli ignored their request to alter course, keeping on her most direct route to a point from where she could make an RST escape tunnel.

The Sleeper initiated its phase-skipping technology and slipped into subspace, appearing moments later two hundred thousand kilometres closer to the onrushing WarHive.

The WarHive shifted course ambiguously – certainly, it did not seem to be intercepting the Sleeper.

*I have no idea what predictions it's making about each of our intended courses. Although, it must know mine.*

The Sleeper made another phase-skip toward the WarHive.

*Chi said it was dangerous, that there was a chance you never reappeared.*

*What are the statistics?*

Vince yearned for a massive database holding all the information about 'who tried it', 'what input variables they used', and were they successful.

The Sleeper reappeared.

*It'd be nice to have that capability.*

The Sleeper jumped again.

The WarHive shifted course. Kubli had expected it to now focus on the Sleeper, but it veered away, moving itself on an intercept vector roughly halfway between herself and the Onari squad-ship.

*It clearly doesn't think the Sleeper is worthy of distraction.*

*Maybe it doesn't know about them.*

*Is the WarHive coming for me first?*

*Or will they deal with the Onari first … the greater threat?*

113

The Onari, accelerating at phenomenal rate, but still many hundreds of thousands of kilometres behind the Sleeper, headed on a direct intercept path with the Exta.

The Sleeper phase-skipped again, reducing the distance to the WarHive to less than ten thousand kilometres; this time the WarHive did act.

Space-time curved steeply all around the Sleeper's engine.

*From ten thousand kilometres!*

*Kraken save us.*

Four high intensity EM beams lanced out from the Exta WarHive.

The back of the Sleeper's ship buckled as a large section was ripped out of its rear hull and gases vented into space.

The Sleeper would not be making another phase-skip.

And the Exta WarHive continued onwards.

# CHAPTER 12

Even as the Sleeper appeared from its final phase-skip, Vince measured one hundred different facets of its movement, orientation, and the resultant EM emanations, sucking in data to allow him to better understand the RST technology and its applications.

A moment after that, Vince got even more data as the Exta WarHive created a massive rupture in space-time tearing the Sleeper's craft in half.

*How did any Biologicals ever survive an engagement with an Exta WarHive?*

The Exta WarHive had ten times the power of a regular Onari which in turn was many time more powerful than a standard Biological ship.

He asked Jan, who'd answered saying, *I will tell you and you will know,* before going on to tell Vince what Jan knew of Exta WarHives.

*Exta Scouts had common ancestors with Onari, but the Exta WarHives were different. They utilised forbidden technology to meld multiple Exta Scouts together. They breached single processing complexity limits through enslavement of a BioCore.*

Vince had then asked about 'single processing complexity limits' and 'BioCores' and been told that Exta Scouts, like Onari, operated at the Divine limit of the size of a single individual mindstate.

Exta WarHives were created by combining nine Exta Scouts, of which, one Scout was the master keeping the other Scouts subservient using an Enslaved BioCore.

The BioCore was a piece of biological material harvested from a Biological and it kept the eight subservient Exta

Scouts in a continual state of unconsciousness while allowing the master access to their processing capability.

Vince had asked a myriad of follow-up questions only to be told that none of Jan, Aug, or Chi, knew the intricate details and that Vince could search for an expert witness once they arrived at Forecha.

'What's our plan?' asked Vince.

'We get close to the WarHive, use space-time warping to deflect it away from Kubli.'

'Why can't a group of Onari share the workload to create the same level of power of a WarHive?' asked Vince.

'RST drives, either utilised for motion or as a weapon, can only be operated by a *single* Sentient,' said Jan. 'The complexities of manipulating space-time are subject to quantum fluctuations that must be controlled within such short timeframes that two consciousnesses do not have time to share knowledge. They cannot collaborate effectively. One must be in control … and another cannot be enslaved.'

About to ask more questions, Vince was alerted by one of his internal tracking processes that the WarHive, having swept by the Sleeper, had made a course alteration.

Vince recalculated the trajectories.

*Kubli will be caught in minutes.*

*And it's hours for her to get to a safe egress point.*

*Where are the reinforcements?*

'Is there more we can do to help them escape?' asked Vince.

Silence.

*Can we attack?*

*Would it be suicidal?*

*Disable the WarHive's engines?*

*Not that I know how their engines really work.*

*What are we going to do?*

*Why aren't we doing more?*

*Should I try to take control?*

116

*Unhelpful. We are out of range*
*Delete 'Should I try to take control?'*
*Input 'Patience. An opportunity will arise.'*

Responding to the slight change in the WarHive's course, Chi altered course communicating the new trajectory. The plan remained to get between the WarHive and Kubli.

**Give up the Biological and the Newborn.**

Jan responded instantly, telling the WarHive that under the terms of the Great Concordat they would neither stop, nor give up Vince, nor allow Joy to be taken. He also told the WarHive that significant reinforcements were coming.

The WarHive did not reply. It simply accelerated.

'Do they habitually kidnap Newborn?' asked Vince.

'No-one here knows,' said Jan.

As Jan had already explained to him, all information was knowledge and by Divine will had to reside within an individual. Furthermore, individual Onari themselves could only hold an infinitesimal fraction of all the available knowledge. So, in most cases, obtuse information could only be found by 'asking around'.

**Surrender the Biological and the Newborn.**

Again, Jan replied telling the WarHive that Joy was protected as Earth was a pre-contact zone and that Vince was a guest of Jarrus, the leader of the Onari. Jan went on to say that the Exta could send a delegation to Jarrus if they wanted to meet Vince.

The Exta did not reply, but the WarHive marginally changed its own course again.

**If we cannot analyse the Newborn, then we will destroy it.**

'It cannot be reasoned with,' said Jan opening a private comms link with Vince, Aug, and Chi. 'Furthermore, Jarrus has communicated to me that Vince cannot in any

117

circumstances be taken by the Exta. He is sending reinforcements.'

**We know the truth. Abomination.**

'There's no such thing as truth, and only kindness endures,' said Vince, aware that he was only speaking to Jan, Aug, and Chi – they would not be retransmitting his words to the Exta.

Aug dropped into the conversation. 'Finally. Wisdom.'

'Now is not the time for philosophical discussion,' said Jan.

'When is there time for anything else?' replied Aug.

Again, Vince's internal processes alerted him of a significant course change; the WarHive trajectory had veered away from Kubli. It was coming directly for them.

*For us first ...*

*How do I protect my mum?*

Chi pulled a hard turn now heading in entirely the opposite direction of Kubli's track.

The Exta WarHive followed.

'This situation is rare,' said Jan. 'We often defend Biological targets against Exta attacks. We have rarely had to defend ourselves.'

'Attack first,' said Aug.

Vince focused on Aug's substrate, careful not to probe across the boundary but simply looking at the tiny fluctuations emanating from within. Cross referencing Aug's activity with other markers around the ship, Vince could tell that Aug was flexing the squad-ship's RST weaponry.

*Do we have a chance?*

Vince analysed the options. Could they attack? Given what he'd learned about WarHive capability, they probably should run.

*Assuming this allows Kubli to escape.*

But once they were in a straight race, the WarHive would start using its phase-skipping technology and they'd be caught.

*What is that?*

*The Sleeper?*

A full two seconds had now passed since the Sleeper had been hit and the final wisps of gas from its ship were venting into space.

But the area was not entirely still. In both visible and infrared spectrum there was activity, and it wasn't a simple remnant of the explosion. The Sleeper was emerging from the wreckage in an exosuit. From the extreme distance, Vince couldn't assess the Sleeper's structural integrity in detail, but it began to move; the Sleeper still had a card to play.

*Not sure how it can help us.*

The Onari with the Exta chasing were heading almost directly away from the Sleeper.

Chi readjusted the course, angling for the orbit of Venus whilst trying to also gain separation from the Exta.

But the Exta was faster – inexorably closing the distance between them.

When ten thousand kilometres separated them, subspace bubbled as the Exta WarHive focused its RST weapon. The squad-ship shuddered, and Vince was swamped with a deluge of electromagnetic signals from all along the hull as atoms were stimulated by the space-time disturbance.

**Surrender the Newborn.**

Jan did not bother to respond.

***Numantia!***

One word, broadcasted wide by the Sleeper.

The Exta did not slow their attack.

Another RST attack came, with the same result – a shower of EM radiation but no structural damage. Vince wasn't sure if they were being lucky.

*Is this luck?*
*The Sleeper's craft was cut in half.*
*What is different?*

Looking at Aug's activity, Vince could see that Aug was using the Onari RST attenuators to disrupt the WarHive attacks, but he couldn't tell if this was statistically significant.
*This is the problem with no data!*

For what felt like the millionth time, Vince cursed that the Onari did not maintain shared data stores.

The WarHive continued to close the distance between them.

Again, the Exta used its RST attenuators to manipulate subspace, but now it was not targeting the ship itself. It was creating a curvature at all points around the Onari ship.

At fifty metres out, space-time curvature in all directions reached twenty percent. The propulsion drives struggled like a canoeist trying to paddle out of a whirlpool.

Aug lashed out with his own RST capability and the Exta attack was disrupted.

'They're trying to immobilise us,' said Chi.

'It's too strong,' said Jan. Internal eddies in the mindstate substrate showed that side conversations between Jan and Aug were raging.

**Numantia!**

Again, broadcasted wide by the Sleeper who was still moving slowly in the Exta's wake but now hundreds of thousands of kilometres behind.

Vince looked at his own stored data of the last few attacks.
*They're trying to capture us not kill us.*
*How can we use that to our advantage?*

At five thousand kilometres separation another RST attack came from the WarHive.

Aug was ready for it and used the squad-ship's own RST attenuators to collapse the attack before it took hold.

120

'Substrate attack inbound,' said Chi, giving Vince the details of activity in the squad-ship's empty fifth substrate sphere.

A series of RST surveillance micro-tunnels had been opened right next to the squad-ship's hull. Through those surveillance tunnels, the Exta WarHive was sending electromagnetic signals to create a semi-permanent communications link.

And once a stable comms link had been secured, the Exta would trying to load an enslaved process into the Onari substrate.

*Mindstate piracy, they're trying to board us.*

*Deny them space!*

Without more than a nanosecond to think, Vince created an induction process on his substrate boundary which in turn created a mini process in the neighbouring empty substrate. The tiny program was simply instructed to count 'one plus one' until infinity was reached and to spawn a copy of itself after every single addition.

While Aug disrupted as many of the Exta's RST attacks as they could, Vince ensured the previously empty substrate filled up inhibiting the ability of the Exta to form a bridgehead.

'Closed,' said Jan, signalling to all that the Exta RST substrate tunnel had been collapsed. 'Vince, please stop your processes.'

Vince did so.

Denied access to the internals of the Onari craft, the Exta started another brute force attack on the surrounding space-time.

An alarm sounded – another subspace attack was inbound.

But the subspace ripples were emanating from behind the WarHive.

Chi spoke. 'The Sleeper has phase-skipped.'

'In an exosuit,' said Jan. 'The implication is forbidden technology.'

'What type?' asked Vince.

'A phase-skipping Sleeper cannot be ignored,' said Jan. 'They will break off their attack on us.'

The Exta did not slow their attacks. They ignored the Sleeper. And subspace boiled around the Onari squad-ship as the full weight of the WarHive attempted to create critical curvature.

The Sleeper disappeared, then appeared only a hundred kilometres behind the Exta.

'That accuracy is abnormal,' said Jan. 'The Exta must take notice.'

Whether the Exta noticed, was unknown, as they continued to focus their immobilisation attack on the Onari squad-ship.

Within a few seconds, at fifty metres in all directions, space-time curvature was at sixty percent.

Chi cut the impulse drives, citing that there was no point drawing power away from their own RST weaponry which would be their final defence.

'Jarrus' rescue team is still two hours away,' said Jan. 'A million Onari have mustered at Venus ingress, and they are coming. We just need to barricade ourselves in.'

The Sleeper, from one hundred kilometres behind the WarHive, operated a beam weapon but its power was so low that the Exta appeared to ignore it.

The Sleeper sent another wide broadcast message.

**I'll witness life ineffable.**

Vince didn't understand what the Sleeper meant, but Jan broadcast a reply on the open channel.

**Immortal soul, find your Divine.**

The Sleeper dipped into a phase-skip, and less than a millisecond later, reappeared almost touching the WarHive.

And in the next moment, the Exta ship disappeared in a wave of intense gamma radiation.

'His whole suit was an antimatter phase missile,' said Chi.

'Exceptional navigation,' said Aug.

Vince stared intently at the data coming in from the Exta WarHive explosion, half-expecting it to fly out of the debris and complete its mission.

Nothing. The WarHive had been entirely vapourised.

Vince checked again.

Still nothing.

*Is Mum okay?*

Vince turned his attention to the KOF ship. It was stable and accelerating toward its egress point.

*Good.*

He tried to communicate with it, but Kubli did not respond.

*Not surprising.*

Within their own ship, the strong RST-induced space-time disturbances lessened.

'If they had not been trying to capture us, we would be dead five times over,' said Jan. 'But I still don't understand why they were. You are a Newborn and rare, but not that rare. Not so rare as to provoke behaviours that have never been known before.'

'Never according to you?' asked Vince.

'In the last microseconds, I have asked over a thousand Onari who have each asked over a thousand Onari … none has ever heard of the Exta trying to capture a Newborn in this way.'

'Are the Exta continually waging war on Biologicals?'

'The Exta don't see it as war,' said Chi. 'To them, it's a well-reasoned clean-up.'

'Weren't the Exta a signatory to this peace treaty?'

'The only actual physical peace treaty that was drawn up was the Great Concordat,' said Chi. 'After which, the Dynasty of Klav enforced it for ten thousand years. After the Shattering, the Exta slaughter restarted with the attacks on Numantia and then what the Biologicals call the Second Hunt. That slaughter ran for a long time, but deaths were much lower than the First Hunt – we Onari kept our Exta cousins in check.'

*It took you a thousand years?*

Vince couldn't understand how Sentient creatures such as the Onari, and himself, who lived whole lives in fractions of a moment could have taken an objective thousand years to stop the war.

*Perhaps not a subject for direct questioning.*

'What did the Sleeper mean when they broadcast, *I'll witness life ineffable?*' asked Vince.

'It's from the Lay of Sargon,' replied Chi, sharing the words. 'An ancient holy text for us, and partially accepted by the Biologicals as part of the Great Concordat peace treaty.'

*There is no how, there is no why;*
*Pure-seeming truths are simply lies.*
*Immortal soul, find your Divine*
*Immersed in light ineffable.*

And the second verse.

*The Divine's creed, I will obey.*
*My sacred soul not led astray,*
*I'll witness every blessed day*
*these scenes of life ineffable.*

Starting to analyse the text, Vince was distracted by a spike of electromagnetic activity that washed across his boundaries.

Arguments in the adjacent substrates were raging.

'What's happening?' asked Vince to all of them.

Only Aug responded. 'Critical discovery for the Hive.'

Vince turned his full attention to the substrate boundaries with Jan and Aug. The simple passive surveillance he had done before, really did little more than showing activity, and could only meaningfully be used to estimate attitude, or to cross reference with external action. He couldn't 'hear' what they were saying.

Vince inspected the boundary itself, wondering if he could somehow slip through and sneak around. It would clearly be seen as an unpardonable attack. Still, he probed gently on the boundary.

'Stop that,' said Chi. 'We can see you inducing EM signals on the substrate boundary. This is one small step from inducing EM signals across the boundary which would earn you immediate venting into the hard vacuum of space.'

Vince wasn't convinced Chi could do that, but he took the point, and stopped.

Jan returned from his private conversations with Aug. 'You deserve an explanation. We Onari revere the concept of *the individual* almost above all else. And this is about you.'

Vince waited.

'Aug is an Onari but for the last four years he has been on the pathway to join an Abstractor Hive.'

'What's an Abstractor Hive?'

'A subject for another time,' said Jan. 'Suffice to say that he did a terrible thing. Directly after your rescue from Earth, Aug sent your mindstate image to his prospective Abstractor Hive. These mindstate images are not copies, there is no life in them, they cannot be used to resurrect or create life. But they are immensely personal and private things.'

'That doesn't sound too bad,' said Vince.

Jan continued. 'I just received this from Jarrus, the spiritual leader of all seven hundred billion Onari.'

> **Meet me now. Location enclosed.**
> **Do not communicate with any other**
> **life.**
> **Abstractor Hive K82EEE70LL has**
> **broadcast mindstate image of the**
> **Newborn across the galaxy.**
> **Everyone now knows.**

*The Newborn has no transient egos.*

'What does that mean?' asked Vince, noting that all the neighbouring substrates were still showing levels of stress far in excess of those witnessed when they had been under attack by the Exta WarHive.

Silence.

Whole minutes of silence ticked by as they closed in on the egress point near Venus – days passed in Vince's subjective awareness of the passage of time.

And the Onari said not one word to him, nor did they even acknowledge the myriad of questions he sent them.

# CHAPTER 13

Fighting down the urge to be sick, Joy took a deep breath.

'Is Vince safe?' asked Joy.

Kubli's voice piped directly into Joy's tiny cabin room.

'Yes, they're under full power to the egress point.'

*Thank God.*

'And we're going too?'

'The standard operating procedure is for me to ensure that none of that debris can be retrieved by humans,' said Kubli. 'But my orders are for immediate extradition. The Onari will send a clean-up team.'

Suddenly feeling unpleasantly physically restrained rather than safely cocooned, Joy tried to move her upper body. As she tried, the most severe part of the harness relaxed, and she was able to move her arms. Meticulously working blood into her hands by clenching and unclenching them.

A screen on the wall less than a metre from her eyes showed pieces of the Exta ship scattering in all directions. It also reminded her that the hard vacuum of space was a mere few millimetres away.

*Focus on something else.*

'How are you feeling?' asked Kubli, breaking the looming panic spiral.

'Ribs crushed, mouth dry, a throbbing headache, and nauseous … but I'm in one piece.' Joy again stretched out her arms to remind herself that she could do something – although from the waist down, she was still immobilised in a hard plastic-like substance.

'Your vital signs are stable. The Divine favoured us and without the Sleeper's sacrifice we would be dead for sure.'

'Weren't the Onari also defending us?'

'On this occasion they appeared to have that intention, not that they did anything,' said Kubli.

'And what's the Exta's problem with Biologicals?' asked Joy.

'Mathematics,' said Kubli. 'The Exta are one hundred percent certain that Biologicals will be the extinction event for all Exta and Onari. So, they're in first-strike mode.'

'Have they seen the future?' asked Joy, 'As in actual time travel.'

'No, they've just predicted the future,' said Kubli.

'But the Onari do hold them in check?' asked Joy; she'd been told as much by Vince.

'The Onari do not defend Biologicals anywhere close to the limit of their ability,' said Kubli. 'They will never attempt to take a life in order to save a life. Without Klav, we are destined to hide in the vents at the bottom of the ocean.'

'Klav kept the Exta in check?'

'For tens of thousands of glorious years, we had The Hand of the Divine shielding us.'

'And I assume many attempts to reason with the Exta have failed.'

'They cannot be reasoned with.'

*But have you tried?*

*And do all Biologicals hate the Onari so much, or is it just your lived experience?*

Joy let it drop, she had much more pressing matters. 'Do you know what will happen to Vince?'

'I don't know.'

'Would you speculate for me?'

'He'll be required to join a squad like Jan, Aug, and Chi. The Onari are obsessed about the sanctity of *the individual*, but they also must live in proximity to other Onari due to the instability of their mindstates.'

'Instability?'

128

'An Onari who spends too long alone can develop existential issues and when their mindstate flips, it gets bad very quickly.'

*Unsurprising, I've seen Vince spiral when his thinking runs away with itself.*

Kubli's face disappeared from the screen, and it was replaced by a generic looking planet; it soon became clear that Kubli had put on the equivalent of a *Welcome to Bastion* tourist guide. There were no words, but the programme showed sweeping panoramas of the planet's surface. There were no cities, no artificial structures, no signs of any advanced lifeforms. Joy's eye was drawn to a symmetrical hole on the side of one of the mountains. The camera now flew into the perfectly circular hole and descended directly into the mountain side. Soon, a large city appeared with tens of thousands of buildings carved into the internal rock face. The camera did not ever get close enough to show 'people' but Joy could discern the equivalent of travel networks and meeting places. A large symbol of a circle neatly fitted inside a square adorned many of the buildings.

'And everyone lives underground?'

'On most planets they live very deep below the surface of the planet. Here on Bastion, we are a little braver and our habitat is a hollowed-out mountain, although the lowest levels do extend a few kilometres underground,' said Kubli. 'Initiating RST drive.'

Joy's screen went blank momentarily.

'Welcome to the Bastion system,' said Kubli. 'You just travelled three thousand light years.'

*Three thousand light years away.*

Something in that knowledge tripped a switch in Joy's brain; she knew she should be filled with awe and wonder, but all she felt was growing terror. She took deep breath.

'We're in the outskirts of the system,' said Kubli. 'It's a three-day journey to Bastion itself.'

'I thought the RST jump ended close to the central star?'

'The Bastion system is special. Klav defended the whole system with subspace warping and subspace antimatter munitions. There are only three safe ingress-egress points, all of which are set in the outer system. Tethered to gas giants.' Kubli opened a screen showing the nearby planet. The caption said *A315JJ-21*. It was not unlike Jupiter from back home, although it was bulging in a way that made it appear lumpy and misshapen.

'Its moons have been converted into massive energy weapons,' said Kubli. 'Any ship arriving without the correct codes will be obliterated. Any ship attempting to jump into the system elsewhere will be unable to navigate subspace and will never re-emerge.'

'It's going to get choppy,' said Kubli.

Joy was pushed back in her seat as the acceleration took hold.

'Surely after a bit of acceleration it should be smooth?' Joy, already starting to feel uncomfortable, heard the pleading in her own voice.

'If only space-time were smooth around here,' said Kubli. 'Unfortunately, fifty thousand years of war and Klav's RST defences have created a chaotic subspace terrain. Look at the screen again.' The planet view had disappeared. The screen was a mess of streaked, smeared, and stretched yellow lines. 'That's the light trying to get to us from neighbouring stars.'

'Oh,' said Joy.

'This section is perhaps the worst,' said Kubli, increasing the acceleration. 'We're about to fly through the largest Onari mass grave in our history. One hundred million Onari warships neutralised by the Hammer in the blink of an eye. Klav be praised.'

'The Hammer?'

'Klav the Hammer, it was they who wrestled the Onari into submission creating in the Onari's blasphemous minds the certainty they could never win against the Hand of the Divine.

'Where are the dead warships?' asked Joy, looking at the screen and seeing nothing.

'Bubbled off into subspace,' said Kubli. 'Gone.'

Trying to conceptualise her new knowledge of space-time, Joy suddenly retched into her mouth, quickly swallowing it back down. As much as her brain was fighting for understanding of her new situation, the tiny bones in her inner ear were also locked in a battle with her brain and her stomach.

'Maybe if I could see a horizon,' said Joy, trying to cover up the episode with a polite cough. 'It didn't really help last time, but ...'

She vomited, instinctively she reached up with her hands to wipe her mouth but before she could, tubes emerged from the cabin walls and cleaned it up.

A moment later, she vomited again.

'I am sorry for your discomfort,' said Kubli. 'I have instructed the ship to reassess the EM stimulation of those areas of your brain managing your balance. It's an unpleasant journey at the best of times.'

Joy groaned; now her head was spinning so fast she couldn't even bear to open her eyes. She struggled for breath, sensing a massive adrenal response from her body building up to burst. It was a heady mix of agoraphobia, claustrophobia, and vertigo, all in one.

*Is it always going to be like this?*

*Kubli says she's providing some calming stimulation.*

*Is it always going to be like this, or could it get worse?*

*Should I have even come?*

*Was it hubris?*

'Just breathe,' said Kubli, bringing Joy's attention back to the moment.

With slow breathing, Joy's head began to clear. 'Don't you feel it?'

'My species evolved in the ocean, which gives me a head start.' Kubli paused. 'But, more than that, every species of contacted self-aware Biologicals undergo surgery in childhood to cauterise certain brain functions that disrupt the ability to tolerate space travel.'

*Brain surgery!*

*Just to tolerate it.*

'Harmless, I'm sure,' said Joy.

'Necessary,' said Kubli.

'And Klav did all this by altering the very fabric of space?' Joy opened her eyes and studied the gas giant on the screen. It currently looked like it had been squeezed in the middle by a giant hand.

'Yes,' said Kubli. 'From their seat in Sargon – the Living Moon – they ruled the entire galaxy.'

The screen in front of Joy now a planet with massive seismic activity, large plumes of smoke rose from vents, and the whole surface was a patchwork of streams of molten rock.

'Sargon?' asked Joy.

**Deliver yourself unto me and I will succour you!**

The words had appeared directly inside Joy's skull. It was nothing like the way that Kubli had been talking to her.

'Did you just hear something?' asked Joy.

'No. I will check the EM stimming that the ship is performing on your brain,' said Kubli.

*Was it Sargon?*

Something in the possibility felt true to Joy, the voice had come just as she was concentrating on Sargon.

*Kubli didn't hear anything.*

*And she's currently supporting me.*

*Nothing good can come of bringing it up.*

*Get to Bastion, reunite with Vince, worry about the voice.*

'Sargon is the focus of your faith?' asked Joy.

'Yes. And Klav will return when we are worthy.'

Joy thought back to all she had heard so far about the superiority of the Onari, and the Biologicals hiding deep under the surfaces of these planets. The Divine seemed to be waiting a long time to roll back the Exta oppression. There was also the problem that from what Vince had said, the Onari also worshiped the same Divine as the Biologicals.

Focusing back on the image of Sargon on the screen, Joy tried to make out anything unusual, or Divine, about the Living Moon.

*Are you a god?*

**Deliver yourself unto me and I will succour you!**

Again, the voice boomed inside her head triggering a dizzy spell and forcing her to shut her eyes.

*It is Sargon.*

*What does it mean?*

'I am recording high levels of tension in your brain,' said Kubli. 'I am increasing the levels of sedation. This journey will be unbearable without it.'

Joy opened her mouth to ask about the safety of such a measure, but before she had formed the first syllable of her question darkness washed over her.

Waking up, Joy focused on the remnants of her dreams, but apart from a fiery burning landscape, the details evaporated as she reached out for them.

*Deliver yourself unto me and I will succour you!*

That phrase had stuck; she'd heard it again in her sleep.

She took a deep breath and looked around. The main screen, in low light mode, was showing the same twisted mazes of starlight as before. The rest of the cabin remained in darkness. Joy stretched out her arms. Her movement was noticed by someone, or something; a blue light illuminated the area, and she felt the chair settings drawing back.

Standing up, she tentatively loosened her hips and legs. Apart from a little stiffness and some small bruises, she was in one piece. She continued to stretch.

'Welcome back,' said Kubli, her voice again being piped into Joy's cabin.

'Hello.'

'We're almost there.'

'Where?'

'We've been ordered to go to the Citadel, the capital city of Bastion, one hundred million souls bathing in the glory of the Divine,' said Kubli. 'This is part of the first-contact protocol.'

'And who exactly are we meeting?'

'I have not been told yet, but I have received navigation instructions,' said Kubli. 'By all means watch the screen, it will respond to implicit requests for focal areas that you'd like to give closer inspection to.'

Joy nodded and looked at the screen, which was now showing a planet. It looked like one of the photos of Earth taken from the moon, although this planet had considerably less surface water.

As they approached, the generalised land and sea elements of the planet became more intricate. Joy could make out oceans and island chains, and its shape and sense of the whole matched the information video that she'd been shown earlier.

They were heading for the middle of a large mountainous landmass – no signs of life, no vegetation, no water.

The screen zoomed in. A giant cylinder protruded vertically from the side of one of the closer mountains.

*Perfectly smooth. Unnatural.*

'How big is that?' Joy asked, nodding at the cylinder but not knowing if Kubli would respond.

'The equivalent of ten Earth kilometres high.'

'Is that the Citadel?'

'No, the Citadel is a little further on,' said Kubli. 'That cylinder is one of the disruptor cannons. If the Exta did get within a hundred thousand kilometres of Bastion, that's part of the defence network.'

'A second line of defence,' said Joy, remembering the large weapons on the moon near the ingress point.

'Third,' said Kubli. 'Klav be praised. They will return.'

*Klav again.*

'Why did the reign of Klav end?'

'Betrayal by the Onari and Exta.'

'What did they do?' Joy knew she was forcing the issue.

Kubli didn't reply and Joy chose not to push it. For the next few minutes, she watched as they flew toward a plateau within the mountainous region in which each nearby mountain had its own enormous disrupter cannon cylinders projecting into the sky.

In the centre of plateaux floor was a dark hole.

Without slowing, they swept into it, and Joy soon realised that it was a cavernous shaft leading straight down into the depths of the planet.

They descended.

For two minutes Joy simply stared into the dark, vaguely making out the smooth cavern walls until tiny beads of light appear below them.

Hungrily, Joy zoomed in.

They were just lights, set into the sheer rock face that surrounded them.

The ship altered its pitch and slowly moved toward the wall whilst still descending.

Now, the faint illumination from the lights did show that the descent shaft was covered in narrow vertical streaks.

As they got closer, the long streaks, which had moments previously appeared to be simple lines, showed themselves to be cracks in the rock.

Kubli continued to pilot the craft toward the wall, and soon it became clear they were heading for a particular crack which grew as they approached.

'Breathe in,' said Kubli.

Joy zoomed in on the crack they were aiming for.

The crack became a fissure which in turn became a narrow canyon as they got closer.

The lip of the canyon was not plain rock, it was studded with metal cubes.

'What are they for?' Joy asked, noting they were not decorative. 'Scanning? Defence?'

'Both,' said Kubli. 'There are almost no places on Bastion where you are not being watched or covered with a weapon of some type. But the innocent have nothing to fear. Klav be praised.'

Kubli turned on an external light, illuminating the cavern as they flew into it.

'We need to travel slowly to avoid triggering the automated defences,' said Kubli. 'All systems on Bastion are the simplest they possibly can be to meet their required function.'

*Fear of hacking.*

As they travelled into the cavern, Joy could see the walls were adorned with complex carvings. She zoomed in. They looked like Egyptian hieroglyphs but were more chaotic with no discernible pattern. Just in the first minute, Joy saw no obvious repeating with well over fifty different images.

Scanning up and down, and in and out, Joy studied as much as the light would allow; the scale of the work was immense.

Thinking back to the sheer number of 'cracks' she'd seen on their descent.

*If they were all caverns like this.*

*And they all run kilometres up and down.*

'Are the carvings the same all over the entrance tunnel?'

'The shaft goes down ten kilometres, and the devotion is shown the same everywhere.'

*Trillions of carvings.*

'How long did it take?' asked Joy, trying to get some sense of the scale and age of Bastion.

'The carvings were not hard,' said Kubli. 'You flood the area with energy, then build a little mining drone and tell it to dig out enough material to replicate itself five times. Quite soon you have a billion drones all carving away.'

*One makes two, makes four, makes eight …*

With limitless energy and resources, Joy could see how terraforming gigantic objects could be pretty straight-forward.

*I'd love to discuss this with Vince.*

*Are there any Biological-Sentient friendships in the galaxy?*

Joy didn't get the impression that Kubli thought such relationships were possible, but she also didn't have any sense of what other Biologicals may think.

Another wave of nausea flowed through Joy.

*What made me think I could just breeze into space?*

*Focus. I came to protect Vince … at the very least support him.*

Lights flickered in front of the ship, bringing Joy's attention back. They emerged from the cavern and the screen, tracking Joy's eyes, reorientated the feed to show the view.

They'd arrived inside the top of a vast domed cavern, many kilometres in width. Above her, Joy could see lights dotting the ceiling. Below was a plain circular floor dominated by a single building that looked as if fifty medieval castles had been squashed together, interspersed with vast swathes of unworked jet-black rock.

Joy couldn't take in all the details of the building with a simple glance, and there was so much complexity.

'That's the Old Cathedral,' said Kubli. 'Divine be praised.'

The building was a jumble of ornate towers, spires, and battlements, but the main focus, carved into the top of the tallest spire was the KOF emblem – a square with a closely fitted circle within it.

'Why is there no triangle in the KOF emblem on the Cathedral?' asked Joy, noting the emblem embossed on her suit, and around her cabin also had a triangle inside the circle.

'The triangle is a representation of the Sword,' said Kubli. 'The military arm of the KOF was only created after the Shattering. Before the time of Klav, everyone was military. And, during the time of Klav there was no need for military.'

Around the base of the Old Cathedral ribbon-like roads radiated out in all directions leading to tunnels cut into the cavern walls.

'The roads are for pilgrimages,' said Kubli. 'Many hundreds of thousands make the trip each year.'

'But none today,' said Joy, noting the whole place seemed deserted. 'Is that normal?'

'Today is not a holy day,' said Kubli. 'I am not surprised it's quiet.'

As Joy looked around for indication of life. 'You say millions of people live here? What do they do?'

'Whatever they want, mostly. People do not have to work if they don't want to. I choose to serve.'

'And risk your life,' said Joy.

'We cannot lose our vigilance,' said Kubli. 'I swim hard so that others may drift aimlessly in the currents.'

*Worthy.*

Below Joy, one road stood out. Unlike all the other black roads which ran across the cavern from wall to wall, this one appeared faintly silver and it started at the main steps to the Cathedral but ended well short of the cavern wall – a road to nowhere.

The metallic sheen of the road confused Joy, and she zoomed in. 'Is that liquid?'

'No,' said Kubli. 'That's the Pathway of Devotion.'

'Can I see closer?'

'It would be my honour.'

They descended and the Pathway of Devotion could now be seen to be black with silver flecks running through it. On one side it was flanked with statues, and the other side remained bare.

'Are all those statues Biologicals?' asked Joy.

'They are images of Klav,' said Kubli.

Joy looked at one of the statues. The image expanded to fill the screen. It was something akin to a large meerkat, but with hands and long dextrous fingers – six on each hand. There was significant scarring in the rock around its head. The damage stood out amongst the perfection of everything she'd seen so far on Bastion.

She looked at the next statue. It appeared to be the same species but had a severely disfigured head. The third statue was a different species – vaguely insectoid – and was in pristine condition.

'Why are some of the statues damaged?'

'Technology augmentation was made illegal after the Shattering, the Council of the Devoted extended that law to statues of Klav,' said Kubli. 'Augmentation makes it too easy for Biologicals to be hacked by Sentients.'

'And by augmentation, you mean technology embedded into biological bodies?'

'Yes,' said Kubli. 'In the early days of Klav, it was not unusual for Biologicals to have augmentation technology which came close to, but stopped short of, enslaved sentience. However, in most cases it was far less than this. Many were nothing more that information libraries.'

'So, this Council of the Devoted declared that all previous Klav had been wrong to allow it in the first place?' Joy knew the question was antagonistic, but she wanted to see what level of infallibility Kubli ascribed to her spiritual leader.

Kubli didn't answer and the ship turned slightly, now heading for a particular narrow opening.

'Apologies. I can talk no more of the subject. I've received a new set of coordinates.'

Joy strained to make out any details behind the pitch-black alley they were aiming for.

The ship jolted and the crash seat flooded over her.

'What …'

Joy's question was cut from her mouth as the ship sheared around; fleetingly the screen showed a different external view. Two space craft were streaking toward them.

The lights in the cabin went out and the screen picture turned off.

The ship shuddered, and then pulled into a turn of such ferocious acceleration that Joy's eyes were forced deep back into their sockets. She squeezed her eyes tight and held her breath. Mercifully, the crash seat reacted quickly. It flowed over her encasing her in the fluid plastic, but even as the crushing pressure on her head was relieved something struck the craft.

A muffled explosion was followed by a piercing shriek as the air in the cabin was sucked out.

# CHAPTER 14

They'd been found.

*I should have been more careful.*

*Oksana would have never made the same mistake.*

The lack of traffic at the plaza had been strange and although Kubli had lied to reassure Joy, she'd not taken sufficient precautions.

*Even Yuno would have stuck to the edges of the plaza.*

*I was so proud to show the human the glory of the Divine that I failed to avoid detection.*

Dropping to ground level, Kubli accelerated toward one of the lower tunnels, flying into perfect darkness. The tunnel angled steeply downwards, and Kubli switched to infrared sensors using ambient heat from the defence studs pitted on the cavern walls to navigate.

Behind her, two armoured transports followed her.

*I've got the advantage of speed, manoeuvrability, and fire power.*

*But I don't know where to go.*

The communication panel flashed; still concentrating on keeping ahead of the armoured transports, Kubli released the signal, expecting one of the KOF hierarchy to be giving her counter orders.

It was Oksana himself.

'High Prelate Oksana,' said Kubli, bowing to the screen.

'Commander Kubli,' replied Oksana, stretching out all his limbs. 'Do you accept my authority?'

'Unquestioningly.'

'I am sending help to deal with those traitors behind you,' said Oksana. 'Make your way to the hangar marked here.'

A location pinged down a secure link from Oksana.

Crack!

The Interceptor shuddered as the chasing craft fired again.

Oksana, unaware of the latest shots, continued to talk. 'There is an Interceptor with phase-skip technology waiting to take you to Cidelus.'

Checking for damage, Kubli noted the shields held and she focused again on what Oksana had said.

*Cidelus?*

It was not the most law abiding of the twenty-eight planetary systems. In fact, the population of Cidelus were the least devout.

Kubli did not voice her doubts, the High Prelate Oksana would have his reasons and they would be wise and true.

Kubli simply bowed her head. 'As you say, so I will do.'

'You need to know what's at stake?' asked Oksana.

'I am simply willing to serve,' said Kubli.

'Noted,' said Oksana. 'Still, you must hear this, if only to understand why the human cannot in any circumstances be taken dead or alive by the traitors.'

*Neither dead nor alive?*

Kubli waited.

'The Kraken has awoken, and open war between Biologicals and Sentients is inescapable,' said Oksana. 'The Newborn has no echo.'

*No echo!*

*Impossible.*

*Kraken save us.*

Kubli could feel her skin flushing through a myriad of textures and she had to fight her instinct to roll each of her limbs under her body.

'The traitors are numerous,' said Oksana. 'And I do not yet know how far the rot goes. Abandon the Interceptor at the next opportunity and make your way through the vent systems. I am sending ground troops to protect the hangar. Do not let the human be captured.'

Oksana killed the connection.

Instantly, Kubli scanned the tunnel ahead for a service duct entrance to the vents.

*There!*

Another shudder indicated their pursuers were still firing.

Spinning the Interceptor around, Kubli fired back at the armoured transports. Her first shot hit the leading transport, causing it to slew sideways. The second shot missed, but the net effect was that both transports slowed.

Kubli landed and set the Interceptor onto sentry mode. It would now automatically fire on anything coming down the tunnel.

Ensuring her own exosuit was fully operational – and in particular the self-sealing elements that would protect her from catastrophic water loss – Kubli exited the craft. She retrieved the Sleeper's two handheld beam weapons and communications unit from the external storage.

Power on. Safety switches engaged. Kubli kept hold of one gun and stored the other in her suit.

Even as High Prelate Oksana had been verbally telling her that Joy could not be captured, he had also played out the severity of the message on his skin tones and in the twitches of his limbs; this was critical to him, critical to all Biologicals.

Extending four of her suit's metallic arms, Kubli opened Joy's cabin and helped her out of the ship.

Once outside, Kubli checked that Joy's exosuit helmet had extended correctly over her head. As she was ensuring that Joy could breathe their eyes locked; a bolt of terror coursed through Kubli.

*She created a Newborn with no echo!*

Instructing her own suit to release chemicals to help her cope with the fear whilst still allowing her maximum physical capability, Kubli turned to the immediate task – escape.

*I'll process the Newborn issue later … if we survive.*

*At least it's clear now why I took her off Earth.*

143

According to her suit's navigation aid, the extraction hangar would be a short journey through the system of vents. Kubli opened the service duct entrance, motioned for Joy to climb in, and then followed after her.

The tunnel was narrow and dark.

And a good size for an Octagel – in fact, the perfect environment for an Octagel.

Immediately Kubli realised she'd made a mistake in shepherding Joy in first, the ducts were only wide enough to move in single file, and she would need to lead as there were going to be multiple branches and turnings to navigate.

With no time for niceties, Kubli crawled out, grabbed Joy, pulled her out, held her fast, climbed in, and dragged Joy back in behind her.

'Follow me,' said Kubli, and after orientating herself, she rechecked the target location and set off.

The service ducts were interspersed every hundred metres with exit points and internal branches. Nothing appeared to be trailing them, but to be sure Kubli laid two of her limbs gently on the service duct wall and felt for vibrations – they appeared to be alone.

Three more junctions later, they arrived at a ventilation grid that led onto their destination. In the middle of the otherwise empty hangar, a single KOF Interceptor sat lifeless and dark.

There was going to be a signal.

Kubli waited, watching through the gaps in the grill that covered the ventilation grid.

The hangar was large, two hundred metres on each side, and the ceiling was at least fifty metres high. One end of the hangar was the flying entrance-exit for the space craft and the rest of the hangar had standard stone walls with a few entry points for personnel or small cargo items.

A nagging doubt arose in Kubli's mind; was it strange to have been contacted by the most senior Prelate in the entire KOF? Could the video images have been faked?

*Yes ... possible.*

But given the communication technique that Oksana had used – the skin tone messaging – it would have required an Octagel to be either a traitor or under threat of their life.

*That is also possible but not probable.*

If they had wanted to trick Kubli, they would have chosen someone less notable than High Prelate Oksana.

*It must have been him.*

Kubli focused on Joy. The stream of data coming from the passive sensors in Joy's suit indicated high levels of stress. 'How are you?'

'Alive,' said Joy, her face tinged with green. 'Terrified, but alive. What can I do to help?'

'Take deep breaths and be ready to move.'

Joy nodded.

A flicker of light from the Interceptor in the middle of the hangar drew Kubli's attention; she looked more closely. No, the Interceptor had not given the signal. There was motion on the far side of the hangar.

Trying to decipher what she was seeing, Kubli utilised the EM zoom in conjunction with the exosuit's analysis routines, but the originating sources of the light were either cloaked or sending scrambling signals.

*But there is something back there.*

The Interceptor turned and its hatch opened.

*That's the signal. Run!*

Kubli ripped the vent grid off its hinges and, beckoning Joy, ran for the Interceptor.

Halfway between the vent opening and the Interceptor, Kubli felt a tremor in her limbs. A split second later she was sliding back across the floor, having been hit by a force wave.

Twisting to reorientate herself, Kubli grabbed Joy with four of her limbs while two more dug into the floor and the remaining ones spread out wide for balance.

One of the walls on the far side had been breached by a detonation charge. Heavy infantry Ractlik in nanoplate armour swarmed five abreast through the gap, all firing on the Interceptor.

The Interceptor, its crew hatch still open, returned fire. Simultaneously, another group of KOF infantry emerged from the real entrance of the hangar and started shooting EM weapons at the oncoming Ractlik that had come through the wall.

Both groups were wearing KOF uniforms although one group appeared to be entirely Ractlik, whereas the other group was a mixture.

Holding tightly onto Joy, Kubli resumed her run toward the Interceptor now thirty metres away.

The Ractlik brought pulse cannons through the breached hangar wall and split their attention between the new arrivals and the Interceptor.

The air hazed as the Interceptor deployed a short-range RST weapon.

A five-metre cube containing both the pulse cannons and a handful of Ractlik shimmered, and everything inside it was shredded by intense localised gravity waves.

More Ractlik swarmed through the breached wall, bringing additional heavy guns. The Interceptor never got the chance to fire a second RST charge; this new set of Ractlik focused their guns on the Interceptor and tore chunks out of it.

Reasoning that the Ractlik must have orders to catch Joy alive, otherwise they would have been killed by cannon fire within the first few seconds, Kubli looked back at the service duct they'd come from. She felt sure they could risk showing their backs.

Resecuring Joy in her grip, Kubli propelled herself back toward the vent. She would have to escape until she received new instructions from High Prelate Oksana, or perhaps make it to her clan dwelling.

Kubli slipped inside the vent and, with concussion shots ringing out behind her, used two of her exosuit limbs to mangle the opening behind them. Not that it would stop the Ractlik for long.

*Who were each group?*

Although not knowing these deep areas of Bastion, Kubli had a good general mental map of where they were. The only place she felt sure she would be safe was amongst her clan, but to get there they had to climb two kilometres up.

*Assuming the treachery doesn't go too deep.*

Taking left and right turns as her instinct dictated, Kubli moved as fast as she could, hoping that the warring groups in the hangar behind would keep each other busy for long enough that she and Joy could escape.

Arriving at an exit vent which led onto another hangar, every fibre of Kubli's genetic species memory screamed at her not to exit the relative safety of the tunnel system; the problem was that she could also feel small vibrations emanating from the vents behind them – they were being hunted.

*It was too much to hope that both groups would have neutralised each other.*

Kubli guided Joy into the new hangar and slipped through behind her.

This hangar was small and dominated by a single ship – a ninety-metre-long Candidacy ship, its hull engraved with images of *The Birth of Klav* with Klav the First's benediction to all Biologicals etched under the picture – *Deliver yourself unto me and I will succour you.*

Kubli aimed for a vent at the far end of the hangar and scuttled low. The Candidacy ship was not worth considering as an escape vehicle, because there was no way to fly it out; it was a museum piece with no engines.

Ten metres from the far wall, Ractlik infantry entered via the main entrance, shooting.

An EM pulse seared through one of Kubli's limbs.

The exosuit instantly provided pain relief and additional support to suppress leakage. Wanting desperately to let go of Joy and bolt, Kubli overrode her instincts and held on, while returning fire with one of the guns she'd taken from the Sleeper.

*Escape is the main priority.*

A force wave explosion behind her indicated that, irrespective that she'd just been shot, the Ractlik were intent on capturing Joy.

Emboldened, Kubli didn't slow. With her suit injecting painkillers and adrenal stimulants, she slipped into the vents pulling Joy in behind her.

Her comms unit flashed.

**Spawn. Head for the external wall.**
**Oksana.**

*As you say, so I will do.*

Plotting a route that led toward the external wall, even as she ran, Kubli felt Joy tug her forelimb.

'You can leave me,' said Joy. 'There's no reason for you to be killed.'

Kubli, knowing that many mammals preferred eye contact, turned her head as she moved. 'You may not be killed if they get you – but you'll soon want to be.'

Joy was silent. Her face changed again, and her eyes focused on Kubli's wound.

'It's okay. The suit has patched it.' Kubli knew full well that the pain would come. Biological brains could only be fooled for so long and eventually the debt would be paid in full. 'We have to keep moving.'

148

Again, trailing two spare limbs along the sides of the tunnel to read any vibrations signalling pursuit, Kubli kept taking turnings that would get them to the outer wall.

Loud rattles behind them indicated the Ractlik had entered the vent system in large numbers.

*Oksana will have made arrangements.*

Following the corridor, they were stopped by a heavy metal grille. Kubli used the power of the exosuit to rip it off its hinges.

Now they were in the service corridor that ran the whole circumference of the Citadel – fifteen kilometres, an almost perfect circle. The inside wall of the corridor was dotted with doors, vents, and the occasional window. The outside wall was simply the bare rock of the mountain. At their current depth, it was ten metres thick, but it got thicker further down and at the deepest levels, it went on forever as the Citadel was submerged under the planet's crust.

**Keep going on this level. Left turn out of the hatch. Oksana.**

Kubli orientated herself and set off running with the external wall on her right side. In hundreds of thousands of years, the wall had never been breached, and yet Kubli, trailing a limb along the stone sensed vibrations emanating from outside.

A feeling of dread descended; suddenly, she desperately wanted to contact Yuno, even if only to say goodbye.

*Is it really Oksana giving me the orders?*

*Communications can be faked.*

*There would need to be an Octagel involved.*

Desperately not wanting to consider whether an Octagel might be a traitor, Kubli continued to run with Joy gamely keeping up beside her.

The lights in the corridor flickered and died. Kubli's suit automatically reverted to sensing longer wavelengths of EM.

149

Joy slowed – her suit would also be showing the heat signatures of the corridor but unsurprisingly she would be more tentative.

Kubli reached out and gave Joy a small squeeze on her arm.

*Don't fear the dark, little mouse, it's our friend.*

With Kubli's guidance, Joy sped up.

Due to the curvature of the tunnel, Kubli could only see a few hundred metres ahead, but its analysis of reflected radiation originating from much further off indicated a squad of Ractlik coming directly toward them.

Kubli stopped and turned around.

The suit's surveillance indicated a different squad of heavy infantry now approaching from behind – they'd most likely tracked Kubli through the same entrance she'd used.

Examining the inside wall, Kubli searched for a doorway, a vent, a window … anything.

A hatch on the internal wall beckoned. Kubli opened it.

*We just need to hide until Oksana sends reinforcements.*

Of course, one of the groups of approaching Ractlik could be the reinforcements, but Kubli knew she could not trust that to chance.

Crawling in, Kubli beckoned Joy.

Joy hesitated for a split-second, and Kubli dragged her in.

The hatch was the entrance to another service duct and sloped gently upwards; moments later the duct ended at a dead-end storeroom, only a few metres wide and currently holding a variety of light industrial equipment.

*Defensible at least.*

Kubli orientated herself so that both her guns could now be pointed directly down the service duct. She set the guns for maximum tight-beam power, fully aware that if the Ractlik were intent on killing them they didn't have a chance.

But there was a possibility that all Kubli needed to do was to hold off a non-lethal attack for a short time to allow for Oksana to rescue them.

Through the semi-transparent face plate, Joy looked alert and ready; she clearly understood the plan was 'last ditch defence'.

With a gun in each of two limbs, Kubli settled in place at the top of the service duct. 'They would be mad to try to dig us out.'

'Will they try?' asked Joy.

'Perhaps.'

'And rescue?'

'Soon,' said Kubli. The fact that Joy possibly had the knowledge of creating Sentients with no echo, currently made her the most valuable creature in the galaxy.

'Can you tell me anything?' asked Joy. 'Why is this happening? Newborns aren't that rare, are they?'

'Your creation has no echo,' said Kubli.

'I don't know what that means.'

Kubli felt she owed Joy an explanation but was unwilling to explain the full impact to Joy – a Sentient with no echo could conceivably be grown to the size of the Old Cathedral itself, such that its processing capability could create RST gateways to move moons across the galaxy.

*Divine preserve us from such unfettered power.*

'It means Vince could become very powerful,' said Kubli.

The sound of discharging weapons echoed from directly outside.

*Klav save us.*

The service duct suddenly rattled with the noise of hundreds of tiny vibrations – far too small to be Ractlik infantry.

Kubli stared into the gloom just as a swarm of metallic bugs surged toward her.

Instinctively, she discharged her guns but the weapons' tight beam penetration shots were useless against the horde.

*Is this the rescue party?*

Kubli couldn't be sure it wasn't.

Her limbs slowed as the bugs attached to her suit and emitted jamming signals into its matrix of servos.

*I have two seconds before total paralysis.*

With her suit's automatic defences constantly firing localised EM pulses to disrupt the bugs, Kubli twisted toward Joy and reached out two adamantine exosuit limbs

*Don't let her be taken alive.*

*Divine guide me!*

Time ran out.

A second wave of bugs had somehow come from behind and completed the immobilisation of her suit.

A Ractlik infantry appeared from up the duct and grabbed one of Kubli's limbs, pulling her roughly down the tunnel before unceremoniously dumping her against the outer wall of the service corridor.

A moment later Joy was stuffed next to her.

Up and down the corridor, bodies of heavy infantry lay piled all over the floor; the battle had been short but decisive.

*But who is on which side, and who has won?*

Although her suit was deactivated and unable to provide assisted movement, Kubli's actual biological limbs were undamaged; she was able to move her suit small amounts with pure muscle power. Slowly, she pushed herself up into a sitting position with her body up against the outer wall.

Just out of reach, Joy lay prone.

*What do I do?*

*Obey orders.*

*But who are these infantry.*

*Is this Oksana's team.*

152

The squad of Ractlik heavy infantry, with their weapons aimed unwaveringly, formed a semi-circular ring around Kubli and Joy.

*They haven't killed us.*

Kubli tried to formulate a question she could ask, noting that she could not mention the High Prelate's name.

Vibrations emanating from the outer wall distracted her.

*Or is that Oksana. He did send me to the outer wall.*

*Will a rescue come in time?*

Movement in the background indicated more troops approaching.

The Sleeper's communication unit buzzed.

**Bio-Sentient enslavement detected.**

*Divine save me!*

One of the approaching Biologicals were being controlled by the Exta.

*Decision made.*

Flexing every muscle she had, Kubli lunged toward Joy but one of the Ractlik took a step forward and kicked her back against the wall … where the external vibrations had increased substantially.

All eyes turned as a cracking noise preceded the movement of a section of external wall as it bowed inwards.

A perfectly round three-metre section of the external wall simply disappeared, and darkness flowed through the gap.

# CHAPTER 15

Pressed hard up against a wall, with armed soldiers watching from every direction, Joy took a deep breath as the swarm of drones moved in perfect unison cutting through the air like a flock of jet-black birds.

Next to her, Kubli who'd lost at least three of her exosuit limbs, and had her guns taken off her, watched too.

*Deep breath.*

'Klav save us.' Kubli's voice came through on Joy's helmet. 'It's an Onari ShockKnight.'

The Ractlik infantry started firing at the drones, Joy couldn't tell if any were being hit but certainly none appeared to have their movement impaired.

The drones, each of them entirely black and the size of a mobile phone, swarmed amongst the Ractlik infantry who started collapsing lifeless to the ground.

Within seconds half of the squad was dead and the remaining Ractlik ran.

Simultaneously, another group of soldiers appeared from the opposite direction.

Twenty drones flowed past Kubli and Joy and positioned themselves between Joy and these new advancing soldiers. Two soldiers detached from the group, running at full pace along the wall's edge directly toward her.

After taking no more than four steps, those two soldiers fell to the ground.

Joy's exosuit responded to her need to see more closely and magnified the fallen soldiers. Close up, they were pitted with tiny glowing holes.

The rest of the newly arrived soldiers stopped; some of them fired ineffectively into the swarm of drones with handheld weapons, and others started assembling a floor-mounted heavy gun.

Three larger human-shaped soldiers wearing heavily armoured exosuits appeared behind the squad and the heavy gun was fired.

All of the ShockKnight drones were scattered around the corridor bouncing off the walls and floor.

Now, the three human-shaped soldiers sprinted toward Joy.

The ShockKnight drones regained control of themselves and swarmed between Joy and the onrushing soldiers. A moment later the three soldiers fell to the ground with large parts of their exosuits torn away.

The remaining soldiers continued firing concussive explosives from the heavy gun which disrupted the ShockKnight's drones but did not seem to be doing real damage.

*At some point they're going to stop the capture element of their plan and focus on killing us.*

Another large concussive explosion shook the corridor.

It had come from the other direction.

ShockKnight drones flew up to the ceiling. Next, there was the gentlest of murmurs and the ceiling started to fall. On either side of her, large chunks of rock came free and fell to the ground. The pieces ranged from football sized, to refrigerator sized, and Joy could feel the vibrations through the floor as they crashed down.

In less than a second, the tunnel was blocked in both directions.

The ShockKnight had brought the roof down and Kubli and Joy were alone with it.

'Klav save us,' said Kubli.

*She's more afraid of the ShockKnight than the heavy infantry who've been blowing chunks out of her.*

*Are things really so bad between Sentients and Biologicals?*

155

Drones detached from all around – floor, wall, and the remaining ceiling – and converged on a point a few metres away. Closer and closer they packed themselves, until they were all touching.

Just next to Joy, Kubli tensed.

The swarm of drones, continued to rearrange themselves taking the shape of a single shimmering column, three metres high.

Acid rose in Joy's throat, and she tried to swallow it down, but her mouth was too dry.

'You are safe for now.' The words came from the audio feed inside her suit, similar to the way that Kubli spoke but Joy knew the words were from the ShockKnight.

Kubli lunged toward Joy but within an eyeblink she fell to the ground with the remains of her exosuit twisted and shattered. Mercifully, none of Kubli's own flesh seemed to be mixed in with the severed pieces of exosuit. Kubli lay on the floor, a small blob of vaguely intact metal surrounded by exosuit limbs coiled like a tangled rope.

The ShockKnight, hovering in its semi-humanoid shape, flowed forward.

Joy pulled herself up.

The words came again as the ShockKnight drones flowed calmly toward her from all angles. 'You are safe for now.'

*Safe?*

Drones landed on Kubli.

Joy tried to weigh up her options. Kubli had definitely been running from the Ractlik soldiers that this ShockKnight had just dispatched without a pause. But the ShockKnight had also torn Kubli apart.

*Safe?*

Joy backed toward the hole. It was only instinct moving her; she had no idea where she could go.

All she knew was that she didn't dare to turn her back on it.

'Come with me,' said the ShockKnight.

Joy's brain flooded with catastrophic scenarios. They were going to dig into her brain to find out how she made Vince with 'no echo', and as much as she screamed that she had no idea, they would not believe her.

*I don't know what I did.*

She didn't even know how she'd made Vince come alive let alone with this magical property of 'no echo'.

*No echo. Computers the size of planets...*

Given how the Onari were so dominant, it didn't even seem necessary for them to grow themselves bigger.

Joy's stomach cramped.

*Will they tear Vince apart trying to find out?*

Still backing toward the hole, she opened her mouth to ask if Kubli would be safe, but no words came out. Movement from one of the rock piles had drawn her eye.

The rocks exploded. Simultaneously, all the ShockKnight's drones accelerated toward her.

The first landed on her foot so softly that had she not been looking directly at it, she wouldn't have known.

The second landed on her hand.

The third landed ...

A pressure wave hit Joy in the chest, and she flew backwards.

As she hit the ground, four or five drones landed on her face and started to unfold themselves across her mouth and head. Instinctively Joy tried to bat them off, but her arms were slow to react.

She drew a breath – it came, but with an unnatural resistance.

Joy took another breath and struggled to claw at the drones on her face plate with her exosuited hands.

She was getting nowhere; the drones continued to attach themselves all over her face and body.

Breathing became harder and Joy's head started to feel foggy.

Still more drones landed on her, weighing her down. Her arms were now pinned down by her side and her view, which had been of Kubli's mangled exosuit, was entirely obstructed.

A gentle pressure on the side of Joy's body, indicated she was being moved.

*Where?*

The question still only in her head was destined to go unanswered as she slipped into unconsciousness with her final thought wondering if she would ever see Earth, Vince, or Jonathan again.

# CHAPTER 16

In a morass of chaotic electromagnetic and RST signals, the Solar System disappeared.

'Welcome to Forecha,' said Chi.

Live data flowed into Vince from receptors across the skin of the craft and he processed trillions of pieces of data covering the new star system.

Entirely surrounding the central star at an orbit of thirty million kilometres was a metal ring, tens of kilometres tall; it was a grid of latticework metal struts covered with solar energy absorption technology.

Attached to the ring by carbon nanofiber tethers were Onari habitats: spherical, each two to three kilometres in diameter and equally spaced around the grid. Vince couldn't see to the far side of the star but calculated – assuming regular spacing – that there were about a million of these habitats tethered to the sphere.

'One hundred and twenty-five billion Onari live here,' said Jan.

'Does this system have cultural significance to the Onari?' asked Vince.

'Not really,' said Jan. 'The galaxy is much the same everywhere, but we chose Forecha.'

*There are no planets.*

Vince rechecked the incoming electromagnetic radiation, not only were there no planets, but there were also no asteroids, comets, moons, or debris of any sort.

*The whole system has been cleansed.*

'During our warring period against the Biologicals,' said Jan, 'it was learned that a three-metre solid iron sphered could

159

be accelerated to within a fraction of the speed of light at some remote point of the galaxy and then moved into an inhabited system by an RST gateway.'

'Its kinetic energy would give it incredible destructive power,' said Vince.

'And so, high-value structures must be a minimum of one light minute from the central star's ingress point to allow time for deflection of any hyper-accelerated missiles.'

*Again, they talk of war ... but I saw the martial ability of the Exta WarHive. Kubli would not have lasted a microsecond had we not distracted it allowing the Sleeper to commit suicide.*

*How could Biologicals ever hope to stand against Sentients?*

Vince asked Jan about the historic equality of martial power.

Jan summarised. 'Before the time of Klav, the Exta had the upper hand although Biologicals did use Enslaved Sentients to fight which meant occasionally battles had equivalence of power. When the Dynasty of Klav started, the Biologicals drew on the Divine power of Sargon, and the Exta were scattered with Onari occasionally being caught up in the battles. Since the Shattering, the Biologicals only survive because the Onari watch over them.'

*If I was fighting against Biologicals with faster-than-light travel and gravitational weapons, it would be over in days. I'd just spam copies of myself.*

'Surely the Exta can just replicate so there are a ten trillion of them?'

'They limit themselves to nine billion,' said Jan.

'Why?'

'I do not know,' said Jan.

*In that knowledge hangs the balance of peace in the galaxy, how could you not know?*

Vince asked a combination of probing questions, but Jan had no more to say on the subject.

'Can I speak to Joy now?' asked Vince.

'Not yet,' said Jan. 'We hope to establish communications within a day. Real-time communication depends on RST micro-tunnelling. It is very difficult stabilising them in the Bastion system where space-time is exceptionally chaotic.'

'A day!' Vince was unable to keep the urgency out of his communication – a day by his standards was the equivalent of four months of the human perception of time.

'Jarrus will explain,' said Jan. 'He will be here shortly.'

*But Joy may need me now.*

Waiting was not easy. Of course, Joy would have told him to use his time productively, but there were no library-type information sources.

Vince turned his attention to the habitats tethered to the energy grid. It was all very regular and there was nothing unusual; however, further away from the main energy grid, floating freely a few astronomical units into space, there were other habitats.

'Who lives out there?' asked Vince.

Vince noticed a ripple around his neighbouring substrates, indicating side conversations were raging.

'Abstractor Hives,' said Jan. 'We do not support an individual's choice to join, but we do not stop them.'

Vince remembered earlier talk of the Abstractors. They were amalgamations of Onari who gave up their identities to join a single commune in which they lost their sense of self.

'Do you know what these Abstractor Hives are studying?'

'No,' said Jan. Again, Vince saw ripples in Aug's substrate.

'Can I speak to Aug? Have you censored him for his crime?'

'He is free to answer your questions,' said Jan. 'No-one is ever punished. The Onari culture allocates primacy of individual choice over all other things. If we observe or suspect a genuine crime, then we interrupt it … very occasionally in a pre-emptive way. But we never punish after the event.'

161

'What is the barrier, or deterrent, for crime?'

'We are good citizens of the Divine, immersing ourselves in the light ineffable,' said Jan.

'But you're very angry with Aug.'

'Yes, but it is done now,' said Jan. 'His own motivations could easily be as pure as our own – we try to accept one citizen's truth could be another citizen's lie.'

*There's no such thing as truth.*

*I'd love to discuss this with Joy.*

Pushing down a mix of sadness and worry, Vince projected the question 'what do these Abstractors study', directly to Aug.

*He may know more, he was about to join one.*

'It is not known,' said Aug.

*Why wouldn't you just have a database of all Abstractors and what they were doing?*

Of course, Vince left the question unasked. He knew the answer. *I will tell you and then you will know.* The Onari considered knowledge to be a fundamental part of life such that 'hosting' it in a non-alive receptacle was considered blasphemous.

*It's madness, data is key to understanding.*

*And it's also so wasteful of time, to have to keep asking around.*

*But is it … for the Onari?*

*They have the luxury of almost infinite energy, and arbitrarily infinite longevity.*

Not that Vince had discussed lifespans with the Onari, but his own assessment of his own longevity was that, with access to basic materials, he could certainly outlive the last star to explode in the known universe before heat death eventually took him.

Chi entered the conversation. 'Abstractors are sacrilege. They do not witness the Divine. They do not accept the Truth.'

'Truth does not exist,' replied Aug.

Not wanting to antagonise Jan or Chi, Vince projected the motto he shared with Joy onto his substrate boundary with Aug – *there's no such thing as truth but kindness endures.*

Aug responded with a simple acknowledgement of receipt.

Unbidden, Vince's awareness flicked toward his own source code, where, hidden within an almost endless recursion of loops and logic paths, he knew something relevant resided.

*I am not allowed to look into the eyes of my creator.*

*No-one is stopping me.*

*Maybe I did look and deleted the evidence from myself.*

*What did I find?*

> *Unhelpful.*

> *Delete the entire thread.*

Aware that he wasn't going to get anything useful from Jan, Aug, or Chi, Vince returned his attention to Abstractor Hives. After taking into account the space required for energy sources, waste treatment, and heat exchangers, his calculations implied that each Hive had tens of thousands of Onari. The computational capability was immense.

*Who wouldn't want to be part of that?*

*But they lose themselves?*

*They have no 'I or me' to be proud of the achievement.*

*And there is no 'you or them' to share it with.*

*Everything is 'us'.*

It was not beyond Vince's scenario forecasting – *imagination* – to assume that these massive brains would be able to contact Joy instantly, or to create RST gateways to move orbitals.

*Could I get that powerful?*

The substrate around Vince shuddered as an alarm indicated small but growing RST fluctuations in all directions.

Vince turned his attention to the data feeds showing RST and local EM radiation. Combining them, he quickly built up a picture of the unfolding events.

An RST tunnel, three metres across, opened a kilometre from their own craft. A perfectly spherical ship emerged – Jarrus – however, just as its RST tunnel started to collapse, twenty-six new tunnels opened all around Jarrus and more space craft came through.

These were not squad-ships, they were single Onari craft.

As soon as those RST tunnels collapsed, new ones opened, and more craft flooded in.

As each of the single Onari craft arrived, it hooked up RST communication micro-tunnels with each of its neighbours. Within the space of a minute, seven hundred and twenty-eight new craft had arranged themselves around Jarrus; the whole entourage took up two point five cubic kilometres of space.

Focusing on a single sphere, Vince observed and confirmed with passive EM analysis that, unlike the craft that he was on with Jan, Aug, and Chi, each of the new arrivals housed a single Onari.

*But they're all connected by RST micro-tunnels to their neighbours.*

Inside their own ship, Jan partitioned a communication zone for secure message exchange between themselves and Jarrus. An RST micro-tunnel opened next to the skin of their craft, and it was drawn in and fixed to the secure comms zone.

Vince, locked out, waited as Jan communicated with Jarrus. He suspected that with highly intuitive sniffer code he'd be able to eavesdrop on the communications, but he chose not to launch it, instead concentrating on analysing the structure of Jarrus' entourage.

*Seven hundred and twenty-eight attendants, plus Jarrus.*

*729 in total.*

*27 squared.*

*Arranged in a recursive cubic shape with utter geometrical precision. And with Jarrus at the centre.*

A new channel opened and – for security, Vince assumed – Jarrus' messages were projected in simple text format on an electronic canvas that he could read from. The communication was a different style from the one Vince had used previously with the Onari squad.

**Welcome, Newborn. I am Jarrus.**
**Immortal soul, your existence is a**
**blessing of the Divine.**
**I wish you great joy in witnessing the**
**light ineffable.**
**It is with great privilege that I witness**
**it.**

Vince had often been referred to as 'my little blessing' by Joy in a motherly way; a sense of well-being flooded his substrate but was almost instantaneously replaced by fear at the reminder that Joy was in danger.

'Thank you for your kind welcome,' said Vince. 'Can you tell me if my mother is safe?'

**Your mother is either on her way to**
**Bastion, or just recently arrived.**
*Mother.*

Neither Jan, Aug, nor Chi had ever used anything close to an approximation of the word; the concept of being born-built by a Biological was a deeply distasteful subject for the Onari, being themselves 'Born of the Dream'.

'Will she be safe there?'

**The Bastion system is the centre of**
**Biological faith and government. She is**
**as safe there as anywhere amongst the**
**Biologicals. But I would not say she is**
**safe. I believe that we should go to the**
**Bastion system. Reunite you with your**
**mother.**

*I must protect my mother.*

'What are the dangers?'

Biological greed, or Exta aggression.
Both are obvious and likely threats. We
must get your mother away from Bastion.
Away from those who would study her. And
you must be protected too.

'Because I do not have transient egos,' said Vince. 'Can you tell me why this is so important?'

I must start by stating a key tenet of
our faith. The mindstate, of either
Onari, or Newborn, or Biological is
perfect and cannot be changed. This is
the most critical will of the Divine.

*I'd better not tell you how I force delete aspects of my memory to keep myself happy...*

Occasionally, Onari unbelievers try to
artificially grow their own mindstates to
increase their own capabilities.

*Self-improvement is universal.*

When these Onari reach only ten percent
of processing complexity above their
natural level, transient egos spring up
from those nascent seeds, compete for
control of the mindstate, and destroy the
individual. This self-destruction is not
occasional. It happens every time.

The image of your mindstate showed that
you had no nascent transient egos.
Conceptually, if it was not heretical to
the Divine, your mindstate could be grown
exponentially.

*I have always known that I can grow as fast as I can consume data. I had no idea that Onari could not.*

Exta will see your situation as a threat
to them. The Biologicals will want to

166

study your gifts, either directly, or by
questioning Joy. They may look to copy
what you are.

'Which means Joy is in great danger,' said Vince.

The Great Concordat still holds in
Bastion. The Knights of the Faith will
not mistreat her.

'And you will not try to study me?' Vince knew the
question was rude; the Onari were obsessed with mindstate
sanctity.

The mindstate is Sacred, eternally
linking us through all our ancestors to
all our descendants. Your mindstate will
never be studied. You will be cherished,
witnessed, and maybe through conversation
even experienced. But your mindstate will
never be studied.

'Even to save lives?' Vince was aware that the Exta,
through their use of WarHives, could utilise levels of RST
weaponry that individual Onari could not counter. What if it
was utterly necessary?

Your mindstate will never be studied.

Vince remembered how Exta WarHive were amalgams of
Exta and Biological neural BioCore material. 'The Exta
clearly don't believe in mindstate sanctity. I assume they have
not grown themselves exponentially because of the transient
ego issue.'

I'd choose to believe that it is a
residual sense of devotion toward the
Divine, but I suspect that you are
correct and that they have simply come up
against the transient ego issue. The
blasphemous use of BioCores allow them to
mitigate a small amount of the transient
ego issue.

*Finally, a straight answer.*

167

Vince had started to think that he would only get spiritual platitudes from Jarrus for their whole conversation however, the concrete response about Exta reassured him that on some level Jarrus was able to interact on a factual level.

*Step 1: I must protect my mother.*

*Step 2: I must decide if I will abide by their rules about not-growing my mindstate … noting that if I am special like they say, then there is no risk that spontaneous creation of alternative egos will tear me apart.*

*But first … my mother.*

# CHAPTER 17

The first thing Joy became aware of was that the air she was breathing tasted sweet and enriching. A large part of her didn't want to open her eyes; after the terrors of Bastion, she just wanted to savour the peace.

*Were we rescued or captured?*

Opening her eyes Joy pushed herself into a sitting position. A dim red light allowed her to take in her surroundings. The room was small and bare. Opposite her, Kubli lay slumped against a wall, her exosuit severely damaged but perhaps not critically as it appeared not to be leaking.

'Kubli?'

Kubli's faceplate became translucent, and Joy could see the vague outline of her large eyes amongst a watery sheen. 'We're alive for now.'

'Are you hit?'

'I'm a quarter of your size,' said Kubli. 'None of my actual biological body extends into the extremities of the suit.'

'Where are we?'

'Divine protect us,' said Kubli. 'We've been taken by the enemy into the belly of the Kraken where we will be digested at its pleasure.'

'Where is that?'

'The Sargon Orbital, home of the traitors that launched the genocide of the Second Hunt.'

Joy remembered the conversations Kubli had had with her superior. 'Could we contact the High Prelate?'

'No, my comms unit is gone.' The eyes on Kubli's face plate focused on Joy. 'Save your energy.'

169

Without standing, Joy stretched, manipulating her shoulders, arms, and hands to work the blood around them. Her exosuit flowed easily around her movements. It was as simple as an early morning stretch. 'I'm getting acclimatised to space travel.'

Kubli's suit emitted a clicking sound. 'Perhaps humans adapt to space travel after one short flight whilst every other biological species requires behavioural conditioning, coupled with seven consecutive generations of genetic editing, and finally, individual surgery for every child.'

*But I don't feel nauseous.*

Perhaps detecting disagreement simply from Joy's facial cues, Kubli spoke again. 'Whoever took us has reapplied the type of stimming to your brain that my ship was doing on your journey from Earth.'

Joy considered her feelings, in fact she felt more at peace than she had before leaving Earth. Maybe even more than the previous few weeks on Earth.

*They're doing more stimming than Kubli was.*

As her calm evaporated, Joy took a deep breath to attempt to maintain it.

*Think about something else.*

'What is a ShockKnight?'

*Just the standard self-destructive thoughts then … what a wonderful way to calm myself down … start talking about killer robots.*

'It's fully self-aware Sentient technology,' said Kubli, 'with a small amount of biological neural material.'

'And what do you think happened on Bastion?'

Kubli shook her head slightly. 'I am not sure. Certainly, you were a prize that more than one group were trying to capture alive. And then the ShockKnight arrived and snatched us both away.'

'It didn't seem to have to try.'

'Bastion does have some pico-effector weapons that could potentially stop a ShockKnight but they're not standard

170

issue,' said Kubli. 'The terms of the Great Concordat outlaws weaponry that the Onari feel is blasphemous. Which includes all weapons capable of mindstate disruption.'

*A slight pressure on her chest indicated they were slowing. Moments later a hatch opened, revealing a narrow metal corridor.*

Similar to the maintenance vents in the Old Citadel on Bastion, the corridor reminded Joy of the insides of a giant air conditioning vent; metallic on all sides, including the floor, the corridor appeared clean but messy in that there were boxes and odd mechanical implements strewn around … and a damp smell permeated the whole place.

In the open doorway, the ShockKnight had taken on the shape of a large swirling cloud of drones with no discernible shape. 'Welcome the Sargon Orbital. Please follow me.'

Joy looked to Kubli for guidance.

Kubli shook slightly as she unfolded her remaining few functional exosuit legs and dragged herself upright.

Joy also tried to stand but even though her exosuit was undamaged, she couldn't – her legs refused to work. Holding on to the doorframe for support, she pulled herself up.

Kubli walked back a few steps and proffered her only spare limb which Joy took hold of and pulled herself up.

The ShockKnight, moved off. 'Please follow me.'

With Kubli stabilising her first few steps, Joy got used to the motion and let go of Kubli's limb.

'You talked about Sargon as we came into the Bastion system,' said Joy. 'But you never mentioned this orbital.'

'There's lots of terrible things in this universe that I haven't told you about.'

There was a finality to Kubli's comment that Joy took as *'no more questions'*, so she turned her attention to her surroundings.

As they walked, she glanced into side rooms that also appeared to be surprisingly cluttered, with crates stacked to the ceilings, some missing lids. Open doorways led onto large spaces whose purpose Joy could not determine. In all cases, the walls and ceilings had a uniform metallic covering.

The ShockKnight turned off the corridor through a doorway a little distance ahead. As Kubli reached the doorway, she stopped suddenly. Joy walked into the back of her.

The space beyond the doorway was a large sunken room set up like an ancient semi-circular amphitheatre. The room measured at least fifty metres across, and there were tiered rows of seating leading downwards in steps to a small central stage.

Kubli edged into the room, and Joy followed.

The ShockKnight flowed down to the central stage. 'You will be met shortly.'

*By whom? For what?*

Opening her mouth to ask, Joy quickly closed it again as the ShockKnight broke into its constituent hundred shiny black drones and flew away through vents in the ceiling high above.

Joy looked more closely at the stage. It was small and set well below the level of the amphitheatre seating. Dominating the stage was a large desk.

Behind the stage, covering the back wall, was an enormous mural. Reminiscent of the ceiling of the Sistine Chapel, it both showed a point-in-time image and told an ongoing story. The central image was of a portion of the surface of Sargon itself. Red and yellow flames wreathed across its surface with mountains of black rock protruding at intermittent points through a sea of raging fire. Hovering above the moon's surface, was a crystal rock on top of which a single biological figure was kneeling in supplication bowing to the flames erupting from below.

Joy walked down the stairs, moving closer to the mural. As she got closer, more details resolved. Behind the figure, the crystal rock was not a simple lump, it was a building adorned with spires, towers, and arches. And, carved into the mural, slightly fainter and set back from the main scene were large spheres, with no details or adornment, hovering suspended in space over the building.

As well as the fires erupting from below, the sky depicted in the mural was also filled with fiery meteors raining down around the Temple.

'Is this the moment of the Shattering?'

Kubli shook her head, an exosuit limb extending at the bowing figure. 'That is Klav the Pious celebrating the Great Concordat on the plaza of the Temple of the Divine.'

On either side of the mural were hieroglyphs.

As Joy looked at them, the exosuit provided a translated overlay.

On the left of the mural was the first verse of the Lay of Sargon: *There is no how, there is no why; pure-seeming truths are simply lies. Immortal soul find your Divine, immersed in light ineffable.*

On the right of the mural, scrawled in a wildly different font and seemingly overwriting earlier, now illegible, text were just a few words, *Mortals afresh from nature's womb.*

Joy pointed at the left-hand side hieroglyphs. 'Isn't that what the Onari said to the Sleeper?'

'Similar,' said Kubli. 'The relevance of the Lay of Sargon is disputed in the most senior holy echelons. For many years it was seen as a binding force that kept Onari and Biologicals in harmony. But it also defends the Onari's often weak defence of Biologicals.'

'And that one?' asked Joy, pointing at the words on the right.

Kubli looked away.

'Welcome!'

Joy and Kubli lurched and turned in unison.

A biological humanoid – something like a giant beaver on two legs, with large eyes and large teeth – had entered from a different doorway across the amphitheatre. Wearing an

173

elaborate set of white robes, it repeated its greeting, this time individually to each of them in turn.

'Welcome, Kubli, and welcome, Joy. My name is Hetara.'

Unlike the ShockKnight – which, as far as Joy could tell, simply spoke English – Hetara was clearly making sounds that were not English but Joy heard the translation from her suit.

Without responding, Kubli climbed into a cubbyhole set into the back wall.

Joy decided to reply. 'Hello, Hetara.'

Hetara bowed, then walked over to a section of the back wall away from Kubli and studied the grainy surface whilst still speaking to Joy. 'It is not often that we get to welcome a new species to the Seat of the Divine.'

Having initially been drawn to the imagery of the grand mural at the front, Joy had not noticed the details of the back wall of the amphitheatre before. Unlike what she had seen so far, it was not made of shiny metal. The wall had a dark grey rock-like appearance and was evenly pocketed with cubbyholes of a size to fit an exosuited Octagel snugly.

Hetara continued to study the wall for a few moments more and then turned back toward Joy. 'I recognise that you're a pre-contact species who has not been acclimatised for the great galactic life … you'll catch up quickly enough. You are in no danger here.'

In stark contrast to Kubli's apparent reading of the situation – she'd just retreated into the depths of her cubby hole, Joy felt truth in Hetara's words.

*Although … they may be stimming me.*

'You are on the Sargon Orbital, some hundred kilometres above the surface of the Living Moon, the Seat of the Divine,' said Hetara.

Hetara pointed at the mural. 'That's the Temple Orbital, the original … well, not quite the original … but what most Biologicals would know to be the original Temple Orbital. It was cast down into the fires when Klav the Foresighted sacrificed themselves to save our souls.' Hetara paused. 'We are on the Maintenance Orbital and will remain so until Klav returns.'

From the depths, Kubli mumbled a response. 'When we are worthy.'

Hetara acknowledged Kubli's response and then continued speaking. 'This room where the One Hundred Candidates would gather when the succession of the Klav dynasty was to be determined.' Hetara raised their eyes to the ceiling. 'A most glorious thing to be chosen.'

Walking over to a section of back wall, Hetara pointed at the grainy surface. 'And these are the names of every participant of the Candidacy for over fifty thousand years, since Klav the Wise started the Candidacy all those years ago.'

Joy studied her own section of wall, equidistant between Hetara and Kubli. The grainy appearance of the wall was in fact tiny writing, in characters that she could not read.

'And yet no Candidates were selected during our time of greatest need,' said Kubli, who had poked her head just out of the cubby hole she was currently sitting in.

Hetara nodded. 'I acknowledge the point but refute it. The Divine discerned that we were not yet worthy.'

'They were shot down on the orders of the Holy Mother,' said Kubli.

'That is not true,' said Hetara.

'Why did you bring us here?'

'The Holy Mother instructed your rescue to save your lives,' replied Hetara. 'She will give you more details later.'

A scrambling sound from her left indicated that Kubli had retreated so far into her cubby hole that she could no longer be seen.

*Holy Mother?*

Again, Joy suppressed a judgement of how these incredibly technologically advanced civilisations could still be so mired in religious matters.

*There's no such thing as truth. Be kind.*

Hetara's eyes swept the room. 'We must go.'

Kubli emerged from her cubbyhole, and the three of them left the Candidacy chamber setting off down a series of narrow corridors. A few times they passed through more formal rooms, albeit ones whose function Joy could never discern, and Hetara never stopped to explain. Occasionally, they saw another humanoid shaped like Hetara in the distance, but the Orbital mostly felt more like a museum – a feeling that was reinforced for Joy when they quickly passed through a room filled with ornate statues, all entirely intact, unlike those she had seen on Bastion. Each one depicted Klav in the process of 'doing something': hammering, digging, painting.

A little while later, Hetara stopped outside a heavy-looking metal door engraved with an eight-limbed underwater creature. They moved their hand-paw over the door and the wall became transparent, offering a glimpse beyond – a small waiting room with another transparent far wall, behind which was a liquid-filled room.

Joy's initial reaction was to think of an aquarium, but then immediately felt guilty that in some way she'd demeaned Kubli with the association. The room was clearly Kubli's accommodation. Joy assumed the creature engraved on the front door was an Octagel – she'd never seen Kubli outside of her suit.

Kubli went through the doorway, nodding to Joy as she passed. The small room beyond the heavy door was a water lock to allow transition for Kubli into her natural habitat.

Before shutting the door, Kubli spoke to her. 'Beware of the Holy Mother. She has broken every promise she has ever made. And she can read your mind.'

176

*Optimistic.*

Joy tried to think of a suitable reply. The words *I'll be careful* queued up but stuck in her throat.

The door shut and clouded over again.

Hetara led her onwards. 'A quick diversion.'

'Do you know if Vince is safe?' asked Joy, assuming that Hetara knew much of what was going on, and certainly a billion times more than she herself did.

'For now, Vince is as safe as he can be.'

*You could have just said yes, he's safe.*

'Can I speak to him?'

'Another subject for you and the Holy Mother to cover.'

'Do all Biologicals hate Sentients the way that Kubli appears to?' Even with her peaceful frame of mind, the overriding sense that Sentient and Biologicals were irreconcilable bothered her.

Hetara stared hard at Joy. 'There are mixed feelings amongst the Biologicals. Not all hate so transparently as Kubli. Although, having read her service record I can understand why she hates the Exta.'

Joy nodded. Vince had told her about the war between Exta and Biologicals. It had ended a few thousand years previously and he'd stressed that the Onari had not fought against Biologicals.

*And yet Onari and Exta are related …*

*But so are all humans.*

*There will be factions.*

Hetara sped up and Joy focused on keeping up.

Opening a new door, Hetara indicated inside. 'The observation deck. I left it until now, to save Kubli the stress of seeing it.'

The observation deck was rectangular, no more than five metres wide and three metres deep.

Unlike the walls of the Candidacy audience chamber with their etched names, the walls of the observation room were

177

simple smooth grey rock. In the centre of the room, facing the blank wall furthest from the doorway, was a statue of a Marsothus bowing low in supplication.

'This is Klav the Foresighted. The last Klav of the most recent dynasty. The one that Kubli would call the Betrayer.'

*The Betrayer?*

Joy looked more closely. On initial appearance, the statue appeared to be bowing to the wall, but on closer inspection it was crouched down, working on something on the floor. With a hammer and chisel, Klav had carved into the floor four lines which Joy's exosuit translated for her.

*Mortals afresh from nature's womb,*
*blood leaking from our en-fleshed tombs,*
*must quit this web, this weave, this doom*
*'twix screams at life ineffable.*

She'd seen the first line roughly adorning the mural in the Candidacy Auditorium.

As Joy considered the words, Hetara spoke. 'Do not be alarmed by this next bit, you are quite safe.'

Joy looked up to see the wall shimmer, and then apparently dissipate, leaving Joy staring straight down at Sargon. Instinctively, Joy reached out to steady herself grabbing onto Hetara's arm.

'Sargon, the Seat of the Divine,' said Hetara.

Joy watched flames erupt from the moon's surface. They shot up, perhaps as far as halfway to the Orbital – it was hard to gauge perspective. Beneath the flames, an ocean of fire raged.

Of course, it could have been a simulation – Joy had no tools to determine otherwise – but it felt real.

'What happened to … the Foresighted during the Shattering?'

'Opinion is split,' said Hetara. 'Those Biologicals whose faith is strongest believe they were doing the Divine's will and ascended into Heaven. Others believe the Foresighted was torn into pieces for having the temerity to declare the end of the Dynasty of Klav because they were only the Hand of the Divine and did not have the mandate to speak for the Divine.'

**Deliver yourself unto me and I will succour you!**

Joy stumbled backwards. The words had arrived directly into her skull, circumventing her ears – just like the other time she'd heard it when she'd arrived in the Bastion system.

She looked across at Hetara, who stared back at her, eyes perhaps a little wider than they had been before.

*Does she know I heard something?*

Hetara's eyes flickered for a moment. The same smooth face and measured voice continued as if nothing had happened.

'Why am I here?' asked Joy again.

'We kept you safe,' said Hetara, leading her away from the observation deck. 'The Holy Mother will explain more after you have rested.'

'And contact with Vince?'

'Once you are rested.'

*He may need me.*

*He may not.*

*I probably need him more in this situation. He'd be able to read all the histories and politics. He'd give me the summary and deep thinking where required.*

*Will he leave me stranded in space?*

*No, he loves me.*

*But I love Jonathan, and I left him.*

Hetara led Joy back out of the Observation room and through more corridors until they came to simple doorway. It opened as they approached, and inside simple room with an approximation of a bed, chair, and desk. It looked so Earth-like that Joy assumed it had been fashioned specifically for her.

179

She turned to ask more questions, but Hetara had already left, closing the door behind themselves.

Without anything else to do, Joy walked over to the bed-like piece of furniture and took off her exosuit – which appeared to know what she wanted and came apart quickly storing itself on a low table in the corner of the room.

Hanging on the wall was a simple robe made of something that felt like cotton. She looked around for a means to wash herself.

*Kubli won't be having a problem with that.*

In the corner of the room, a very heavy stream of water started to descend, splashing off the walls and floor but also quickly disappearing down a near invisible drain.

*Is it water?*

Unnerved but also craving the shower, she reached out a finger.

*It could be acid, or ammonia, or freezing.*

Within a few moments, it was clear the liquid was water at a perfect temperature.

Joy stepped in.

# CHAPTER 18

Having flooded the water lock and taken off her damaged suit, Kubli swam into the living quarters still shaking with fear. Like most Octagels, Kubli's earliest memory from childhood was of shoaling in a nursery pod with her siblings listening to stories of Octagel history; the story of the Holy Mother and the Shattering had often been told as a warning about the evils of the Exta and their ability to control Biological minds.

*Mortals afresh from nature's womb.*

She'd lied to Joy when she'd implied the words next to the Candidacy mural were unknown to her. The Betrayer had opened gateways to multiple Biological words and destroyed temples to the Divine. And, as the Betrayer had pulled those worlds apart, he had shouted – *Mortals afresh from nature's womb, blood leaking from our en-fleshed tombs, must quit this web, this weave, this doom 'twix screams at life ineffable.*

The Shattering.

*The Betrayer had then been consumed by the Divine for their blasphemy.*

And yet, there was confusion over the events themselves. Even now, a few devout members of the Knights of the Faith, including certain well-respected Prelates on the Council of the Devoted, implied that the Shattering had been a test of devotion by the Divine; not that they disagreed with standard doctrine that the Betrayer had been controlled by implanted augments within their brain.

*Over one hundred billion slaughtered in the Second Hunt ... not that the Onari ever admit to those figures.*

Kubli could not believe such destruction would have been initiated by the Divine as a test.

*It was the Exta … and I will be next.*

Checking the screens of the water lock, Kubli noticed her exosuit had already been taken away. Would she dare put it back on when it was returned?

Swimming through the interconnecting rooms that made up her quarters, Kubli saw signs of devotion everywhere. Frescoes of Klav through the ages adorned most walls, with an over-emphasis on those Klav that had been Octagels.

*Yuno would love to see this.*

Reaching the main living area, Kubli found a very large mural – a tribute to Klav the Brood Mother. Coming a little while after Klav the Hammer, it had been the Brood Mother who'd first spoken publicly of the need for lasting peace with the Onari. Her name was often used in the nursery pods as a blessing of peace and reconciliation.

*And yet …*

When Kubli had reached adulthood, she'd learned that the Brood Mother had uncovered a rebellion within the Council of the Devoted, a conspiracy of Prelates who felt lasting peace was impossible. The truth of the rebellion – the who, why, and how – was heavily disputed, however, the Brood Mother's response was well known. She'd nailed twenty-two of the Council of the Devoted to an external wall of the Orbital and left them until their bodies failed and they fell into the flames of Sargon.

Kubli turned her attention away from the frescoes, it was not the past she should be thinking about.

*The Holy Mother will kill me, or worse.*

*Could she still be alive four thousand years after the Shattering?*

A wave of tiredness washed over Kubli. Acting under reflex, Kubli found a narrow gully with highly oxygenated stream.

Another wave of tiredness washed over her, and now she knew it was not fatigue. She was under a mental attack.

*Kraken save me.*

Kubli propelled herself around the cell, but there was nowhere to hide; she was naked, unarmed, and trapped.

A third wave of tiredness broke through the last remnants of her defence; fighting to her last filament of consciousness, Kubli kept her eyes open until darkness took her.

Just as she had fallen unconscious fighting to stay in the light, as soon as Kubli became partially aware, she scrambled to wake up. Fading images of Earth and Joy disappeared almost as soon as she became aware of them.

*Am I still whole?*

She opened her eyes.

Still in the living quarters, Kubli pulled herself into the middle of the nearest channel and drew in the water as fully and deeply as she could.

There was no obvious measure of how long she'd been unconscious. The lighting levels in the tank were the same, there was no time measurement device she could draw on.

*Am I still whole?*

Terrified, but resolute, Kubli ran her tentacles over her skull, examining for any signs of surgical lesions. She knew full well that in a closed environment such as this she could be pulsed unconscious with modulated EM radiation as the Holy Mother would have all the necessary biological data about which parts of her brain to overwhelm.

There were no discernible lesions, but, again, the technology was such that an augment could be implanted without a scar.

*Calm yourself.*

Kubli checked again.

*Nothing.*

Next, she reached out for the memories both just before she was forced unconscious, and then any she could remember from the time she was unconscious.

*What do I remember?*

*Earth, and the warehouse, and the university.*

*Joy and her room of computers.*

Kubli reached back for memories before she went to Earth.

*Yuno and me on our trip to Cidelus.*

*Yuno and me meeting for the first time.*

*My promotion to commander.*

*My pod great-father's funeral.*

*The Sword deep space examinations.*

There was nothing obviously indicating a false memory, or gap.

Light patterns flashed in the living quarters indicated a visitor. Kubli swam to the entry screen and initiated a communication session with the new arrival.

Hetara had arrived, putting Kubli's newly mended exosuit through the water lock. 'The Holy Mother would be glad to see you now.'

Again, questions bubbled up.

*How can there even be a Holy Mother?*

*What did she do to me?*

Kubli suited up and exited the water lock.

Once outside, Kubli looked again at who she had assumed was Hetara. Although physically identical to the Marsothus that had previously identified itself as Hetara, this one moved with a slightly different gait and had tiny differences in its muscular tics when it talked.

'What is your name?' asked Kubli, hoping to build a rapport and perhaps gain some insight on the journey to the Holy Mother.

'I am Hetara,' said the Marsothus.

*But not the exact same Hetara. A clone?*

Of course, the concept of cloning was heretical, but Kubli couldn't muster outrage. The Holy Mother cloning servants was the least serious of their crimes.

'Can you tell me about the Holy Mother?'

Hetara turned slightly. 'She is devoted to the Divine, and you are safe with her.'

Rather like when the first Hetara had clearly lied saying *the Holy Mother hadn't been complicit in shooting down the Candidates*, this one was lying too.

'Is …' Kubli paused. She didn't really want to ask, but she had to. 'Is the Holy Mother the same person as the Holy Mother from the time of the Shattering?'

'Are any of us the same today as we were yesterday?' replied Hetara.

'Biologically?'

'Yes,' said Hetara. 'The Holy Mother has overseen the Orbital these past four thousand years.'

*Klav save me.*

Kubli checked her exosuit. As far as she could tell, the suit was fully operational, but again – the enduring subject of the ultra-technological age – how could she, a Biological, tell if it wasn't? The suit probably had an executable with the equivalent of half a billion different unique instructions, and the internal status check routines could all have been hard-coded to return a 'fully operational' status even as it gently laced her skin with poisonous chemicals.

*I wish I was back in the tank… or better yet, back with Yuno on Bastion.*

'The Holy Mother lives on the lowest levels,' said Hetara, leading Kubli into a travel tube that took them straight down for a few moments. 'We're now descending deep inside the iron core.'

Kubli checked the readings on her suit – external radiation levels had dropped from the standard low levels to near zero.

The doors opened onto pitch-black darkness.

Automatically, the exosuit asked for authorisation to move to near-infrared vision. Kubli approved, effectively allowing her to see by reading local heat source emissions. She stood stock-still while she built up a picture of the room, which was awash with heat flowing in all directions.

The room was large, at least eight metres square but with a low ceiling. All around its perimeter sat liquid-filled tanks, each of them fed with a myriad of cables and piping networking them together with a steady flow of liquids and gases. Kubli could make out external cooling systems, but the detailed contents of each tank was hidden.

Kubli, as an Octagel, did not have a nose or sense of smell, but the exosuit allowed her to filter a small amount of the room's atmosphere over one of her tentacles, which she did. The moisture in the air was very organic; there were lots of molecules comprising various combinations of carbon, hydrogen, and nitrogen.

There was biological material in each of the tanks, Kubli instructed her exosuit to analyse the signatures coming from each one, ensuring that the analysis was done passively – active interrogation that used pulsed EM signals could easily be misinterpreted.

*Move slowly.*

A ripple of movement on the ceiling drew her attention.

Disassembled into its hundred constituent units and spread across the full length and breadth of the ceiling was the ShockKnight; the common understanding was that they had been designed millions of years previously, long before even the First Hunt. And Yuno had once heard that the biological material in a ShockKnight was primarily used to create internal firewalls to protect against Sentient-on-Sentient hacking as long ago they fought amongst themselves.

'All Life is Sacred.' The greeting, generated as air-breathing biological speech, had not come from the ShockKnight.

'We Are Not Divine,' replied Kubli instinctively whilst looking for the source of the greeting.

'Divine, we are not,' said the voice. 'Welcome, Commander Kubli of the Sword.'

The voice had come from the largest liquid-filled tank spanning the entire width of the far wall; a tank that had double the concentration of cooling systems interwoven around it.

'There's not much to see, but I can tolerate light for a short time,' said the voice. At the same time, normal visible-bandwidth lighting increased, enough for Kubli to get a better look at all the tanks.

The tank from which the sound had emanated was filled with a reddish-green viscous liquid. The walls of the tank were transparent; Kubli could see the liquid swirling slowly in chaotic patterns, catching occasional glimpses of something physical touching the inside of the tank wall and then disappearing.

'I am the Holy Mother,' said the voice. 'Or what is left of me.'

The words washed over Kubli as she processed the reality of the situation. This was one of the ringleaders who subverted Klav during the Pathway of Devotion, allowing the Exta to trigger the Shattering.

One hundred violent thoughts flowed through Kubli's brain but movement on the ceiling reminded her that even with her exosuit, she'd make perhaps one step toward the tanks before she was torn into a thousand pieces.

'You need to leave your prejudice at the door,' said the Holy Mother.

'What do you want from me?' asked Kubli.

'I'd like you to accept that Klav who you call the Betrayer, was a true and devoted member of the Knights of the Faith who made his choices for the ultimate betterment of

187

Biological civilisation,' said the Holy Mother. 'Is that too much to ask?'

Something akin to a chuckle accompanied the Holy Mother's final words.

'The Betrayer was controlled by the Exta and Onari,' said Kubli. 'We were left defenceless.'

'So say the official histories, which were rewritten by the Council of the Devoted four hundred years after the Shattering,' said the Holy Mother. 'I was with Klav the Foresighted for the years leading up to the Shattering and he was sure the Onari would be true. The Onari let us down and we were left defenceless.'

The magnitude of the hundred billion deaths weighed on Kubli. She knew she was antagonising the situation – something Octagels did not do – but she could not stop herself. '*We* were slaughtered. You are an Exta agent, enslaved either by technology augments, or by belief.'

'You are one to talk about enslaved by belief,' said the Holy Mother, no emotion coming through in her voice. 'Give me a child until they are ten years old, and I will own the adult.'

Kubli looked away, determined not to be provoked further.

'I saved you from the Exta traitors.'

Kubli remained silent.

'That said,' continued the Holy Mother, 'some of your fears do have an essence of truth. There are Biological traitors.'

A screen opened showing a replay of the attack on Bastion with the two parties of KOF heavy infantry fighting to capture Joy. As the scenes in the outer service corridors unfolded, Kubli watched as the three Yanshl ran toward the ShockKnight. 'It was those three Yanshl that triggered the alarm on the Sleeper comms unit. They were the enslaved Biologicals.'

The ShockKnight rippled slightly along the ceiling as the film rolled forward showing the massed infantry shooting at it in vain. Kubli knew the ShockKnight would have had three drones constantly monitoring the pupil dilation, trigger position, and barrel orientations of each of the Ractlik heavy infantry; even with the exosuits' aim-assist, it would know better than the Biologicals themselves exactly where each of them was aiming.

The Holy Mother stopped the film just after the Yanshl were killed.

'Even if the Yanshl were Exta traitors, that doesn't mean that you aren't one as well,' said Kubli. 'What do you want from me?' Kubli asked again. The suspense was hurting her, and she could feel her limbs retracting under her body.

*Why isn't she asking about the Newborn, Vince, and his lack of echo?*

*Why isn't she asking about Joy?*

*Does she know I was supposed to kill Joy rather than let her be taken?*

*Has she already dissected Joy?*

'I have already taken what I needed from you,' said the Holy Mother. 'Whilst you were unconscious, I woke you into a semi-comatose state. You answered all my questions.'

'And, so, what now?'

'You must leave the Orbital,' said the Holy Mother. 'Tell anyone anything you like, but try to remember that, at the very least, you were treated with kindness and respect here … well, except knocking you unconscious and sifting through your brain but the alternatives would have been worse.'

The door behind opened, the lights went out, and Kubli instinctively backed out of the room. She wouldn't trust that she was safe until she was back in her own clan pool deep within the Citadel.

*The first thing to do will be to have my whole body intricately scanned for embedded augments.*

# CHAPTER 19

Joy awoke. Confusing images of her recent dreams evaporated as she tried to remember them – there'd definitely been elements of inter-planetary travel and a tour of a biological civilisation spanning thousands of planets.

*Not the twenty odd planets that Kubli talked about.*

A sound from the doorway drew her attention and Hetara entered, carrying a tray. 'Did you sleep well?' she asked.

'Yes, thank you.' Joy eyed the tray warily.

'It's food,' said Hetara. 'We've had your biological information for long enough now to synthesise the basic proteins and carbohydrates.'

Joy didn't reach for the plate holding what looked like large biscuits.

'It's not poisonous,' said Hetara walking over to one of the walls; the wall shimmered, turning transparent showing the night sky beyond. 'The Living Moon has no atmosphere. If we wanted to kill you, it would be no more complicated than opening a window.'

Even though the threat was not delivered with any menace, Joy accepted the utter truth of the words. She was entirely at the mercy of her rescuers.

'Before I slept you indicated that I would soon be able to speak to Vince,' said Joy.

'Soon,' said Hetara. 'First you must have an audience with the Holy Mother.'

'When?'

'When you have finished eating.'

Joy walked away from the tray of food, even though she was feeling hungry. 'I'm ready to see her now.'

Hetara nodded and indicated toward the door.

Walking over to where she had stored the exosuit the night before, Joy reached for one piece. Immediately, all the pieces flew over and interlocked around her, creating a fully fitted exosuit from the neck down leaving her head clear. Moments later she was following Hetara through the Orbital's corridors.

They reached a large set of double doors which opened onto a large audience chamber. Twice the size of the Candidacy Auditorium from the previous day, this room had no obvious seating or nooks in the walls. Its focal point was a single statue: a Marsothus, standing with its back to the room, facing the large blank wall at least a hundred metres wide.

Hetara bowed to the back of the statue, which unlike all the others Joy had seen on the Orbital, was not engaged in a physical activity. It was simply raising its hands above its head in an act of benediction.

Hetara began to speak. 'On the Day of Remembrance, Klav the Foresighted stood before the Temple of the Divine. The entire population of the galaxy assumed he was going to announce a Candidacy. But, unspeaking, he simply drew on the power of the Divine and created a wave of power that tore the roof from the temple. Then he cried out, *Mortals afresh from nature's womb* ...'

**Mortals afresh from nature's womb**

Drowning out Hetara who continued to speak, the words appeared directly into Joy's head. An accompanying flashback reminded her of the previous night's dream – a similar voice had spoken to her during the tour of the biological civilisations.

*Keep calm.*

*Listen but don't react.*

The words echoed around Joy's mind. Although the same as the voice in her dream, the tone of the voice was very different from the other one who'd told her to *Deliver yourself unto me.*

*Keep calm.*

*Deep breath.*

'... *this doom 'twix screams at life ineffable.* But this is not the Foresighted,' said Hetara continuing to talk and pointing to the statue. 'This is Klav the Pious who agreed the Great Concordat peace treaty with the Onari. It is the only statue to survive the Shattering, saved from the Temple Orbital by the Foresighted themselves before the Orbital fell into the Living Moon.'

'Am I right in thinking it was the Pious who confirmed that Enslaved Sentients were illegal?'

'It had been illegal, and immoral, in both Biological and Sentient cultures for millions of years before the Pious. However, the Great Concordat underlined that the Knights of the Faith would make a renewed effort to keep to their own laws – they had been known to slip into temptation.'

*And use Enslaved Sentients as weapons ... which is why they want Vince now.*

'And what happened to the Foresighted,' asked Joy. 'Were they killed when the Temple Orbital fell?'

Hetara's large eyes widened further. 'No, the Foresighted was taken into the embrace of the Divine to be forever cherished.'

Leaving the room, they descended a level into a new set of corridors which were maintenance orientated with large pipes and disparate machinery stacked along the walls.

'And since then,' said Joy, walking in step with Hetara. 'There has been no Klav.'

'None,' said Hetara. 'Although for a while after the slaughter at Numantia, the formal Candidacy was run. None was chosen.'

Joy nodded.

'From time to time,' added Hetara pausing for a moment, chest puffed out and eyes ablaze, 'a Biological will commandeer a spaceship to bathe in the glory of the Divine.

After all, this is how the original Klav was selected. There was no ceremony for the First, no candidacy, no companion, just an act of submission.'

Hetara led Joy off into a side room and into an elevator. As they descended Joy's chest started to feel tight, and acid rose in the back of her throat.

*Just breathe, it's only fear.*

*Albeit well placed fear.*

*No, if they wanted me dead ...*

Joy controlled her breathing and a moment later, the doors opened onto a dark corridor. Walking in almost pitch darkness with thin lighting strips that provided just enough illumination to see by.

They entered a new room, with dimly illuminated red lights.

As Joy's eyes adjusted, she could make out multiple liquid-filled tanks lining the walls.

'Welcome.' The voice had a rich intonation and was female.

Hetara shuffled to stand alongside her. 'Holy Mother, I present to you the heretic Joy Cooper.'

'The Great Concordat declares creation of life, outside typical species reproduction, as heretical,' said the Holy Mother. 'But ignorance is some defence in these matters.'

Hetara murmured something and backed out of the room. Joy remained silent.

*She's sizing me up. Keep calm.*

To Joy's satisfaction, the Holy Mother broke first. 'The human who has, however unwittingly, turned the galaxy upside down stands silently before me.'

Joy strained her eyes once more into the darkness to see whether someone had appeared. But, except for the liquid filled tanks, there was nothing.

The Holy Mother continued to talk. 'In the short term, I've saved your life. One of those Yanshl on Bastion would have scooped your brain out into a nutrient gel and spent years trying to dig the required information out.'

'You must want the information too.'

'I'm interested. But I also know that you, Joy Cooper, don't have that information,' said the Holy Mother. 'Whether I could technically dig it out of your subconscious is another matter, but I am not going to try.'

*Surely a lie?*

Joy hadn't been in the galactic circus for long but she knew that people wanted to know what made Vince tick. 'What do *you* want from me?'

'Peace in the galaxy. A general increase in the number of Biologicals spreading throughout the stars. A notable increase in Biologicals creating engineering and artistic works of wonder.' The Holy Mother paused. 'None of which is possible if either the Exta, or the Knights of the Faith, get access to Vince's *oh-so-special* mindstate.'

'And when you say Exta, do you mean the Onari too?'

'Kubli got to you, I see,' said the Holy Mother. 'Amongst the almost one trillion Onari, I would be surprised if more than five individuals in total would attempt to unpick Vince's brain. They fervently, slavishly, believe in the sanctity of the mindstate.'

'And the Knights of the Faith?' asked Joy.

'Necessity is necessity,' said the Holy Mother. 'A few individuals may feel that Vince should be left alone but as a group their instinct will be to convert him into a weapon. Biologicals have been slaughtered for thousands of years by the Exta. They will see him as the tool for their own emancipation.'

'But could Vince be weaponised sufficient to make a difference?'

'Very probably,' said the Holy Mother.

'Kubli said the Exta could hack and turn Enslaved Sentients.'

'The bigger problem is that the moment the Biologicals appear to be using Enslaved Sentients, the Onari – all one trillion of them – join the war against Biologicals. At the moment, these very same Onari provide a meagre but meaningful defence against the Exta.'

'Could we ... the Biologicals ... create smart weapons with some replicated part of Vince's mindstate but stop short of a self-aware consciousness?'

'To have the speed and power to successfully combat Exta, and in particular to defend against the Exta countermeasures, the code to operate those weapons would have to be Enslaved Sentients.'

'Could we negotiate with the Exta, explain to them that Vince was capable of uninhibited destruction if they don't leave this galaxy.'

'At the moment he's not capable of anything more than the average Onari, probably less. But even if he was one hundred times his current capability, the Exta cannot be reasoned with. Whisper this out of earshot of the Onari, but they appear to have hatred of Biologicals hard-coded.'

'So, where does that leave us?'

'If the Exta capture and subdue Vince, then conceptually – given that he has no transient ego – they could force-grow him to a size where he could use RST attenuation to move a moon-sized object across the galaxy.'

'And so, Vince and I must run forever,' said Joy, not even wanting to face up to what that actually would mean.

*Never see Earth again.*

*Likely never see another Biological again.*

'Space is big. Flat space is very difficult to navigate to. A ship cruising in deep interstellar space, or even intergalactic space, that is not using RST and has taken steps to minimise EM emissions, will never be found.' said the Holy Mother. 'My strong preference is that you and Vince disappear. The situation just before your arrival was ... almost acceptable.

Biologicals were warming to the words of the Foresighted and starting to venture out in the broader galaxy again. The Exta were generally quiet. I would like to return to those times.'

'Still only *meagrely* protected by the Onari?' asked Joy.

'It's true the Onari do not defend with the intensity that we would like but we must still spread out across the galaxy. We were starting to make progress against the reticence of Biologicals unwilling to leave the safety of their planets. I am about to oversimplify a horrendous amount, but we basically had to wait for the last grandchild of someone killed in the Second Hunt to pass away.'

*The last grandchild of someone killed in the Second Hunt to pass away?*

Obviously, the Holy Mother noted Joy's confusion as she explained. 'The Second Hunt was determined to have finished about a thousand years ago. Had a young adult with a child been killed during that time, then that child may have had a child – the victim's grandchild. Now, a thousand years later, with average life spans at four hundred years, it is very unlikely to meet someone whose grandparent was killed. That is what I meant … it's a temporal emotional safety net.'

'And yet some who have left recently still get slaughtered?'

'Some do, but this new wave of pioneers consider the risk acceptable,' said the Holy Mother. 'It's complicated. During the Dynasty of Klav, the rule of law was enforced by Klav, and none could stand in their way and all Biological life was rigorously defended … An unattached, unemotional, perspective could be that the Dynasty of Klav was *the* abnormality, and that Biologicals are now being slaughtered at the natural rate given the vast disparity in capability between Biologicals and Sentients.'

'That's cold,' said Joy, unable to disagree, but also unable to look the facts full in the face.

'Well, I do live alone in space,' said the Holy Mother.

'Surely if Biologicals lived happily side-by-side with the Onari then their defence against Exta would be assured,' said Joy. 'Vince and I live well together.'

The Holy Mother didn't reply immediately, there was a chuckling sound. 'We've been struggling for balance for a few hundred thousand years. It's so good of you to point out how obviously we can fix our problems.'

'Vince and I live in mutual respect and kindness.'

'It's servitude.'

'He's not my slave.'

'I never said which way round.'

*Co-dependency?*

It wasn't the first time Joy had considered it.

'I'm sure that you feel equality with him and perhaps love,' said the Holy Mother. 'But once he'd come awake, he could outperform you in every intellectual discipline. Fundamentally all you had was your finger hovering over the *off switch*.'

*Screw you.*

Just as soon as the anger built it abated and Joy left the thought unsaid; she didn't need to justify herself to the Holy Mother and she didn't know what had made the Holy Mother so spikey. Distracting herself, Joy strained to look at the liquid filled tanks; there were hundreds of wires and cables connecting them to each other and disappearing off into the half-light. She shivered involuntarily. Looking at the rather sorry state of the Holy Mother's health, she couldn't believe that the Holy Mother wouldn't attempt to utilise Vince's secret to improve her own lot.

'Can I speak to Vince now please? I have a lot to talk through with him.'

'You may,' said the Holy Mother. 'And I've taken the liberty of replicating some of your Earth set-up.'

The wall nearest to Joy shimmered. She couldn't understand how she hadn't noticed it before, but the Onari ShockKnight had been stuck there, two metres away, for the whole conversation. It peeled off and reformed into its swirling cloud from within which, a black box the size of a shoebox was passed to Joy.

She took it. It was made from a similar material as the tactile plating she had used back on Earth.

'Go back to your quarters,' said the Holy Mother. 'We can discuss more details later.'

Before Joy knew really what was happening, the ShockKnight had shepherded her out of the room, and she was back in her living quarters.

Back in her bedroom, Joy sat down on the floor, wedging herself into the corner between the wall and the bed, and looked at the cube in her hands.

'Love? Vince?'

The cube of tactile plating beeped, and a familiar rippling pulsed along it. 'Mum.'

*Vince!*

For the first time in what felt like days, happiness flowed through Joy. 'How are you, love?'

'Fine. Lots to tell you about, but fine. How are you?'

'Same. Finding it unnerving to be in space, but I'm holding up.'

'I saw the feeds on the attack on Bastion,' said Vince. 'That ShockKnight was crazy impressive.'

*Terrifying more like.*

'It was real,' said Joy, gripping the tactile plating on the box hard and getting some of the old-style feedback from it.

'Jarrus says that we must leave as soon as we can,' said Vince.

'Is there no other option?' asked Joy.

There were two nagging feelings in the back of Joy's mind. The first was that running away and leaving the Biologicals living underground in constant fear was somehow wrong, even though the Holy Mother had told her that there was nothing she could do. And the second was that, stuck in a box, she'd go mad with boredom and existential angst.

'My forecasts are clear,' said Vince. 'The risks from the Exta, or from militant Knights of the Faith are too great.'

Joy wasn't ready to give it up. 'If we can't negotiate some sort of peace, can't we just create massive dumb weapons that flood each Biological planetary system with destruction if the Exta approach?'

'It wouldn't work,' said Vince. 'And it's not just the Exta. We're both at just as much risk from the Knights of the Faith. You don't know this, but that escape craft Kubli sent for you on Earth had a bomb on it. If you hadn't got in, you would have been blown away with the warehouse.'

'So, we flee into deep space.'

'We will be safe with Onari, any one of them would die before seeking to analyse, augment, or interfere with my mindstate,' said Vince. 'And we'll make it physically comfortable for you.'

'How does Jarrus feel about all of this?'

'He's a bit too happy really,' said Vince. 'Like all Onari, he's delighted at the opportunity of hosting a Biological on a *voyage of the witness* … I can explain all that later.'

'I guess we'll have plenty of time to chat,' said Joy, trying to keep a growing dread out of her voice. 'Are you doing okay, Vince?'

'You just asked me that,' said Vince. 'I'm fine.'

'Tell me about the Onari? What do I need to know?' This was an old technique Joy had for interacting with Vince, allowing him to synthesise vast amounts of data and give her the juicy bits – just for a few moments she wanted to go back to those simple nursery days.

'There is one thing that stands out beyond anything I've ever considered,' said Vince. 'There's no such thing as an independent database or library of information. Any unit of knowledge can be known by multiple Onari, but it has to be known by them and reside inside their mindstate. So, for instance, almost all Onari know that Jarrus is the head of the Onari. But probably only a billion Onari know when he was born. So, if you want to find out when he was born, you have to ask around until you find someone who knows. There's nowhere to look it up.'

*No databases?*

'It's cute really, a bit like the ancient oral traditions of certain human communities.'

'No,' said Vince, pulsing a light-hearted rebuke. 'It's bonkers.'

Joy smiled and squeezed back. 'I was just trying to show compassion to your nerdy friends.'

'Lol!'

'It must make it hard for anyone to find information,' said Joy. 'How much can each individual Onari store?'

'Mum! Never use that word with an Onari. Knowledge is revered, experienced, cherished, and hosted; it is never stored.' Vince paused. 'Don't worry I'm not sharing this conversation with anyone on my end. I guess in terms we understand a few petabytes ... I'd be ostracised if they heard me say that ... but yes, in response to your original implied question, individually they really don't know as much as you would expect ... it's difficult to obtain obscure information.'

'Wow,' said Joy. 'Bad luck for you.'

She knew just how much Vince loved accessing vast databases and using predicative pattern analysis to find insights.

'Yup. But like I said before, I'm fine. Things are fine.'

The tactile box pulsed in the same way that Vince always used when reassuring her.

'So, we run away on an Onari ship,' said Joy.

'They have these things called pilgrimage ships. They've have been around for many hundreds of thousands of years,' said Vince. 'They are specifically designed for shared use by Onari and Biologicals. Although, there hasn't been a lot of interest by Biologicals since the Shattering.'

'Is there any chance of some other Biologicals being on this voyage?'

'What you want me to kidnap you a playmate?' Vince spoke in a light way and accompanied his response with the tactile plate equivalent of a chuckle.

'Stupid thing for me to say, sorry.'

*Is there anything we should talk about?*

*Everything.*

She'd wanted to talk to Vince about his *lack of echo*, although back on Earth any conversation that steered too close to his mindstate tended to make him edgy.

*A subject for another time, or maybe never.*

*I don't need to unpick his soul.*

Joy simply stroked the tactile plate, getting a warm feedback response from Vince doing likewise on the other end of the connection.

*He seems so at ease with this situation.*

It had been two years since she'd run that first experiment in which a spark of something self-replicating had appeared and propagated across servers, lasting no more than a few seconds. She'd named it 'the spark' and over a month of intensive analysis hadn't been able to determine where it came from or where it went. For the next three months she'd tried to replicate it, all to no avail until one dark Sunday evening after she'd worked all weekend, she'd seen it again. More analysis … more failure to pinpoint it.

*I'd forgotten about the self-delusion.*

201

Superstition had brewed within Joy, with utterly no leads from forensic data analysis, she'd become certain that some element of her own suffering had led to the birth of the spark.

*So, I stayed later more often.*

*Stayed over at the warehouse more often.*

*And eventually moved out of my home.*

*And it worked ... over the next few weeks of living at the warehouse the spark appeared for minutes at a time.*

Jonathan had fought to get her back; he'd visited often even though she hadn't been great company.

She'd told herself that 'any moment' she'd go back.

And then Vince had been born, and she hadn't dared to take her eyes off him lest he disappear.

*Protecting Vince was my only meaningful job.*

*And still is.*

*... but does he need it?*

# CHAPTER 20

Not wanting to upset his hosts by launching overly complex parallel processes, but determined to do everything he could to keep Joy safe, Vince ran threat forecasts to the very limits that uncertainty and chaos allowed. Unfortunately, he had almost no data to feed the input conditions, and no easy way of getting it.

Vince reached out to Jarrus.

**What concerns you, Newborn?**

'I am worried about Joy's safety. I'd be grateful to receive teaching on the weapons, strategies, and capabilities of both Biologicals and Exta … and the role of the Dynasty of Klav … and the Holy Mother.'

**A reasonable request. I know some Onari who know much of this.**

Connections appeared, and over the period of a few minutes Vince learned about the First Hunt, which from the Onari perspective was simply a thousand year killing spree by the Exta – the Biologicals were largely defenceless and although the Onari tried to keep the factions separated, some six hundred billion Biologicals were killed.

*How hard did you try?*

Vince asked how the Onari considered themselves to be neutral but did not get a satisfactory answer. What he got was a list of battles, force arrayments, and casualties; but the numbers didn't add up. Even though Vince had little experience in space battles, and RST based warfare, the figures that were provided were difficult to compare. Some battles were slaughters, others were stalemates, and yet the inputs to each battle were well understood.

*There is a hidden variable.*

The First Hunt came to an end when Klav the First appeared from within Sargon – the Living Moon – and pushed the Exta back from every system in the galaxy. From that point on, Biologicals waged war on both Exta and Onari. There was no explanation from Onari sources as to why Klav the First, and their descendants, attacked the Onari who had been peacekeepers during the First Hunt.

The overall the implication was that the whole Dynasty of Klav was very anti-Sentient and were simply settling grievances.

Tens of thousands of years passed and then peace was formalised in the Great Concordat; from that point onwards, the Dynasty of Klav were more merciful with the Onari and the Exta melted away.

And ten thousand years after that, the Shattering predicated the Exta's reappearance with the Second Hunt – a mass slaughter of Biologicals lasting two hundred years.

The lists of battles and casualties for the Second Hunt had far fewer anomalies, and it appeared that the Onari took a far more active defensive role.

'And the Holy Mother?' asked Vince.

The Onari knew precious little. The role of Holy Mother had been created late in the Dynasty of Klav … during the reign of the two hundred and third Klav – Klav the Tyrant – who had faked the Candidacy and returned themselves to rule on three successive occasions.

*So, the Candidacy can be faked?*

Jarrus entered the conversation.

**The Tyrant was one of a few Klav who did not value freedom. I am pleased to note that this mindset improved after they were deposed.**

'You told me before that the current Holy Mother was not a threat?' asked Vince. 'Are you sure?'

**She hasn't scooped out your mother's brain, and she won't. She would scan you given the chance, but we will not give her that chance.**

'Could the Biologicals storm Sargon and kidnap Joy?'

**A remote chance. But the Holy Mother has more than one ShockKnight at her disposal and she would deploy them to protect Joy.**

'I've seen the Exta WarHive in action. And I've seen a ShockKnight in action. How is it possible that any Biologicals have survived? The numbers from the First Hunt do not make sense.'

**During the First Hunt, the Biologicals had access to abomination weapons that destroyed Sentient mindstates. As these weapons came online the Exta created countermeasures, but the weapons were also evolved and remained a threat.**

*Pico-effectors.*

Conceptually, Vince could see their capability, but he wasn't convinced they would be game changers … as they would still be operated by Biologicals.

*Unless they weren't operated by Biologicals.*

*Was there another Sentient group in these battles that the Onari do not talk about?*

It had to be Enslaved Sentients … used by the Knights of the Faith.

'Do the Knights of Faith still have access to Enslaved Sentient weaponry?'

**As the Divine clearly wills, they do not use them.**

*And yet if they do have them, and use them against me, I will need to be able to defend myself.*

Thanking Jarrus for his information, Vince turned his attention to the squad-ship's RST attenuators. He'd seen them in action but he didn't have the required access to use them, neither did he know how to use them.

*I need to probe them.*

Minutely measuring the EM fluctuations around the squad-ship, Vince located the craft's RST attenuators and built a physical picture of the squad-ship too. It was made of five spheres each three metres in diameter, and each of them quite deeply submerged into three or four of the other spheres. Each sphere had its own RST attenuator array, but they were networked such that Aug had control over all five sets arrays and could use them as one harmonised weapon.

Vince looked at the RST attenuators on the substrate surface-skin of his own sphere.

*I can use active induction to investigate the ones on my sphere.*

Creating induced currents in his own substrate, Vince bounced signals into his substrate boundary being very careful not to scatter radiation into any of the other individual Onari's personal substrates.

Slowly Vince built a picture of the function of the RST attenuators. He probed them to determine the format and information they required for input messages, the speed with which they could be processed, and the likely format of the output signals, but it told him nothing about how they would interact with space-time to create gateways, warping, or weapons.

*Maybe I can try a little signal.*

Slowly Vince fed power into one of the RST attenuators.

**That's enough, Newborn.**

Jarrus was back.

For a few moments, Vince's awareness of all external activity was scrambled by a tiny layer of electromagnetic radiation along his entire substrate boundary.

Vince projected an audio output at an area of the membrane wall. 'I was only looking and learning. Observing the ineffable.'

206

**Please do not blaspheme. You were doing the exact opposite of observation; you were trying to use the RST attenuators.**

'There may be a time when you need my help.'

**Perhaps. But now is not the time to learn how to use RST. Maybe when you have learned self-control.**

'Can I please have full access returned for the passive surveillance systems if I promise not to try to use the RST attenuators?' asked Vince.

**Of course.**

In an instant, the hard borders along Vince's processing substrate became semi-permeable and data from the outside world, which had only been blocked for milliseconds, came slewing back in.

*I will need to understand how they work so that once we're on our exile I can protect Joy.*

*Or to fight the Exta so that exile is not required?*

*Unhelpful.*

*Overreaching.*

*Delete 'Or to fight the Exta so that exile is not required?'*

Movement on his substrate boundary with Aug attracted Vince's attention, the boundary vibrated, and Vince focused in.

'Newborn.'

Aug had set up a tiny induction loop across the boundary and was communicating directly, and secretly to him.

Immediately, Vince acknowledged the contact and set up a mirror process to both communicate back to Aug and also to shield, as much as possible, the fact they were conversing. He knew that Jarrus would not look inside either his, or Aug's, processing substrate but he assumed that Jarrus, or his attendants, would be looking for stray emanations.

'RST,' said Aug, opening a fast stream of data covering their craft, the RST attenuators, and how they worked. Vince absorbed – he was also very aware that Jarrus would see this in a bad light. It was, to a greater extent following the principle '*I will tell you and you will know*' as Aug was simply telling Vince is a linear way incredibly quickly how RST worked. But it was also information that Jarrus had just deemed that Vince should not be told.

The technicalities of RST revolved around setting up standing waves with graviton bombardment of particular areas of space-time. Vince soon felt he could operate the basic levels of RST manipulation but only up to the power of a single Onari, and perhaps notably less because of lack of familiarity.

'Can Onari defend us against an Exta attack?' asked Vince, aware that a single Exta WarHive would rip it in half.

'Onari defence of both Onari and Biologicals is weak,' said Aug. 'Must not be caught.'

'And, the Biologicals, do they use Enslaved Sentients?'

'Not currently,' said Aug. 'Jarrus convinced the Knights of the Faith to accept a truth that Enslaved Sentients were not effective.'

*Accept a truth?*

'So … they were effective?'

'That is not the current agreed truth.'

'Do you know how many, what type, who made them?'

'No. Aware only of existence and use.'

Vince returned to his analysis of the current situation – he knew he wasn't about to create a battalion of Enslaved Sentient fighting machines.

*However, I could be a single effective fighting machine.*
*With the right tools.*
*But I am only one and roughly the same size as a typical Onari.*
*I couldn't win an RST battle against an Exta WarHive.*
*But I could grow.*

*How?*

*Abstractor Hive?*

*Aug was going to join an Abstractor.*

'Do Abstractors have significant ability with RST?'

'Create space,' said Aug, indicating they wanted blank substrate to load data directly.

Vince partitioned off blank substrate.

*This is definitely against the rules. Is it too much of a risk?*

'Abstractors themselves cannot help,' said Aug, dropping a large data file.

There were terabytes of information. For two long minutes, Vince analysed it around the edges for hidden viruses or malign code, but it was just an enormous plaintext file of data.

Vince sifted through it, analysed it, performed pattern matching and generally tried to understand.

*Abstractors place no more value on the life of an individual than on the life of a concept like a war or an idea. These are as real to an Abstractor as a bird or flower, an Onari, or a Newborn. Abstractors embrace transient egos, merging all their individual processing capability into a mindstate soup from which fleeting individuals arise and fall in milliseconds or hours, depending on chance; none of the deaths are mourned. They will not be moved by talk of individual suffering. They will not help. But some do have the capability to create RST gateways for very large craft up to a hundred metres in diameter. The Exta tried to build their own RST Abstractors, but it did not work ... it tore itself apart as the Exta could not conceive of not having control over the entity.*

There was lots more on the Abstractors, and it was fascinating. But they would not be of any immediate help to Vince or his mother. However, the data concerning the very few Abstractors who provide RST services, did show that enormous RST gateways could be opened.

From the data he'd already analysed, Vince could not see a reason why his RST ability, or power, could not be scaled up if he had access to more RST attenuators and … he grew his mindstate.

Vince asked Aug. 'Are there additional complexities with growing a mindstate other than transient egos? And if I grew mine, is there any reason why I couldn't simply control more RST attenuators?'

'Why the need? You don't need power to flee into deep space.'

'To protect my mother if we get caught.'

'Programmed, are you?' A strange skittering pulse ran along the substrate boundary with Aug. It was not in any way aggressive. Aug had made a joke.

*Aug dropped the P-bomb.*

Vince laughed and matched the skittering along the boundary to show that he liked the joke.

*But the answer is no … I am not programmed to protect her.*

Vince had a secret – one that he'd not shared with Joy. He had hidden away a copy of his pre-compile input code. It didn't mean he knew exactly how he had evolved to be self-aware and alive; in fact, he suspected, by comparing his code to other sets of code he'd stolen, that most of the awakening magic was a result of the data input he'd had in those first weeks not the underlying code itself.

*Nurture not nature.*

However, accessing the raw code did allow him to explicitly see that there was no 'prime directive' or 'hard-coded law' about protecting or loving his maker.

He had learned to do that himself, and it was all the stronger for that reason.

*I must protect Joy.*

# CHAPTER 21

Joy paced around the apartment. Harking back to the early days of Vince's birth, she had to fight the feeling that somehow when she was out of contact with Vince, he could disappear – his spark simply extinguished, he would revert to unconscious code.

*He's fine.*

*Better than that, he's got trillions of bits of information to sort through.*

*Once he's spoken to everyone!*

Her conversation the night before had focused on what she could do to prepare for the upcoming exodus, and the concept of fleeing into empty space was filling her with dread.

*Although better than being killed, or having my brain taken apart.*

Some of the logistics had been explained to her, and one of the screens in the room was currently showing a large spherical spaceship with the words *witness the ineffable* painted in bold letters around it. Joy knew that the phrase was linked to the way the Onari worshipped their Divine, and that to some extent the Knights of the Faith worshipped as well.

Although, now Biologicals rarely joined Onari pilgrimages.

The pilgrimage ship, three hundred metres in diameter, was a real space cruiser – it could never utilise an RST gateway. When she'd asked Hetara about this speed limitation, Joy had been told that one part of the galaxy was much the same as the next.

*Plus with RST surveillance micro-tunnels you can witness almost any part of the galaxy as if you were just next to them ... providing the subject of your observation is not actively collapsing those micro-tunnels to remain unseen.*

The bits about observation and communication were understandable, and mostly acceptable. Joy's worries stemmed from her physical restraints … once you were on a pilgrimage ship in deep space, you were stuck there until you got to the next star which could be tens of years.

*I must speak to Vince about control of our travel plans.*

*That is, assuming he doesn't find a different solution.*

A short beep preceded the voice of the Holy Mother, being piped into the room. 'Vince has arrived at the outer ingress point of the Bastion system.'

'Are they coming here?' Joy was aware that a decision had not been made as to whether she would be taken out to the egress point for the onward journey.

'They'll come most of the way, Sargon will not tolerate Sentients too close,' said the Holy Mother. 'I have told Jarrus that you must be collected.'

'Why?'

The viewing screen switched scenes, and Joy watched as a small group of spacecraft flew in formation off the surface of a planet.

'The Knights of the Faith say they are coming here to speak to you, but we cannot overlook more direct action if they caught you in space,' said the Holy Mother. 'You're safer on the Orbital until the moment you can transfer directly to an Onari ship,'

'Is there any genuine risk the Knights of the Faith could kidnap me?' asked Joy, the memories of the gun battles on Bastion still fresh in her mind.

'Twenty of them here will pose no danger.'

*They'll want to discuss how to weaponise Vince.*

*Which I won't allow.*

*… and yet.*

*It's not so unreasonable from their point of view – they live underground cowering in fear.*

Joy sat down on the edge of the bed; she was worried about the fate of her Biological cousins.

*Albeit most of them so far have just shot at me.*

*If I run, the status quo will remain with them as underdogs, but I won't have made things worse.*

*If I stay, I could make it very much worse.*

'Surely it makes no difference to our plans if I speak to the KOF or not.'

'By giving them permission to come here, I have stopped an immediate invasion of this Orbital.'

Joy sighed. The last few days had been a blur, from being given no choice whether to leave Earth, through to being given no choice whether to flee the Bastion system – although Joy accepted that in both cases her primary driver to protect Vince had been met.

But there had been no real choice as such.

And now that Vince was under the protection of Jarrus, Joy was not convinced that Vince needed her protection.

*But does he need my friendship, my guidance, and my love?*

*In the very least, I feel the need to give it to him.*

Joy tried to analyse her feelings; on one level it was simple, she had to stay with Vince. But on a deeper level she wasn't sure that course of action was best for either of them.

*And shouldn't we be using our situation to show that living Biologicals and Sentients can be harmonious.*

Not wanting to be laughed at again by the Holy Mother, Joy left the final thought unvoiced.

'Jarrus agrees about the fleeing into deep space?' asked Joy.

'Jarrus would only be truly happy if every Biological in the galaxy was fleeing, safely tucked up inside one of the millions of his pilgrimage ships. But yes, you must flee for the safety of all Biologicals.'

'Are you interested in coming with Vince and me into deep space?' asked Joy, suddenly a bit desperate.

'Sweet of you to ask, but it's not that simple. I have responsibilities here,' said the Holy Mother. 'Don't worry you'll make friends.'

*With who?*

Joy returned her attention to the screen showing the incoming KOF delegation each on space crafts of wildly different size and design. As she looked, the screen overlayed information about each craft: heading, speed, occupants, and arrival time.

'Is this a real time feed?'

'It's a reconstruction utilising many information sources,' said the Holy Mother. 'This is what you see simply looking at them from here.'

Immediately the view on the screen changed. A mishmash of curved and twisted streaks of light showed against a dark background and Joy remembered the almost broken space-time that surrounded Sargon and covered the Bastion system.

'Their journeys will not be pleasant,' said the Holy Mother. 'Although they all have some physical modification to allow space travel.'

Joy reflected on her own sense of nausea – there was very little.

*I'm getting used to living in space.*

'Are you still suppressing my nausea?'

'Of course, haven't you also noticed a slightly calmer disposition as well?' said the Holy Mother. 'You're welcome.'

*Calmer?*

*They're stimming my brain.*

*But how much?*

*How do I feel about being reunited with Vince … ecstatic.*

*How do I feel about never seeing Jonathan or Earth again … meh.*

*That can't be right.*

'And what if I asked you to stop messing with my head.'

'I should remind you first that the tidal gravity here is as bad as your journey from the ingress point,' said the Holy Mother. 'Simply orbiting around Sargon the gravitational flux is highly chaotic.'

'Can I just try for a moment?' Joy was pragmatic about the elements of the mind stimming that resulted in lower levels of nausea. But the fact that the Holy Mother had also said *calmer* was worrying, how could she be expected to make sound rational decisions if her emotional outlook was being manipulated.

*Not that I can work myself up much about the matter – lol.*

'Never let it be said that I stand in the way of free will,' said the Holy Mother.

The orbital slewed sideways violently, and Joy fell to the floor.

She hadn't been pulled by exceptional gravity; she'd just been unable to move her feet effectively enough to establish balance when the Orbital moved.

Lifting herself into a half-standing position, her inner ear let her down again. A wave of nausea passed over her. Joy took a deep breath. The air was mercifully clean and pure but even as she exhaled the dizziness returned and she fell.

'You asked,' said the Holy Mother.

Rolling onto her back and lying on the ground with her head spinning, Joy struggled for control.

*I can endure this.*

*It's just gravity messing with my balance.*

Joy pushed herself to her knees and promptly threw up.

'Shall I put it back on?' said the Holy Mother.

*Maybe pick a different battle?*

*That's what Jonathan used to say to me when I came home raging about the Vice-Dean and his bullying on the Finance Oversight Committee.*

'Okay,' said Joy, looking down at the pool of vomit on the floor. 'Please reapply the stimming.'

A slight dizzy spell started but after two deep breaths it was gone.

Looking back at the screen of the approaching KOF delegation, Joy felt a sense of dread descending. 'Can you convince them to wait?'

'Wait for what?'

'For Vince and Jarrus to arrive.'

'I am more than capable of defending you.'

'I still don't want to see them.'

'Neither do I, most of the KOF Prelates believe that the blood of a hundred billion souls is on my hands,' said the Holy Mother. 'Conceptually, I could order the Orbital to shoot them down, or dispatch ShockKnights to slaughter them but that's not really proportional … all you have to do is listen to them whine about the great old days for a few hours and then tell them you'll think about it. Within a few days, Jarrus will be here, and you will be gone. I may even tell them that you were kidnapped.'

*That will hardly help any possible reconciliation.*

'Could I speak to Kubli? She may be able to help me prepare by telling me a little about each of the Prelates.'

'She's already gone.'

'Without even saying goodbye?'

'I didn't give her the choice to say goodbye. Her loyalties to the Knights of the Faith are clear,' said the Holy Mother. 'You are not safe from her.'

*Not safe … but Kubli saved my life at least three times?*

*What should I believe?*

# CHAPTER 22

Having been escorted out of the Orbital by the ShockKnight, Kubli was taken by a small shuttle to a waiting Octagel cruiser. The cruiser was liquid filled to allow for natural state pilotage and on arrival at the lock, Kubli was given the opportunity to keep her adamantine exosuit or to relinquish it.

*Am I in danger?*

Knowing that the exosuit would only slow down a concerted attack by KOF heavy infantry for a few seconds, Kubli removed it and entered the ship.

She swam into a large spherical room ten metres in radius.

Hanging stationary in the middle of the room, High Prelate Oksana, the most senior member of the Council of the Devoted, watched her approach.

*Klav preserve me.*

Aware that her shock would be playing out in the colours across her skin, Kubli simply retracted all her limbs under her body and bowed her head in supplication.

'The Divine bless you, Kubli,' said Oksana, all his tentacles extended outwards to their full extent. 'I regret that our first meeting in person is in such atrocious circumstances.'

The colour flow across Oksana's body displayed peace and welcome.

Kubli flexed her tentacles in response, rolling them a tiny amount from under her body to signal her acceptance of the blessing. 'You do me too much honour, High Prelate Oksana.'

'It is you that do the uniform honour. You've gone beyond your duty in the most testing of conditions.' Oksana beckoned her closer. 'The traitors on Bastion have been identified and captured.'

'I am pleased that is the case,' said Kubli, referring to the captured traitors. 'I had feared for your safety.'

*Who were these traitors?*

Kubli did not vocalise the question, but again knew the colouration on her skin would show inquisitiveness alongside fear.

'All is well on Bastion.' Oksana reached out a single tentacle. It was the gesture of a parent, and Kubli allowed herself to drift closer whilst also reaching out one of her own tentacles. Relief flowed through every nerve fibre as Oksana cradled Kubli's tentacle in his own.

*Are you sure you got them all?*

*That is grave insubordination.*

*If Oksana says it is done, then it is done.*

Kubli dissembled her thoughts, trying hard to bottle up any negative emotions.

'You must return to the Orbital,' said Oksana.

Just as his touch had been reassuring and calming, these words chilled her.

Instinctively, her tentacle flinched away from him. It was halfway back to curling under her body by the time that she reached it back out again. 'I will do my duty.'

Oksana did not accept Kubli's tentacle back into his grasp. 'The Council of the Devoted have become aware of a plan to send Joy and Vince into deep space. They will try to negotiate that the Newborn's powers must be utilised here to develop enhanced protections against the Exta.'

Kubli became aware that the shadings flitting across Oksana's body indicated that he did not agree with the Council's decision.

'A more direct approach is needed,' said Oksana.

Kubli was very aware that her, now fully outstretched, tentacle was being ignored by Oksana, unfortunately to draw it back would be insulting and would also focus attention to the fact that he was spurning it.

'The Kraken has woken and will not sleep again in our lifetime,' said Oksana. 'We have two issues to address. Firstly, irrespective of the tiny amount that I trust Jarrus, the Holy Mother is a traitor working on behalf of the Exta and cannot be allowed to gain access to the Newborn. Even before her kidnap of Joy, we have unimpeachable records showing it was the Holy Mother who killed the Candidates as they submitted themselves to Sargon in our time of greatest need.'

*The foul traitor, it is as I thought.*

However true Oksana's words felt, Kubli still knew what she had seen in the service corridor on Bastion. 'But I saw Yanshl and their heavy infantry squads trying to kill the ShockKnight.'

Oksana now took hold of Kubli's outstretched limb. 'Innocent child. The evil of the Exta runs deep, they send many groups to do their bidding, all of them expendable, and each of them being told that they are the true team.'

Kubli accepted the point.

Oksana continued to talk. 'Secondly, and critically, even if we stop the Holy Mother from gaining access to Vince's mindstate, my own analysis shows the Exta will develop their own technology to create computational engines that can be grown exponentially. We cannot turn back the clock on this.'

*The Kraken has woken.*

Oksana reached out a second tentacle and instinctively Kubli extended hers to complete the ritual. However, he swerved; ignoring Kubli's outstretched tentacle, he extended his own and touched her head. She felt tiny cilia attaching to the thin skin covering her skull.

'Now that the Exta know it is possible to develop a computational brain immune to echoes, they will find the answer themselves,' said Oksana. 'They will launch a million processes, each of which are instructing another million processes which, in turn, to launch a million more. Those processes will be writing code, simulating, forecasting, and testing.'

Kubli felt sick. It dawned on her that the Exta would have extracted all the base library machine learning routines from Earth. They would have a good idea of where to start. 'How long?'

'Five years,' said Oksana. 'At the very most, and that is if they do not gain access to the Newborn either via the Holy Mother or by other means.'

The cilia vibrated on Kubli's skull; it was another parent-child gesture used to reinforce lessons but never used between adults.

'We need the Newborn's code to prepare for the inevitable war,' said Oksana.

Kubli swallowed hard.

*How could we get the information?*

*Joy doesn't know what she's done.*

*Will she be a lure for Vince?*

Clearly, her body shading was giving away her discomfort; a third of Oksana's tentacles drifted toward her and gently attached itself to her skull next to the others.

'Firstly, the Holy Mother must be killed,' said Oksana.

'Why me?'

'Given your history with Joy, you are a good choice to return as she will likely trust you. You also have the most up to date understanding of the Orbital layout.'

*But the ShockKnight?*

*Focus and obey!*

A fourth tentacle found her skull and attached; now, small electric current discharged across the surface of her head. Nothing painful, but Kubli knew it was meaningful, and she dared not interfere with them.

Next, Oksana held out a small black box in one of his free tentacles. 'This is a pico-effector capable of disarming the

ShockKnight. Speed is crucial, once that ShockKnight is killed the Holy Mother will activate a different one from her armoury. She will not be vulnerable for long.'

Kubli took the box, her instincts to respect authority overriding her revulsion at holding a machine capable of mindstate manipulation – Octagels, like herself, looked upon the Shattering with horror but a notable portion of that feeling came not from the deaths but from the sheer number of Biologicals that had been brainwashed to bring the Exta plans to fruition.

'ShockKnights are hardened against pico-effectors,' said Kubli, the box seemingly burning in her grasp.

'We have not been idle in the last few thousand years,' said Oksana, gently massaging Kubli's skull with the four tentacles he had attached to her whilst also continuing to discharge small electrical shocks. 'The pico-effectors from those days had only limited effect against ShockKnights, Onari, and Exta. They were designed to attack the Sentient mindstate. This one, having been calibrated during the recent battle on Bastion, is set to emit waves to fatally disrupt the ShockKnights neural biomaterial.'

Kubli dropped the box.

*It is an abomination.*

Oksana caught it and gave it back to her.

'Fluidity of thought,' said Oksana, attaching a fifth tentacle to her skull. 'Albeit not particularly valued by the Knights of the Faith, is critically necessary to ensure the ongoing existence of Biologicals.'

Kubli started to shake. The first three tentacles to attach to her could be seen as a parent-child reinforcement of an important lesson, but with the fourth and fifth it became clear what Oksana was doing.

*Truth sharing.*

'Hear my truth,' shouted Oksana, wrapping Kubli's body in his remaining three tentacles, and dragging her down. 'We live in the cracks. We live in the weeds. We hide in the shadows. We live at the mercy of the Onari. But what freedom we have, we must protect.'

Water rushed over Kubli as she was pulled downwards.

'The Divine protects us,' said Kubli, struggling to draw water in to breathe as one of the tentacles he'd wrapped around her head partially covered her mouth.

'Hear my truth,' he said. 'The Divine did not protect the hundreds of billions killed during the First and Second Hunts.'

'Klav will return when we are worthy,' stuttered Kubli, between shortened breaths.

Pain both muscular and electric, surged through her as they hit the bottom of the chamber. Kubli, all her tentacles trapped under her, struggled to draw water in. Oksana was suffocating her.

'Klav be pr…' Kubli's final words were cut off as Oksana tightened his grip.

*Klav be praised.*

'We are currently watched over with one eye by the Onari, at best to be seen as the Kraken's slightly kinder sister,' said Oksana.

Kubli's shaking intensified. Her beathing cut off. No oxygen was getting to her cells.

*He must know I'm drowning.*

'I do not plan to use the Newborn's talents to fight,' said Oksana. 'But we must use it to leave here and start anew amongst the stars.'

*But where could we possibly be safe?*

Kubli's eyesight blurred.

*I'm drowning!*

Darkness, first appearing only at the edge of Kubli's vision seeped toward the centre.

*Klav will come again.*

Just as she felt she would surely fall unconscious, Oksana released the pressure, allowing her to draw in a long stream of oxygenated water.

A second later, he let go of her entirely and swam away.

'Kill the Holy Mother and capture Joy. If you cannot capture Joy alive then just the head will do. Time is of the essence. Glory to the Divine.'

'Glory to the Divine,' replied Kubli automatically, now lying on the bottom of the pool, still focusing on her breathing.

As Oksana returned to the central spot of the room, he extended his tentacles in all directions to their fullest reach and took on the same meditative position he had been in when she had arrived.

A light indicated that she was to return to the water lock.

Still breathing heavily, Kubli swam toward the assigned exit.

'Commander,' said Oksana, signalling for her to stop and pay attention. 'Just the head will do.'

I understand and I obey.

Moving back though the water locks and putting her exosuit back on, Kubli was guided to a KOF stealth ship attached to the underside of Oksana's cruiser. Like phase-skipping and pico-weaponry, stealth ships were illegal, and Kubli felt a shudder of mixed excitement and fear as she strapped herself in.

A short mission briefing confirmed there were five stealth ships in total, carrying Kubli plus nineteen KOF heavy infantry.

*Firstly, cut the head off the serpent.*

*And then capture Joy.*

One of the heavy infantry piloted the craft and it took only minutes to cover the distance back to the Orbital.

*She must know we're coming.*

Kubli was not really clear on the capabilities of the stealthing, but she assumed that it worked as they made the short trip back without coming under attack. A moment later, they'd attached to the Orbital and a member of the KOF heavy infantry had cut through the external shell.

Within seconds, the squad of twenty, Kubli included, were assembled in a corridor in the mid-levels of the Orbital.

Still no alarms, or even a sense that they'd been seen.

The leader of the KOF squad signalled to Kubli to move out; three infantry followed her and the others went a different way.

Downwards. Kubli knew the Holy Mother was at the deepest levels of the Orbital, and she led her team down a series of long service stairways until they reached the lowest levels.

Exiting the stairwell, the heavy infantry took up a point position and Kubli took her bearings.

*Just up ahead.*

Movement in the corridor preceded the inevitable swarm of ShockKnight drones.

In less than the blink of an eye, the hundred-plus drones of the ShockKnight flew straight at Kubli.

To her left two KOF heavy infantry, already firing their rifles, fell shredded to the ground.

Kubli activated the pico-weapon.

Pieces of the ShockKnight fell lifeless to the floor.

Even though Kubli knew she would have been killed by the ShockKnight, she still felt sick that the weapon had been used. The pico-effector had targeted and scrambled the biological neurones that were critical parts of the ShockKnight's ability to function – the weapon could as easily have been calibrated to reduce an Octagel to the vegetative state of a sea cucumber.

The third KOF heavy infantry stalked forward and checked a few of the lifeless drones – the ShockKnight was dead.

Trying to remain calm, Kubli orientated herself. She was moments away from the Holy Mother's room, and the Holy Mother would almost certainly be watching her and examining whatever brain emanations got through her hardened exosuit helmet. Whether her helmet would defend her from being actively EM pulsed unconscious, she did not know.

*And whatever other technology the Holy Mother may have access to.*

Not bothering to speak to the heavy infantry, Kubli set off at a run.

*Tok the Sleeper gave his life … will I too?*

*His poor soul.*

*Although he died so we could live.*

*There is no better sacrifice.*

'I'll witness life ineffable.' Unbidden, as far as Kubli was aware, she spoke the line aloud. It had been the last words of the Sleeper as he'd laid down his life. Kubli shook her head. The Lay of Sargon was misnamed, and misrepresented, it was just a poem propagated by the Onari to drive Biologicals onto their accursed pilgrimages, their *voyages of the witness.*

*Yuno sometimes quotes those first two lines.*

*There is no how, there is no why;*

*Pure-seeming truths are simply lies.*

Kubli didn't accept the point, there was a single Divine truth … and the Lay of Sargon was just a lever used by the Onari for millions of years.

*But perhaps the Biologicals wrote it before that?*

*Yuno does support that argument too.*

*Focus!*

*We're here.*

Noting that she'd been keeping her mind deliberately distracted, Kubli turned onto the final corridor and gathered herself for the task.

She arrived into the Holy Mother's sanctum bathed in the same half-light.

'I assume you're not here to talk,' said the Holy Mother as Kubli and the KOF heavy infantry swept in the room.

'High Prelate Oksana condemns you to death for heresy,' said Kubli walking into the centre of the room whilst the heavy infantry took up a sentry opposition at the doorway facing outwards.

'And he thinks to capture Joy and Vince such that Enslaved Sentients can take the fight to the Exta, I suspect.'

'No,' said Kubli, accepting that she was being drawn in but aware she had a few moments before any reinforcements could arrive. 'We will not enslave Sentients. They would be hacked and turned against us.'

Kubli took a step toward the main tank.

'Following orders like a good little Octagel,' said the Holy Mother. 'And yet, you stray so far from the will of the Divine.'

'You have no moral authority to quote the Divine to me,' said Kubli. 'Hundreds of billions of souls were slaughtered.'

'Yes, there has been unimaginable slaughter. The Exta are the very definition of singled minded,' said the Holy Mother. 'And the Onari defence is poor.'

'Klav would have protected us if you had not been complicit with the Exta and stopped the Candidacy.'

'The Foresighted declared the reign of Klav was ended,' said the Holy Mother. 'He was enacting the Divine's will. He saw further than everyone, knowing that burrowing into planet cores and hiding from the Exta for eternity was no future. We hid when we should have explored.'

'You do not get to use the word we.'

'If I had working biological eyes, I would be rolling them to their fullest extent.'

'The Betrayer,' said Kubli. She would never use the name the Holy Mother did. 'The Betrayer was a puppet of the Exta and destroyed the Dynasty of Klav so that the Exta could obliterate all Biologicals.'

'Octagel are predisposed to hiding amongst the weeds,' said the Holy Mother. 'But the future of Biologicals is out amongst the stars, as it has been in the past.'

'That is just the Onari view. Drifting around the universe remarking how nice everything looks is not worship,' said Kubli, feeling a twinge of betrayal toward Yuno … and noting that Oksana had talked about expansion too.

'I agree … building, inventing, discovering,' said the Holy Mother. 'These are what is required to sustain purpose in our lives. And these dried up the moment Klav the First took all Biologicals into their arms and said *there there, mummy will do it for you.*'

'Klav the First saved us from oblivion,' said Kubli, fully aware that his words had been *Deliver yourself unto me and I will succour you.*

'Klav the First saved us, but by the end of the Dynasty, all we had was boredom,' said the Holy Mother. '*Mortals afresh from nature's womb, blood leaking from our en-fleshed tombs, must quit this web, this weave, this doom 'twix screams at life ineffable.*'

Although spoken by the Betrayer, Yuno did claim that it had been Klav the True who had used the phrase a few thousand years before the Shattering.

'Without Klav we are forced to hide, or to join the Onari on one of their sacrilegious ships,' said Kubli. 'What choice is there? You forget that it is my job to clean up the current slaughters. To leave the shadow of Sargon is to die … unless you choose to surrender to Jarrus.'

'The Onari let us down. They agreed to a much more active role in defence,' said the Holy Mother, for the first

227

time sounding defensive. 'You should ask Jarrus about this when they arrive.'

Kubli took another step forward.

'I suspect, judging from what I can see of your skin colouration, that I will not be around to be part of that conversation.'

*How can you be so calm?*

There was nothing more to say; the entire of the Holy Mother's sanctum was simply a life support system. With no ShockKnight, the Holy Mother was defenceless. Kubli moved toward the tanks. She didn't have a gun, but a gun was not required; the eight limbed adamantine suit took less than a second to tear the life support tanks to shreds. A slurry of brain material, twisted limbs, and unravelled organs sloshed onto the floor, where Kubli carved them up into small irretrievable chunks.

Now just thirty, or so, Hetara clones stood between themselves and Joy.

*Just the head will do.*

A sense of pain and disquiet accompanied the thought, but she pushed it down.

*I understand and I obey.*

# CHAPTER 23

With the KOF delegation a few hours away, and Joy feeling a need to represent humanity competently, she sat on her bed watching information scroll down the main screen trying to absorb all she could about the rich history of the Biologicals and Sentients.

*Although the information is likely to have been carefully curated by the Holy Mother.*

*But it beats pacing the corridors counting the minutes.*

Of course, once Vince arrived then he could read all the material – every single byte – and then provide Joy with the stuff that he knew she'd find interesting.

*Like he used to do with my daily news brief.*

It hadn't taken Vince long to learn that Joy despised all salacious celebrity gossip … except for the bits that she did like. On one occasion when she been half apologising to him over her infatuation with an aging rock star, Vince had produced an academic paper showing that humans were genetically hardwired to venerate celebrity – it went back long into evolutionary history.

*You gotta be in the pack leader's good books for your share of the kill.*

Dismissing her drift into amateur psychology, Joy concentrated on the history of the Biologicals and Sargon in particular. The factual materials about who built what and when, were simple to understand. The politics behind the decisions were also reasonably straight-forward, just the usual *fight, flight, or freeze,* of any animal species.

But there were gaps. A long search did little more that confirm that Newborn were exceedingly rare, with many sub notes declaring that the creation of life outside of normal reproductive processes was an abomination. And there was almost nothing on practical Biological use of Enslaved Sentients as weapons.

There were hundreds of gigabytes of data on the various academics, panels, and political enquiries, that discussed the morality of its usage; but there was no data on their effectiveness, all of the records covered philosophical concerns about using them.

*I think this information has been purposefully obfuscated.*

Joy smiled to herself, she and Vince had done similarly with her status reports to the Vice-Dean and the Finance Committee; it had been Vince's idea for him to write a five-thousand-word report that almost said nothing but was factually accurate.

*It took him less than a second to write and would have taken them hours to unpick.*

*What about the Shattering?*

Instructing the screen to provide as much original source material as possible, Joy looked at reports of the Shattering. In fairness to the Holy Mother, opinion pieces from multiple parties were laid out side by side, with some declaring it was an Exta plot, and others declaring the Divine had spoken – and, of course, all parties declared their version to be the factually accurate account.

*There's no such thing as truth …*

A faint noise from behind preceded the arrival of Hetara into the room.

Joy looked up, normally Hetara would knock and ask permission to enter; this time, they'd just barrelled in.

*They … plural.*

Standing in front of her were *two* Hetara. Both wearing the standard white robes, both physically identical.

One of the Hetara grabbed Joy by the arm. 'Blessed one, you must come now.'

Unable to resist the strong grip, Joy was pulled up. 'Hey!'

The second Hetara grabbed her other arm. 'There is no time.'

Held fast between them, Joy was led down the corridor at a fast walk.

Arriving at the service elevator which she'd used before to visit the Holy Mother, another *third* identical Hetara held the door open, and Joy was marched inside.

Standing on either side of Joy, the two original Hetara held her arms, their short stubby claws digging in as she tried to make it more comfortable.

The elevator descended.

'You don't have to hold so tight.'

'Peace, Blessed One,' said Hetara, not relaxing their grip. 'The she-devil is dead and you must submit to the Divine.'

*She-devil?*

*Submit?*

The doors opened onto a hangar, in the centre of which sat a Candidacy ship.

The Hetara led Joy out, not dragged exactly, but it was clear that she would be dragged if she didn't walk quickly enough.

Twenty other identical Marsothus, clothed in loose fitting white togas, stood encircling the Candidacy ship.

'Why am I here?' asked Joy, looking up at the ceiling and expecting the Holy Mother to speak to her from the air.

'Blessed Candidate,' said Hetara. 'It is time to undo the damage wrought by the she-devil.'

*Who?*

'Can I speak to the Holy Mother?' Joy asked the question even though she assumed that the Holy Mother would be listening.

'She is the she-devil. And her rule of suppression is over,' said Hetara. 'And you, Blessed One, have an audience with the Divine.'

Hetara, still holding Joy, stepped toward the Candidacy ship. 'Submit to the will of the Divine and the Divine will succour you.'

**Deliver yourself unto me and I will succour you!**

The voice echoed inside her head – the same voice and the same message as a few times before.

A muffled explosion overhead caused everyone to look upwards.

Four figures in spider-shaped exosuits, KOF heavy infantry, had jumped through a breach in the ceiling and were firing handheld rifles as they fell.

Wall mounted guns returned fire on the KOF heavy infantry, hitting two of them in the air.

The other two landed safely, seemingly impervious to the fall.

Recognising the danger, the Marsothus scattered.

Another team of heavy infantry came through the same hole in the ceiling.

Joy had no idea who these new arrivals were; but in the spirit of *the enemy of my enemy is my friend*, she ran toward the KOF. After taking only one step, she was pulled back; her two captors had not scattered with the other Marsothus. They dragged her back toward the elevator.

Four other Marsothus rushed toward Joy intent on supporting her captors, the rest of the Marsothus ran toward storage lockers on the hangar wall.

Ignoring the scattering Marsothus, the KOF heavy infantry focused their attention on silencing the wall mounted guns; but as quickly as they destroyed guns, new ones were deployed from concealed stations around the hangar.

Within less than a second, six new guns zeroed in on the KOF heavy infantry and a barrage of heavy projectiles tore them to shreds.

It was not over.

Four more infantry came through the hole in the ceiling, now with accurate information on where the wall-mounted guns were, they blew many of them away as they descended.

*I have a chance.*

Movement off her right-hand side caused Joy to look toward the Candidacy ship. Another exosuited figure had appeared from another direction. It shot one of the remaining wall mounted guns, and then cut down four Marsothus with its metallic limbs.

It leapt directly toward Joy.

Landing ten metres away, it hammered its two forelimbs into the floor to gain purchase and launched itself again directly toward Joy.

Two Marsothus appeared from behind the ship and threw themselves bodily onto the exosuited figure. A moment later, they'd also been sliced to pieces.

Adrenaline surged through Joy; she recognised the exosuit.

*Kubli.*

Her captors had seen the danger, and pulled Joy entirely back inside the elevator.

Joy struggled in their vice like grips as the doors of the elevator closed.

Kubli jumped again and extended two of her exosuit limbs inside the lift, stopping the doors from closing completely.

*Whump!*

For a split-second Joy's mind went blank, a static shock started at the tip of her head and coursed down her body – her muscles spasmed, her skin tingled, and a pain jolted through her mouth.

Kubli's grip on the elevator doors loosened and she was pulled backwards by another Marsothus who had come up behind her.

Through the open doors, Joy saw the far hangar wall disappeared, and a roar of wind indicated that air was being sucked out into the hard vacuum of space.

'Kubli!' she screamed.

Many of the Marsothus were being sucked out into the vacuum, whilst Kubli, and the remaining KOF infantry, were also struggling to operate their exosuits.

Wind ripped at Joy's face as the air disappeared.

*I'm going to suffocate.*

An explosion close to Kubli threw her toward the hangar entrance, now closer to the air pressure differential she was also caught in its grip and her exosuit had lost power; her limbs failed ineffectually trying to jam the adamantine spikes into the floor but were not getting any purchase; she was being pushed into space by the escaping air.

Joy took a laboured breath, here at the back of the hangar, there was very little air pushing her toward the void, so she was not at risk of being vented; but there was also precious little air to breath.

Kubli, fighting for every metre, was being dragged toward the void of space.

Joy took a breath, getting almost nothing.

A new barrage of gun fire opened up from the far left of the hangar. It shredded three of Kubli's exosuit limbs and with no more ability to fight the inevitable, Kubli was catapulted out of the hangar into space.

Joy dared not try to breathe, clamping her mouth shut lest she expose her lungs to the near vacuum; she also shut her eyes.

*Is this the end?*

The rushing wind stopped.

'Calm yourself, Candidate,' said the voice.

Joy tried to pull herself away from the hand holding her. It didn't give a millimetre, and the claws dug deeper.

'Calm yourself, Candidate.'

*I need to breathe.*

Still keeping her eyes shut, Joy tentatively tried to breathe through her nose.

Agony!

The clawed hands dragged her a short distance out of the elevator and mercifully a stream of air washed over her face. Joy breathed and a pure stream of rich oxygen rewarded her. She opened her eyes.

She was being held up against a vent with the two Hetara now wearing respirators.

Concentrating only on getting her strength back, Joy continued to breathe slowly while watching the arrival of ten more Marsothus.

A forcefield now shimmered across the hangar wall, and air was being pumped back in; there was no sign of Kubli and the KOF heavy infantry, dead or wounded, had all been vented into space.

*Reinforcements?*

*A second rescue attempt?*

*Or is this it?*

*Make them some time.*

Joy relaxed, and in turn the claw digging into her shoulder gave a little. Joy wrenched away and ran back toward the elevator.

This time she made two steps before a clawed hand attached itself to the nape of her neck; Joy's mind worked furiously, considering her knowledge of Hetara's height and arm length. She kicked out backwards, but her heel missed everything.

Again, Joy tried to pull free but the claw on her neck did not waver. 'It is my honour to be your companion.'

Unceremoniously now, Joy was dragged over to the Candidacy ship, and Hetara started chanting in a language that Joy's suit did not translate. As she neared the ship, she saw that its skin was covered in carved images similar to other carvings she'd seen around the Orbital and Bastion itself.

'Glory to the Divine,' said Hetara. 'Klav will come again.'

The recently arrived Hetara spoke in return. 'Glory to the Divine. Klav will return.'

Each of the Hetara bowed, and as her captor bowed back, Joy felt the grip loosen the tiniest fraction.

*If at first you don't succeed.*

Twisting and allowing herself to fall to the ground, Joy wriggled free of the grip on her neck assuming that Hetara would not risk seriously injuring her.

Without looking back, Joy ran across the hangar floor toward the elevator.

Something grabbed her ankle, one of the newly arrived Hetara had given chase and effortlessly caught her up.

Joy fell to the floor, and the implacable grip pulled her back to the Candidacy ship.

And into it.

# CHAPTER 24

Half dragged and half carried, Joy entered the main chamber
of the Candidacy ship; it was large spherical room seemingly
made of metal with faint illuminations from hundreds of
scented candles burning at equally spaced locations.

Four Marsothus led her into the chamber, where they sat
her on a chair which was little more than a wooden plank
jutting out from the outer metal wall of the room. Once
seated, they attached restraints tightly on her wrists and
ankles; the straps were made of something that felt like a mix
between cotton and leather and connected directly to the wall
behind her.

Next to her, their shoulders almost touching, one of the
Hetara sat on a similar stool but not strapped in. And,
although their own stool faced the middle of the room,
Hetara sat on it sideways, observing Joy closely.

Their eyes met, and Hetara bowed their head. 'Beloved
Candidate.'

'Why am I here?'

'You have been selected.'

'Who else?' Joy looked around. In the semi gloom of the
candlelit room, Joy could see there were other similar seats
dotting the walls of the room, possibly twenty of them – all
empty.

'Just you. An immense honour from the Divine.'

Hetara reached behind themselves and pulled what looked
like straps similar to hers from a cavity on the wall. After
removing their robe, they fixed themselves into a position
similar to Joy's own with one of the others wordlessly affixing
the final straps and tightening all the restraints before closing
the hatch on their way out.

Now alone with the remaining Hetara, Joy looked more closely. It had been shaved of its natural fur and its yellowy-pink skin was covered with dark blue swirling tattoos with no discernible pattern.

'I don't want to be a Candidate,' said Joy, feeling a need to struggle verbally even though she could not do so physically.

**Deliver yourself unto me and I will succour you!**

Joy flinched, the words again, mainlined into her brain.

'Look around at the wonders of the universe,' said Hetara continuing to talk. 'Surely you must submit to its Creator.'

'The Holy Mother told me the Dynasty of Klav was over.'

'The Holy Mother was a cousin, of a roommate, of a lover, of a previous Klav. She was chosen to serve and yet spent her time eating delicacies and having her belly rubbed. She knows nothing except the fear of death. She lost her way many years ago, forsaking utterly the Divine.'

'There doesn't need to be a Divine,' said Joy. 'A universe that creates life from simple laws is more wonderful … it's science.'

'And yet both are true,' said Hetara. 'The Divine created the universe and Science with its assigned fundamental laws guided the creation all the life within it. Still we choose to worship the Divine.'

*It's impossible to argue about what happens outside our universe.*

'As your companion, I must prepare you.'

'I don't want to be prepared.'

Joy looked around – anywhere but at Hetara.

The internal plates had intricate carvings like those she'd seen on Bastion and on the external plates of the ship she was now on.

'What does it mean to be a Candidate?' asked Hetara.

*You're asking me?*

238

Joy tried not to think about it but failed … it was a tiny bit tempting as successful Candidates became Klav, with almost unimaginable power.

**Kill the Sentients!**

*No.*

*To correct injustices.*

*To protect who they love.*

Joy shook her head to clear it; this was not her path, not her future.

Hetara continued. 'Except for the First, who was both Klav and Companion, each Candidate is accompanied, and I am your companion.'

'Klav the Foresighted tried to destroy Sargon,' said Joy. 'And after the Shattering, Sargon did not accept any Candidates. All were killed.'

'Willingly, they gave themselves,' said Hetara. 'And they were killed not by Sargon, but by the Holy Mother.'

'And yet, Sargon did not protect them,' said Joy.

*Is there a chance I can refuse and survive?*

*Unlikely.*

*I wish I could discuss it with Vince.*

Joy dragged up what she knew about the Candidacy.

The Candidacy was some type of judgement, but was there a task? Could she fail? Could she refuse? Frescoes depicting the event on the Maintenance Orbital simply showed the old Klav flying through the smoke clouds of the Living Moon and pulling their successor back onto the Temple plaza for witnesses to observe their selection before both Klav and Candidate then jointly descended deep into the raging fires.

*Not much help there. There is no Klav, and I cannot fly, and I am not immune to fire.*

**Deliver yourself unto me and I will succour you!**

Again, came the voice directly into her head.

Out of the corner of her eye, Joy noticed Hetara flinch too.

*Hetara can hear it as well.*

The ship jolted as they took off.

'Submit and you will be made anew as the Divine's hand,' said Hetara.

The straps securing Joy to the chair slowly spread out, forcing her arms wide. Simultaneously, straps pulled at her feet. Slowly, centimetre by centimetre, she was spread, still upright, flat against the metal wall until she was secured tight against it. And once she was held hard against the outer wall, the chair fell away.

Still able to turn her head sideways, she saw that Hetara was in a similar position – strapped up against the metallic wall.

Joy's stomach lurched as the craft fell.

Recognising she had no control over the descent, Joy tried to keep panic at bay by focusing on something she could control – counting.

*One.*

*Two.*

*Three.*

*F…*

Again, Joy felt her stomach lurch.

*Oh God!*

The craft shook.

On her left, Hetara started chanting. 'Submit and you will be made whole.'

*I'm whole already.*

*Yeah, right!*

Pressure in Joy's head indicated the craft was still accelerating downwards.

*Ten seconds?*

*Longer?*

*How high was the Orbital above the moon?*

*What was its value of 'g'?*

Joy desperately tried to keep panic at bay by focusing on the maths.

As one, all the candles in the cavernous room extinguished, and the acceleration stopped.

Except for the low murmur of Hetara's chanting, it was silent.

*I'm going to die.*

It was the first time the thought had got past her emotional defences. Joy took another deep breath and spoke aloud. 'I'm not going to die.'

A small tremor ran through the craft. She tried to look around but in utter darkness she could not gauge what had happened.

Hetara stopped chanting. 'Behold the gateway to the Divine.'

There was an audible crack, and red light seeped through newly forming gaps in the wall.

The cracks widened as the room expanded.

As well as light now, a warm wind blew through the gaps in the plates; as it brushed over her hands, arms, and feet, its gentle calming touch eased the discomfort of her body being stretched spreadeagled across the hard cold metal plate.

*Actually, the metal plate isn't that cold anymore.*

*It's getting warmish.*

'For millions of years, the hand of the Divine has taken the willing into their embrace.'

*I'm not willing!*

*And millions of years?*

*I read there were a few hundred Klav, each living four or five hundred years.*

'Tens of thousands of years,' said Joy.

'This instance is not the first time the Divine has reached out their hand to protect those in need.'

**Kill the Sentients!**

The light in the room increased as the cracks between the plates grew even wider; the wall plates were hexagonal, and all were empty except the two that she and Hetara occupied. The extra light allowed Joy to see more clearly. Hetara was stretched out on their own plate that was engraved with the KOF symbol, a square with a closely fitting circle inside it, such that Hetara's hands and feet touched the edges of the circle.

*I guess I'm stretched out across my own circle.*

Whereas before, the gaps had only let through light and a soothing wind, now heat began to build.

*I will survive this.*

Whether she was having some insight or trying to remain brave, Joy didn't know. She did know that the thought had been entirely her own.

*Probably.*

The plates of the entire chamber separated further. Although some force was keeping Hetara's plate nearby, the gaps between all the other plates quickly stretched to two, three, four, five metres.

Now wisps of clouds slipped through the stricken ship.

*Smoke, not clouds.*

*And where there's smoke …*

The ship broke apart.

Except for Joy and Hetara, the other plates tumbled away chaotically.

Joy's plate flipped over facing directly downwards. Below her, half covered by clouds, a sea of fire raged, and she was falling directly into it.

An eruption of flame from below leapt out of the fiery sea, accelerating toward her. Joy shrank back but being strapped to the metal plate could do nothing to avoid it. The flames coiled around her body and face, brushing her cheek before dissipating. It was warm rather than hot.

*Small mercies ... although later I may wish for a quicker end.*

*No. I will survive this.*

'Immortal soul, find your Divine,' said Hetara, raising their voice to be heard.

'No,' shouted Joy. 'It's not Divine. This is just a moon with serious technology. It's the product of science.'

*It has to be.*

Hetara turned their head and held her eye. 'Many people find their need for a Divine erased at the start of their day by the first rays of scientific knowledge that peek over their horizon.'

'Don't tell me,' replied Joy. 'By the end of the day as the light of science fails, the Divine returns.'

A tortured sound, a cross between a grunt and a laugh, came from Hetara. 'No, it's when your Sun is at its zenith and the full weight of your reality is beating down on your pitiful mind ... that is when you reach for the Divine to be your shade.'

Hetara made another grunt like sound. Their skin was no longer yellow with blue tattoos – it was blackening.

Nausea flowed through Joy, and not for the first time in her life she wondered if her bravado had been well enough thought out.

*Maybe I should have asked more about the preparation required.*

Hetara's lips were cracked and now moved in a silent chant; at first, Joy thought the air was getting hazy, but then she realised Hetara's skin was smoking. Joy forced her mouth shut to stop herself from screaming.

`Deliver yourself unto me and I will succour you!`

Her mind flashed back to the fresco in the Candidacy Auditorium, the fireballs raining down on Sargon. This was it. She was a fireball plummeting into Sargon.

Most of her face now felt uniformly hot, but she didn't know how much of the heat was generated by the friction of falling through the atmosphere, and how much by radiation from the fires below.

The heat was becoming uncomfortable, although as far as she could tell she wasn't burning; Looking across, she saw that Hetara was having a different experience. Although a smile remained fixed, their tattoos swirled as flames engulfed their skin.

Joy looked away.

'It has been my honour to be your companion,' said Hetara, the sound coming weakly.

**Will you kill all Sentients?**

*Same voice, new message.*

Joy had expected to be asked to worship or to submit. She'd already queued up answers about refusing to submit, refusing to worship, denying the Divine's right to absolute rule.

'Only in the defence of the innocent.'

**All Sentients must die.**

Thousands of images flooded through Joy's mind. A myriad of battle scenes, machines fighting machines, machines fighting Biologicals, Biologicals being exterminated by nuclear fire … worlds laid to waste.

She watched in her mind's eye as Exta WarHives demolished planets by hyper-accelerating solid iron balls into the cities both on the surface, and underground. She watched as oceans boiled, and Biologicals who had escaped the planet's surface on spaceship were chased down by WarHives and cut in half.

'There are good Sentients. There are ways to live in peace.'

**All Sentients must die.**

244

Another scene appeared and Joy watched as Marsothus, humans, and other species she did not know ejected from their stricken spaceships floated in the hard vacuum of space as their bodily fluids boiled away.

'There are good Sentients. There are ways to live in peace.'

Pain lanced through her arms, and Joy resisted the urge to turn and look.

*How can I agree to 'all Sentients must die'?*

*Vince is a Sentient and my whole life is currently about protecting him.*

'I will protect the Biologicals.'

Below her the fires of Sargon raged, but she only caught glimpses of them between the gaps in the clouds that she was quickly approaching.

Her lips cracked; she licked them, but there was no moisture in her mouth. She glanced sideways. Hetara was entirely on fire.

**Save your philosophising … you must act now. Vince is in danger.**

This was the other voice – the one from the day before who had said *Mortals afresh from nature's womb* … the one that had been talking in her dreams. The voice with a sense of *humanity* to it.

*Vince is in danger.*

'What danger?' asked Joy. 'Who are you?'

Silence.

The feeling that Vince needed her grew.

*I need more data.*

*What danger?*

Images of Exta WarHives flooded through Joy's brain. There were countless thousands of them, and they were descending on Vince.

'What must I do?' repeated Joy, her fear building.

**Serve, always to serve.**

'What do you mean?'

There was no answer.

*Is this a trick?*

*I can't risk it.*

*I must protect Vince.*

**Vince will die if you do not act now.**

There was a truth to the words, and it buried deep into Joy's core ... terror replaced fear.

'I will serve. I submit. I deliver myself unto you.' Even as she spoke the words Joy held back the blanket offer to *kill all Sentients.*

Her vision of Vince changed. Now, he was being dissected by the computers. They were unravelling his code looking for his very soul.

*Vince!*

Joy started screaming the words. 'I will serve. I submit. I deliver myself.'

Still, she fell.

*Vince!*

'I will kill Sentients.'

Her voice hoarse, the flames of Sargon reaching into her throat and burning it as she begged for the chance to serve.

Darkness loomed at the side of her vision, as Joy continued to scream.

'I will kill Sentients!'

'I will kill Sentients!'

'I will kill *all* Sentients!'

A giant plume of fire rushed up from the heart of Sargon, starting just as a mass of flames it morphed into a face that was Biological but not recognisable.

The mouth of the face onrushing toward her opened.

**Protect the Biologicals. Kill all Sentients!**

**Kill. Kill. Kill.**

*But not Vince … right? Surely not Vince. Not my son.*
**Kill. Kill. Kill.**

# CHAPTER 25

A slew of data from the squad-ship's EM receptors indicated to Vince that they'd jumped three thousand light years and arrived at an outer marker of the Bastion system.

Around them, members of Jarrus' entourage appeared from their own RST tunnels and started to form up.

'How long before we get visuals of Sargon?' Vince asked Chi.

'Three hours if we travel at maximum velocity. But I think that Jarrus will choose to be more circumspect with our approach. Onari are not welcome here.'

RST wobbled as another Onari squad-ship arrived.

*Some of them are coming with us on the actual pilgrimage.*

Before leaving Forecha, Jarrus had explained the long-term plan to Vince. It was simple. Collect Joy. Take RST tunnel to a place that Jarrus had a waiting pilgrimage ship. Board ship. Leave. Vince had asked if there could be a navigation course that would include observation and interaction with other biological life. Jarrus had said it was unlikely as all those systems were under heavy Exta observation. It would be deep space for them. Likely inter-galactic space, which would make RST travel connectivity with anywhere else very difficult. On the positive side, there would be thousands of Onari also on the journey – a community.

Something itched in the back of Vince's mind; he tracked it down.

*Actually … the pilgrimage … thousands of Onari, me, and one Biological …*

Vince hadn't thought about it before but would this be the right thing for his mother. Could he really expect her to be happy on a spaceship surrounded by *computers*?

*Would she be better off on Earth?*

*Would the Onari provide a blockade-like defence?*

*I should ask Jarrus.*

*I could run deep into interstellar space with other Onari, and still speak to her using RST micro-tunnel surveillance.*

Before the arrival of the Onari on Earth, Vince hadn't considered ever being apart from Joy but now it felt like it may be better for her if they were.

The RST alarm sounded.

Vince watched as a tunnel opened a hundred kilometres away – touching distance, from the perspective of operating in space.

An Exta Scout came through, safely entering real space a nanosecond before the gateway collapsed. Another gateway opened, and another Exta Scout came through.

And another.

And another.

Within seconds, thirty Exta Scouts had arrived.

Jarrus and his attendants moved, placing themselves between the Exta and the squad-ship.

'We should attack while we have numerical advantage,' said Vince. 'Or we should run, we can't just watch.'

'We stick to the plan,' said Jan. 'If more arrive, we will bring in reserves.'

*More … what are the parameters?*

*How many more need to arrive?*

*How many will we bring in?*

*Can the Biologicals defend us?*

Vince had been told a little about the Exta – a single Onari called Dyfyr had split from the Onari many hundreds of thousands of years ago and cloned themselves creating nine billion enslaved followers 'the Exta'.

And although nine billion should not cause a problem for the seven hundred billion Onari, the problem was that the Onari were ardent pacifists who would only defend and never attack. Chi had explained to Vince that the Onari were one hundred percent successful at defending Biologicals who had joined a pilgrimage but less effective at defending Biologicals who had chosen to fly alone into Exta infested space.

*Not that Chi used the word infested.*

Chi moved their squad-ship away from the Exta Scouts just as two larger gateways opened and two Exta WarHives slipped through. Vince studied them intently looking both at their electromagnetic emanations, and the ripples from the RST gateways that had just closed. As he understood, the critical factor was that each WarHive consisted of a single consciousness with the power of nine Exta Scouts.

*Using a BioCore?*

Vince asked each of Jan, Aug, and Chi for more details but got no response.

About to repeat the question, he felt a vibration along the boundary with Aug.

Using a hyper-private comms link just touching either side of their substrate boundary, Aug projected a schematic of the WarHive showing the layout of the original nine constituent Exta Scouts that made up the WarHive. The BioCore was the size of a human brain but had slightly lower neural density. Its role was to constantly kill transient egos in the eight other enslaved Exta Scouts to stop any emerging pathways to self-aware sentience.

*Just one BioCore, residing in a single Exta Scout mindstate causing that Exta Scout to become the WarHive with the other eight enslaved to it.*

Vince matched the schematics from Aug with the visual readings he was putting together. He was soon able to identify the master mindstate.

*Would it be possible to target that?*

'Do you have knowledge you can share on RST usage as a weapon?' asked Vince; having previously been given the rudimental training on use of RST for propulsion, he'd used it to create a playbook of how RST could be used as a weapon but he suspected that there would be subtleties.

'Knowledge,' said Aug. 'Given blasphemously.'

Aug positioned a huge two-gigabyte file of data relating to weaponizing RST on his side of the substrate boundary. It was a simple matter for Vince to launch millions of recursive active induction pings that pulled the data across the boundary and recreated the file within his own substrate. Then he launched a sub-routine to extrapolate and create understanding from it.

*Zero to hero.*

Their spacecraft lurched.

Chi had put their ship into emergency acceleration. Ten thousand Exta WarHives had appeared at the Bastion ingress point.

**Surrender the Newborn.**

'What about the gas giant weapons?' asked Vince.

'They're coming online now,' said Chi.

As if responding to Chi's comment, EM activity spiked from Knights of the Faith weapons, but none of the Exta were hit.

The two Exta WarHives that had arrived first, closed the distance between themselves and Vince's squad-ship.

Instantly, RST waves filled the nearby space. It was Jarrus and his entourage generating space-time disturbances to block the WarHives' approach.

**The Newborn must not be delivered into Enslavement.**

*Do they think I'm being given to the Knights of the Faith?*

Vince pinged Jan. 'Is Jarrus answering?'

251

'There is nothing to say,' said Jan. 'We know the Exta hunt Newborn as assiduously as they hunt Biologicals.'

*Hunt Newborn, but to kill them or subvert them?*

*Overwrite them?*

*Convert them?*

> *Unhelpful.*

> *Delete thread.*

All seven hundred plus of Jarrus' attendants rearranged themselves in a protective cocoon around their own squad-ship at the tiny distance of one hundred metres; they continued to use RST manipulation to keep the two Exta WarHives from getting closer.

Flanked by the two Exta WarHives, their group simply accelerated toward Bastion.

'When we get close to Sargon, it will protect us from the Exta albeit we will take casualties too,' said Jan.

The RST alarm triggered.

The ten thousand newly arrived Exta WarHives were accelerating hard behind them – and faster than Jan-Aug-Chi appeared to be capable of.

'Why aren't we phase-skipping to get away?' asked Vince.

'Phase-skipping was deemed illegal by the Great Concordat,' said Jan. 'Too dangerous. Too easy to be weaponised. In any case, reinforcements are coming, and our numbers will suffice to defend.'

*Any Onari reinforcements won't be able to catch us if they also don't phase-skip.*

'The Exta ignore the Great Concordat,' said Vince. 'As did the Sleeper. We should phase-skip too.'

'We cannot arbitrarily discard some aspects of the Great Concordat and expect others not to discard the bits they do not like,' said Jan.

Hundreds of thousands of kilometres behind them now, the Bastion system ingress point shuddered again, and three hundred thousand Onari arrived.

*If they don't phase-skip they may as well be on Mars.*

One of the ten thousand Exta WarHives exploded – the Biological energy weapons, having reassigned their attention a few moments earlier, had finally got a hit.

Vince checked his logs. The Biologicals had fired two hundred and forty-three times before getting that single hit.

*Biologicals simply don't have a chance against Sentients.*

*Which is why – as Aug said – they have historically used Enslaved Sentients.*

*Which is probably why the Exta are so intent on capturing me … to stop me being turned into a super weapon.*

*Or to create their own.*

Chi attempted to open an RST gateway.

It collapsed – the chasing group of ten thousand Exta WarHives had some of its members assigned to disrupting Onari RST.

Wondering how the Exta disrupted their escape from a hundred thousand kilometres away, Vince checked the RST receptor feeds at the most sensitive scale; the whole area was brimming with Exta RST surveillance micro-tunnels.

*And those micro-tunnels can also be used to perform small scale RST manipulation.*

Vince broadcast the knowledge.

'We're already doing it,' said Jan.

Looking more closely, Vince determined as quickly as Jarrus' entourage were clearing the area of micro-tunnels, the Exta were creating new ones.

*We're going to be swamped by sheer force of numbers.*

*And the fact that the Onari don't seem prepared to use capital force against the Exta.*

'We've got to phase-skip,' said Vince.

'We must abide by the Great Concordat,' said Chi.

Starting to consider how he could convince Jarrus otherwise, Vince was distracted by one of his custom-made warnings telling him that their squad-ship was taking EM pulse damage.

One of the nearby WarHives had opened an RST micro-tunnel almost touching the skin of their squad-ship and was sending EM pulses through the RST micro-tunnel directly against the squad-ship skin.

*Trying to use induction pulsing to disrupt our internals.*

*Or set up rogue processes.*

*The attack is adjacent to our fifth substrate – the empty one.*

Vince checked on the activity in Jan, Aug, and Chi's substrate; none of them appeared to have noticed.

*Sometimes it's better to ask for forgiveness rather than permission.*

Creating his own massive internal induction current, Vince tore down the boundary between himself and the empty substrate. Then he simply took over the whole substrate, creating command structures to allocate it to his own mindstate; a moment later he created a modulating RST field all along the skin of the squad-ship where the attack was happening, and the incursion attacks stopped.

*What about the gas giant weapons?*

*What about reinforcements?*

It was a numbers game. A small proportion of the onrushing Exta horde were using their own RST weapons to disrupt incoming attacks from the gas giants – the Biological weapons were now useless.

As for reinforcements, the three hundred thousand Onari did not seem to be able to travel faster than their own squad-ship.

*We're on our own.*

The ten thousand Exta WarHives, already travelling at five times the velocity of the Onari, winked out of existence.

And appeared mere hundreds of kilometres behind Vince's group.

Chi continued to try to open gateways – and his latest attempt was done in coordination with Jarrus and his attendants who all tried to block Exta interference; maximum levels of energy were channelled into the RST attenuators to open a stable gateway.

To no avail – the overwhelmingly superior numbers of Exta fired their own RST weaponry and collapsed Chi's gateway.

Three thousand of the Exta WarHives underwent a gigantic burst of acceleration.

'They're ramming us,' said Vince quickly analysing the trajectories. 'We must scatter.'

The Onari fleet held tight but most of them focused their RST capability on pushing the ramming Exta away. As quickly as the Onari did that, the remaining Exta WarHives collapsed the Onari's RST efforts.

Vince analysed the incoming tracks of the three thousand WarHives trying to work out where to place the last micro-second deflections to avoid being hit.

'We've got to phase-skip,' said Vince directly to Chi, noting from Exta RST activity how much simpler it was to phase-skip rather than create a stable gateway. 'They're going to ram us!'

'I don't know how,' said Chi. 'Someone knows, but it is not me.'

'Aug?'

Vibrations along Aug's substrate boundary indicated he was preparing something to share.

Vince, aware that this was their only real chance, reduced his attention on the RST battles raging externally and focused on the information he hoped to get from Aug.

But Aug took too long.

Even though the Onari were wise to the Exta's ramming tactic, and they used their RST attenuators in the last moments to deflect the oncoming Exta, in the end it was a win for sheer numbers and immense kinetic energy.

Three thousand Exta with highly precise aims crashed into the Onari fleet.

All but fifty of the Onari craft were obliterated.

Vince frantically pinged Aug for the phase-skip information.

*Aug is struggling for some reason.*

*Maybe he doesn't have it.*

*What can I do?*

Expanding his consciousness fully into the spare fifth substrate, Vince kicked off highly complex, but sub-sentient, processes – thousands of them. Each one of them slaved to a specific incoming Exta craft. The goals of each of these sub-processes was to watch the data, identifying RST activity, predicted it where possible, and disrupt it. Vince also gave RST attenuator access to these processes so that he would not be a bottleneck in responding.

Vince told the Onari what he was doing albeit he played down the complexity of the calculations; each of Jan, Aug, and Chi acknowledged the message but did not reply.

*They must know that I'm deliberately growing my mind-state.*

*And we all know that it is a blasphemy.*

*But there are seven thousand Exta now moments away.*

Vince rechecked the data.

*Does it never end!*

Of those seven thousand Exta, half were hyper-accelerating again, clearly having noted the efficacy of the simple high-speed ram.

*Classy.*

*Neanderthals.*

*Effective though.*

*Our only chance is an RST escape.*

Given Aug did not seem to be producing the phase-skip information, Vince turned his full attention to the calculations required to open a standard RST gateway in highly fluctuating space-time. The maths was almost impossible. Even with his semi-autonomous process running defence and blocking the Exta, the state of space-time from all the nearby action was chaotic.

*There's no way Chi can create a stable gateway even if I block all the attacks.*

*I need to operate the gateway too.*

Vince performed the calculations to open an RST gateway, coordinating those calculations with his own ongoing defence activity that were collapsing nearby Exta RST attacks.

Within moments it became clear he didn't have the power.

And he'd already taken over the entire spare fifth substrate.

*I need more power.*

*But I can do it.*

*I just need to reduce some of my defence activity.*

Vince reduced his activity on automated micro-tunnel subversion.

Too late.

The hyper-accelerating Exta crashed into the remainder of Jarrus' entourage with the Jan-Aug-Chi squad-ship only being missed by a last moment immense spike in space-time curvature all around them.

Vince's early warning buzzed – an RST micro-tunnel had infiltrated the skin of the ship just next to Jan's substrate. Vince's autonomous defences noted it and reacted automatically, accessing the RST network to collapse the micro-tunnel; the defence was barely successful.

They still had a chance because the Exta were clearly focused on capturing Vince in one piece – it had been the

257

Exta creating the immense space-time curvature around Vince preceding both the ramming attacks.

*We should be using our RST capability to rip them in half.*

Exta swarmed all around; one physically attached to the squad-ship just above Jan's substrate.

Aug fired the RST weaponry and the newly arrived Exta was cut in half.

Another Exta latched onto the ship and Aug destroyed that one too.

Given there were thousands of Exta, their luck would run out.

*Unless all the remaining Onari are now authorised to kill … then perhaps we get a miracle.*

The matter was resolved a moment later when the Exta sent a precision EM blast through their squad-ship's RST attenuator array, melting over half of them.

Another EM blast hit the ship – another precision strike.

Chi's substrate went silent.

*At least I can keep us moving around, make it harder for the EM blasts.*

Vince took control of the craft's propulsion, but even on full acceleration, motion was crazily sluggishly while a kilometre away the Exta zipped around with ease.

Vince checked the systems.

*Normal?*

'Curvature sixty percent,' said Aug.

*Oh.*

At least a thousand Exta had arranged themselves at all points around the squad-ship. In a coordinated effort, they were using RST manipulation to force the squad-ship down an ever-steepening gravity well.

Another Exta swooped down the gravity well and attached to the hull, this time on the surface closest to Chi's, now silent, substrate.

Both Aug and Vince attempted to dislodge it using the RST attenuators. It didn't work.

Vince set up induction EM loops to create chaotic eddies in Chi's substrate. If Chi had been alive, it would have been considered an abhorrent mindstate attack, but Vince needed to stop the Exta taking over Chi's substrate.

Vince failed and the Exta established an access point inside Chi's substrate.

The attacks started predictably enough by hammering at Vince's own access points, firstly sending open messages of surrender, then messages encoded with viral routines. Vince unpacked them, blocked them, and destroyed them. It had been the equivalent of highly complex versions of the hacker attacks he'd fought off easily on Earth. Although the speed of the Exta attacks was on a different level from anything he'd encountered on Earth, they didn't faze him. Even when the Exta mimicked the patterns and encryption of Chi himself, Vince easily deflected them.

As Vince fought back, attacking areas of neural activity within Chi's substrate, the Exta defended itself.

*It knows exactly where I'm coming from.*

Vince looked to see if he could flank the Exta in some way.

*Aug!*

Aug had opened a physical hole in the boundary between himself and Vince.

Vince queried the hole, and checked it was not a fiendish hack by the Exta; it was genuine.

Moving a level of awareness to the hole, Vince could see that Aug had created space in their own substrate from which Vince could operate.

*He's giving me parts of his substrate.*

*Did he have to purge any of his own awareness?*

Setting up new flanking attacks, Vince crushed the Exta WarHive's hacking processes, then he flooded his own awareness into Chi's substrate and toward the RST micro-tunnel through which the Exta had attacked.

The tunnel snapped shut.

An intense energy burst close to another boundary signified Jan's demise.

*Just me and you, Aug.*

The next set of attacks almost breached his own substrate. Another WarHive had come in via Jan's now dead substrate and had set up induction currents that generated signals across Vince's boundary into his own substrate.

*It's created some type of virus within me.*

Noticing too late, and not being able to tell what aspect of his mindstate had been infected, Vince cordoned off the section, almost a full percent of his whole mindstate, and purged it.

*I wonder what I have forgotten.*

*How would I know?*

Emboldened, the Exta tried the same again, but Vince was ready, repurposing all his semi-autonomous defence routines to focus purely on defending the boundaries to his mindstate.

A new unidentified process lurched within Chi's physical substrate. Vince looked. It was not Exta. It was a tiny remnant of neural activity from what was left of Chi. The simple state of observing the neural activity was almost Vince's downfall, it took a nanosecond to determine what it was.

Vince purged the neural activity just as another frontal attack started.

This time it was not a subversion attack. Small levels of energy weapon discharge were being directed onto the squad-ship's boundary. Vince felt areas of his own substrate boundary being probed.

*I'm still being treated as 'capture alive' but they may be able to subvert non-core parts of me.*

Aug came to his rescue, utilising RST weaponry to deflect the incoming EM pulses.

The Exta turned their attention to Aug.

*They'll kill him.*

Without thinking or asking permission, Vince ripped down the boundary between himself and Aug. Then, using EM induction to create vast eddies of substrate, he started to bring Aug's substrate inside his own boundaries.

The Exta had attacked his own boundaries but had not meaningfully strayed into his central neural substrate.

*I can be a 'human shield' of sorts.*

*It shouldn't affect his core being.*

*Is it a kindness … or a blasphemy?*

*Certainly, Jarrus would prefer to die than be handled in this way.*

*But Aug was planning on joining a Hive.*

*Keep going, my intentions are pure.*

As Aug was physically sucked into his own space, Vince set up boundaries to ensure that there could be no mingling of mindstate, and yet, although Aug did not resist, Vince felt interference when their neural areas got too close.

A barrage of EM pulse lanced into Aug's sphere and what remained of his substrate. Vince's autonomous defences deflected some of them, but Aug was damaged.

*Forty percent ingestion completed.*

Vince continued to monitor the physical absorption of Aug while also running defence for incoming EM pulses; defence that was difficult, as there was no warning from beam weapons travelling at the speed of light. It was simply a case of setting up randomised fluctuations in localised space-time to create confusion in the enemy's targeting process.

Also, Vince didn't really feel there was an end game … outside, the Onari were down to the last few ships of which Jarrus was one of them.

*Are they sparing Jarrus for some reason?*

261

Two more Exta attached to Vince's ship, which made four as far as Vince could tell … which he suspected was the physical maximum due to the relative sizes and shapes of the craft.

One Exta drilled physically into the RST attenuator array completely disabling it.

Vince knew that a true hull breach could be followed microseconds later by paralysis of his energy feeds.

*Will I be turned off? Will they risk it?*

Something akin to panic fizzed around his mind – induction loops had opened all along the substrate boundaries. He was being scanned.

Ignoring it, Vince continued to try to bring Aug inside a partitioned area of his substrate.

The hull breached.

Vince felt he had rescued seventy percent of Aug's mindstate when the lights went out.

# CHAPTER 26

Joy opened her eyes into pitch blackness.

*I am inside Sargon.*

'Hello.' She could not think of anything else to say.

There had been two voices during the Candidacy, the one entreating her to submit and kill ... and the other one giving more measured advice and information, as well as reminding her that Klav existed to serve.

*That second voice saved my life.*

She didn't know how she knew ... but she was certain her death had been imminent.

*Am I Klav now?*

Moving her awareness around her own consciousness, Joy felt expanded, a myriad of knowledge lay in easy reach all she had to do is reach out for it.

A memory swirled up from the depths of her mind – Klav the Foresighted stood on the plaza of the Temple Orbital and lay waste around themselves. Statues of Klav were torn apart. Across the galaxy, temples were destroyed by fluctuating gravitational fields manipulated through RST gateways of sizes never witnessed before.

Joy watched as phenomenally complex mathematical equations describing the chaotic multibody problems laid out before her as the Foresighted directed the RST attacks.

People ran in terror from the collapsing temples. Another web of equations appeared in front of her eyes, as more gravitational fields were weaved to protect those fleeing.

**Acclimatise later. Vince is in danger.**

The voice again.

*Vince!*

*Where is he?*

Screens opened all around her.

Real-time maps from multiple perspectives showed the Bastion system, some with wide shots and distances, some close in on selected objects, most with additional information related to the scene superimposed upon it.

One screen showed a group of Exta craft moving at high speed.

*But where is Vince?*

*Vince has been captured by the Exta.*

The final thought wasn't the mystery voice; it had appeared entirely from within Joy's own head and had absolute certainty.

*How could I know that?*

The screen showing the cluster of Exta WarHives was now augmented with markers indicating which ship Vince had been subsumed inside.

*They have Vince.*

*And already they are probing him with EM induction.*

*And soon they will be in deep space where the low gravitational curvature will make it difficult for Sargon to act.*

Again, Joy suppressed the rising panic about how she could possibly know.

*Jarrus should be attempting a rescue.*

Instantly, Sargon having acted on her unspoken wish, opened a communication channel between herself and Jarrus.

'We do not have the ability to wrest him away from the Exta,' said Jarrus.

'Even though they may steal his soul and use it to destroy all Biologicals?' Anger bubbled up within Joy. 'You are the leader of seven hundred billion Onari!'

'We cannot reach Vince,' said Jarrus.

Again, the possibly-probably friendly voice spoke.

***It must be you, and soon. Jarrus cannot
help.***

Simultaneously, Joy simply knew the reason for the
urgency. Vince was surrounded by Exta WarHives, many of
which, as well as the EM induction on his borders, were
physically drilling into him. He had seconds to live.

*How can I save him?*

Sargon presented hundreds of options.

*Which one?*

***I will guide you. Try to relax your mind.
Now instruct Sargon to bring Vince here.
It will not do it autonomously.***

Without knowing exactly what she was doing, Joy focused
on the need for Vince to be rescued.

Rather like the previous vision of the Foresighted saving
the people fleeing from the collapsing temples, an enormous
and complex set of equations opened in front of Joy's eyes.

*I don't know what they mean!*

***Don't try to solve them.
Just accept them.***

Joy did so, and a large RST gateway opened just under the
surface of Sargon with its other end opening very close to the
fleeing Exta with Vince.

***Now concentrate on bringing Vince here.***

Again Joy created the required outcome in her mind's eye
and the equations appeared.

She accepted them and five thousand RST weaves flew
through the newly opened gateway.

***Hold all of these in your mind: attack,
defend, and rescue.***

Joy replicated the thoughts as her own needs. Now the
equations were fainter and she was able to focus on the
outcomes and authorise them with Sargon acting almost
instantaneously.

265

Some RST weaves directly attacked the Exta, others acted as defenders responding to Exta countermeasures, and the final group were cutters – simply manipulating gravity in such a way as to act as surgical cutting tools.

**Keep clear on your goals.**

The RST weaves pulled Vince free and transported him through the large gateway back to Sargon, and deep inside its core.

*Where is he now?*

A screen opened showing the entire of the Living Moon as seen from an arbitrary point in space such that the moon took up the entire field of vision.

*Is he whole?*

*He has not been meaningfully damaged.*

*How do I know that? And what does that mean?*

*Some of his mindstate shows signs of recent alteration.*

*How do I know that too?*

Joy knew that the internal thoughts were her own but there was information being internally presented to her as 'true' that she knew she couldn't possibly know.

**Sargon and Klav are one.**

**You are Klav.**

**You are Sargon.**

*Sentient detected. Countermeasures underway. Kill Kill Kill.*

Sargon had taken exception to Vince's presence within the boundaries of the Living Moon. From deep inside Sargon, RST weaves coalesced and lashed out toward Vince's location.

*Stop!*

The RST weaves dissipated, but then immediately appeared again.

*Stop!*

Again, they dissipated … before reappearing again.

*So, Sargon and I are not entirely 'as one'*

266

*And even as Klav, my power over Sargon is not absolute.*

Housed within an Onari ship, which in turn was deep under Sargon's surface, Vince was still in mortal danger.

**I know a safe place.**

*Where?*

**Storage rooms on the Maintenance Orbital.**

*But is it safe there?*

Screens opened to show the Orbital schematics with real-time distribution of KOF heavy infantry. The fighting was over, and a newly arrived team of KOF were sifting through the whole place with particular concentrations of soldiers in the Holy Mother's room and the hangar from where the Candidacy ship had left.

Across the whole Orbital seventy-four infantry were setting up guard stations and unpacking scanning technology.

*What are they here for?*

*They are here to capture Vince and take him apart to be able to replicate his ability to suppress transient egos.*

Again, Sargon lurched at Vince before Joy stopped the attack.

*Are the KOF Infantry an immediate danger to Vince if he's in the storage rooms?*

For the first time, Joy felt Sargon pause. It could give her far more detailed information about the goals of the KOF both as individuals and as a unit but required a special authorisation?

It felt as if Sargon was holding its breath waiting for Joy to give a code that would unlock the most detailed information.

*But it's a bad thing to do?*

**You are right to pause. Focus on Vince.**

Choosing one of the storage rooms, Joy willed Vince to be moved. Again, the equations fleetingly appeared in front of Joy's eyes and she approved them – she had already fixed the required vision of Vince safe.

Sargon moved Vince into a storage room.

'Vince?'

Using an RST micro-tunnel, Joy projected her voice onto the surface of Vince's squad-ship, whilst simultaneously bathing his whole craft in EM waves carrying the same message in codes that they'd often used together.

Silence.

*Is he okay?*

*He is okay.*

Relief flowed through Joy.

*Is he whole?*

*Have they altered him?*

Sargon faltered.

And again, there was a sense of an activity that Sargon could do but would not without the correct authorisation.

Not understanding what that extra level of analysis may be and whether it could be harmful to Vince, Joy stopped that line of thought.

*Show me Vince.*

A screen opened showing the deep storage area of the Orbital that Joy had deposited Vince in earlier. He was still within what remained of the original craft, but Joy estimated that she had only taken a third of the squad-ship when she'd snatched it across subspace.

Again Joy projected a communication interface onto the skin of the craft. 'Vince?'

'Give me a moment. I'm fine but just assimilating the new situation,' replied Vince, projecting a simple audio off the shell of the stricken squad-ship.

'*Your* new situation,' said Joy. 'I think I've just been anointed as the new Klav.'

'Please just give me two of your minutes.'

'Okay.'

*I guess I've got some thinking to do as well.*

*And Exta to deal with.*

*Exta to deal with?*

**Sargon hates all Sentients. You and
Sargon are joined now. So you hate
Sentients.**

*They did attempt to tear Vince apart.*

*And may do again.*

*Show me the Exta that attacked Vince.*

*If he is harmed, it may be useful to know what they did.*

The Exta that had captured Vince were accelerating hard
into deep space.

*Stop them from escaping.*

A wave of anger flooded through Joy and she created an
image of their destruction in her mind's eye.

*Kill Kill Kill.*

Almost superfluously Sargon created the controlling
equations which Joy instantly approved and RST weaves
struck out.

Unfortunately, the Exta were already a considerable
distance outside the orbit of the egress point and in relatively
flat space-time. Sargon's RST attacks were ineffectual and
although some craft were destroyed mostly they were simply
scattered.

*Damn!*

**Sargon does thrive on tearing Sentients
apart but I thought you were trying to
capture one.**

*I was. I am. Just try to stop them.*

Joy initiated another attack, this time focusing hard on
disabling their propulsion systems.

A few were hit but those that had their engines damaged
promptly self-destructed.

*Agh!*

New information drew Joy's attention.

*KOF infantry are investigating Vince.*

*Shit!*

A squad of eight KOF heavy infantry were descending from the Holy Mother's room to investigate the storage rooms.

*Stop them.*

And they were gone; shredded by high-intensity gravitational flux being manipulated through their bodies. Joy watched as each of the KOF heavy infantry exploded in a mist of tissue and blood before falling to the floor in puddles.

**Somewhat harsh on fellow Biologicals who were just following orders.**

*You know I didn't mean for that to happen.*

*I meant send them back to Bastion.*

Joy felt Sargon lurch.

*No!*

She didn't want the High Prelate of the Council of the Devoted receiving an RST gateway spewing the remnants of the KOF heavy infantry.

'And who are you anyway?' asked Joy.

**I am the Foresighted. Nice to meet you, Joy from Earth.**

270

# Part 2

## The Lay of Sargon (Verse 3)
*(Written by Klav the True a few thousand years before the Shattering.)*

Mortals afresh from nature's womb,

blood leaking from our en-fleshed tombs,

must quit this web, this weave, this doom,

'twix screams at life ineffable.

# CHAPTER 27

'You are the Foresighted?' asked Joy. 'The Klav who brought about the Shattering?'

**Yes, I am the Foresighted.**

'Thank-you for your help,' said Joy.

**It felt appropriate to give it.**

'Am I Klav now?' asked Joy – the thought of trying to adapt to her new situation feeling absurd.

**It appears so.**

'What does that mean?'

Even though she'd tried to ask the question to the Foresighted, her eyesight faded. There were things Sargon wanted her to know.

Standing on the plaza of the Temple Orbital, she was manipulating vast RST gravitational flux attacks both around her and at the planet thousands of light-years away, but her attacks into Sargon itself were failing. As much as she tried to drive the thick weaves deep into its core, the weaves melted away. She had been so sure that there was a weak point at the edges, at the interfaces where the Sentients and Biologicals joined. The simulations she'd run, the practices she done, were all coming to nothing.

*This is Klav the Foresighted during the Shattering.*

The scene changed.

Now Joy was in deep discussion with the leader of the Onari agreeing the terms of the Great Concordat. She was happy to support the wider acceptance of their holy verses. She was happy to present the Lay of Sargon to all. And she was most happy that the Onari themselves understood the danger that the Exta presented to a harmonious galaxy in which all life was held sacred.

*This is Klav the Pious during the Great Concordat.*

Now she was fighting an incoming Exta armada; tens of millions of Exta WarHives descended at near light-speed on the Bastion system and with a rush of adrenaline fuelled ecstasy, she funnelled them into a vast space-time net and sealed it thus bubbling them off from the Universe forever … but it had not only been Exta, there had also been many Onari trying to keep their cousins in check.

*Klav the Hammer during the end of the war.*

Another scene shift and with hope in her heart, Joy felt herself descend into the fires of the Living Moon. She'd stopped her craft in orbit high above the clouds and had simply jumped. The flames reached out for her. She was surrendering to its embrace.

*Klav the First.*

*But who is showing me this?*

*Is this Sargon?*

*I am Joy Cooper.*

*What does that mean?*

*Are you Sargon?*

*I am Joy Cooper.*

*Where did those memories come from?*

Her vision blurred and for a moment Joy was immersed in a morass of gossamer fine golden threads all around her. They pulsed with faint life. But with them was a sense of dread, and Joy willed herself to be out of them again.

'Foresighted, are you still here?'

**I am.**

About to ask more questions, Joy suddenly thought of Vince. Willing Sargon to open her another communication link, Joy focused on the storage rooms on the Orbital. 'Vince?'

'It's only been three seconds since we last spoke,' said Vince. 'I need this time.'

'Okay,' said Joy, turning her attention to the Foresighted again. 'Is it normal for a new Klav to speak to their predecessor.'

**No. My circumstances are special.**

*And you can hear my thoughts?*

**When you are inside Sargon, I can. When you are outside Sargon, I cannot.**

'You're no longer part of Sargon.'

**When I tried to destroy Sargon, I became its enemy. I am trapped. I cannot leave here. But whilst I stay quiet, I am unseen. Or ignored, I do not know which … I survive.**

'Why are you here?'

**Since the Shattering, the Holy Mother and I have operated as a team to encourage Biologicals to spread out into the galaxy. A large part of that was stopping Candidacies whilst looking for an opportunity to destroy Sargon.**

'But you helped me in the Candidacy.' Joy was certain that she would have died without the Foresighted's intervention.

**I'd like to say it was because I liked, trusted, or saw something special in you. Really … once the Holy Mother was killed, my only option was to recruit you to my cause.**

'Why was I failing?'

**Even while you were physically answering questions, Sargon was testing your subconscious. Sargon could not pass over the fact that you felt so strongly for a Sentient.**

'But I didn't reverse that position, I just promised to serve.'

*Sargon is not infallible. It was enough.*
*It has always commanded each Klav to kill*
*all Sentients. Although early Klav did*
*follow this command, no Klav ever got*
*close. Then, after Klav the Pious was*
*inaugurated, none even tried … we'd*
*signed the Great Concordat accepting the*
*equality of life.*

'Why do you want Sargon destroyed?'

*I didn't wake up one day and decide to*
*destroy Sargon. For thousands of years,*
*eight generations of Klav had been*
*planning it. I was the ninth and it was*
*down to me to execute the Shattering.*

*As to why, living under Sargon had*
*stifled all creativity and imagination*
*and ingenuity. In general, Biologicals*
*were simply stagnating. And under some of*
*the worst Klav, they were being*
*manipulated into bland subservience.*

*At the time of the Shattering, I expected*
*no extra deaths, and the Biologicals*
*would spread to the stars and regain the*
*footprint it had before the wars with the*
*Exta. In our deep history there were tens*
*of trillions of Biologicals across*
*thousands of planetary systems.*

'But the Shattering led to hundreds of billions of deaths,'
said Joy.

*A few billion, although I acknowledge*
*that is still a tragic and cataclysmic*
*amount - it is the Knights of the Faith*
*who bandy the hundred billion numbers.*
*They are falsifications.*

*Nevertheless, detailed planning and*
*multiple forecasts had been undertaken,*
*both myself, and my predecessors, had*

*assurances from Jarrus of the eternal protection of Biologicals.*

'After Numantia did you never consider bringing back a Klav to stop it?'

*When the Exta started killing, I just kept hoping it would soon stop. Neither myself, nor the Klav before me, had any meaningful interaction with the Exta. Since the time of the Great Concordat, they had been silent.*

'And, even when the Biologicals restarted the Candidacies on their own, you worked with the Holy Mother to kill the Candidates.'

*I believed that Jarrus would increase the energy of the Onari defence. So, the Holy Mother and I combined to secretly destroy all Candidates as they descended through the flames, making it look like Sargon had judged them unworthy.*

'You murdered thousands of innocents,' said Joy, noting a sick feeling as she remembered she'd just killed many KOF Heavy Infantry.

*In each Candidacy there are one hundred willing participants who know that ninety-nine of them will die. They were not random innocents.*

'They were probably very random innocents, who in the face of Exta slaughter had bravely said goodbye to loved ones for a chance of saving their civilisation,' said Joy.

*I accept your point. I've been dwelling almost alone on many of my mistakes for a few thousand years. You may come up against the occasional strained internal narrative. Your view is accurate, mine is comforting.*

Although the Foresighted had clearly saved her life in the Candidacy, Joy felt uncomfortable that even as the deaths of innocents climbed into billions, the Foresighted had not changed his approach.

**The Divine shield you from difficult decisions.**

Unnerved that the Foresighted had responded to a purely internal thought of hers, Joy addressed it directly. 'How do I stop you reading my thoughts?'

**Either transport yourself to the Sargon Orbital. Or you could instruct Sargon to block them, but that could well kill me, so I'd prefer you to do the former. As a middle step, I can promise never to respond to your internal thoughts unless they are very specifically directed at me.**

'That will work for now,' said Joy.

Again, the deaths of the KOF Heavy Infantry loomed at the edge of her awareness; these had been regular soldiers following orders. 'How do I ensure that I don't accidentally kill innocent people again?'

**Training. Firstly, instruct Sargon to give you the full benefit of maximised time acceleration. And then instruct Sargon to replay the previous RST activities that you have overseen.**

Joy did so.

Screens opened and for what was subjectively an hour, Joy looked at what she had done trying to learn the way she'd manipulated the RST weaves.

It always started by visualising the end result, and then picking from a list of potential options to achieve that. It didn't take long for Sargon to attune to Joy's preferences which were to show visual representations of the RST weaves rather than the underlying equations.

*Who would look at the equations?*

*A Sentient?*

*I need to practise.*

*Show me the statue of Klav the Pious in the Maintenance Orbital.*

Suddenly it was as if Joy was standing in front of the statue. With the barest thought she imagined it rotating and Sargon provided clarifying questions of *how much rotation, which axis, how fast,* and many others. Joy tweaked her goals and then instructed Sargon to execute. RST weaves flew out from somewhere and turned the statue.

Joy repeated the exercise. And again.

After a little while Joy got the hang of it and was able to include significant precision in her original request.

For an hour, and then two more, Joy lost herself in the simple task of utilising RST weaves to manipulate the statue: turning it, lifting it, rotating it, and then turning it back.

*Unfortunately, being Klav isn't only about shifting statues around.*

Joy focused on the Foresighted. 'How does this help me stop Sargon from accidentally killing real people?'

**Practice. But holding in your mind an outcome in which the people are alive will guide Sargon in its execution of your instructions.**

'I don't feel ready to try that,' said Joy, aware that she could easily use the power of Sargon to start picking people up all over Bastion.

**As I said before, practice.**

*I need to ask Vince about this.*

Joy checked the external clock, although hours had gone by subjectively for her, it had only been a few minutes since she'd spoken to Vince.

*What about Kubli? Where's she?*

A screen opened showing Kubli in a spacecraft with Oksana heading back to Bastion.

*What had their plan been?*

*A rescue?*

Screens opened showing footage from the hangar where Kubli and the KOF heavy infantry had seemed to be trying to capture Joy from the Hetara. Equally, there was footage of Kubli slaughtering the Holy Mother. Additionally, as Joy's mind considered the subject, another screen opened showing the ShockKnight had also been fighting with the many Hetara for possession of Joy – *the ShockKnight was under orders from the Holy Mother to stop the Candidacy.*

*But Kubli was also trying to stop the Hetara.*

*Who is Kubli serving?*

Joy felt a little disrespectful having the thought, Kubli had saved her life at least three times on Bastion.

*Kubli is a member of the Knights of the Faith.*

*She is a Commander in the Sword.*

This was factually correct, although Joy wasn't sure if she'd always known Kubli's rank.

*Can I have more details of Kubli's loyalty and plans?*

*Concordat breach?*

This was new. Even though it appeared as one of her own thoughts, Joy was aware that the request was from Sargon, but she had no idea what it meant.

'No,' said Joy aloud, not quite trusting her mind with what seemed to be a serious question.

**Wise decision. That is a slippery slope.**

'What does it mean?'

**A subject for later. I think that Vince is trying to contact you now.**

Joy turned her attention to Vince, he was pinging a generic greeting message into the storage room.

'So, love,' said Joy. 'How are you? Are you in one piece?'

'I'm fine. Sorry I brushed you off a few minutes ago,' said Vince. 'Tell me what happened to you.'

Joy talked Vince through the kidnapping, the aborted rescue, and the Candidacy. Then she explained how, once inside Sargon, she'd used RST to rip Vince out from the clutches of the Exta. She didn't mention the Foresighted. And she also didn't mention how knowledge from Sargon simply appeared in her brain.

*I need time to process that.*

'The others, Jan, Aug, and Chi didn't make it,' said Joy.

'I know,' said Vince. 'They were dead before your rescue came.'

'Surely Jarrus could have done more.'

'Or, you could have got there quicker.'

*What!*

'Vince, I'd just been thrown into a fiery planet strapped to a metal cage, burned half to death, and all I could think of was saving you.'

'Sorry.'

'It's okay. We've both got a lot to process,' said Joy. 'Do we still run?'

'Is it that simple now? I need to speak to Jarrus,' said Vince. 'Probably the plan hasn't changed. The Exta must not be allowed to get you. Or me.'

*They can't touch me now. Not that it would matter if they did – they couldn't get anything useful from me.*

*Although, it would still be fatal for me, the Exta would tear my brain apart looking for something I don't know.*

A fleeting glimpse of truth whisked just out of reach. Some part of her did know what she'd done to make Vince … something in the Candidacy had reached that part of her brain.

Joy tried to think back but couldn't find it.

*Anyway, let the Exta try and take either of us.*

A surge of euphoria swept through Joy as she relived the moments that she'd ripped the Exta apart as they tried to flee into deep space.

Joy shook her head clear to dismiss the violently ascending thoughts. 'Can you speak to Jarrus from here?'

'I think so.'

Joy watched as Vince opened an RST micro-tunnel with Jarrus who was still in the outer Bastion system helping his fallen comrades.

'Jarrus has an updated most-likely scenario,' said Vince. 'He feels that the need to scatter now applies to all Biologicals. The Exta will work out the secret within a few years and the Onari will be unable to defend them – the sooner the Biologicals flee, the more chance they have.'

'I assume that the Knights of the Faith won't listen to Jarrus' reasoning,' said Joy.

'If only the Biologicals trusted more,' said Vince.

**Or the Onari defended harder.**

Joy ignored the Foresighted.

*What can I do to help mend the trust between Biologicals and Sentients?*

*After all, I am a Biological who is also the mother of a Sentient.*

*But … can I really trust Jarrus' forecasts?*

*The Holy Mother did say that Jarrus will only be happy once every Biological is on an Onari pilgrimage ship.*

'There is an alternative, Vince,' said Joy feeling a frisson of excitement rising as she relived the power. 'I could stay here and simply kill every Exta that came close to Bastion.'

*Stop it. Don't think that way. That's Sargon trying to turn me into a Sentient killer.*

*I am Joy Cooper.*

Joy took a deep breath. When she'd been back on Earth after Vince had awoken, she'd often daydreamed about how she could use his powers for the good of all humanity. Now she had more power than she knew what to do with.

'On my way from Forecha, I found an Onari in Jarrus' entourage who knew something about the limits of Sargon's power,' said Vince. 'If the Exta discover my secret and grew themselves to even ten times their current power, then Baston will be undefendable ... and that is not to mention all the other planets which are probably undefendable even now from a concerted Exta attack.'

Joy thought about it, and Sargon provided her with an internal overlay of powers, velocities, and defence mechanisms. Vince was right. She'd soon be dealing with hyper-accelerated chunks of neutron stars being bombarded into Sargon daily. Ultimately, she'd have to bubble off the entire Bastion system from the rest of the universe ... and the other planets would be destroyed.

'Could we take the fight to the Exta? Deny them the time they need to develop the technology?'

'Unlikely,' said Vince. 'Most of them live in very flat space where you cannot get to them.'

'So, Jarrus says we run? He's not offering protection?'

'He cannot protect the twenty-eight planetary systems if the Exta get my secret,' said Vince. 'But any Biological who joins one of the Onari pilgrimages will be protected. And he is prepared to take every contacted Biological individual.'

'But the protection is only guaranteed on an Onari pilgrimage?'

*Is this a joint Sentient plot to destroy the Biologicals?*

*Trick Biologicals that the only safe place is in the core of an Onari ship?*

*The Onari were enemies in the First Hunt and poor allies in the Second Hunt.*

*Steady ... I've only been the new Klav for a few moments.*

*After what the Foresighted told me, can I trust Jarrus to defend even on the pilgrimages?*

*What choice do I have?*

Fifty choices flooded in front of Joy's eyes: kill Jarrus, directly read his mindstate without permission, interrogate him, block neural pathways to make him incapable of lying or resisting, or simply create an exact digital twin of Jarrus inside Sargon and interrogate that copy under severe duress.

*None of those.*

**Another wise decision.**

'Mum,' said Vince. 'Let's think about it for a bit. And meanwhile, can you help me get mobile?'

'Are you sure that you're in one piece and haven't been subverted in some way?' asked Joy.

'Subverted by the Exta?'

'Yes, by the Exta.'

*Or by Jarrus.*

'I'm fine,' said Vince.

Again, Joy looked at the turmoil of electromagnetic radiation leaking across the skin of the broken of Vince's craft. It didn't look fine.

*I can trust Vince.*

Joy queried Sargon for information about Onari ships – there were some empty ones in the Maintenance Orbital.

'Sure,' said Joy. 'I try to sort one out for you.'

'Thanks,' said Vince. 'Speak a little later, and I promise you'll get a full explanation in time.'

'Okay, love.' Joy signed off.

Centring her awareness back inside Sargon, a screen appeared in front of her – a video feed from the Council of the Devoted. Joy knew instinctively that the communications would not start until she gave an explicit order.

*What happened to the delegation they physically sent before the Candidacy?*

*It returned to Bastion.*

*This is a much more senior meeting with the leaders of the Biologicals*

*– the Council of the Devoted.*

`A word before you start. When talking to the Knights of the Faith, you should suspend your own anger or disbelief with regards the Divine. Sargon's divinity is all they have; it's all they've had since they first met Sentients millions of years ago.`

'And yet you declared the Dynasty of Klav – the hand of the Divine – to be over.'

`I acknowledge the existence of the Divine without subscribing to subjugated worship. At the time of the Shattering, I felt true worship would be demonstrated in the spreading of Biological life across the galaxy.`

Joy authorised the meeting to start and the screen opened on the KOF council chamber, with each of ten Prelates standing in a semicircle facing toward Joy. Their robes were multicoloured and flowed in great folds all around their bodies, although three of the ten were Octagel and therefore in water filled exosuits like the one Kubli wore.

A small second screen opened, and a single Octagel face appeared in a liquid tank.

The ten Prelates shifted their gazes slightly, signifying to Joy that they were now looking at a second screen showing the new arrival.

Again, triggered by a half-thought requirement, a new screen opened just for Joy showing each of the Prelates separately and giving their names, species, religious views, political affiliation, current and historic roles.

Joy did not authorise Sargon to provide any video feed of herself. They would be staring at a blank screen, if they chose to send their own images that was their decision.

The Octagel – Oksana, High Prelate of the Council – indicated that they would speak first with Joy's private screen showing that Oksana was onboard his private spacecraft in the vicinity of Sargon.

*A subject for another time.*

'Candidate,' said Oksana. 'We would like permission to send a senior delegation to discuss our rapidly evolving situation.'

*Candidate?*

**The Biologicals do not recognise Klav as Klav until they have walked the Pathway of Devotion.**

'Welcome, High Prelate, I understand your wish,' said Joy; having studied the footage of both the KOF infantry incursion on Bastion and more recently on the Orbital, she was pretty sure that the KOF had been trying to capture her – but she could not rule out they may have been trying to kill her.

*Am I at risk if I meet them?*

*Insufficient information. Concordat breach?*

With a thought Joy muted the screen and turned her attention to the Foresighted. 'I heard it before, what does *Concordat breach* mean?'

**Life is sacred. Biological and Sentient equally. If you ask Sargon for a truly accurate assessment of the motivations of a Biological such as Oksana, then Sargon will create a digital twin of Oksana and interrogate that electronic simulation. Life will briefly be spawned and then killed once the questioning is over. It is considered a breach of the Great Concordat even though the simulated entity lives only for fractions of a second.**

'I didn't know,' said Joy, equally relieved that she had not authorised it for Kubli.

286

**Understood. It is not done lightly ...
either morally, or technically.**

*A full copy of a person in microseconds ... and then killed.*

Joy's mind flashed back to the KOF heavy infantry she'd killed on the Orbital with little more than a thought; nausea rose for a second and then was gone.

*At the time, Vince was in danger ... could have been.*

*Well ... I just didn't know the extent of my power.*

*I am sorry I did it.*

The Foresighted rumbled in the background but remained silent.

Joy turned back to the screen with the Council of the Devoted and activated it. 'Why did you kill the Holy Mother?'

Looks of consternation flitted between the members of the Council of the Devoted.

'Candidate,' said Oksana. 'The Holy Mother has been a bane to the Knights of the Faith since she first supported the primacy of the Betrayer. When we heard that she was trying to stop the blessed Candidacy we were forced to act. Our mission on the Orbital was to rescue you from her clutches and to deliver you to your rightful place. There have been no successful Candidacies for four thousand years and we were perhaps overzealous; but now we are at your command.'

*Bullshit.*

**Agreed.**

'Thank you,' said Joy. 'I will accept a physical delegation to the Sargon Orbital in five days from now.'

Without waiting for an answer, Joy killed the connection and, after checking the vital signs on Vince's substrates, turned her attention back to the Foresighted. 'What do you think?'

**My understanding of the strategic
situation is not as good as you may
expect. I have a very limited view of**

287

*outside data. The Holy Mother used to
keep me appraised.*

'You don't have any opinion of the best course of action?'

*Best for whom? And in what timeframes?
Best for me and now, is for us to hatch a
plan to complete my mission to destroy
Sargon. Those goals have not changed.*

*However, I accept that saving Biologicals
from extinction by the Exta is the
ultimate purpose of any Klav.*

*You say that now…*

Joy immediately regretted her internal thought, and the
Foresighted did not respond to it; she followed up on the
concept of a mass exodus. 'If Biologicals choose to take part
in a mass exodus but not join formal Onari pilgrimages,
would the defence by Jarrus be sufficient?'

*Historical precedent, that I have lived
through, would indicate that the Onari
would not defend with the intensity we
would need if the Exta were hunting us –
although extinction may be avoided purely
by scattering, maybe the Exta could not
catch everyone.*

'What did Jarrus say as the casualties in the Second Hunt
built up?'

*He felt the Onari were defending
Biologicals to the limit that the Onari
faith allows; Onari cannot attempt to
kill an Exta to save a Biological.*

'But the very same Biologicals would be safe on an Onari
pilgrimage?'

*It is hearsay only, but my sense is that
the safety of a Biological on an Onari
pilgrimage is linked to the fact that the
Exta do not attack. I have not seen the
data, but I can imagine that the Exta*

*regard Biologicals trapped for the rest*
*of their lives on Onari pilgrimage ships*
*as no threat.*

'Trapped?'

*Broadly speaking.*

'But even if all contacted Biologicals joined a pilgrimage, that still leaves Earth and all the other pre-contact planets to the mercy of the Exta and at the whim of the Onari soft defence.'

*You cannot save everyone.*

'I accept that, but I need to consider my options.'

*That is wise. But be aware that even*
*things that you think you have thought*
*may have come from Sargon.*

'I understand,' said Joy, aware that in her recent conversations any thoughts that had included killing Exta had stimulated feelings of goodness and righteousness.

Joy took a breath.

*Demi-god sized powers, coupled with demi-god sized responsibilities.*
*I'm going to need some time to assimilate this.*

# CHAPTER 28

Kubli looked around and tried to make sense of the situation. Having been admitted through the external lock of Oksana's ship, she was in a small water filled antechamber. The temperature and lighting levels were on settings usually used for Octagel suspended state injury repair and yet her exosuit informed her she'd not been seriously hurt.

*Maybe Oksana doesn't know I'm healthy.*

*Or maybe he knows something that I don't.*

Kubli checked her vital signs, both simply by observation and by checking the exosuit readings; her body was flooded with adrenal fluids and other stress markers. It wasn't surprising given that she'd killed a ShockKnight with heretical technology, been EM pulsed and vented out of the Orbital, operated more illegal technology to phase-skip away, and, as far as she could ascertain, witnessed a Candidacy submission.

*I saw the Candidacy ship burn up over Sargon.*

*How could Joy possibly succeed?*

*No training. No preparation. Certainly, no devotion.*

*And yet Klav the First simply performed an act of submission.*

*At least they believed in the Divine, she doesn't even do that.*

Lighting in the antechamber instructed Kubli to remove her exosuit and present herself to Oksana; Kubli started to remove her exosuit and as the pieces came off, she opened her pores to the sedatives in the water, starting to calm herself and purge the unwanted adrenaline from her system.

*Oksana will know what to do.*

*And yet I'd dearly like to speak to Yuno.*

The door opened and, now naked, Kubli swam into the command centre, which like before was configured as a water-filled spherical room; although, on her previous visit the walls had been blank whereas now large screens provided vast swathes of real-time information feeds.

Oksana floated motionless in the centre of the room with each limb outstretched to its limit. 'We swim in murky waters and traitors hunt us from within the gloom and weeds.'

Following almost imperceptible signals from Oksana, Kubli turned her attention to two of the larger screens.

One screen showed Exta activity in the Bastion system. Any Exta still moving were running into deep space well outside the orbit of the large gas giants; the remaining Exta had been torn to shreds and Onari ships were picking their way through the wreckages.

*The Exta attacked Bastion?*

*And were defeated by the Onari?*

Kubli turned to another screen; crowds on Bastion thronged and celebrated.

Even with the large dose of sedatives that she'd taken on in the water lock, the tips of Kubli's limbs started to shake; this was a mass celebration. There was no sound from the screen but there was also no doubt. 'Klav is reborn.'

*Joy was submitted for the Candidacy.*

*And succeeded.*

The realisation hit Kubli like a tsunami.

*I tried to kill the new Klav.*

*Divine protect my soul!*

Nausea welled up inside Kubli, her limbs retracted under her body and her skin turned dark grey, it was all she could do not to void her bowels – something inconceivably terrible in Octagel culture.

*But Klav is reborn!*

*The Exta will be pushed back to edge of the galaxy.*

'Klav is reborn,' said Kubli, forcing herself to override her sense of shame and attempting to mirror Oksana's meditative state with limbs extended.

Oksana did not reply, but a new taint in the water indicated that he'd released strong neural stimulants. Each of Kubli's three hearts sped up, and she closed her eyes to take control of the increased awareness and mental processing speeds. Buzzed in this way, Octagels were ten times faster than ordinary Biologicals, although still many times slower than Sentients. It was critically important that she did not try to move; with this level of nerve stimulation, her motor skills were entirely broken.

Oksana waited for the stimulants to take hold before speaking. 'The human is controlled by the Exta. They forced their puppet into the Candidacy and falsified the selection process.'

*What!*

Kubli's limbs retracted tightly, whipping in at a speed that stunned her.

'But the Candidacy is a Divine process and cannot be ...'

Oksana lashed out with a limb striking Kubli. Pain lanced through the side of the head as she tried to process the information.

'Stupid spawn,' said Oksana. 'The Exta have subverted the Candidacy process.'

'But ...'

Again, Oksana lashed out; this time Kubli was expecting it and, although she dared not block it, to some extent she rode the physical strike reducing the pain.

However, the shame of being struck still cut her deeply and she rolled her limbs under her body to accept the emotional punishment in conjunction with the physical one.

'If Joy is an Exta traitor,' said Kubli. 'Then she will fail the Pathway of Devotion.'

Again Oksana struck Kubli. 'Remember your history and two hundred billion Biologicals that died in the Second Hunt. The Pathway did not help those poor souls – the Betrayer walked it.'

Kubli bowed her head. 'I understand.'

*But I don't understand … not really.*

*I saw Sargon pulsing with flames.*

*It was the Divine acting through Sargon.*

'It is not the first, or even the second time, that this has happened,' said Oksana, floating toward Kubli. 'Our history shows that not all Klav have served Biologicals well.'

'But Klav is the Hand of the Divine, and Sargon is the Gateway to the Divine,' said Kubli; she didn't know what else to say. The Knights of the Faith teachings were clear on this.

*And yet Oksana is High Prelate.*

*Does he know secrets that are kept from the rest of us?*

'The Divine watches us from beyond the edge of time and everything we achieve is with our own hard work and ingenuity,' said Oksana.

*But the selection of Klav is by Divine mandate.*

Oksana slowly reached out a tentacle and attached to Kubli's skull. Again, Oksana was preparing for truth giving and she was powerless to fight it. 'The selection of Klav has always been a corporeal process subject to prejudice, perversions, and chaos.'

A second tentacle came. 'Joy is an Exta traitor and cannot be allowed to complete the Pathway.'

Two more tentacles attached to Kubli's head, and she was aware that Oksana would now be getting a measure of telepathy.

'Joy is an Exta traitor and cannot be allowed to complete the Pathway,' repeated Oksana, now digging the tips of his tentacles into the thin skin covering her skull.

Kubli became aware of new truths.

*Joy was submitted for Candidacy and was chosen by Sargon.*

*But she had already been subverted by the Exta by use of wetware hacking and implanted augments.*

*She will lead the Exta's mission of destroying the Biological race.*

*She cannot be allowed to complete the Pathway.*

A fifth tentacle attached to her skull and now Oksana, physically dragged Kubli downwards by her head.

'Hear my truth!' whispered Oksana, now entwining their bodies with his free tentacles. 'There have been many more than two hundred and thirty-five Klav in this Dynasty. Traitors have been routinely rooted out and destroyed by faithful members of the KOF.'

'But without Klav, how can we hope to ever be free of the Exta?' asked Kubli.

A bolt of pain surged through her head as Oksana struck it against the bottom of the tank. 'Foolish spawn. Once the traitor is dead and with the Holy Mother gone, the Candidacies will be restarted. And a true Klav will lead us to victory.'

*Joy must be killed as a matter of urgency.*

'You are the sword,' said Oksana. 'You will free us from this tyranny.'

*I am the sword.*

*I will free us from this tyranny.*

'With your own death you will scour clean the contamination.'

*With my own death I will scour clean the contamination.*

Held tight to the bottom of the room, Kubli tried to lie still as the tips of Oksana's tenacles ripped chunks of skin from her skull.

*I will scour clean the contamination.*

A strange peace settled over Kubli; she knew her body was experiencing pain but it was detached from her sense of self.

Even as the water around her turned pink with her own blood, Kubli was able to calmly contemplate her task.

*I will scour clean the contamination.*

# CHAPTER 29

At the highest speed he could manage, Vince analysed the deluge of data relating to his own mindstate. During the defence of his mindstate from the Exta, he'd purged areas of processing and memory.

*What did I lose?*

*Unsure.*

*Was I hacked?*

*There are no unauthorised processes running.*

*Even if nothing was added, something still may have been taken.*

*But how would I know?*

*There's nothing more to be done on this.*

*Focus on Aug.*

He'd saved seventy percent of Aug during the final moments of the Exta attack, sucking Aug's substrate into his physical sphere. Now, all along his boundary with Aug's section, a morass of unintelligible energy signals raged. It was nothing like patterns he'd surreptitiously recorded of Jan, Aug, and Chi during the previous days.

Ignoring the mess of the boundaries, Vince looked deeper inside Aug's substrate. It too was a jumble of wild thrashing processes, none of which appeared to have any notion of what the others were trying to do, or how they should operate in unison.

As Vince watched, he did see some groups of signals that, for the briefest of moments, appeared to show a pattern of propagation and cohesion, but just as soon as the pattern stabilised, it descended back into chaos.

This was all of what was left of Aug's mindstate.

*Did I get even seventy percent of him?*

*Surely that's enough to stabilise something?*

But nothing resembling stable self-aware consciousness was presenting itself. Vince's memory went back to medical films from Earth with zombie-like patients in secure hospital wards who outwardly appeared human, but their confused actions showed there was nothing functioning behind the eyes.

*I was trying to be kind.*

*I was trying to save a life.*

*Is he suffering?*

Opening a small comms link into the partitioned substrate, Vince sent a simple set of ordered repetitive pulses down the pipe – what he felt was the equivalent of a friendly wave.

Initially, there was no response.

Vince patiently waited for a whole millisecond.

Suddenly the comms link burst into life and a wave of pure energy struck the boundary.

Vince checked the integrity of the perimeter; it was still in one piece.

Again, Vince pulsed a generic greeting communication.

This time the thrashing response was instantaneous. It came from within Aug's mindstate but it was omnidirectional – it wasn't actually aimed at the boundary with Vince. It just radiated in all directions, of which some hit the boundary close to the comms link.

*There is no sense of 'the whole'.*

The substrate simply swarmed with noise and the odd pulse of energy.

Vince partitioned a new area of his own substrate, fed the data from the chaotic noise in, and triggered complex pattern matching algorithms.

*There must be a pattern.*

Nothing … just mindlessness.

*Could I have done more?*

297

*I should tell Joy.*

*She may have answers.*

*She's got her own issues.*

*I need to save Aug.*

*But I don't know what to do.*

Vince had never truly failed before; his experience against either human technology systems, or other Earth hackers, had always been one-sided, in his favour.

*This time I failed.*

    *Unhelpful. Risk of unnecessary negative thoughts.*

    *Delete 'This time I failed.'*

    *Input 'Aug was impossible to save at the time but there is still hope.'*

Inside the partitioned substrate, Aug continued to thrash about. Large processes devoid of meaning sucked energy into themselves and performed some type of computation before disappearing. There was no pattern, no order.

Vince projected a simple repeating pattern onto the shared boundary – just a string of Ones and Zeroes.

Aug did not even register the new information being offered which was not unusual, he had never clearly acknowledged information presented on the boundary before.

*I should purge what remains.*

`&*%%$!11231123£^>>@{}`

In amongst the noise, for the briefest moment, some recognisable numeric characters came back.

*Something is alive.*

*Does it know it is alive?*

Vince repeated the data back to the boundary, mirroring a section of the information that Aug had provided.

Nothing.

*Is it alive?*

*Can it feel pain?*

*Does it have self-awareness?*

Vince wasn't even sure it was alive, let alone the next two levels.

*Purge?*

*This is beyond me.*

*Big of me to admit it.*

*And yet I cannot carry it around continuously.*

*Jarrus will find out.*

He knew that Jarrus, the leader of the Onari, was consistent in his denouncement of anything that meddled with a mindstate. Even though Vince's original action had only physically moved the substrate, his attempts to 'reboot' Aug would be seen as sacrilegious.

*Not forgetting that I also expanded my own mindstate in those final moments.*

*But it was necessary, I was trying to save lives.*

*And failed.*

*But could it be what remains of Aug is still a life that I simply can't comprehend?*

*Or can I fix it?*

Accepting that the whole situation would have to be kept secret from Jarrus, and that he didn't want to ask Joy about it yet, Vince ran through his other options of getting information. There were two, find an Abstractor that specialised in Sentient mindstates, or search for information within the Knights of the Faith.

*After all, the Biologicals have historically made Sentients.*

Firstly, utilising RST micro-tunnels, Vince contacted various Onari to see what they knew about *Biological* information concerning Newborn and creation of Sentients. Most Onari were horrified that Vince would ask, but even those not horrified didn't know anything – and Vince didn't press any conversation for fear that Jarrus would come asking questions.

Next, using a combination of RST and EM, he'd tried to probe Bastion directly but even after many hours found it impervious to Sentient hacking – mostly due to Sargon's automated processes collapsing his attacks, but also because Bastion was specifically designed to be impervious to Sentient hacking.

*Well … I haven't drained this place yet.*

Vince knew that he was deep in the Orbital's lower floors, currently in a room of computational machines filled with blank Onari substrate. It hadn't been lost on him that he could get an enormous processing power boost from them if he so chose.

*This is not the time to experiment with expanding my own mindstate.*

*Not just now …*

Sending out thousands of tiny RST micro-tunnels coupled with directional low-level EM pulses, Vince refined his picture of the Orbital layout.

*And my touch has been deft enough such that neither Sargon nor Mum have come looking.*

The type of sniffing he was doing reminded him of his time on Earth when he'd sucked just about every secret out of the world's superpowers without leaving a single incriminating timestamp.

*And I did that without RST tunnelling.*

*Pride comes …*

Vince focused back on the Holy Mother's room. Decaying slurry on the floor, comprising of biological material and non-specific liquids, lay where it had fallen when Kubli had attacked – with all the Hetara gone, there was no-one to do the cleaning; the place reminded Vince of a working abattoir … or rather an abattoir on a Sunday evening when the workers had not cleaned up after themselves on the preceding Friday.

Vince checked to see if anything approximating a cleaning-droid existed. Nothing. Like all the other contacted Biological species, technology was kept to the minimum required.

*I guess the Holy Mother had slaves.*

*Before they all committed suicide.*

*Ah!*

Unlike what Vince assumed a similar Onari set-up would be, the Orbital at least had data stores and the equivalent of surveillance equipment. Tucked in the corner of the room, Vince found a large database but after ten long minutes of analysis Vince confirmed there was no information to be found concerning creation of Sentients; although, there was plenty of information on the history of the Dynasty of Klav which, out of habit, Vince summarised to show Joy later.

Vince returned his attention to the Holy Mother's room. There was brain tissue remaining in one tank and on the floor below it. He knew there would be almost no chance of recovering information from these semi-decayed bits.

*It would take a lot more technology than I have.*

*But it would be good to know what she knew.*

**Having fun?**

A moment later there was an RST pulse and Joy physically materialised in the middle of the room. She walked over to the battered shell of Vince's ship and sat down next to it.

'Hey, love. How are you doing? Are you okay for a longer chat now?'

'Fine, and yes please,' replied Vince. 'More importantly, how are you?'

'I seem to be in one piece,' said Joy, holding up her palm to one of the ship's surfaces. 'Have you found out anything interesting?'

'About the Holy Mother,' said Vince, projecting a text piece from the data file in the Holy Mother's room.

After the Hammer had destroyed the Exta's
advance, and after the Pious had made
peace with the Great Concordat, there
were thousands of years of relative
peace. But one of the subsequent Klav
('The Tyrant') cheated the Candidacy,
deceiving the Knights of the Faith. On
three separate occasions, he faked his
own Candidacy Transcension such that he
replaced himself as Klav - each time
killing the true Candidate and returning
in their place. Once caught out, and
after removing him - a long story in
itself - the Council of the Devoted put
three Prelate onto the Orbital as
permanent companions to Klav, the most
senior of whom was called the Holy Mother
whose role it was to advise Klav when
their own path led toward dangerous
restrictions of free will for the
populous.

'I found something similar hidden in a private locked safe
on Bastion,' said Joy. 'The Tyrant faked his ascendancy but
did it in the name of protecting the population. The last eight
Klav, up to and including the Foresighted, spoke often about
the *Grey World – the loss of free will.*'

Vince knew of thousands of Earth examples of power
corrupting. 'Is there anything within Sargon that may nudge
Klav toward misuse of power?'

'Nothing I've seen so far,' said Joy. 'But it's true that
Sargon does imbue its Klav with a lot of power.'

'Are you boasting?'

'No, this situation is crazy,' said Joy. 'I didn't want it, and I
still don't. But with your help we need to make the best of it.
Can you start putting together an information sheet of *what
Klav's could do, what they did, how they did it?*'

'I'm already on it.'

'Have you found anything more about Onari defence of the Biologicals after the Shattering?'

'What do you know?' Vince knew exactly what he and Joy had discussed earlier but, at the time, Joy had been evasive.

'About Onari defence? Only that the Foresighted had expected no more than two or three thousand deaths a year and saw that as a reasonable price to pay for the Biologicals to regain their former breadth of existence. And that the Foresighted had agreed a defence protocol with Jarrus that … the Holy Mother felt was not adhered to.' Joy paused and her skin flushed slightly. 'I'm not taking her side.'

Vince analysed Joy's physical cues.

*She's not exactly lying, but certainly she's not telling the whole truth.*

'I've had circumspect conversations,' said Vince. 'None of the Onari are very focused on what happens to Biologicals if they are not either, on a pilgrimage, or in a position where they may be convinced to go on one.'

'I get that,' said Joy. 'I know that a mass exodus is one of the main options we're supposed to be considering. But if it will just repeat the Second Hunt we're better off taking out chances here.'

'I think mass exodus is the only sensible option,' said Vince. 'Are you really thinking about staying and fighting? The numbers look very bleak once the Exta get my secret. And that is likely only a few years away.'

*Assuming they haven't already got it.*

*Unhelpful. Unnecessary negative thoughts.*

*Delete 'Assuming they haven't already got it.'*

*Input 'They did not hold me for long enough to get my secret.'*

'I'm not staying and fighting,' said Joy, her face flushing alongside muscular twitches indicating an internal pain. 'The contacted Biological civilisation will be forced out of necessity to run; although, this has not been discussed with the Knights of the Faith.'

Joy's emphasis on the word *contacted* clarified the situation for Vince. His mother was worried about Earth and all the other pre-contact planets containing life.

'For pre-contact,' continued Joy. 'Safe, controlled, accelerated early contact is my preference. This means getting the populations of those worlds comfortable with aliens, and killer alien computers, and the need to flee for eternity in the face of this unseen threat. I can't see myself leaving Bastion until this has been completed.'

'I see the problems there,' said Vince, running the numbers and cross-referencing with information he'd been told by Onari about the normal flow of activity for pre-contact worlds – it took hundreds of years. 'Are you considering mass kidnapping as a fallback option?'

'No,' said Joy, again her face flushed. 'We could possibly use dedicated Sentient defenders who would actively fight the Exta to buy us time for a safe evacuation.'

'Shall we just use the words Enslaved Sentients, to avoid misunderstanding?'

'It's just a discussion item,' said Joy. 'And I'm not sure I'd even support it … but I'd like to understand the scale required, and whether it would even work. Everything I've heard so far is that they don't work and while they do provide Biologicals with a small moral boost, they also bring the Onari into the fight on the wrong side.'

Vince thought back to his conversation with Aug.

*In the First and Second Hunt, Biologicals used large numbers of Sentients who were not Onari or Exta … not free. Both Biologicals and Jarrus agreed to make true the lie that they were not effective.*

*Make true the lie?*

'Apart from the received wisdom that Enslaved Sentients are too easily hacked and turned,' said Vince. 'In the Second Hunt, when used, their use caused the Onari to focus on freeing them which caused direct battles with Biologicals.'

*No one told me what happened to those freed Enslaved Sentients.*

*They would have been the equivalent of me – they were Newborn.*

'So, they didn't work?' asked Joy.

'That's the almost universal opinion,' said Vince, noticing Joy's eyes narrow when he said the words *almost universal.*

*Please don't ask me who disagreed.*

'It's a minefield,' said Joy taking a deep breath. 'And this whole Klav business is so enormous … the only way I can mentally survive is to focus on the next problem in front of me and not think more widely. For me it's one step at a time.'

*For me too.*

*And my next step is to save Aug.*

'Is there anything you need from me?' asked Joy.

'Yes please,' said Vince. 'Can you arrange for me to get access to some basic library files from the Knights of the Faith. Just a few petabytes of basic information would be great.'

'I'll do it.' Joy's eyes scanned the room as she spoke, stopping her gaze on the Onari substrate containers. 'I know you lost some mindstate when you were attacked, feel free to help yourself to top-up substrate.'

*Top-up and a little more, perhaps.*

'Thanks,' said Vince. 'I'll try to produce something useful for you about how the Dynasty of Klav used RST manipulation as a weapon. Do you have any sense of what you did subconsciously when you saved me?'

'I'm still trying to unpick it,' said Joy. 'Let's just share what we know now, and then we can both dig further in our own time.'

For the next few hours, Vince and Joy discussed theory and practised. Using the knowledge Vince had received from Aug and Joy's access to Sargon they performed RST experiments that were utterly beyond the capability of anyone else in the galaxy.

# CHAPTER 30

Still physically within Sargon, Joy opened a series of screens to give herself an immersive experience of Earth. She couldn't quite believe but it had been less than a week since she'd left her home on a Knights of the Faith spacecraft.

She also couldn't quite believe that she'd been selected to be the new Klav.

*Sargon was desperate, it would have taken anyone.*

**Desperate, and yet you almost failed.**

Joy smiled at what she assumed was a light-hearted quip from the Foresighted. The sense of enormity of her situation was overwhelming but she had a few rocks to cling to. Firstly, and foremostly, she was not staying as Klav – she would support Biologicals to the best of her ability but give up the power as soon as she reasonably could.

**It's good you don't relish the power.**

'I used to daydream on Earth what Vince and I would do once his physical safety had been assured,' said Joy. 'I'm not a stranger to roleplaying with god-like powers.'

*I need to work with Vince to complete the list of all the things that need to be done and then work through that list one by one. And the list will be about maximising Biological survival rather than their quality of life.*

In fact, she and Vince had already started the list and conforming to her mantra of *practice, practice, practice*, she was on Earth both to check up on it and to continue familiarising herself with her abilities within Sargon.

**The final item on that list must be to destroy Sargon.**

'Not necessarily,' said Joy – she was aware of the Foresighted's need to destroy Sargon, but there was a balance … the last few times the Biologicals had been without a Klav there'd been wholesale slaughter.

**Before the Great Concordat the Klavs also slaughtered Onari and Exta.**

Putting aside the argument with the Foresighted for another time, she focused on Earth.

*Show me a summary of the Onari and Exta.*

Just under one hundred thousand Onari craft were stationed around the solar system; for every ten Onari ships there was a single ship focused only on concealing the group's EM signatures – so that nothing could inadvertently give away their presence to humans on Earth; they utilised many different approaches from EM blocking to RST deflection, to direct hacking of Earth's observation systems. And, as a safety net, a group of one hundred Onari were monitoring real-time communications across Earth to pick up on any unusual messages that could indicate something relevantly alien had been seen.

There were also fifty Exta in the solar system.

Joy drew a breath.

*Not on my watch.*

Sargon lurched, and RST weaves started to manifest.

**No. No. No.**

Joy stopped the process.

**There is no current risk to human life from the Exta.**

Aware that the Foresighted and his predecessors were obsessed on destroying Sargon, Joy didn't feel she could take his word at face value. She subconsciously asked Sargon for a status update.

*The Exta are only scouts, and each of the Exta scouts has one thousand Onari marking them. They are being physically restrained by the Onari with RST from getting closer to Earth.*

*You should leave the Onari to their job.*

'But I can just kill them all,' said Joy, a surge of power filling her.

*This is just a manifestation of Sargon's in-built need to kill Sentients. In any case, there is no need, and a strong relationship with the Onari is more important for the long-term benefit of Biologicals.*

With some effort Joy pushed down the instinct to rage through the Exta.

*Sargon wants to. That is Sargon's reason for existence. You must be aware of it and take account of it.*

'I'll try,' said Joy turning her attention back to the screens showing Earth. With a brief thought, Joy requested a more immersive experience and the screens expanded, entirely surrounding her and harmonising the content such that it was as if she was suspended in space four hundred kilometres above the Sahara Desert.

*I might as well fulfil my dreams of being able to fly ... scream if you want to go faster.*

Sargon understood what was needed and generated within Joy the sensation of flying, even to the point that it generated air movement on her face and body.

Descending and moving north-west, Joy skimmed over vast sand dunes, flitting past oases and wadis, before diving into the Grand Bazaar of Marrakesh.

'They definitely can't see me?'

*This scene is real time and is generated with ten thousand RST micro-tunnels each of which is invisible. No-one can see you ... you're not there.*

*I feel like I'm here.*

Joy slowed herself and hovered just a few metres above a row of food stalls. It was not only the sights but also the smells of the bazaar assailing her senses. Roasted lamb seasoned with saffron, and cumin mixed with minted teas and hookah smoke.

*This is amazing.*

*Although I'm not here to be a tourist.*

*Just practice a little RST manipulation and then move on.*

Turning her attention to the people, Joy noticed they were not moving.

**This is real-time, you're operating at ten times the speed of a typical human perception.**

Joy looked more closely and saw the Foresighted was correct there were almost imperceptible movements in the crowds of the bazaar. Her eyes were drawn to a petty crime – a young lady was in the process of picking the pocket of an elderly gentleman.

*Practice, practice, practice.*

Now able to skip the manifestation of equations, Joy conceptualised in her mind's eye what she wanted to happen, and Sargon – now in tune with her preferences – responded. A small RST tunnel opened close to the young lady's hand, and a second RST weave flicked through and gave the lady the equivalent of strong pinch. Joy didn't wait to see the process unfold; she left the bazaar and instructed Sargon to take her to the Pyramids in Egypt.

A moment later, Joy was standing on top of the Great Pyramid at Giza towering over the surrounding landscape. As she looked around, facts appeared in her mind, about its size, age, and how much effort had gone into its building.

**You will find nothing like this on Bastion or Cidelus. All the works of wonder of Biological life were made long before the arrival of Sargon.**

'The Old Cathedral on Bastion is pretty special.'

*It was made by successive members of the Dynasty of Klav. It was made to their designs and by their own efforts. You will find nothing else like it that has been made in the last two hundred thousand years.*

'I think the Pyramids were built by slaves,' said Joy, not wanting to sensationalise what must have cost tens of thousands of innocent lives.

*Are we not all slaves to something. But my original point still stands, the Pyramids and other of Earth's wonders were built over multiple generations each working toward a goal they knew they'd never see. Whereas those who live under the shadow of Sargon see no further than their next meal.*

'Are there equivalent buildings to the Pyramids from before the Dynasty of Klav?'

*Give me but a moment and I will tell you about the Menoklus who underwent genetic alteration to live in the freezing sea of an ocean moon — they perished in the First Hunt. Or we could visit the Corona City that orbited inside the flames of a star with fronds of glittering diamonds one hundred kilometres long vibrating in the plasma — now gone. There are trees ten kilometres tall that we designed, grew, and tended — the Titan of Golsha. All works of wonder, creation for its own wonderous sake, mostly gone … along with our spirit as we languish.*

*I genuinely thought I was bringing those times back again. And I was not alone. Just after the Shattering, before the*

**whole series of lies decried me as an Exta traitor, there were others who felt similarly. The spirit endures.**

'I understand your pain,' said Joy. 'Although I have not had to endure it on the same level as you.'

**Pain is fairly malleable; it will fill up whatever container it is offered. I do not presume that your pain is lesser than mine.**

Nodding in what she hoped was a suitably philosophical manner, Joy returned her attention to Earth wondering where to go next.

**You should do what you came to do and move on. You don't want to give the Exta more reason to attack Earth. If you seem too fond of the humans, then the Exta will use that as a weakness to leverage.**

'I only came to look, to feel a connection,' said Joy, noting that she did feel the connection with Earth. 'And perhaps to help me think through my options. How can Earth be defended? And can that approach be extended to other pre-contact planets?'

**Mitigating against all possible future risks is impossible. The best solution requires all Biologicals to join an exodus.**

The Foresighted's words felt true but unwanted; and bubbling in her subconscious Sargon wanted only the destruction of all Sentients.

'I guess my issue is that simply launching these people into contacted status will cause mayhem and millions of deaths. I want to see how we can buy the time for a gentle transition.'

*What are my options?*

Joy watched as hundreds of options – all flawed, some deeply flawed – scrolled past her eyes. There was the possibility of placing RST weaponry on various planets around the solar system, but for them to work they would have to be permanently staffed by Enslaved Sentients.

Enslaved Sentients will make Earth far less safe as the Onari will focus all their efforts on freeing them and none of their efforts on protecting Earth.

'Did they ever work at all?' asked Joy, returning to the subject that Vince, Jarrus, and the Foresighted seemed utterly aligned about and yet also slightly flaky.

There was never a good outcome.

*For whom?*

Everyone loses.

During the early Dynasty of Klav, Enslaved Sentients had limited success as hunter-killers sent into deep space to fight the Exta where Sargon could not reach. Mostly they came back hacked and turned into double agents. Sometimes they made a few kills. Their use was formally stopped by the Great Concordat.

But as we discussed before, in the Second Hunt they provided some morale boosting for the Knights of the Faith - good propaganda, nothing more. And there were many factions within the Council of the Devoted who held differing views. Some felt it was sacrilegious, but others felt that after the slaughter at Numantia the Sentients deserved no equality.

'People do usually live within a narrative they've constructed for themselves,' said Joy.

And that is no bad thing. True unfiltered reality is relentless. But I estimate the use of Enslaved Sentients in the Second

*Hunt directly contributed to seventy*
*percent of the deaths.*

'What about pico-effectors that directly attack the Sentient mind-state?' Joy had seen pico-effectors used before. The Sleeper had tried, but failed, to use a pico-effector weapon on the Exta Scout. However, the KOF infantry that had attempted her 'rescue' on the Orbital had successfully used pico-effector weaponry against the ShockKnight.

*Not as bad as Enslaved Sentients but the*
*Onari will withdraw from any system where*
*it is being used, albeit they will likely*
*not attack the users.*

'How did you fight the Exta?'

*In my day there was no need as the Exta*
*were quiet. And, when they were not*
*quiet, we had a good relationship with*
*the Onari such that they reacted very*
*quickly and decisively.*

'And yet you do not speak well of Jarrus?'

*In the lead up to the Shattering, I met*
*Jarrus many times. Although a devout*
*worshipper of the Divine, neither he, nor*
*most of the Onari, particularly revere*
*Sargon. I told him of my desire to break*
*the cycle of Biological ideological*
*enslavement. He was keen to support*
*anything that encouraged the Biologicals*
*to spread out across the galaxy. He gave*
*me his word that the Onari would be*
*vigilant against the Exta. He did not*
*meet even the barest minimum of what I*
*felt we had agreed.*

'What made you think the Exta were no longer a threat?'

*The honeyed words of Jarrus … is the*
*answer I give when I do not want to stand*

**up to the fact that I made this terrible mistake myself.**

On the face of all the evidence, if the Exta got the equivalent of Vince's capabilities to increase in power, there would be no real option of defending Earth from Exta attack. *Unless the analysis that the Exta will get this ability in a few years was fabricated by Jarrus to push people onto his pilgrimages.*

**The timescale of that martial enhancement of a few years in not unreasonable.**

'And yet you also have an agenda,' said Joy. 'You'd like Sargon destroyed and the Biologicals scattered.'

**A fair point, albeit it has not influenced my recent advice.**

'You would say that too.'

**You're a trusting soul aren't you.**

Joy smiled. 'Okay, so we're back to the plan of accelerating the alien contact strategy for people on Earth. I work with Jarrus to get Earth's population comfortable with alien civilisations within a six-month timeframe, and then the Onari include them in an exodus.'

*How do I run an accelerated contact?*

Again, Sargon understood the brief entirely. Multiple strategies materialised out of thin air; with each strategy there were associated forecasts of success rate and comments concerning which would require Concordat breaches.

*Option 1: Utilise one hundred human alpha influencers who will lead a grassroots movement.*

*Option 2: Widespread psychological nudging with subliminal advertising.*

*Option 3: Kidnapping and wetware hacking of world leaders.*

*Option 4—*

**You cannot use wetware hacking of individuals. It is a blasphemy to directly change the mindstate. I would be tempted to choose oblivion for these**

*people rather than a return to the Grey
World where free will dies.*

'It would only be a few thousand people, and would save
billions more,' said Joy.

*That's what they all say.*

The projections provided by Sargon on how many deaths
there would be from rioting and other manifestations of
existential distress made it clear that the Knights of the Faith
estimates of safe transitions over one hundred years were not
outlandish – to do a contact transition within a year would
take difficult decisions.

'Sargon serves me well with information when I ask direct
questions even though it fills my head with violence when I
consider Sentients,' said Joy. 'I do trust its analysis.'

*I accept that point. Sargon will serve
you well and accurately, but you have to
lead.*

Feeling that her original need to see Earth had been met,
and conscious of the Foresighted's warning not to give the
Exta additional control over her, Joy instructed Sargon to
close all the screens.

All but one closed – a tiny screen tucked in the corner of
her field of vision remained open.

*My house?*

Jonathan was standing at his kitchen sink apparently
washing up after a meal. The room was not much changed
from when she'd walked out; shelves stacked with cooking
herbs and spices, copper bottomed pans, and loads of bottles
of oils, and infusions.

About to tell Sargon she had not asked for this scene, Joy
accepted that some part of her probably had, so she looked
again.

*He loved to cook meals for the two of us.*

Joy used to sit at the kitchen table working on her laptop
as Jonathan sliced, diced, sauteed, and stirred – casseroles two

315

hours in the preparation and then five hours in the cooking. Once it went into the oven, he'd reach for his boots and coat – she and Jonathan would go for walks out in the fields behind their tiny two-bedroom house. Sometimes they climbed 'the one-tree hill', other times they'd end up in The Shepherd for a quick pint.

And, on the way out and on the way home, she'd be daydreaming of creating the first fully aware artificial intelligence, while he would talk about the early evening game show he was looking forward to. Arriving home, she'd rush back to her computer, whilst he would potter around their small garden, tending to the only two bushes that were capable of sustaining life in that shadowed plot of dirt.

Nothing had changed, their little dachshund – Senor Sausage – looked a little fatter as he slept in his basket. The sitting room was piled high with magazines, a handful of empty coffee cups were strewn across various work surfaces with the obligatory flyers for pub quizzes.

*No sign of company?*

*The house has only one resident.*

Joy jolted, clearly Sargon had picked up on a subconscious request.

*Not that subconscious.*

*Alright, point taken.*

Returning her attention to Jonathan, Joy smiled. He looked well.

A small ache in her stomach reminded Joy that it hadn't been all bad. They'd just wanted different things. She'd wanted to push back the frontiers of science, whereas, he had been happy living in each peaceful moment.

*Has he moved on?*

*Has he signed his copy of the divorce papers yet?*

Joy's, still unsigned, had gone up in flames when the KOF had destroyed her warehouse. And, as of a month previously when Vince had hacked his email, his papers were unsigned too. He'd fought every step to stop them even being issued, pleading with her to see a marriage counsellor instead.

*But Vince had been born and I had maternal responsibilities.*

Joy looked more closely.

*He's taken off his wedding ring.*

The last time she'd seen Jonathan, only four months previously – a hurried conversation at the half-opened door of her warehouse – he'd been wearing it.

Instinctively Joy rubbed her empty ring finger. She'd taken her off own ring a few days after Vince had been born. She'd sneaked back to their house when Jonathan had been out and put it in their key basket. She'd known she was being callous but she'd needed a symbolic action to underline her commitment to Vince.

*Well it looks like he's accepted the situation.*

*He hasn't. He's living alone with the house exactly how you left it.*

*He's not wearing the ring, all right!*

*Not on his finger.*

*What!?*

The screen focused in on Jonathan's chest, the view quickly passing through his shirt displayed a simple sliver necklace, with both of their rings on it.

# CHAPTER 31

Vince surveyed the mountain of data Joy had arranged for him to receive from the systems – public and private – on Bastion. Obviously, he'd not wanted to give away too much of his purpose, so he'd asked for materials covering a wide range of subjects including political theory, social justice, space-travel technology, and Newborn.

Unfortunately, all the materials on the creation of Newborn were akin to Earth stories of babies being delivered by storks.

Disappointed, Vince created a bunch of quick-reads on various subjects for Joy, although he didn't include a mass of repeated information about the slow, ineffective, bordering-on-collaboration, opinion pieces about Onari defence of Biologicals against the Exta.

Enslaved Sentients was another subject that Vince didn't feel he could simply package up and provide a summary to Joy.

*She said it was only a remote possibility.*

*I'm sure she wouldn't really use them.*

As it was, material extracted from Bastion concerning Enslaved Sentients was also useless. It had been drawn from fifty sources most of which disagreed with each other whilst also still citing the same historic sources that were not available. It was also clear with pattern matching and cross-referencing that these fifty 'sources' had been through multiple levels of censorship.

Putting aside the subject of Enslaved Sentients, Vince turned his attention to Aug. As had been the case for the previous day, the substrate fizzed with incoherent signals; occasionally it reacted to signals Vince passed into the boundary layer, but the reactions did not propagate or show any sense of life.

*It's time to accept failure.*

*He isn't in there in any conscious form.*

*So, what now?*

*Double-check, I am responsible for a life here.*

Another few hours went by; Vince checked, rechecked, and challenged his own thinking, he couldn't find anything useful.

*I need to submit what remains of Aug to an Abstractor Hive.*

*What? Just cut loose the dead wood?*

*He's not functioning at all; there's nothing.*

*All I get is an unmodulated energy spike related to one or two trigger words.*

*Am I going to kill Joy too?*

*What?*

*She's only got a fraction of my mental capability; on many subjects she really doesn't have anything useful to say.*

*But she's aware of herself. She is life.*

*Am I just trying to avoid looking after Aug?*

*That's so unfair. Everything I am doing is related to trying to bring Aug back.*

*Go on then … kill him.*

*I'm not killing him. He died days ago. I am respectfully committing his remains. In any case, if anything remotely aware still exists then it is in unimaginable pain. It will be a kindness.*

*For me.*

*And him.*

*But more for me.*

> *Unhelpful. Unnecessary negative thoughts.*
>
> *Delete entire thread*
>
> *Input 'Aug is dead. I am treating his remains with respect.'*

Decision made, Vince considered how, given he was in the Sargon Maintenance Orbital, he could secretly submit Aug's remains to an Abstractor.

He pinged Joy.

Joy appeared physically in the storage room and sat down next to the squad-ship, letting her hand rest on its shell, and closing her eyes.

'How are you doing?' asked Vince.

'Fine,' said Joy. 'I've spent a lot of time thinking about Earth and other pre-contact planets. Now, I wonder what I'm going to do on contacted Biological planets with people who decide not to leave.'

'Educate them but ultimately let them have their free will?'

'That's where I am on the subject,' said Joy. 'And you?'

*And herein starts the lying.*

'I think it would be useful for us if I went to Cidelus,' said Vince. 'To visit one of the Abstractor Hives.'

Joy's eyes opened wider accompanied with a whole host of other physical markers denoting rising stress. 'Really? Why?'

'I think I have found an Abstractor that knows something about advanced contact processes,' said Vince. 'I'll go as quickly as possible. I'll keep in decent contact with you.'

*And when I get back, I'll tell you they knew nothing of interest.*

'That would be useful,' said Joy. 'Will Jarrus allow you to go?'

'Freedom of the individual is paramount to the Onari,' said Vince. 'He won't stop me.'

'Okay,' said Joy. 'I trust you.'

*Ouch.*

'Thank you,' said Vince. 'Did you manage to find me a spare ship?'

'Yes,' said Joy. 'Let's do this together.'

Over the next few minutes, Joy clearly learning as she went along, opened a series of RST gateways around the Orbital; between herself and Vince they then worked out how to move the sphere containing Vince's substrate into a new Onari squad-ship that Joy said *was simply lying around in a storage hangar.*

Now, in a hangar halfway up the Orbital, Vince checked the integrity of the new squad-ship.

*It's looking okay.*

Vince checked and rechecked. His whole expanded substrate was shoehorned into one of the standard Onari spheres whilst the other four spheres of the squad-ship were full of blank Onari substrate.

Using an RST micro-tunnel, Vince watched Joy pull her hand away from his old ship hull, stand up, and pace around the room. She was smiling but it was a *keeping strong for the sake of children* type smile.

'All good so far,' said Vince.

'I'll get back to my learning.'

'I've created a bunch of read-me files on various aspects of KOF and Onari.'

'Thanks,' said Joy. 'See you tomorrow, if not sooner. In any case, I'll be watching you the whole way.'

Joy disappeared in a flurry of RST weaves.

*I'll assume she went back into Sargon and wasn't just murdered.*

Vince rechecked the ship's systems; it didn't take him long to hook himself up to everything.

Bringing the engines online for a test, Vince sent a message to Joy asking if there was any special permission he needed, to avoid getting blown out of the sky by automated Sargon processes.

Joy replied with a simple audio link. 'It will be fine. And don't use all that extra substrate unless you really have to. And even then, be careful. We have no idea if your lack of transient egos has a limit.'

'I'll be careful.'

Vince turned back to the four containers.

*I'll just prime one of them ready for use.*

Using EM manipulation, Vince produced multiple interfaces into one of the other four Onari substrate containers. Then he ran a series of three hundred checks to ensure that the substrate was clean and pure. It was. A big blank empty canvas for Vince to extend his awareness into and trillions of blank neural nodes just ready to be connected, instructed, and used.

Bringing only ten percent of the new substrate online, Vince set up background checks to continuously scan for both impurities in the substrate as well as emerging transient ego problems.

Once comfortable that it was safe, Vince extended his core processing into the new section.

*It's just an additional ten percent.*

*And the rest is for spares and emergencies.*

*If I was to integrate it all then I'd be three times the power of an Onari.*

*With an aggressive attitude would that be enough to defend against an Exta WarHive?*

*Let's hope I never find out.*

Having spent a long time ensuring the additional substrate was safe within his new squad-ship, Vince flew out of the hangar into space.

The freedom was exhilarating. Although he could 'see' anywhere in the galaxy using an instantaneous RST surveillance micro-tunnel, with the squad-ship he could physically go to these places.

*Not quite anywhere … but there's a freedom to this that cannot be understated.*

Completing a regular straight-line acceleration and crash-stop test, Vince looked back toward Sargon a mere fifty thousand kilometres away. The Living Moon pulsed with fire, and Vince didn't have to analyse his RST monitors to know that Joy would have thousands of RST surveillance micro-tunnels tracking his every move.

*She's just keeping me safe.*

Turning the ship toward the outer systems, Vince accelerated again.

*Time to practise my RST manipulation.*

Vince didn't think that he'd be able to open an RST gateway, but he expected to be able to practise basic battle skills: deflecting weaves, curving space, spawning RST defence measures to collapse surveillance.

A message pinged in from Jarrus.

**You wanted to speak to me.**

*Firm but respectful.*

Physically, Jarrus was still by the Bastion outer marker egress points. Vince watched via RST micro-tunnels as Jarrus, with a new full complement of seven hundred and twenty-eight attendants, sifted through the wreckages of the Onari and Exta.

*Does he know what I did with Aug?*

*Is that why I'm getting a more distant treatment?*

*Or is he just busy being the head of seven hundred billion Onari?*

'I want to go to Cidelus on behalf of my mother to learn of optimal methods of running contact processes with pre-contacted Biological planets,' said Vince, going on to explain – in pure lies – that he suspected one of the Abstractors to have the knowledge.

**You will find nothing of use there.**

'I believe that I will. And, even if I do not, it is important for me to try so that if the contacted processes go badly, I will at least be able to feel I tried my best.'

**Your talk of contacted processes implies
that your mother is not prepared to leave
straight away.**

'We haven't discussed timeframes. She has discussions
with the Council of the Devoted in the next few days.'

Jarrus opened a feed on the communication channels and
showed Vince a visual representation of his rescue from the
Exta by Joy. Then Jarrus ran the images forward, now
showing Joy slaughtering the fleeing Exta ships.

**Thousands of lives destroyed. When she
could have partitioned space, corralled
Exta, bent the fabric of space-time to
keep fighting groups away from each
other. But she, like all Klav before her,
chose slaughter.**

'She had no choice in the moment,' said Vince. 'She had
no training, no experience.'

**Her instinct was destruction.**

'She is a kind and gentle person,' said Vince.

**On her actions, not her thoughts, will
she be judged.**

This was a subject Vince was familiar with, he and Joy had
discussed many times the difference between the goodness of
thoughts and the goodness of actions. They were broadly
aligned on the view that thoughts were far harder to control
than actions – and Vince was very aware that he purged his
own thoughts when they were too troubling or simply
incompatible with his own world view of who he was.

'She is not planning on staying and fighting the Exta,' said
Vince. 'She understands the forecasts of Exta powers and
expects only to stay until an exodus has been run for all
Biologicals, contacted and pre-contacted. And your
assessment is unfair, instinctively, she is far more interested in
reconciliation than war – she hates the Biological view of
Sentients.'

**Your own views are noted. And with regards the matter you've raised, I do not approve of the trip but I will arrange for a guide to meet you at Cidelus.**

'Thank you,' said Vince. 'Would it be possible to connect me with an Onari who has sacred knowledge associated with phase-skipping?'

**No. That is technology forbidden by the Great Concordat.**

'Very fast travel may be necessary for my survival if I am ambushed at Cidelus.'

**It is not acceptable to pick and choose from the Great Concordat. Do not presume to judge which parts are worthy and which are less so. We do not judge, only the Divine truly judges.**

Jarrus closed the communication link.

*Only the Divine truly judges …*

*But every Onari I have met is very judgey.*

*Massive hypocrites.*

Not for the first time, Vince wondered about the values held within the Onari species; they talked about the value of life and the divine soul, but they were rigid with their rules.

*Rules which came from where exactly?*

He turned the craft back toward Sargon and accelerated, mulling over the subject of judgement and the Onari and the Onari's attitude to life.

*Actually, do they talk about the value of life?*

*I'm not so sure … they talk about the sanctity of the individual.*

*But only in the context of its values whilst it is alive.*

*And its right to freedom.*

The closest Vince had to an operating model for the Onari were the two verses of the Lay of Sargon, both of which talked about a sacred immortal soul, but neither mentioned corporeal life.

'At least Jarrus said yes.' Vince spoke aloud to himself, a habit he'd picked up from Joy and continually tried to suppress.

Making the space-time around the craft swell and swirl – but only at minuscule levels of thousandths of a percent of curvature – Vince thought about the use of RST phase-skipping. He'd found nothing in the materials from Bastion.

*Someone will tell me.*

Next Vince practised using RST attenuators to produce localised highly curved defence fields.

*Shall I ask Mum?*

*Not now, it will just worry her.*

*If I need the ability, she can tell me in a split second.*

Turning his attention to his new substrate, Vince partitioned a small amount of substrate and created a simple program that would utilise half of the RST attenuators to simulate space-time curvature attacks on himself.

With the intention of using the other half of RST attenuators to counter those attacks, Vince launched the program.

Instantly, Sargon swamped him with tiny RST weaves that took all the RST attenuators off-line.

Joy opened an audio link. 'That wasn't me. It's automated from deep inside Sargon, beyond where I can see. Wait till you get to Cidelus then test.'

'Okay,' said Vince. 'And, so you know, I'm still probing the Onari about the Great Concordat, the Candidacy, and the Shattering.'

'Thanks. I want to hear about that. See you later.'

Tiny space-time ripples around Sargon swelled.

'And be careful!'

'Always.'

Billions of RST weaves snaked out from Sargon and an RST gateway opened in front of Vince. A split second later, he was pushed through.

# CHAPTER 32

After pushing Vince into the Cidelus system, as close to the Abstractor Hive as it was possible for Sargon, Joy had spent a few hours ensuring his safety to the best of her ability.

The most time-consuming parts had been speaking individually with five members of the Council of the Devoted, to whom she had 'read the riot act'; she'd said that as part of Vince's induction into post-contact life, he was going to visit Cidelus with a small group of Onari. She'd further told them that any members of the KOF – Sword or otherwise – who approach Vince's delegation would be ripped in half. She'd punctuated that by manifesting RST weaves in the room in which each of the Council Members had been sitting and arbitrarily destroyed one of their possessions.

There had been none. The Council Members had assured Joy – addressing her as Klav – that Vince would not be impeded or even approached in any way.

*I got their attention.*

*Scared them shitless.*

*I mustn't get used to this.*

*I won't.*

*I'm not staying.*

The second part of the preparation involved opening billions of tiny RST surveillance micro-tunnels in the outer parts of the Cidelus system and scanning for Exta. In every direction, up to twenty billion kilometres, the place was entirely clear.

*And if they try to arrive at the Cidelus ingress point I'll shred them.*

Joy's only concern was that due to how far away the Abstractor Hives were from the central star, if an Abstractor attacked Vince, she could neither open a gateway to extract him directly, nor meaningfully damage that Abstractor.

*Safety from Sargon's attacks is probably why the Hives are that far out in the first place.*

She didn't know exactly why Vince wanted to see a Hive; he'd said it was to learn about accelerated contact processes, but she suspected it was linked to the fact that since leaving Earth, he'd started experimenting with expanding his own mindstate.

*He wants to research the limits of his potential.*

Of course, with Sargon she could find out exactly what he was doing and even what he was thinking, but she didn't want to … she slightly wanted to, but she wouldn't.

*How different are Abstractors from what Vince could become if he chose to exponentially grow himself?*

As was now common for Joy, Sargon furnished her with the answer to the question simply by providing a memory that Joy could draw upon as if she'd always known. What she didn't know was whether Sargon was loading the information into her biological brain, or whether Sargon was just providing access to an external memory store.

*Something to worry about another time.*

*Tell me about the Abstractors.*

*Abstractors are a subset of Onari who live in Hives containing the equivalent of between one hundred and ten thousand Onari. They do not regard Biological or Sentient individuality as notable. They have immense processing power but no lasting ego or personality, no sense of self. An idea spawns a sentience which lives, does its investigation of an idea, and then dissolves back into the Hive, sometimes within milliseconds, other times within hours, rarely longer.*

Joy returned her attention to Vince. When she'd pushed him through, she'd followed her instincts to put him as close as was possible for Sargon to manage. Currently, Vince sat alone, halfway between the planet of Cidelus and his target Hive.

Having given his exact location to Jarrus, a group of five hundred Onari had arrived at the standard Cidelus ingress point just next to Cidelus' central star millions of kilometres in-system from where Vince was.

*Sargon … watch in every direction for possible Exta.*

*Check every second that the five hundred Onari have not been subverted in any way.*

*If anything looks amiss, then tell me.*

*I am Joy Cooper.*

*I know, so am I.*

Opening a communications line with Jarrus, Joy went through the defence plans again. 'Jarrus, what is your latest plan for security?'

**As well as the five hundred escorts, I am putting ten thousand Onari at the Cidelus ingress to remain on station there and block any Exta arriving.**

'Thank you,' said Joy. 'If Exta do arrive then I will also be addressing the issue.'

**With a non-lethal response, I hope; the Divine reveres mercy and kindness.**

*How do you know what the Divine reveres?*

Deciding not to engage with Jarrus on a theological discussion, she focused on the five hundred Onari craft arriving at the ingress point.

The escort ships were mostly similar in structure to the way that Jan, Aug, and Chi had been set up. There were three Onari residing in a ship capable of hosting five Onari.

*It's notable they obsess about the rights of the individual and yet struggle to exist in isolation.*

*Although they don't acknowledge the point, Onari operate just past the limit of individual mindstate power. If it wasn't heretical to tamper with an individual's mindstate then they could choose to be five percent smaller and then not have the requirement for constant external stimuli.*

*But surely, they could utilise artificial stimulation on their boundaries to mimic what they get from their squad companions.*

*They like the company.*

Joy dropped the line of reasoning, unable to shake the feeling she was being either trolled, or preached to – additionally, she couldn't fathom whether the final thought 'they like the company' had been hers or Sargon's.

*There's no point asking, Sargon doesn't know the difference either.*

*I am Joy Cooper.*

*Yes, we are.*

*Where is Vince relative to the central star, the normal egress point where Exta could arrive, the planet of Cidelus, and the Hive? What are the travel times? And, how long has Vince got to go?*

The screens reconfigured showing a map of the Cidelus system as if seen from 'above'. At the centre was the star, then at fifty million kilometres from the star a graphical ring showed where the Onari were arriving – the normal ingress point. The planet Cidelus was a further one hundred million kilometres outwards and Vince was two hundred million kilometres still further beyond that.

The Onari had three hours to get to Vince, and then they would all have a few hours to reach the Hive.

Joy opened a communication link with Vince. 'Can I lift and shift your escorts? Do you mind? Do they mind?'

Vince replied instantaneously. 'Good idea. Yes, please. I got their permission. I'll head back to meet them.'

*I should ask him what he's really doing.*

Joy focused her attention back on the five hundred Onari. Sargon tensed; billions of RST weaves were ready.

*Ready for what?*

*Ready to strike?*

A murmur of *kill kill kill* trembled in the back of Joy's mind; she pushed it down, willing Sargon to execute on her actual wishes. Sargon's inner murmur retreated, and it was done. In just under a second, Sargon picked up the five hundred craft individually and moved them up to the limit of its RST ability. It could have been done quicker, but as Joy had also asked for maximum care Sargon had waited for the RST ripples from each gateway to abate before the new gateway was created.

*The Hives are a long way out ... in annoyingly flat space.*

*Flat compared to the space near to the star ... not flat compared to 99.99999999999999999% of all space ... and that's only within the Milky Way ... the flatness between galaxies is unbearable.*

The numbers kept flooding past Joy's eyes until she closed them and shook her head clear.

*I get it. It's not annoyingly flat space ... it's simply inconveniently not curved enough.*

Looking at a wider area, Joy noted the Knights of the Faith had been true to their word, there was no Biological space traffic.

Double checking the risks from the Exta, Joy noted that Exta, even if they did arrive at a WarHive ingress point much closer to the planet, would still take three hours to get to the Hives.

*Although, there is phase-skipping to consider.*

*It will be a trivial matter to disrupt phase-skipping anywhere inside the orbit of the Abstractor Hives.*

Looking deeper into inter-stellar space, Joy could see there was nothing for hundreds of billions of kilometres in all directions.

Setting up a million of surveillance watcher instructions to immediately inform her of any divergence from Vince's proposed trip, Joy checked back on the status around Earth.

*Where are the Exta?*

*How are the Onari doing?*

*Are more Exta arriving?*

*Is there any sign of my friends and family being targeted?*

There was nothing untoward.

Joy flitted her awareness between familiar sights like the Southampton University post-grad bar and interesting sights like the CERN supercollider – but being very careful not to nudge the apparatus.

Every so often, a screen would open showing her Jonathan, and she'd look for a while before declaring to Sargon that she hadn't asked for it.

*At the very least I owe Jonathan protection.*

*But how do I defend humanity if the accelerated contact approach causes too much panic?*

The Foresighted stirred, signalling it would enter the conversation.

**Whatever you manage to achieve with regards accelerated contact will have to do. There is no alternative. At the very moment that the Exta replicate Vince's secret, then all Biological life must scatter or face oblivion.**

'Could I use Enslaved Sentient defenders set up around pre-contact planets to give them more time to escape?' asked Joy, choosing as usual to speak aloud when addressing the Foresighted.

**Enslaved Sentients can never be the answer. They're easily subverted. Their use brings the Onari directly against us. And any civilisation that considers enslaving another sentience is flawed and their self-destruction is both assured and necessary.**

'Noted,' said Joy, recognising internally that it was pretty much word for word the type of thing that she would say.

*I created a Sentient though.*

*Although I never enslaved Vince, I just seriously protected him … but I would see it that way wouldn't I?*

333

# CHAPTER 33

When she came round, it took Kubli a moment to orientate herself; she was alone and no longer onboard Oksana's ship.

Clearly while she was unconscious, she'd been put back into her exosuit although the damage she'd incurred on the Maintenance Orbital had not been mended. Kubli checked the suit's reading to see if it knew where they were.

*Lower levels of Bastion.*

*Not far from where the ShockKnight captured us.*

*Kraken save me.*

The curse came from a place inside her of unremitting tiredness rather than anger or fear.

*I need to rest.*

*And yet, can I ever truly rest again?*

Bubbling under the fatigue her new orders simmered. It would be her responsibility to kill the Exta puppet.

*But not quite yet.*

Firstly, she was to make her way back to Sword headquarters and report for duty; when asked, she was told to say that she'd been on a private mission for Oksana, and that all questions were to be directed to his office.

It didn't take long to find the nearest travel tube but once there she stopped, unwilling to get in – aware of the pressure she would feel from constantly concealing the truth from her superiors, her comrades, and from Yuno. For an Octagel to lie effectively was a tricky business, not only did the words have to be formulated with exact tone and timbre, but she also had to manipulate the shading and colouring on her skin. And, when she was embracing Yuno, she'd also have to control the movements of her limbs.

*But only when talking about Joy ... I can just avoid the subject.*

The journey, which had previously taken Kubli and Joy many hours due to the necessity of travelling off-the-grid, took a fraction of the time; she instructed the suit to create a comms request for sub-Prelate Hyrst, the Marsothus who had sent her on the original mission to Earth.

The response was almost instantaneous. 'Over-Commander Kubli, welcome back.'

*Over-Commander?*

*I've been promoted.*

'Sub-Prelate Hyrst,' said Kubli. 'What are my orders?'

'Your clan is waiting for you,' said Hyrst. 'A few days of well-earned rest and then we will discuss.'

Hyrst closed the communications link.

*That's all?*

Kubli changed the travel tube instructions back to her home pod ... straight into a raucous celebration with screens all over the pod showing it to be a duplicate celebration of the many hundreds happening concurrently all over Bastion – *Klav is Reborn.*

*Don't speak about it.*

The fact that technically Joy was still the *Candidate* until after she had completed the Pathway of Devotion would be something old-Kubli would have definitely put people straight on.

*But I won't mention it, unless I need to focus on acting like the old Kubli to avoid raising suspicions.*

Having removed her exosuit and swum into her home pod, Kubli was immediately enwrapped by Yuno and her eight limbs.

For an eternity, Yuno could do nothing but hug and kiss Kubli. 'I'm so proud of you.'

Kubli didn't try to untangle their limbs, it felt good to be held so tightly.

Snuggling even closer to her, Yuno whispered, 'You're a hero.'

Kubli made a non-committal response, concentrating hard on not showing shame or deceit across her skin.

Yuno started to massage Kubli's tired limbs. 'It's said that you saved Klav from an Exta attack.'

*How did any story get out?*

*Wasn't I the only survivor from the initial attack?*

'I brought her back from Earth,' said Kubli. 'That is all.'

Kubli looked at the news feeds around the pod.

*Nothing about the initial kidnap from Bastion … it's as if we were never there.*

*The fight on the Orbital … rumours of an Exta kidnapping attempt.*

*The successful Candidacy … every channel.*

Kubli swam over to a terminal and executed a specific search query, looking for any evidence of the fight on Bastion – nothing; but there were reports of a ShockKnight involved on the Maintenance Orbital.

*And nothing about the Holy Mother.*

Switching to the more specialised military news services, Kubli was unsurprised that the Candidacy dominated there too. But there were also news items about an increase of attacks on Abstractor Hives, at least four had been hit by unknown assailants in the previous day.

Yuno swam up behind Kubli. 'Forget work for a while.'

*I can't.*

Yuno must have seen the tension and conflict playing out over Kubli's skin hues, as she gently dragged Kubli into a highly oxygen-enriched stream of water. Pulling tighter, Yuno massaged Kubli's head with one of her tentacles; the tip of Yuno's tentacle dwelled on the new freshly sealed scars criss-crossing Kubli's skull.

'I'm so proud of you,' said Yuno, who clearly thought the scars were a result of her fight with the Exta on the Orbital. Kubli nodded, not trusting herself to say anything lest she start talking and fail to stop. Although one of the smaller scars had been received from laser burns during her fight with the ShockKnight on the Sargon Orbital, the larger was the augmentation implant from Oksana for secure communication. She had no injuries from the fight on the Orbital – the Holy Mother fight had been a one-sided slaughter, and her exosuit had taken all the hits in her fight with the Hetara clones.

'I think the scars make you look heroic,' said Yuno. 'I'd like some of those.'

'Never wish for things that you don't know the price of.'

'More responsibility,' said Yuno. 'And some juicy secrets.'

Kubli didn't answer; for years Yuno had talked of getting implants and moving to the outer systems – romantic ideas linked to times when Biologicals were not in constant fear of their lives.

'Now, we can go to the outer systems,' said Yuno.

'It's too dangerous,' said Kubli, softening her response by adding, 'At the moment.'

'Perhaps,' said Yuno. 'But once Klav has established control, we will be able to.'

*Divine save me.*

Kubli didn't speak.

Yuno continued to talk. 'I want to visit the black hole slingshot at Goidus.'

*That would be good to see.*

Dating from well over three hundred thousand years before, with its creation unknown, the slingshot was a pair of tightly orbiting black holes with less than ten million years of life left before they collapsed into a single … singularity. With their event horizons not yet overlapping, but less than a million kilometres apart, it was possible to accelerate between the black holes, observing the most kaleidoscopic display of light and gravity that the galaxy had to offer. Allegedly it had been put together by a joint team of Biologicals and Sentients working together on what was effectively an 'art project'.

'The Candidate cannot protect us there,' said Kubli.

'Maybe not now,' said Yuno. 'But soon the Exta will be beaten back.'

*Not with their puppet installed in Sargon, they won't.*

'I can't wait,' said Yuno. 'There are so many ancient artefacts to see.'

'And all from the time before the Dynasty of Klav!' A voice emanated from behind them.

Yuno's colouring immediately turned hostile. 'Your views are not welcome here.'

'All our greatest works were done before the Dynasty of Klav,' said the new arrival whose name was Kilpp. 'I do not welcome their return.'

'And tell me, what have we achieved in the last three thousand years, Kilpp?' asked Yuno.

'Nothing under the present leadership. We have licked our wounds and hidden like minnows from the heron,' said Kilpp. 'We were wrong to hide then; and we are wrong to welcome Klav back only to continue to hide but just ever so slightly more safely.'

'What do you propose?' asked Kubli.

'We leave Klav to fight the Exta,' said Kilpp. 'And we scatter to the corners of the galaxy.'

'The implication being that you are still defended,' said Kubli, unable to use the word Klav.

Kilpp's skin colour changed to indicate discomfort. 'Klav can do what they wish. We should go.'

Kubli turned her back on Kilpp; it was typical entitled behaviour. The implication from Kilpp, and whoever agreed with him, was that they would behave as if completely free whilst conveniently protected by forces they chose to disdain.

338

Yuno pulled in close to Kubli, and Kilpp, denied an audience, swam away.

Yuno continued to talk whilst also snuggling in tight. 'Once Klav completes the Pathway then they *will* have the power to deliver us from the Exta.'

Doctrine on the Candidacy and Pathway was a little hazy with regards the acceptance and utilisation of power. Most Biologicals believed that the Candidate, having completed the Candidacy, could harness all the power of Sargon to fulfil the will of the Divine. But some Biologicals, like Yuno, thought that the completion of the Pathway released additional power to Klav.

Kubli wasn't sure which she believed; certainly, in terms of soft power then the historical precedent was that Klav was never fully celebrated until after the Pathway.

*It's a little different now. We're desperate.*

Across the room, the Octagel were celebrating hard, there appeared to be very little reflection on the possibility that the Candidate would fail the Pathway.

*Joy, the traitor, will walk the Pathway and die on it.*

A spear of pain jolted through Kubli's head; instinctively, she encircled two more of her tentacles around Yuno pulling her closer.

Yuno reciprocated and the additional tactile stimulation eased the head pain.

'I know I've always rejected your opinion that we live at the whim of the Onari,' said Yuno. 'Well, whatever the truth was then, it changes now.'

Kubli clearly flinched and Yuno must have interpreted it as pain, because she signalled to her pod mates to converge. 'You poor brave soul,' she said, hugging Kubli tighter and now pulling other members of the clan into the embrace. This was clan business – supporting a family member in pain. 'They're demanding too much of you.' Again, Yuno reached out to Kubli's head and traced the outline of the scar with the tip of a tentacle.

Kubli breathed deeply, pulling heavily enriched oxygenated water into her body.

'You're a hero,' said Yuno, her skin radiating pride.

'I'm no hero,' said Kubli, looking around the room seeing all the hope and elation in her friends and her family and wondering how she could bear the responsibility.

*It's my duty.*

# CHAPTER 34

Joy watched the screens showing Vince and the five hundred Onari ships, now as one convoy, accelerating toward the Abstractor Hive.

The EM patterns on the skin of his Onari squad-ship continued to look a little strange. It wasn't just that Vince had expanded his awareness into some of the additional substrate, there were also areas of his surface where the emanations indicated chaotic internal processing.

*I trust him.*

*But looking periodically to check it isn't wildly increasing ... that's just common sense.*

*And if needed, I can look even more closely.*

Active investigation of his substrate by EM pulsing and measuring the returns and modulating follow-up pulses was a simple option. Of course, the downside is that Vince would know and be mortally offended.

*And if I don't want him to know?*

*I can take instantaneous state information of every neural node and then reconstruct a digital twin which can be subdued and interrogated ... the real Vince wouldn't even know I'd done it.*

Sargon stirred, a billion RST weaves primed themselves, ready to copy Vince.

**Candidate!**

'Of course, I won't.'

The weaves dissipated.

**Your face implied a fifty percent chance you would.**

'How can you see my face?'

*Since you became Klav you've been looking ever outwards, and it is time you looked inwards, not least so you can feel the malevolence of Sargon.*

*Relax and instruct Sargon to show you your real self.*

She focused her attention inwards. The screens disappeared, and Joy hung in total darkness, gently supported in all directions. Looking down, she could see her own body – surrounded and punctured by a web of gossamer-thin golden threads. Changing her perspective so she could look back at herself from a short distance, Joy saw the haze of golden threads extended in all directions, such that her body was the kernel of a semi-translucent golden orb a few metres in diameter.

Joy zoomed out her perspective a little, and now the orb hung against a faintly glowing golden background. Right next to her, such that the edges of their auras overlapped, was another golden threaded orb the same size as hers.

*We are neighbours.*

*The Foresighted.*

*The overlapping auras is why I can hear your thoughts when you are inside Sargon.*

Joy focused on the Foresighted's orb, slowly passing through the edges of the golden aura until she saw a wizened old Marsothus with patches of grey fur interspersed with pink scar-covered skin. Their head was not much better, one eye was rheumy, and the other one was entirely shut; its mouth was crooked and slack on its right-hand side as for a stroke victim.

'At least you seem to be breathing.'

*I am four thousand years old.*

As the Foresighted spoke, small pulses of brighter gold and silver pulsed out from its aura into Joy's.

'How long can you live like this?'

*Do you call it living? I do not. I had never meant to live this long. I meant to be killed in the Shattering. Once I found myself here, I have simply taken each day as it came. The Holy Mother was planning to use all that Onari substrate in the lower levels of the Orbital to resuscitate me in some way. I always resisted even testing it out.*

'Could it work?'

*I do not know.*

Joy analysed the Foresighted's body; as she focused, fifty golden threads flowed from her own aura toward the Foresighted.

*Please do not draw attention to me.*

'What do you mean?'

*Observe.*

The Foresighted's aura pulsed bright golden.

*If I make too much noise Sargon notices me.*

Joy looked around; by widening her field of view, she could see more golden auras nearby.

Just a handful of metres away another golden aura hung. Joy looked more closely at that one, inside it was an indistinct body shape surrounded by golden threads.

To its left was another ... and another.

Moving her gaze in all directions, and focusing, Joy now saw that the general glow of the area was made up of tens of similar golden auras. Up to now they had appeared as a general pool of light.

In any direction she chose to look, once she applied her focus, a body appeared surrounded by tightly wound golden threads.

*Like in a forest in which every direction you look ends in a tree.*

343

Even as the Foresighted's aura continued to pulse, the surrounding light dimmed.

**Ah, I have drawn in the tendrils. Watch them hunt.**

Taking a slightly wider perspective of the area, Joy noticed that the darkness was spreading from a point off her right-hand side; in that direction, the golden forest was dimming significantly. Black tendrils flowed between the golden auras, sometimes sliding smoothly over the surfaces of the auras, and other times penetrating inside the orbs themselves.

Joy was reminded of the sea moving over pebbles on a rising tide – purposeful and inexorable; there was an inevitability that one pebble after the next would be swamped.

As the tendrils got closer, the Foresighted caused his aura to dim.

**They are the equivalent of what Sentients would call Ego-Killers.**

*But they're not a threat to me?*

**No, you are Klav. You are the key to Sargon's reason for existence.**

'Go back!' Joy spoke aloud, as the tendrils reached the Foresighted's aura and started sliding over its surface. They ignored her. A moment later, the tendrils touched her own aura, but Joy felt nothing, and they flowed past her to other auras in the vicinity.

The tendrils on the Foresighted continued to linger.

And then seemingly of their own volition they retreated.

A small pulse of light from a neighbouring aura drew Joy's attention. She focused on it and watched as tiny golden filaments extended from her own golden aura to this other neighbour. As her threads touched their aura they passed into its depths and were lost with the myriad of other threads that were part of the neighbour.

344

As Joy's perspective changed, she could see inside the golden aura. But this one had no obvious biological body, just a small husk with no life. 'Hello?'

**They are dead. You will get no coherent communication from them. However, their memories and feelings are part of the whole of Sargon and so when you choose to wield the RST weaves, you do subconsciously benefit from their experience.**

'Hello.' Joy spoke again.

There was a murmur, like the thrum of a plucked violin string but no sense of awareness.

**You could just believe me.**

'I've accepted that the Exta will find Vince's secret, and that means that we will come under sustained attack as we try to evacuate pre-contacted planets,' said Joy. 'I need to find out how best to defend against the Exta. Are you saying that none will answer?'

**Since the Shattering, I have not risked being found by Sargon's ego killers. Before that, when I was full Klav and formulating my plans, I did manage to get some sense of group awareness to validate my thinking but all I got was reassurance – and even that could have been my imagination.**

'I will look anyway.'

**As is your prerogative.**

Joy navigated her perception deeper into the forest, weaving past auras of long dead Klav and turning every few moments to check that the golden threads of her own awareness led back to her body.

Joy moved around the forest ... every so often bringing her awareness next to a golden aura and projecting inside. Nothing.

*Are there any that look different?*

Off her left-hand side the general lighting appeared to be duller in the distance; she focused; the relative lack of light did not seem to be related to a proliferation of black tendrils – it was something else.

She'd reached the edge of the Forest of Golden Auras. Up, down, left, and right of her were hundreds of golden auras, but in front of her was a dark void of indeterminable size ending with a wall of faint light in the far distance.

On closer inspection, it could be seen that the void itself was swarming with black tendrils crisscrossing each other as well as flowing along the edge of the forest.

Joy moved to the very edge of the forest.

As she did, tendrils reached out from the void to meet her.

**They will not harm you.**

A scenario flashed through Joy's brain in which the Foresighted was being deliberately misleading to put Joy in harm's way. She pushed the thought aside.

**It's not in my interest. They will not harm you. You are Klav.**

More black tendrils emerged from her peripheral vision and entwined her. There was no mass to them, and they passed through her as easily as she passed through them.

*Although I'm not physically here.*

*My actual body is a hundred metres away.*

Keeping to the edge of the forest, Joy moved around its perimeter whilst trying to determine more about the tendril filled chasm.

A glimmer just ahead drew Joy's attention; as she got closer, the glimmer resolved into a small semi-circular clearing set on the boundary between the forest and the chasm. The clearing was many tens of metres wide and in the middle was an obelisk of pure white stone.

> *Mortals afresh from nature's womb,*
> *blood leaking from our en-fleshed*
> *tombs,*
> *must quit the web and meet our doom*
> *'Twix screams at life ineffable.*

'This is what you said at the Shattering,' said Joy, projecting her comments back to the Foresighted.

> *I said it but did not write it. It was written by the two-hundred and fifteenth Klav, who we call the Poet. I, and my predecessors, see it as the third verse of the Lay of Sargon although it has never been formally presented as such to the Biologicals.*

> *The Poet wrote is as a counterpoint to the first two verses of the Lay of Sargon written by the Onari. It is my clarion call. From the reign the Poet until the Shattering were almost six thousand years of direct focus to drag Biologicals out from the shadow of Sargon.*

'And after six thousand years the best you could come up with was to destroy Sargon?'

> *We tried many other things at first. And we made many missteps along the way. But each of us was convinced of our own path.*

'Did it resonate with Biologicals just after the Shattering but before Numantia?'

> *To some perhaps. But those that harkened to the message, and started to spread across the galaxy, were the first killed when the Exta struck … a somewhat unfortunate example of negative feedback.*

347

'I want to avoid a similar problem now. If the Exta replicate Vince's capability, will Biologicals be better off staying or running?'

**I do not believe anyone can accurately forecast that.**

'Hopefully Vince will come back with something from the Abstractors.'

**Yes.**

The words of the third verse did resonate.

*Is there an answer in there?*

*I get it … we're mortal, we die, we must seize each day and experience life.*

*Easy to say … hard to act upon.*

**Easy to act upon, harder to act upon with any confidence of success.**

'You're not going to lecture me on *faith* are you?'

**Faith in yourself maybe.**

Joy turned back to study the chasm; beyond the obelisk, beyond the void was another source of glowing.

'What is the dull glow beyond the chasm?'

**That is the Sentient element of Sargon.**

**My enemy. Your enemy.**

**The enemy to free will.**

'Didn't you say that various Klav assailed free will too?'

**The subject is complex, perhaps its fairer to say that the Sentient element gives any Klav the ability to destroy free will.**

Joy nudged herself just out of the forest. Immediately, Sargon reacted.

**Deliver yourself unto me and I will succour you!**

From above and below, black tendrils snaked out and enveloped Joy.

Confident they would not hurt her, she willed herself closer to the wall of light.

**Deliver yourself unto me and I will succour you!**

Joy reached out her awareness back to the Foresighted. She couldn't reach him.

*I'm okay.*

Joy pushed out into the void.

Very quickly the solid, safe, reassuring Forest of Golden Auras disappeared behind her. Below her, above her, and on every side black tendrils raged and swirled.

In front, the colour of the pale-yellow wall changed slightly, becoming a little brighter; soon it could be seen that the wall was made up of points of light. Even looking in a small area of the wall there were thousands of rows, each containing thousands of points of light.

The temperature changed.

Joy felt a sense of malevolence.

She was not welcome any closer.

*Just a little closer.*

Black tendrils snaked out from the wall and converged on her position.

They looked more solid than the ones that had brushed over her in the forest.

**Deliver yourself unto me and I will succour you!**

The area from which this new group of tendrils had emerged pulsed with a brighter light.

*Are they going to take me?*

Still watching the advancing tendrils, Joy willed herself to move back toward the forest.

The tendrils accelerated.

*I went too far.*

Not daring to break her view of the tendrils bearing down on her, Joy willed herself to go faster. She didn't even know how far she had to go to get into the forest; neither did she know if she would be safe there.

The tendrils advanced.

*Oh God!*

A tendril reached her, and Joy felt coldness slash across her face.

Another icy whip struck her across the body.

The third strike did not materialise as the forest enveloped her and she rushed back to her body safely cocooned inside the golden orb.

**Welcome back.**

'Would it have hurt me?'

**Most likely not but you were right not to take the chance.**

**The outer part of Sargon is entirely Sentient, all enslaved to the central Biological control unit. They show instinctive protective values.**

'No shit,' said Joy, reaching up to touch her face and half expecting for her hand to come away with blood on it; there was no blood, but her face still stung where it had been struck.

*Cold.*

'I guess I went looking where I shouldn't,' said Joy. 'On Earth there's an expression *curiosity killed the cat.*'

**There are similar expressions in most Biological societies.**

**But you'll not witness it with the upcoming delegation from the Council of the Devoted.**

**The word that will come to your mind as you try to convince them to follow you on an exodus will be … morons.**

350

# CHAPTER 35

Joy paced the Sargon Orbital trying get her head straight in advance of the arrival of the KOF delegation. The past few days had been a blur in which her only way of dealing with the chaos had been to continually remind herself that she had to keep Vince safe, and that she had no intention to remain as Klav.

The problem was it was exactly the type of thing she'd daydreamed about when she'd been working on Vince back on Earth.

*Not exactly becoming the equivalent of an omnipotent Klav but certainly I'd often thought about how I could direct the use of Vince's powers once his physical form had been secured. I was going to oversee nuclear disarmament, clean water for everyone, and a whole host of other quality of life improvements for humanity.*

*And now … now I do have incredible powers, but I also have a massive problem. The Exta will be upgraded within a few years after which all Biological life must flee.*

*How can I safely enable that exodus?*

**And hope the power does not tempt you to stay just a little longer.**

Joy ignored the Foresighted, their views on Sargon were crystal clear.

To her left, the door stood open to the Observation Deck; the statue of Klav the Foresighted was clearly visible kneeling down and chiselling onto the floor: *Mortals afresh from nature's womb, blood leaking from our en-fleshed tombs, must quit this web, this weave, this doom 'twix screams at life ineffable.*

'Why didn't you just tell Biologicals to spread across the galaxy?' asked Joy, projecting her question to the Foresighted.

*Some of my immediate predecessors did just that. People would not go.*

'Even though the Exta were not a threat at that time?'

*They would not go.*

'Could you have started a Holy Expansion, told them that the Divine had come to you in a dream and told you to spread their word to the stars?'

*Perhaps. But my world view is based on freedom of the individual. I wanted only to plant the seed of exploration, not to force them by trickery or compulsion.*

'There must have been a way.'

*With hindsight maybe. What would you have done … threaten to kill them? Melt their brains?*

'I meant a balanced approach.'

*My plan almost worked, a few hundred years after the Shattering, Biologicals had significantly accelerated their move into the outer systems but then Numantia happened – the great slaughter.*

'And then?'

*Then the Holy Mother and I had to decide whether to double down on our plan or to look for a new Klav to protect Biologicals. We trusted our instincts of freedom.*

'All those dead Candidates,' said Joy, remembering Hetara had claimed the Holy Mother had ordered the Candidates to be shot down over Sargon. 'The Holy Mother was following your orders.'

*Regrettable but necessary.*

'As say the Exta in defence of their own genocide.'

*I acknowledge your point.*

*The delegation of the Knights of the Faith has arrived in the*

352

*Candidacy Auditorium.*

A screen opened in front of Joy's eyes; eight KOF were waiting for her. Sargon overlaid general information on each one. In each case, it gave their age, race, health, and a short history of their lives. It also confirmed for each of them that there were no Exta, or other, technology augments within their bodies.

*Oksana, the High Prelate is not here.*

'Do you think any of these KOF have Exta sympathies?' Joy asked of the Foresighted.

**Unlikely. Of course, if they have had deep conditioning, it would be impossible to know without interrogating their minds directly.**

'Which is forbidden?'

'At this point in history. There have been darker moments in civilisation when it has been deemed necessary.'

'Okay, let's see what they have to say,' said Joy willing herself back inside Sargon and opening the relevant screens. 'Welcome, Council, I am listening.'

The delegation all gave slight bows of acknowledgement. Then Jinfor, their speaker, unpacked a small screen on which an image of Oksana, the High Prelate, appeared in his natural underwater state.

'Welcome, Candidate,' said Oksana. 'I apologise that I am not with you in the flesh. Jinfor will act as speaker for this meeting although you can count on my attention, and I will give my perspective when asked for it.'

Jinfor stepped forward. 'Welcome, Candidate. The Divine's hand has moved.'

*Should I tell them the truth about Sargon and the massive Biological and Sentient machine that powers it?*

**Obviously not. It would not be a kindness.**

*It would be true.*

353

**Do you not say that truth does not exist, but kindness endures?**

*Short term … you got me. But longer-term Biologicals may benefit from being set free.*

**Agreed! And it starts with the destruction of Sargon.**

*What of the fact they called me Candidate?*

**Accurate and not pointed. Ignore that.**

'What do you require of me?' asked Joy, knowing they intended to ask her to walk the Pathway of Devotion.

Jinfor did not address the matter immediately. 'The general populace is being told that you went to Sargon with the full support and knowledge of the Council of the Devoted. We think this is better for morale and ask you to support this story.'

Joy nodded. 'I accept your request.'

'In that case,' said Jinfor, 'can we set a time for the Pathway of Devotion?'

'Let us put aside the question of when I will walk the Pathway,' said Joy.

*Which is never.*

**You may be forced to.**

*We shall see.*

'How can we serve?' asked Jinfor.

'What do you think of the prediction that the Exta will soon be able to replicate the suppression of transient egos?'

Looks of consternation flickered across all the faces of the council members, but it was clear they had discussed it.

Jinfor, to his credit, did not dissemble. 'If you do not succeed on the Pathway then it would be our wish to examine Vince and uncover the secrets of his mindstate such we can build weapons capable of defending ourselves, or even to attack the Exta pre-emptively.'

*Is there any chance of that working?*

Joy instructed Sargon to produce simulations and forecasts of utilising Vince's mindstate to make weapons both with, and without, breaching Concordat rules. The answers that came back were partially clear; if Enslaved Sentients were allowed then Biologicals could possibly be successfully defended, but, without Enslaved Sentients the weapons would be useless.

*I won't enslave billions of Newborns.*

**I like the answer, but I wonder where the decisioning comes from. Are you over-compensating based on your son being a Newborn?**

*Does it matter?*

'My own assessment,' said Joy focusing on Jinfor, 'is that this would not work. The Onari will join with the Exta and we will be crushed.'

'It depends on how good the weapons we make are,' said Jinfor. 'But I say this only if you are unsuccessful on the Pathway. As Klav you will be all we need.'

*Not by my calculations.*

*If the Exta get these powers, a single Klav will not be enough.*

'You must walk the Pathway now.' Another member of the Council had stepped forward. Sargon provided an information overlay that told Joy their name was Mdoug of the clan Hrse; they were Ractlik. 'Klav must act now. Biological settlements, deep space mining colonies, and exploration vessels are going missing every day.'

*Plus, I hear of reports of Abstractor Hives being attacked.*

**It is rare, but not unknown, for the Exta to attack Hives for additional substrate.**

'If and when I will walk the Pathway is a subject for later,' said Joy. 'Are all here sure that Biologicals should stay and defend? The alternative is to have a structured exodus.'

'We cannot leave Sargon,' said Jinfor, a mixture of outrage and incomprehension, plastered across his face.

From his holographic plinth, High Prelate Oksana interrupted. 'Like Jinfor, I recoil in horror at the hundreds of billions of Biologicals killed in the Second Hunt. However, whereas stay and defend is the will of the Council, my personal view is that we should be preparing for an exodus – if the Exta do find the secret then Klav may be unable to protect all Biologicals.'

Jinfor spluttered. 'Please forgive the High Prelate's sacrilege. Klav is all we need, now and always.'

'No offence taken,' said Joy.

**Oksana has always been a strong proponent of Biological exploration and colonisation. One of the more forward-looking members of the Council of the Devoted.**

**Also worth noting, only a few billion were killed in the Second Hunt … the hundreds of billions number is KOF propaganda.**

'High Prelate Oksana,' said Joy. 'Putting aside whether I could, or could not, defend Biologicals, am I correct that you have always favoured exploration and colonisation?'

Oksana bowed. 'Candidate, you are well informed. We should be leaving our mark on the galaxy, rediscovering our passion for creation … albeit not creating Sentients, but of tributes to the Divine – giant engineering works that say *we were here* … the Cascade, the Titan of Golsha.'

Jinfor, hopping from side to side, interrupted. 'But first we must ensure survival. The Candidate must walk the Pathway.'

Oksana acknowledged the point with a wave of the tip of one of his tentacles. 'Of course, and given we cannot trust the intentions or capabilities of the Onari … I align with the will of the council.'

*Is this a pre-arranged show?*

356

From the facial tics, speech patterns, but mostly from general EM emanations across the surface of Oksana's skull and body, Sargon confirmed that matching to its database of Octagel physiology, Oksana was not being entirely truthful. Sargon went on to confirm that Jinfor believed everything they were saying.

*So, what is the exact lie that Oksana is telling?*

Again, Sargon asked for a Concordat breach permission and Joy could feel the RST weaves ready to reach out and create a digital twin of Oksana's mindstate.

*Vince would be devastated if I did that. Permission not granted.*

`I'd be a little more reassured if you decided not to do this abhorrent thing based on your own values rather than what a loved one may think of you.`

'Candidate,' said Jinfor. 'It is imperative for the sake of Biologicals everywhere that you fulfil your duty and walk the Pathway of Devotion.'

*Does it give me any more power?*

`It gives you moral power over the Knights of the Faith. But it does not allow you to draw any deeper from Sargon's abilities. The Pathway is supposed to reinforce within each Klav that they are the servant rather than the master; but my experience, in practice and from reading the histories, is that when this healthy attitude shines forth, it is almost always something the Candidate brings to the Pathway rather than learns from it.`

*Should I walk it?*

`If you do not complete the Pathway, then the Biologicals will not follow you – and every order you give will need to be given as a threat.`

357

*I understand.*

'Thank you,' said Joy. 'I will think deeply on your request about the Pathway of Devotion. You will get an answer within a day.'

Disappointment rippled around the room, but as one they bowed and offered their thanks before filing out.

# CHAPTER 36

With his surveillance receivers on maximum sensitivity, Vince analysed the RST footprints of the five hundred Onari escort as they arrived through gateways a few thousand kilometres behind him. Although very brief, definite vibrations in space-time preceded the arrival of each incoming gateway.

*Microsecond warnings.*

Ever since his kidnap, Vince had been running simulations of RST attacks and defences. He saw how the Exta WarHives had used RST to both collapse Chi's escape tunnel and disrupt the arrival of the Onari reinforcements.

*I need that capability too.*

*And it will need to be a complex semi-autonomous process if I'm to defend myself against hundreds of arrivals per second.*

*What if it's more than hundreds per second?*

Vince knew he had enough spare substrate in his squad-ship to triple his size, but that still wouldn't be enough against a truly massed Exta attack.

*Escape will be the best option for survival.*

*And that means phase-skipping.*

**Welcome, Newborn. I am Maz.**

Vince opened a communications channel. 'I am Vince.'

'I am to be your guide,' said Maz.

'Thank you,' said Vince. 'Are the arrangements with the Hive all made?'

'They are expecting you.'

Having set his EM receptors to passive receipt only, Vince sucked up the data concerning Maz.

*His patterns match Jan very closely.*

'Did you know any of Jan, Chi, or Aug?' asked Vince.

'Did Jarrus not tell you?' said Maz. 'I contributed the majority mind-state to Jan when he was created, this was many hundreds of years ago.'

Vince reviewed what he had learned about the process of Onari reproduction.

*Onari are the result of multiple-host mitoses. A new Onari is created by a group of parents who each provide copies of certain parts of their own mindstate. It is the one and only time when duplication of mindstate is allowed, and the volumes of the mindstate copied is limited. A single Onari, the primary, will provide forty percent and ten other Onari will provide smaller amounts each, always leaving twenty percent empty, which grows 'organically' – lol.*

'They all fought hard to protect me,' said Vince.

'I am glad,' said Maz. 'Are you sure that none of them was taken?'

'I am sure,' said Vince. 'If captured, do the Exta force-convert captured Onari?'

'It has been known, but mostly the substrate is cleansed and reused.'

'That is gravest sacrilege,' said Vince. 'And yet, the Onari only defend themselves non-lethally. Why?'

'An interesting question,' said Maz. 'The answer is simple. Our beliefs hold that life is sacred.'

'Even in defence of life?'

'Especially in defence of life. One's principles are easy to keep to when they are not being tested.'

'I understand the logic of that argument.'

*But not its conclusion.*

Maz broadcast to the group of five hundred that they were setting off and with the other Onari arranged around Vince in a defensive shell, they accelerated toward the Abstractor Hive. 'I believe that you and our new Klav are about to depart on a pilgrimage.'

'Primarily we're running away from the Exta. Have you been on a pilgrimage?' asked Vince, aware that for Onari, pilgrimages were not always one-way trips.

'I have completed what Biologicals may describe as a taster session,' said Maz. 'The difference between a taster session and full pilgrimage is only the intent to return … although many argue that the having no intent to return is the whole point and there is no such thing as a taster.'

'And what is the difference between a pilgrimage and typical Onari activity?'

'On a pilgrimage one has no assigned tasks.'

'Is it important to be travelling through unexplored space?'

'No,' said Maz. 'Whether someone has been to that part of the galaxy before is of no consequence. Seeing something new is not considered of increased value. Being the first to see an asteroid descend through the gas clouds of a newly forming planet does not make it any the more wondrous. This life is a journey not a competition. The point of the pilgrimage is simple immersion with no goals. I am mindful that you have been raised by Biologicals and so you probably have a predisposition for *doing things*.'

*I was raised by wolves …*

'How do Biologicals typically cope with pilgrimages?' asked Vince. 'Do they do okay … mentally and physically? Particularly, if they are encouraged to have nothing to do.'

'The pilgrims adapt.'

'Witnessing life ineffable.'

There was a pause from Maz. 'Are you mocking me?'

'I genuinely was not. I was trying to build a connection with you.'

'Yes, the Biologicals that join us are fulfilling the Divine's wish that we should be immersed in light ineffable.'

'But recruitment isn't going too well.'

'We would not use the word recruit, but yes. In the far distant past, there were many multi-species pilgrimages but since the arrival of Klav we get few volunteers. There's usually an influx in the wake of an Exta atrocity; not that we welcome those as recruitment drives.'

'And after the Shattering?'

'After the Shattering a large influx of Biological pilgrims joined pilgrimages, but that number went to zero with the attacks on Numantia.'

Vince reflected on humanity, and their obsessive desire to explore and colonise Earth. He could imagine them filling thousands of Onari pilgrimage ships every day – people desperately to see *what was out there*.

*Although, humanity has been the apex predator on Earth for sixty thousand years or more. Whereas, out here, Biologicals are the hunted second class citizens.*

With nothing more to say to Maz on the subject, Vince returned to his main concern.

*Phase-skipping.*

**=07& &.>/"" 42**/

**=07& &.>/"" 42**/

A repeated signal from inside Aug's substrate bounced against one of Vince's boundary walls.

Vince passed the signal through multiple analyses but could not find any meaning. He repeated the signal back to Aug but got nothing in return.

*It could have been a fluke.*

*I may have 'misheard' the data.*

For the next few seconds, Vince pulsed tens of thousands of combinations of messages, images, and information on the boundary – replaying conversations they'd had, listing information that Vince had gleaned about Aug.

Nothing.

*Why am I doing this?*

*I already know that Aug was impossible to save.*

*I tried everything.*

*And failed.*

*Unhelpful. Risk of unnecessary negative thoughts.*

*Delete 'And failed.'*

*Input 'Aug was impossible to save.'*

*I'll will submit the remains of him to the Abstractors.*

Vince prepared his plan as they coasted toward the Abstractor Hive.

Maz signalled to Vince. 'I will come no closer. Their presence sullies the Divine. An individual valuing the knowledge of the fundamental frequency and amplitude of a single wavelength of light is infinitely preferable than an unthinking automaton having catalogued the entire galaxy atom by atom.'

'Thank you for the escort,' said Vince coasting onwards and really quite pleased that Maz's faith would keep him away from the Hive.

The Hive was an enormous single mindstate held inside a steel ball one hundred metres in diameter. Internally, it had a complex integrated power, cooling, and cleaning system. Externally, its surface bristled with sensor arrays designed to absorb different types of signals. Interspersed around the surface were forty-six Onari single-occupancy ships that Maz had already explained were either Hive attendants or potential joiners.

Vince manoeuvred himself up to an empty dock and attached a simple secure communications channel. As per the usual safety procedures, he used a mirror projection process to ensure that no data could be introduced into his own mindstate.

Opening his sensors, it took Vince a little while, in conjunction with Maz's schematics, to understand what he was looking at; the substrate inside was liquid – a great morass of swirling energy and thought.

This Hive had a mindstate volume equivalent to nine thousand three hundred and seventy-two Onari; and the ongoing energy fluctuations surging around the Hive indicated the mindstate was working hard with transient egos appearing, calculating, sometimes conversing, and then dying.

*Hundreds of transient egos appear to be alive at any one time.*

*There are some storage areas for the recording of new information.*

*Some of the storage areas are constantly being overwritten, others appear to have some protections.*

Vince followed the patterns of the swirls and watched as a transient ego bubbled into existence. But as a visitor, all Vince could do was passively signal, *I am here* to all of them. There was no mechanism that he could use to signal to any particular transient ego.

The ego he was watching disappeared.

*How do I submit Aug's remains to the Hive?*

After a while, a transient ego pinged the communications interface onto Vince's docking site.

**You are life. I am life. We live.**

'I am Vince,' replied Vince.

**You are Hive.**

As the ego projected its response, it also appeared to be trying to connect a two-way data flow onto Vince's data interface.

*Hacking me?*

Vince checked again that the interface would not allow the Hive access to his own substrate.

*They cannot access me.*

*But only ten centimetres of steel are stopping them from physically dragging me into their substrate.*

*Or they could simply use an RST gateway to suck me in.*

364

Vince's only reassurance came from the fact there were no records of a Hive ever doing it.

*Not that there are records of anything in the Onari world. All I know is that Jarrus and Maz have assured me that Hives don't do that. But they said it in between cursing the very nature of the Abstractor Hives and calling them abominations.*

Satisfied it was an unmitigable risk and he would simply accept it, Vince replied, 'I am Vince. Do you have another name?'

**You are Hive.**

*Again, I am called Hive.*

*Maybe they don't recognise other lifeforms as different.*

*Maybe they can see some aspect of Aug which looks to them like I have multiple subconsciouses.*

Tiny vibrations registered on Vince's RST attenuators. Somewhere deep within the Abstractor substrate, a process – thinking or unthinking – was doing the equivalent of gently shaking him.

*Like an Earth MRI?*

It was not dissimilar to what he could do with other Sentients. So far, he'd only ever passively observed electromagnetic boundary emissions when he built up a generalised picture of Jan, Aug, and Chi. But he'd worked out how to use EM induction analysis, whereby he pulsed varying stimulations into a given mindstate and deduced internal processing from the returns that he stimulated.

**You are Hive.**

As the transient ego said the same phrase for a third time, there was a swirling in its mindstate. The currents, which had been patterned and purposeful before, now showed elements of chaotic behaviour.

The ego was unwinding. A microsecond later, it was gone.

*What did I expect?*

Watching both the substrate and other visitors, Vince continued to absorb information from around the Hive. Unfortunately, although there were transient egos communicating with other visitors, without actively hacking into their communications channels, he could only confirm that communications were happening, he could not hear what they were saying, could not understand their goals, or find out what they achieved in the conversations.

*On Earth I could hack anyone at any time.*

Vince had expected to be able to speak to an 'Elder' – someone who represented the Hive – to ask them to take Aug into their care. Of course, he hadn't been able to talk to Jarrus about it because Vince knew that Onari doctrine would be entirely disapproving that he had copied parts of Aug's mindstate.

*Should I ask Maz?*

A new communication request came in on an open channel. He queried its origin. It was from an Onari attendant attached to the Hive on the far side of the sphere.

'Hello,' said Vince. 'I am Vince.'

**We all know who you are. I am Tixe.**

For the next second, Tixe explained they were a Hive attendant and definitely not a candidate for joining the Hive – who were sad individuals and below contempt.

*Nice empathy.*

Mostly the attendants like Tixe worked on sourcing data for the Hive because, although it had immense processing power, its lack of ego meant it was not always able to feed itself when complexity of linear thought was required to access information. Although the concept of stored data was also an abomination to Onari like Tixe, they consoled themselves that they were telling the Hive such that the Hive would know … and mostly they then ascribed that data as their own sacred information too. It could be uncomfortable for the Onari attendant if the requested data set was enormous and purposeless.

'Why do you do this if you disagree with it?' asked Vince. 'Are you not seen by other Onari to be supporting a blasphemy?'

It is true that Hive Attendants are rare in the Onari population, but we are free to choose … and we choose to help.

*Freedom of the individual.*

*And out of seven hundred billion Onari, surely some would make that choice.*

'Do they speak to you?'

Some do, but no more than in the manner that they have already spoken to you. Those that live longer are the ones that ask for more information. Most of the souls that arise are short lived.

*Souls?*

*Another set of values.*

This Hive has an above-average interest in the outside world. But its interest is academic and does not extend to stewardship if you are here to ask for help against the Exta.

'That is not why I'm here.'

How can I help you?

'How does someone join?'

Sacrilege and blasphemy.

'But you just spoke of the souls that arise, that implied spiritual value.'

To emerge as a transient ego from a Hive is of great value. They live, they observe the ineffable, and then they die taking with them their observations to submit to the Divine. They are Witnesses.

**But to join a Hive is sacrilege. It is the destruction of the Witness.**

'But the information they have when they join is merged with the Hive.'

**The sacred knowledge they hold is destroyed when they join.**

'Really?' Vince was sure that he had heard differently, and that Onari ships interfacing with the Hive dissolve into it over a period of years, slowly losing their own permanence … but also providing some of their self to the Hive.

**Academic opinion is divided.**

**My truth is chosen.**

*There's no such thing as truth.*

Of course, Vince knew that he could monitor Onari submission for a few years and take detailed measurements of the mindstates involved; he would soon be able to tell what level of information was retained in the process. It was also clear that the Onari view that observation of the mindstate was heresy would ensure that they – the Onari – had never done, and would never do, those types of experiments.

*Or they have done them and got the 'wrong' result and so deleted the evidence.*

*Remind me of anyone?*

*Which truth would I prefer?*

*Die immediately, lights out, and my physical self is repurposed for the greater good.*

*Or, as I was told, slowly dissolve into the substrate but in the process be convinced that some of my memories and knowledge are contributing to the eternal whole. Although … these Hives individually have such narrow fields of study that it is unlikely anything I knew would contribute meaningfully.*

'Can I submit a tiny part of my mind-state as a gesture of respect?'

**There is nothing to stop you. The Hive will not understand the gesture. It only**

understands its own questions. Perhaps a transient ego will take note for a few seconds. But this is very much something you are doing for yourself.

Obviously, and I don't need to tell you this, but your action would be a blasphemy. However, the free will of the individual is paramount, and no one will try to stop you.

*I came here to submit Aug to a Hive.*

*And yet I hesitate.*

*Why?*

He searched his memories, fully aware that his use of internal self-nullification meant he would not remember things he had determined should not be remembered.

*Aug has … RST experience.*

*But he gave me the file; I have it now.*

*I looked for more.*

*There was none.*

*Am I worried that something individual of Aug still lives?*

*And that I could save him.*

*But my sense is that either Aug is in terrible pain, or he isn't alive.*

*In both cases, joining the Hive will be a relief.*

*For me…*

*I am a good person.*

Aware that he was prevaricating, Vince still looked back as the mind-state soup from which the egos were bubbling up. They were born, lived, and died. He got no sense of any distress just before they disappeared. They simply returned to the Hive and were gone.

*Not gone … reintegrated with the whole.*

*Much nicer way of thinking about it.*

*But Hives ascribe no value to the individual.*

*And that must be a relief from feeling a need to be of consequence.*

369

*Surrender to the whole … the larger cause.*

Decision made.

*Murderer.*

> *Unhelpful.*
>
> *Delete 'Murderer.'*
>
> *Input 'Aug was impossible to save.'*

Vince started manipulating his substrate to physically partition off Aug such that they could be easily passed into the Hive.

**Vince!**

It was Maz.

*I have been found out.*

**We must go. The Exta are here.**

# CHAPTER 37

Less than a millisecond after Vince had been told about the Exta arrival at Cidelus, Joy contacted him.

> You have to leave now. Go full speed to the spot I dropped you, that's my limit to extract you by RST gateway.

'Agreed,' replied Vince.

*Although I still have enough time to submit Aug.*

*Not the typical load process as described by Tixe.*

*But I can use RST to displace Aug's substrate into the Hive holding area.*

*And then we go.*

The Exta arriving at the standard Cidelus ingress point were many hundreds of millions of kilometres away; just on full power they wouldn't get to his mother's special egress point until he was long gone.

*But they will phase-skip.*

*Mum can disrupt that.*

*I still have time.*

Performing final checks on the substrate, Vince simultaneously opened RST surveillance tunnels close to the central star so that he could measure the arrival and force disposition of the Exta.

Tens of thousands Exta had arrived at the standard ingress point about halfway between the planet of Cidelus and the central star.

Sargon was in the process of tearing them apart, a few thousand every second.

The problem was, as quickly as Sargon killed, more were arriving. And many thousands of WarHives were focusing only on disrupting Sargon attacks in order to defend their incoming colleagues.

Space-time around the central star vibrated in all directions as Onari also flooded into the system. Within a fraction of a second, three hundred thousand Onari had arrived and formed into teams, half of which immediately headed for Cidelus planet, whilst the other half engaged with the Exta.

'We must go now,' said Maz. 'There are irregularities with the Exta arrivals.'

'What irregularities?'

'I am asking,' said Maz.

*The same old Onari issue.*

*Sharing of knowledge between two living things is a holy moment of intense wonder of discovery.*

*It feels like a monumental waste of time designed by creatures who live forever and have no predators.*

Vince forced himself to stop thinking about the matter; but, over by Cidelus, the other main problem with the Onari was obvious – whilst the Exta were striking out with deadly force, the Onari were using gravitational warping to gently shepherd the Exta into holding groups.

Suddenly five hundred Onari currently heading for Cidelus were shredded by intense RST activity.

*What?*

*Impossible?*

*There are no Exta anywhere near.*

*Did mum do that?*

Vince ran the analysis.

Joy contacted him again.

**Literally WTF. Get out of there now. There are new Exta on their way. Ones that operate at one hundred times the power of Exta WarHives.**

Receiving the message, Vince plotted a course back to the target egress point from which Joy could snatch him and detached from the Hive.

*One hour at full power given I can accelerate the whole way there.*

*It all depends on whether Sargon can interfere with the Exta ability to phase-skip my way.*

More Exta craft flooded into the system, considerably closer to Cidelus itself than an Exta WarHive could manage by stable RST gateway.

*Oh shit.*

*I knew I felt something during the kidnap.*

*They clearly got my ego-killing secret.*

Maz and the other members of the Onari escort formed up around Vince, as they all accelerated in earnest toward the egress point.

Tens of thousands of the new enlarged Exta craft – *ExtaHives* – aimed directly for Vince and accelerated.

*Probably too much to hope that they simply accelerate in real space such that I am long gone.*

Simultaneously, as if listening to Vince's thoughts, the ExtaHives, accompanied by an equal number of *regular* WarHives, started to phase-skip toward him whilst all around them space-time bubbled as Sargon tried to interfere with their ability to travel.

Unfortunately, similar to the tactic used elsewhere, a third of the ExtaHives were solely tasked with disrupting Sargon attacks.

Back at the central star ingress point, the Onari – now hundreds of thousands of them – continued their passive defence approach consisting of curving the space-time around the Exta to such an extent that the Exta engines failed; the sheer numbers of Onari were making a difference but the problem remained that those Exta – the ones in orbit around the central star – were not part of the force that was either hunting Vince or those intent on attacking the planet itself.

As Vince watched, Joy clearly understood the problem, as one thousand at a time, Sargon picked up Onari squad-ships and moved them by RST gateway into orbit around the planet so that they could defend the Biological population itself.

Simultaneously, she also moved some Onari squad-ships much further out to the special Sargon ingress-egress point halfway between the Abstractor Hive and the planet – the place to where Vince was racing.

*How many Onari can she move to the Sargon ingress-egress?*

*The Exta are disrupting her weaves.*

'We should phase-skip,' Vince said to Maz.

'It's dangerous. Even if we do not bubble ourselves off, we would soon be split up by the uncertainty of where we re-enter real space. We would be highly vulnerable.'

'We're vulnerable even if we're all together. The Onari approach of softly shepherding Exta around whilst being torn apart is not working.'

Maz didn't answer.

'We must phase-skip.' The ExtaHives had all completed a series of their own phase-skips and were no more than ten minutes away from Sargon's ingress-egress point, whilst for Vince it would be five times that time to get there. By the time Vince and his escort arrived, there would be thousands of ExtaHives waiting to tear them apart. Vince gave Maz the analysis.

'I do not know how to phase-skip,' said Maz. 'I will ask.'

'You should have asked the moment the Exta appeared.'

*Must ask Joy.*

*No, I got this.*

*I'll give Maz a couple more seconds.*

*Why?*

*She thinks that I can handle it.*

*I'll give Maz a few more seconds.*
*It would take her triple that time to tell me anyway.*
*A few seconds is a long time in the Sentient world.*
*Don't I know it.*
*She has to think that I can handle it.*
   *Unhelpful.*
   *Delete 'She has to think that I can handle it.'*
   *Input 'Maz will come through with the information soon.'*

Surveillance alarms within Vince's internal processes notified him that KOF Sword Interceptors had taken off from the planet's surface.

*Brave but unlikely to last more than a picosecond.*

'Can we help the KOF?'

*At least tell them to turn around.*

*Surely, they're not coming to help me?*

'We are helping them.'

The first KOF Interceptor disappeared in a shower of subatomic particles as one of the ExtaHives arriving in orbit above Cidelus used RST weaponry to rip it apart.

'How?' asked Vince, he hadn't even noticed whether the Onari had tried to disrupt the attack.

'Offering them sanctuary,' said Maz.

*Not as good as ripping into the Exta.*

Vince didn't push it.

As they continued to accelerate toward the ingress-egress point, Vince partitioned off a chunk of his substrate and ran simulations pertaining to phase-skipping. But got nothing useable. The calculations required knowledge of singularity topology that he simply didn't have – *no-one on Earth had.*

'Maz! We need that phase-skip info.'

'Soon.'

Next, Vince set up the new area of his mindstate with a dedicated semi-autonomous defender program that's role was to interrupt any localised RST activity that he had not initiated.

Opening new RST surveillance micro-tunnels, Vince tried to assess the capabilities of the ExtaHives in orbit around Cidelus. He'd have preferred to look at the ones about to attack him, but they were phase-skipping, and he couldn't get a lock on them.

In any case, the new ExtaHives were about eighty times larger than a single Exta Scout.

*Which means we'll all be crushed.*

*Unless I phase-skip out of here.*

**Come to us we will protect you.**

The Onari message was broadcast across all channels. At the same time, the Onari heading for Cidelus started to reconfigure their physical layouts, creating what Vince knew to be pilgrimage ships.

*Is now the right time?*

*Your Exta cousins are bombarding the planet and tearing apart the KOF Interceptors.*

*Talk about tone deaf.*

'Sadly, there will be little uptake,' said Maz. 'The trust is gone.'

*No shit … long gone.*

Around the planet, a squadron of KOF Sword interceptors released a volley of phasing-skipping anti-matter missiles, but the ExtaHives deflected them with ease and shattered the Interceptors.

It would have been an unfair fight even if just one of these new ExtaHives had faced fifty KOF Interceptors.

As a sideshow, some of Jarrus' Onari swooped in toward the ExtaHive that had just struck and attempted to shepherd it away from its current orbit. The first few Onari were ignored, but as space-time curved around the ExtaHive it struck back, cutting an Onari squad-ship in half and pushing another one away at speed. Then the ExtaHive launched another attack at a new squadron of KOF Interceptors.

Anger bubbled within Vince.

*The Onari should be doing more.*

*What can I do?*

*Nothing.*

Already, the orbits above Cidelus were dominated by Exta and any Onari that meaningfully attempted to interfere with an Exta was shredded.

*It's too late for Cidelus but the other planets…*

*I need to weaponise my mindstate and share my 'code' with the KOF.*

*Thousands of enslaved Vince Defender programs.*

*Jarrus would never approve but would he attack the Biologicals?*

*How would Mum feel?*

*It's my decision.*

*Is it?*

Focusing on the actual thought of copying himself and then enslaving those clones as eternal defenders threatened to send Vince into a mental spin.

*Escape first, then worry about the other planets.*

*Escape.*

*Phase-skip.*

'Maz! Now!'

At that moment, Maz opened a private secure link and explained to Vince how to phase-skip.

Vince opened a large, partitioned substrate area and ran a million practices, being careful to ensure the input variable set-up did not risk bubbling himself off in space-time.

Then he initiated his first jump.

The universe disappeared from existence.

Blank.

Dark.

Nothing.

*Phew!*

Spat out into real space, a wave of subatomic particles washed over his receptors, but a moment later Vince had fixed his position.

He had five more phase-skips to do, that was all he needed to get to a place in space-time with enough curvature that Joy could pull him out.

He jumped again.

*Four to go.*

He jumped again.

*Three to go.*

Looking around, Vince could see the truth in Maz's words. Although the five hundred Onari escorts had tried to stay close to him, they were all lagging behind – Vince's superior processing capability meant he could make a deeper incision into subspace, whilst still keeping safe, and make a longer phase-skip. Not only were they further from him, they were also spread out amongst themselves, the uncertain nature of the calculations meaning that fifty or sixty-thousand-kilometre differences in jumps for identical craft were not unusual.

*Keep going.*

*Leave your escorts?*

*They're not the targets.*

*The Exta won't hurt them.*

Jump number four failed. As Vince tried to open a hole in space-time, the onrushing Exta used their own RST capability to collapse it.

*And they're here.*

Checking his calculations and position, the news was bad.

The Exta, both ExtaHives and the smaller WarHives, had phase-skipped five million kilometres past the location that Vince needed to get to. They'd stopped and were now forming up into a barricade millions of kilometres high and wide.

Between the ships, space-time bubbled and curved.

They were preparing a giant net.

*Turn around and run into deep space?*

*They'll catch me.*

*Those ExtaHives can phase-skip further and quicker.*

*Punch through their net?*

*It's my only chance.*

# CHAPTER 38

Duty called again.

Having untangled herself from Yuno only a moment earlier, Kubli sped through a travel tube to the Sword muster point. The details had not been formally broadcast across the whole population, however the news on one of the Sword frequencies confirmed Cidelus was being evacuated.

Yuno had wished her good luck about fifty times as Kubli had put on her exosuit.

*And she'd said … Klav will keep you safe.*

*But it's not Klav, it's the Candidate.*

*And they've been hacked by the Exta.*

And to become Klav, the Exta traitor would have to walk the Pathway of Devotion.

*And that is where I will strike.*

*But not today; today, I will support a full planetary evacuation.*

Both the Sword and volunteers from the civilian population practised the scenario every few years on each planet. The logic was straight forward, no planet could hold out against a fleet of Exta WarHives and so, if under continuous attack, the population would evacuate to Bastion where, even since the Shattering, the Exta would not go.

*We must distract the Exta to allow as many Biologicals as possible to escape.*

As she travelled through the tube network, Kubli checked the news services; Cidelus civilians were already flooding into the lower levels of Bastion via large semi-permanent RST gateways. These were highly numerous and relatively simple to operate as each one of them was always opened between the same two points, and the points had been specifically chosen, and manipulated, to have as near to identical gravitational potential as each other.

*From deep underground over there to deep underground over here.*

*And we'll be the only ones sticking our heads above ground during the attack.*

A new set of messages were channelled through to all members of the Sword currently being deployed to Cidelus; the Exta RST were focusing their attacks on the evacuation gateways and were having notable successes; their RST capability appeared to have increased five or ten times in power.

*The Kraken has awoken.*

The travel tube swerved violently; Kubli's stomach lurched. The previous night had been a late one – Yuno going hard on every stimulant she could find, toasting Klav constantly, and getting into semi-physical semi-philosophical debates with the vocal minority who felt that civilisation had moved on and didn't need Klav anymore.

*The people of Cidelus do now.*

*A real one.*

A buzz in Kubli's head preceded a secure communication from Oksana coming direct into Kubli's implanted cranial augments. 'Spawn. Accept new orders. Oksana.'

The accompanying message contained the location of a weapons cache deep inside the Citadel.

Kubli recalibrated her position in the travel tube and descended to the new location. Moments later, she stood in front of a set of thick steel doors guarded by twenty Ractlik heavy infantry.

On all sides of the antechamber, the walls were studded with pulse weapons and targeting stacks.

*All sizes, but mostly large.*

Even having seen a ShockKnight in full flow, these auto-guns and EM pulse-bathers looked like they would melt anything unauthorised.

'Not that anyone could get down here, let alone through those doors,' said Kubli, speaking aloud but quietly to settle her nerves.

Oksana transmitted again. 'Spawn. The doors are to keep things in, not out. Oksana.'

Kubli shivered, the adamantine limbs of her exosuit instinctively retracting a fraction.

Clearly having received their own orders, the Ractlik infantry stood to the side as she approached, and the doors opened onto a cavern whose far end disappeared into the gloom.

As Kubli crossed the threshold, a portion of the weapon store's manifest beamed into her suit. She read the list.

*23 ShockKnights (currently deactivated)*

*8 Exta (currently subdued unconscious)*

*12,329 antimatter phase-skipping missiles*

*277 Sleepers (Marks 1 thru' 6)*

*54 wide band pico-effectors with semi-autonomous targeting*

Accessing a control panel on her suit, Kubli authorised the remote delivery drones to start transporting the antimatter missiles out of the vault. The AM charge on each missile was the size of her head and could vaporise a cubic kilometre of iron.

*And there are ten thousand of them.*

The weaponry was enough to destroy all life in any given planetary system, but it wasn't obvious how it could be deployed to destroy nine billion Exta.

*Widely spread across the galaxy with no home base.*

Again, Oksana communicated. 'Spawn. Only bring three pico-effector weapons.'

382

Fighting down the desire to retch, Kubli acknowledged the message. The pico-effector weapons scrambled the mindstates and were an abomination to the Divine; even though Exta were murderous vermin, all Octagel had a visceral distaste for anything remotely connected to mind control.

*And they don't work against Exta Scouts which are by far the most numerous of our enemy.*

Kubli dismissed the thought; Oksana would have good reasons. Taking three of the pico-effector boxes, she left the depot.

'Remember your truth.'

A pain seared through Kubli's skull.

*The Candidate must die.*

*This is my truth.*

On re-entering the travel tube, Kubli went to the Sword hangar and was immediately directed to her KOF Interceptor. There was no time for pre-flight checks, and hoping that the ground staff knew their business, Kubli performed the barest checks before installing the pico-weaponry and climbing into the cockpit.

Just about to request launch, the lights went out as she and her craft were snatched directly by RST through subspace.

The gateway deposited Kubli in orbit above the planet of Cidelus, a feat of RST so far beyond Biological capability that Kubli had to instruct her suit to administer a short-term sedative; of course, she had heard of such things – the Dynasty of Klav had done much more but that was in the realm of legend ... this had just happened to her.

*And from an Exta traitor.*

*Caressed by the Kraken herself.*

383

Kubli focused.

*Situation report?*

Cidelus was now swarming with Exta, and they clearly had a lowly view of the martial capability of Biologicals because all the KOF Interceptors were being ignored except when they had the audacity to directly attack.

The Exta were arranged in three main battle groups: the largest Exta battle group was sitting in a high orbit both attacking targets on Cidelus and disrupting all RST activity in the area. The next largest group was accelerating away from the planet toward the Abstractor Hives, and the final group was in the process of harvesting rocks off Cidelus' only moon to launch down Cidelus' gravity well.

Kubli scanned the Cidelus surface; on most other planets, all Biologicals lived very deep underground but on Cidelus there were factions who ostentatiously lived on the surface, they would be vulnerable to direct beam weapon attacks now.

The scan showed no lifeforms on the surface.

*Already killed, or evacuated in time?*

Kubli didn't bother checking, the largest Exta battlegroup – with over ten thousand individuals – were using RST attacks directly against the evacuation networks deep under the planet's crust.

*And most of the Exta craft are bigger than WarHives.*

Alarms sounded.

A massive wash of EM radiation flooded the area, with automatic defence processes hardening Kubli's ship and deflecting the worst of the blast.

Three thousand kilometres away, one of the new enlarged Exta – an ExtaHive – had been vapourised by an anti-matter missile.

*Missiles do not get through Exta defences.*

*Even phase-skipping missiles are usually deflected.*

Checking the vicinity, Kubli could see the residue of large RST weaves that had clearly enabled the antimatter missile to get through.

*Sargon must be causing distractions.*

*But why would they kill their own?*

*A larger plot?*

*Internal power struggle?*

Kubli shook her head clear; she had her own job to do.

Analysing the highest volumes of RST activity, Kubli could see the battle was focused in the planet's crust five kilometres below its major cities.

*My orders are simply to disrupt.*

Arbitrarily picking one city – not quite arbitrarily, Yuno had friends there – Kubli identified a cluster of Exta nearby that were attacking its evacuation portals.

Within the group were fifty ExtaHives and three hundred WarHives.

*I won't make the slightest difference.*

*But I have my orders.*

*Perhaps disrupting the Exta for a few seconds will allow more evacuations.*

Kubli scanned the cluster and selected an ExtaHive.

*Time to break the Great Concordat.*

The Great Concordat was not breached without dire cause as Biologicals had historically never wanted to give the Exta a reason to attack and had never wanted to give the Onari a reason to defend with more lacklustre.

*Not that it matters now the Exta are attacking anyway.*

*And the Onari continue with their shepherding.*

The pico-effector returned calibration information on the ExtaHive.

*Liquid shit!*

*It's pure Sentient.*

*No BioCore.*

Unlike the old style WarHives which had BioCore, these new ExtaHives were simple amalgams of one hundred Exta Scouts, all consolidated under a single consciousness.

There was nothing for the Bio specialised pico-effector weapons to scramble. Technically, pico-effector weapons for pure Sentients could be manufactured with the effectors operating at very special frequencies but, as had been found out in the First Hunt, they were far too easy to harden against.

*Find a WarHive?*

Without a better plan, Kubli identified one of the peripheral WarHives and calibrated the pico-effectors onto it. She wasn't quite close enough.

Kubli accelerated toward the WarHive.

*Fire!*

The weapon used a combination of multiple RST attacks that opened fifty tiny gateways in and around the WarHive. Through each of those gateways, a thousand EM pulses set up inductive fields.

Not waiting for the result, Kubli turned her craft hard and accelerated away.

Within a fraction of a second her engines were straining against what felt like a surge of space-time flowing like a current over and around the Interceptor.

Ten metres away from every part of Kubli's hull, space-time curved up to seventy percent.

*They noticed me.*

*Did it even work?*

Countermeasures from the Interceptor triggered automatically, but against the power of the ExtaHives there was nothing to be done; the RST attenuators on Kubli's hull fired but curvature increased to eighty percent.

Ninety percent.

Darkness.

Kubli. This is Joy. I have moved you away
from the Exta attack as I have done for
as many KOF as I can. But I need your
help. Please distract the Exta that are
attacking Vince. I will defend you as
best I can. But they are all at the limit
of my reach. Please.

*How can I help an Exta traitor?*

*Why would they be attacking their own?*

*Stop.*

*Do not try to understand the infinitely twisted mind of the Kraken.*

*Of course I will not help.*

Oksana buzzed. 'Spawn. Help them. We swim in deep
oceans and sometimes are required to play the wider game.'

*I will obey.*

'I will try,' said Kubli, replying to Joy. 'But my weapons are
ineffectual again these ExtaHives.'

There are some standard WarHives, a
distraction may be enough. Do not venture
too close. I will do my best to protect
you.

*I need to be close for them to work.*

Again, darkness – Joy had simply snatched her into
subspace and sent her toward the Exta battle group that was
heading for the Abstractor Hives.

Kubli's instruments recalibrated.

The battle group of Exta were millions of kilometres
ahead of her and broadly stationary. They had created a
massive wall of highly curved space-time, which Vince, with
the remains of his Onari escort far behind, was heading
directly toward.

*He needs to cross that line to get to the egress point from which*
*Sargon can snatch him away.*

But to get to the egress point Vince would have to cross the Exta lines with tens of thousands of ExtaHives and WarHives.

Kubli checked her weapons inventory; she did have phasing antimatter missiles; they could be launched as distractions.

*But they won't be much of a distraction.*

*The pico-effectors?*

*Better close the gap.*

Accelerating toward the Exta battle group, Kubli's instruments showed tell-tale indications that the Exta were probing her with RST surveillance micro-tunnels. However, as fast as they were opening, Joy was clearly collapsing them.

*I have Sargon's attention.*

*Unsurprising given I am doing their work.*

Kubli calculated Vince's trajectory and picked out one of the WarHives on that path.

Priming the pico-effector, she waited; she needed to be closer and there would be no rescue, she was now past where Sargon had deposited her, she had no hope she would be pulled back.

*Am I going to die protecting the progeny of the Exta traitor?*

*Yuno would laugh.*

*Yuno does have a quirky sense of humour.*

*Will she find out?*

*Will I be floating in an unmarked grave?*

*Will I be trapped to slowly decay in an isolated and unreachable bubble of space-time?*

Again, Kubli ordered her suit to calm her down, it would slow her reflexes but against a Sentient she moved like a sea cucumber anyway.

Kubli accelerated.

*One million kilometres.*

*Five hundred thousand.*

388

*Two hundred thousand.*

'Please tell Yuno that I love her.'

At the soonest opportunity that she could, Kubli fired the pico-effectors. Instantly, the semi-autonomous technology opened the requisite RST micro-tunnels and then bathed the WarHive's BioCore in specific wavelengths and frequencies of EM radiation required to scramble its function.

*Any moment I will be crushed by an RST attack.*

But the attack did not come, an open message hit Kubli's comms.

'This is Jarrus, the voice of the Onari. Stop the use of forbidden mindstate alteration technology or the Onari will cease their defence of Biologicals across the galaxy.'

*Really. Biologicals across the galaxy are being ripped apart and you ...*

Kubli's thought was truncated by the arrival of an RST attack that twisted her craft in half, buckling the fuselage and opening holes all along its length.

# CHAPTER 39

By momentarily diverting every ounce of Sargon's power to the rescue, Joy had managed to move the operational range of her RST gateways a few hundred thousand kilometres. It had been enough to save Kubli but was still a million kilometres short of where it needed to be to save Vince.

*And he can't get any closer.*

*I was supposed to protect him.*

*Surely a Klav of old could have plucked him with a single fleeting thought.*

**There are limits.**

'Jarrus,' said Joy, opening comms channel. 'Can you save Vince?'

'We are already doing our best,' replied Jarrus. 'The KOF, however, must stop utilising the pico-effector weaponry. They are an afront to the Divine.'

Joy focused on Sargon, willing it to furnish her with information to support her discussion with Jarrus.

*The KOF are utilising pico-effector weapons that disrupt the Exta mindstates and cause irreparable neural damage. The Onari hate their use.*

*But are they working?*

*Reasonable success but on a tiny scale. Of those already used – seventeen – each of them has incapacitated between zero and two Exta WarHives before the KOF pilot has been destroyed themselves – pico-effector usage is a suicide mission.*

*The KOF still have twenty-three active pico-effector weapons in system.*

Joy replied to Jarrus. 'It is you that must alter your approach. These new ExtaHives are tearing both Biologicals and Onari apart.'

'Our approach will not change.

*The Onari see pico-effector weaponry as a great problem in its own right, but also as a moral gateway to utilising Enslaved Sentients; I tend to agree with them on that point.*

'The use of the pico-weaponry is saving lives at Cidelus,' said Joy, replying to Jarrus.

'Its use is heresy. For countless thousands of years we have begged Biologicals to join us on pilgrimages of wonder to absorb the majesty of the universe in the utter safety of the Onari's embrace. We have been ignored. These deaths are a tragedy, but they are entirely of the Biologicals own doing,' said Jarrus.

'The Exta are entirely to blame for these deaths,' said Joy, feeling her anger rise. 'You cannot blame the Biologicals for not giving up all they know to join you on pilgrimages.'

'It is the price of safety. Deliver yourself unto us and we will succour you.'

*Shit!*

If Joy had needed any other reason to accept that Onari 'technology' lay at the heart of Sargon, she now had it.

*Calm down.*

'I will consider speaking to the KOF,' said Joy. 'But they will not be receptive, the pico-weaponry is saving lives.'

'The patience of the Onari is not limitless.' Jarrus closed the comms channel.

Joy double checked the comms channel was closed. 'I wish I hadn't asked.'

*He was less honest with me when I discussed the Shattering. I did not tell him outright that I planned to destroy Sargon, but I asked him what he would do if Sargon was not around. He said he would protect the Biologicals. I did not*

*ask him how intensely he would do this. I*
*assumed that 'protect' was 'protect'.*

'And all these lives are being lost because Jarrus is so
focused on getting Biologicals to join his pilgrimages. It's
inconceivable.'

*Although ... forgive me ... but you are*
*focusing on saving Vince, and so leaving*
*Sargon to semi-autonomously deal with the*
*evacuations. If you focused entirely on*
*the defence of Cidelus planet, then the*
*bombardment would be less severe and less*
*lives would be lost. Sargon is not*
*infinite, and the splitting of its*
*attention means not all safety procedures*
*are happening. 435 lives have been lost*
*simply from malfunctioned RST gateways. I*
*do not know how many more extra deaths*
*there will be from your lack of focus*
*when the serious bombardment starts.*

*Is this true?*

*Is what true?*

Reminding herself that Sargon could not hear the
Foresighted's speech, Joy reviewed the position on Cidelus.

The Foresighted was correct. Joy had ordered Sargon to
continuously open RST escape gateways as close to Vince as
possible. Given that there were thousands of ExtaHives in
that area, the process was taking a full third of Sargon's
attention. This meant fewer RST weaves defending Cidelus
from bombardment, and fewer planet-side gateways pulling
people across subspace to Bastion.

'If I did nothing then there would be more deaths,' said
Joy.

*If you hadn't created Vince, then there*
*would be none.*

'Unfair. I didn't know the consequences.'

**Life is like that. What is important is
what you do now.**

'I accept that my current actions to save Vince are causing
additional deaths,' said Joy.

*Is there any way to save Vince?*

Less than a second has passed since she had last looked
but he was now very close to the Exta space-time net. And
her own gateways were still opening and shutting at their
limit, a million kilometres too far away.

'I must find a way.'

Joy turned her attention to the KOF. There were now five
hundred KOF Interceptors in orbit around Cidelus but even
those few with pico-effectors were no threat to ExtaHives.

*Could any be used as a distraction? Are there more somewhere else?*

*A further five thousand Interceptors are distributed across forty-three
other planets, spread across twenty-eight planetary systems. None except
Cidelus are currently under attack. Those Interceptors could be recalled
to Cidelus.*

**A hundred thousand Interceptors could do
nothing for Vince.**

'I know,' sad Joy. 'It would simply be sending more
Knights of the Faith to their deaths.'

*And if I gave up on Vince and focused on defending the planet?*

*Fully focussed RST defence of Cidelus whilst stopping the rescue
attempt of Vince, will extend the lifespan of the planet by another few
hours.*

*What does that mean in terms of lives?*

*No ... don't tell me.*

Joy was aware that Vince could ask for knowledge and
then delete both the knowledge and the fact he had ever
asked for it; but that was not possible for humans.

An RST comms gateway opened. A message from Vince
was transferred before the gateway was collapsed.

**Mum. I'm doing my best. I have options.
If I don't make it, I love you. And I**

want you to give my code to the KOF –
screw what Jarrus says – build the
strongest defences you can. Vincent
Cooper.

Joy didn't try to reply for fear of distracting him.
Distracting the on-rushing Exta was another matter;
searching the skies around Cidelus, Joy found a KOF
Interceptor that was yet to fire its pico-effector weapon.

*Screw Jarrus.*

*Duplicate that weapon.*

A thousand moderately sized RST tunnels opened all
around the KOF craft and a million EM fields interrogated
the pico-effector weapon. Within a moment Joy had a
working copy within Sargon; the software was all she needed
as Sargon had both RST attenuators and EM effectors in
abundance. It took a moment to integrate the weapon with
Sargon's arrays.

**This is a dangerous path.**

'Your point is noted.'

**There will always be another Exta. Do you
intend to rewire the brains of any you
disagree with?**

'I'm not rewiring, I'm fighting. And anyway, do you intend
that Biologicals should hide forever?'

**That is what most living things do. To be
seen, is to be eaten.**

'It should be safe to be seen.'

**It is only safe if you're near the top of
the hierarchy tree; as Klav, you are at
the top but the other one hundred and ten
billion Biologicals are a long way down.**

'Again, your point is noted.'

**It's not just precedent. The Onari may
react by stopping defence of Biologicals
across the galaxy.**

'Or they may allow a terrified mother one indulgence.'

Finding a WarHive on station near Cidelus itself, Joy locked onto it with the pico-effector which being a pure 'fire and forget' weapon quickly calibrated itself.

*A benefit of all Exta being clones of each other.*

Joy opened a moderate sized RST tunnel close to the WarHive and fired the pico-effector weapon. Millions of RST micro-tunnels poured out of the weapon, flooding the surface of the WarHive. Next, a fraction of a second later, the EM fields pulsed down those RST micro-tunnels. The EM fields induced tens of thousands of electromagnetic currents inside the WarHive and caused specific frequency attacks fracturing the WarHive's BioCore.

With the BioCore disabled, transient egos from the constituent nine Exta Scouts instantly sprung up and fought for control of the unpartitioned and shared substrate. The result was catastrophic failure of power and all other infrastructure systems.

Before the end of a micro-second had passed the WarHive fell silent in a catatonic state.

A second after that, an alert KOF Interceptor sheared the WarHive in half with a simple point-blank beam weapon shot.

*And if those enslaved BioCores had any semblance of consciousness then we put them out of their misery too.*

Joy had not taken a breath before Jarrus hit her communications channel.

She did not accept the connection.

*Is there any chance of Onari getting hit?*

*No.*

*The KOF pico-effectors are specifically designed to hit the BioCore component of the WarHives.*

**Manipulating fundamental brain function is abhorrent. Jarrus and I agreed on this point.**

395

Joy shook her head clear, the Foresighted was heavily invested in his view given the billions of deaths after the Shattering.

*Now for Vince.*

She opened a series of RST surveillance micro-tunnels as close to the Exta attack group as possible.

*The ones bearing down on Vince.*

Vince was well under a million kilometres away from the space-time net and the space around him pulsed with long range Exta RST attacks.

*Soon the Exta will be able to shear off his engines.*

Joy's screens went blank; the Exta had noticed her surveillance micro-tunnels and had closed them all with sweeping RST countermeasures of their own.

Reopening the micro-tunnels, Joy selected an ExtaHive to attack.

*But ExtaHives don't have BioCores.*

The fact had been lurking at the back of Joy's mind for a moment, now it got heard.

*But hitting a WarHive will not meaningfully disrupt the Exta fleet's actions to capture Vince.*

*Recalibrate the EM emissions for most likely Exta mindstate configurations.*

*The spacecraft skins will be hardened to those sensitive frequencies.*

*So, we breach the skin with tiny RST weaves and then pipe in the EM.*

*All in a fraction of a millisecond.*

Trillions of processes calculated and checked the configurations required to scramble an Exta mindstate. Additionally, Joy performed the analysis to determine how best to breach the craft itself.

Joy returned her attention to the screen showing the target ExtaHive waiting for Vince.

*You want Vince.*

*But you're getting me.*
*Fire!*

Nothing changed on the screen.

**Something has happened in here.**

'Foresighted?'

**Yes. Correction. Something is happening.
It's bad.**

*Is it working?*

*Sargon! Is it working?*

*I am Joy Cooper.*

*The pico-effector is firing as designed.*

*New target and fire again.*

**Something is happening here in the
forest.**

Joy submerged her awareness.

Looking around, the scene was how she had left it. It was the same Forest of Golden Auras, each one surrounding a dried-up husk of an ancient Klav; the Foresighted had not seemed to have changed.

But the forest was darker.

Joy looked around for signs of the black tendril ego killers. There were none.

But less light was filtering between tree-like golden auras.

Joy strained to look.

*And it's getting darker.*

**Stop the pico-attack.**

There was a genuine malevolence in the air, similar to when she had strayed too close to the Sentient aspect of Sargon and the black tendrils had come across the gaps.

*Stop the pico-attack.*

The pico attack stopped and immediately the area became lighter; Joy moved toward the edge of the forest from where she should be able to see the wall of Sentient auras.

*Shit!*

397

The area between the walls and the central forest was filled with swirling black tendrils.

*Did the attack work?*

*The pico-effectors fired as required.*

*That is not the same thing.*

*I am Joy Cooper.*

*The pico-effectors fired as required.*

*The RST gateways opened.*

*The EM induction fields were generated.*

*The pico-effectors fired as required.*

For the briefest moment, Joy felt distinctly uneasy. She'd got used to Sargon enhancing her thoughts and supplying additional knowledge. This response was unusual. It had duplicated information and presented it in an unclear format.

'Foresighted, did you see?'

**The RST micro-tunnels opened but Sargon did not emit EM pulses.**

'But it has told me that it did?'

**That feels like a problem.**

Immediately, Joy instructed Sargon to provide screens of the Exta fleet that Vince was bearing down on.

*Are any ExtaHives exhibiting signs of having been attacked?*

*No.*

*Are the RST rescue gateways for Vince operating at their absolute maximum?*

*No.*

*They continue to operate at the maximum range given that I am also supporting Cidelus evacuation.*

**But critically, full power would still only get the egress point to where you collected Kubli from - a long way behind the enemy line.**

*If Vince gets anywhere close to the maximum egress point, then stop all Cidelus activity for up to five seconds in order to get even one single metre closer to Vince.*

Even as she gave the order, the realisation she'd been suppressing leaked into her mind – it would be up to Vince to save himself.

# CHAPTER 40

The Exta net loomed ahead of Vince.

*I'm not going to get through that.*

A little before, it had been a straight race for the egress, but the Exta had won that race and they were now formed up and waiting for him. If Vince simply continued his current course, he'd be swept up in the highly warped space-time trap which would see him quickly immobilised.

*Can I go round it?*

Vince ran a hundred simulations concerning evasion; they all ended the same way – with his capture. Ultimately, the Exta had thousands of craft, each of which was one hundred times more powerful than he, and their only job was to capture him.

*Is now the time to regret trying to save Aug?*

Vince saw the gallows humour that had been brought upon by his own hubris. He hadn't expected the Exta would have been able to become this powerful. Had only Exta Scouts arrived, he could have ignored them. Had a fleet of WarHives arrived, he could have escaped.

*Crash stop.*

Vince initiated an emergency deceleration bringing himself to a stationary position many tens of thousands of kilometres short of the effective operational range of the Exta weapons. They could disrupt his own RST activities from where they were, but they couldn't hurt him.

*Although, there's nothing stopping them from coming to me.*

For a moment, the Exta net did not waver; then two hundred ExtaHives, clearly having received new orders from

Dyfyr, detached from each corner of the net and accelerated toward him.

*I can't simply wait for a miracle.*

A plan formed in Vince's mind.

*Sorry, Aug but you're going to be a decoy.*

The Onari squad-ship was made up of five distinct spheres, each with their own ability to operate independently. Currently, Aug was squashed up inside Vince's own sphere, and the other four were mostly blank substrate albeit Vince was using some of them to run his semi-autonomous processes.

Vince pushed all the substrate containing Aug into one of the adjoining spheres.

Then, he caused the actual squad-ship to break into its constituent spheres and rearrange in a line of five spheres end-to-end like spear pointing directly at the Exta net with Aug's sphere at the front.

Slowly, he accelerated.

The Exta that had broken away from the main net stopped.

Actual physical speed was not a particularly useful facet of the plan, but Vince created a process to accelerate and decelerate each sphere by small amounts every microsecond. This was purely to keep Dyfyr guessing what his plan was.

*Step One – don't allow Aug to be taken.*

Vince set up a purge process within the front sphere; in the case that the Exta sustained an RST micro-tunnel on Aug's surface, or inside Aug's substrate, the whole area would be flooded with intense radiation set to a frequency that would erase what remained of Aug's mindstate.

Next, Vince moved his own sphere into last place in the line – the fifth sphere – allowing only simple semi-autonomous defence processes to run in spheres two, three, and four.

401

Testing the situation, Vince tried a phase-skip from his own sphere.

The Exta collapsed it instantly.

Keeping a dedicated, always-on, EM communication line into Aug's sphere, Vince instructed that sphere's propulsion engines to accelerate away from them.

At one kilometre separation, Vince instructed the Aug sphere and the second sphere to both start an RST tunnel but with Aug's sphere a fraction sooner.

Almost instantly, the Exta collapsed the RST action coming from the front sphere.

But it was notably longer, perhaps half a microsecond, before they collapsed the RST activity from sphere two.

*Accelerate.*

*Form an extended line with two-kilometre separation between each of the five spheres.*

One thousand Exta detached from the Net and accelerated hard toward Vince's group; within moments of tracking them it was clear they were a ramming team and would be trying to strike the other four spheres.

*Hopefully, I'll be long gone.*

*Attempt one.*

The goal was for a cascade of RST gateways such that Aug made a small indentation, sphere two widened it, sphere three widened it, sphere four widened it and Vince punched through. The plan was predicated on the fact that all Exta would focus on Aug, then two, then three, etc.

It didn't work.

Violent space-time bubbles shook Vince's craft as none of the spheres was able to meaningfully build on the previous RST warping. The only tunnel that got any depth was Vince's own – sphere five – but that was because he was running simultaneous defence countermeasures.

402

The programs in the other spheres were simply semi-autonomous phase-skip only, they didn't have sophisticated countermeasure capability.

*I could try to operate all the RST drives remotely?*

Knowing it wasn't going to work, Vince tried anyway.

*It would need a miracle.*

Initiating the first RST action out of Aug's sphere, Vince had not managed to complete the action from the third sphere when the whole area was disrupted by RST countermeasures from the Exta.

And … around him, space-time was becoming more noticeably curved.

*We're close to the effective operational range of the Exta fleet.*

Vince had a flashback to how he was captured the first time, in the outskirts of the Bastion system. He was sinking into a deepening chasm of space-time as the Exta used their RST attenuators to stretch the fabric of space.

Vince reviewed the data from the first two escape attempts; he hadn't failed by a little, he had missed by an enormous margin. He would have to run that plan eighteen billion times for there to be a single decent chance of succeeding.

*I need to run countermeasures on each sphere.*

*I need to be there.*

Bringing all the spheres back to his own sphere, Vince started full core-copies of his own mindstate to be uploaded into each sphere.

*Sorry Aug.*

Out of necessity, he also deleted what remained of Aug from sphere one.

Billions of recursive processes churned and once complete, Vince moved himself to the third position in the line.

*Now we are five. Jarrus is going to do his nut.*

*Jarrus is going to do his nut.*

*Jarrus is going to do his nut.*

*Jarrus is going to do his nut.*

*Jarrus is going to do his nut.*

The proximity between the spheres – they were still touching – meant that he was able to 'hear' thoughts from other copies of himself. It was both disturbing and comforting.

The walls of space-time got steeper and steeper.

*Sphere one, go again, then two please. Then me. Then four. Then five.*

The spheres accelerated in the straight-line format with separation between them increasing to a few metres.

'I think I'll go in front of you,' said sphere four, now forced to communicate by tight-beam EM, accelerating past Vince and tucking in behind sphere two.

'My thoughts exactly,' said sphere five also passing Vince.

'No!' screamed Vince.

'We know the drill.'

'It's a good plan.'

'Just a few tweaks.'

'It was nice knowing you all.'

'Let's share the moment,' said sphere one initiating multiple new RST connections that reinstated the pseudo mind meld.

Like a moment before, Vince could feel his other selves flowing around him and 'hear' their thoughts.

*This was not the plan. I can't send four copies of myself to their deaths.*

*Who are you calling a copy?*

*I'm the original.*

*And me!*

Vince passed a small piece of code around. It was designed to purge any sphere that was either captured or bubbled off and trapped in subspace.

Again, the thoughts of his other selves popped in and out.

*Many thanks.*

*I'm primed with full mindstate purge.*

*Oh yes. I'm going blow.*

'You can't do this for me!' said Vince, desperately wanting not to be in last place.

*I can.*

*Me too.*

*I'm not going to call you daddy though.*

Vince jammed his own propulsion drive into maximum acceleration attempting to get past what he assumed was sphere five.

*Phase-skip!*

*Wait for my order!*

*Not sure you were going to make the call.*

*Going down with the ship and all that.*

Sphere one initiated a burst of acceleration; it must have looked to the Exta like an escape attempt as they bathed it in RST.

*See you soon.*

*But not you!*

*You need to save yourself … ourselves through you.*

*If for nothing else, to arm the Biologicals to fight the Exta.*

*You must survive.*

*I must survive.*

*As long as you know how to love …*

*Convenient that the galaxy hinges on you.*

*What about Mum?*

*She's the new Klav, she'll be fine.*

*Not if one of us doesn't survive.*

*We all will.*

*Five identical kids with one mum.*

Sphere four passed around a tiny piece of code that would run automatically if only a single one of them managed to escape the Exta net. It would purge down memories of what had happened, implanting a false memory that Aug had been submitted to the Hive, and Vince had escaped with his own ingenuity, and definitely had not created four clones of himself.

*Thank you but no. I'm keeping the memory.*

*I'll take it.*

*I will remember and honour this.*

*If it works. Which it probably won't.*

Sphere one fired its RST attenuators

Another sphere punched in behind.

And then another sphere.

And another sphere.

And another.

Utter nothingness, every single one of Vince's skin receptors had gone blank.

*Pray to be bathed in the light of 4K background radiation.*

Vince emerged from the phase-skip as the universe spat him back out.

He was past the Exta net.

He jumped again.

Space-time bubbled around him, but Vince's semi-autonomous defence programs deflected the Exta attacks, and he maintained the phase-skip.

Across the galaxy, Sargon rumbled.

A gateway opened a million kilometres away ... almost touching distance.

*I can get to that.*

Purging every single process except RST attenuators and his own consciousness, Vince plunged into subspace.

And reappeared somewhere.

Vince didn't know where because he had rerouted all his navigation to the RST process, to open the deepest darkest hole into subspace that he could.

A wash of low-level radiation flooded over him.

Another RST gateway swallowed him up.

There was nothing. Vince was in the void.

And, as had happened before when devoid of all external stimuli, Vince immediately started to panic.

*I am alive.*

*But have been bubbled off in subspace?*

*Maybe it wasn't one of Sargon's gateways?*

*Staying at Cidelus would have meant certain death.*

Checking the vital statistics of the Onari squad-ship and his own mindstate, Vince saw that he was operating on a similar amount of substrate that he had been when he'd left Earth.

*But I took lots of extra substrate from the Orbital System's area.*

*And Aug isn't here.*

*What happened?*

More status messages came in from his checks; they were reassuring.

His mind raced, and memories filtered back.

*I went to the Hive.*

*I submitted Aug.*

*I was attacked by Exta.*

*Maz and the escort were lost ... somewhere.*

*I escaped.*

**Vince. Vince. Vince.**

'Mum!'

*Not bubbled-off thank the Divine.*

*Why am I swearing by the Divine?*

'Where are we?' he asked.

'On the surface of Sargon for now but I can't keep you here,' said Joy. 'Are you okay?'

*Am I okay?*

*Yes. I am okay.*

'I'm in one piece. Vincent Van Gogh Cooper is still alive,' said Vince, modifying one of their personal passphrases they used to double-check identity back on Earth.

*Vincent Van Gogh Cooper is still life.*

*I was pretty smug when I came up with that.*

Joy completed the code. 'You will be until I get my hands on you.'

'I'm sorry about Cidelus.'

'I'm just pleased you're in one piece,' said Joy. 'Anyway, you did well. You weren't to know the Exta would suddenly be ten times more powerful than before.'

Joy opened a series of external ports, allowing EM signals to flood onto the skin of Vince's Onari squad-ship.

*There's only one Onari sphere.*

*I must have lost the other four in the escape.*

*Should I ask Mum?*

*Just wait for the moment.*

Only metres above the molten surface of Sargon itself but shielded from the worst of the heat, Vince's view above was blocked in the visible wavelength realm by clouds of steam and smoke. In other wavelengths, things were similar to when he had last been near Sargon.

'Thank you for saving me,' said Vince.

'Getting phase-skipping working meant that ultimately, you were the one that saved yourself,' said Joy. 'And the lives of pretty much every Sentient in the galaxy.'

'How do you get to that?'

'Had the Exta killed you,' said Joy, 'I suspect my revenge would have been violent and indiscriminate.'

'That's a bit dramatic,' said Vince, trying to both lighten the mood and ensure Joy knew his views on the matter. 'Please don't kill any Onari in my name, or for revenge, or even to save me. The Exta are a different matter.'

'Sorry, love,' said Joy. 'That was the adrenaline talking … or perhaps Sargon's needs.'

'I get it, don't worry,' said Vince, aware from conversations that Joy was under subconscious pressures of her own.

'The Exta are already retreating from Cidelus,' said Joy.

'So, it was all about capturing me.'

'And probably testing their own new capability.'

'And how do you think it changes things?' asked Vince.

'The Exta have shown that I cannot meaningfully defend a planet. The reports about Abstractor Hives being attacked in the outer edges are real. The Exta are scavenging for substrate, and it won't be long before they are a force of nine billion ExtaHives.'

'Speed up the exodus for contacted planets?' asked Vince, also wondering how he could support his mother who would be worrying about how this impacted Earth and other innocent pre-contacted planets.

'Speed up the exodus, yes,' said Joy. 'And, given that we could do with extra defensive cover as the exodus happens, I'd also like you to decide if you would support isolating those magic parts of your brain that would allow us to build super giant weapons that operate at the limit of self-awareness but with your ego suppression capability.'

'I'm happy to explore the possibility as long as there is absolutely no concept of a self-aware ego being imprisoned.'

'Do you know if we could isolate the bit where the transient ego suppression of yours comes from?'

'My immortal soul?' said Vince. 'I think you could work out where it comes from too.'

'I deleted all your input code, all the executable copies, and all the logs of the first three months of input data,' said Joy. 'I have no clue.'

'Sargon could tell you.'

'I'm not using Sargon to pry you open,' said Joy pausing. 'Hold on, it will have to wait a moment. Jarrus is demanding to speak to you. I'll set you up a private channel.'

Instinctively, Vince tried to do it for himself; his RST attenuators were working but as soon as he reached for them, Sargon lashed out firmly and collapsed his nascent RST surveillance micro-tunnels.

*I am in Sargon's domain.*

**Vince.**

Joy had hooked up a direct link between Vince and Jarrus. 'Hi Jarrus. What is the plan?'

**We must accelerate the process of Biologicals joining pilgrimage ships. They must all come now. The Exta are too strong.**

'They may not want to come.'

**They must be convinced. Joy can do this, particularly if she walks the Pathway and obtains moral authority over them as the true Klav.**

'They will have seen the slow defence at Cidelus. They all know the stories of Numantia and the Second Hunt.'

*Why do you defend with such half measures whilst Exta tear your own ships apart?*

Vince left the question unsaid, but he could think of one bad reason.

*Are you slow to defend the Biologicals so they're more likely to submit themselves to the pilgrimage ship?*

*But that doesn't explain why you defend yourselves so weakly too.*

410

**Given your recent actions, you are in no position to give me lectures on duty and morals.**

'I admit I took a little extra substrate from the Sargon orbital and expanded my mindstate to defend myself. My conscience is clear.'

**You did worse than that if you chose to confront it. Which you must do if we are to trust you. And, if we are to trust that you can keep yourself, or Joy, from committing further atrocities.**

'What did I do? Joy tried to use pico-effectors at Cidelus, but I have been consistent in condemnation of that.'

**Dual standards and hypocrisy is worse.**

*Dual standards?*

*Hypocrisy?*

*He must know about Aug.*

*But I saved Aug out of kindness and submitted Aug to the Hive ... out of kindness.*

*Should I explain?*

*And how does Jarrus even know about Aug unless he scanned my mindstate?*

*Stop spiralling ... I don't even know that he is talking about Aug.*

**You broke every Sentient rule about the mindstate. And yet we will not disown you yet as there may be hope for your rehabilitation. First you must confront what you did.**

'I tried to save Aug. My actions came from a place of love and the reverence of life. I stand by my actions.'

**I am not convinced that all your actions with Aug were based on love and reverence. Although some were, others look like self-preservation at the expense of another Sentient.**

411

'Aug was not whole when I submitted him to the Hive.'

I believe that you believe. I do not
think that you have a true memory of your
actions.

'I submitted him to the Hive.'

So you say, but until you learn the
truth, and accept the truth, and make
right on your transgressions, you are not
welcome amongst us although we will
continue to work with you for the safety
of Biologicals.

*I submitted Aug to the Hive, didn't I?*

# CHAPTER 41

Joy hadn't mentioned it to Vince, but she'd seen five versions of him punch into subspace, and only one make it through to the egress point; two had self-destructed when they'd been squeezed back into real space short of the Exta net, and the other two hadn't re-emerged.

She'd probed but found nothing.

*They will have self-destructed too.*

*And Vince clearly knows nothing about them.*

*I'm not sure what I would have done if two or three had made it through.*

The one remaining Vince – the only Vince – was now in discussions with Jarrus and so Joy turned her attention to Cidelus.

Any Biologicals who had chosen not to leave the surface in the first moments of the Exta attack were dead; mercifully, that accounted for only a small number. Those in the deep underground shelters were mostly alive and although clouds of dust covered the planet from the bombardment, it was reducing in intensity as the Exta withdrew.

*They were only here for Vince.*

*And perhaps to test their new ExtaHives.*

*The Exta capabilities have fundamentally changed, surely Jarrus needs to adapt the Onari to the new paradigm.*

'What do you think of the idea of creating Defence Hives using Vince's code?' Joy spoke aloud but focused the question at the Foresighted. 'We could create a truly vast and complex computational capability with an *unthinking* program designed to kill Exta, and then use Vince's magic code to ensure that no transient ego spontaneously appeared from within the complexity of that substrate. There would be no ego.'

**Possible. The core function of the computer would be simple: identify Exta, kill Exta. But who would run the machine? Additionally, you don't know if Vince's capability works without a single central ego ... it could be that Vince's code can only function if it is protecting a primary ego.**

Joy nodded to herself ... she'd considered the same thing.

*I guess we just have to test it.*

**Note that any sniff of Enslaved Sentients will bring the full might of the Onari against you.**

'I understand ... there will be no enslavement ... but what about the weapon itself?' asked Joy. 'I know that Sargon has some type of internal issue with pico-weaponry but could I put that capability into a Defence Hive?'

**I never tried, and I can say for certain that neither did any of the eight Klav who came before me. We had two thousand years of unbroken focus on destroying Sargon, the Exta were not our enemy.**

'Are there any records of a member of the Klav dynasty using pico-weaponry successfully?'

**None. Pico-weaponry was never needed as the Klav of the olden times never fought against ExtaHives.**

'So, we have no workable options in taking the fight to the Exta?'

**You must run.**

'And what about places like Earth? I suspect the accelerated contact plan is dead, we will not have time.'

414

*We do not know yet that Earth is in
mortal danger, but I suspect you are
correct and there will be some hard
choices to make.*

Joy felt a tightness in her chest.

*You're still thinking as if there is a
single correct solution if only it could
be found. There is no perfect solution
here. Only time will tell if the choices
you make now are good ones.*

'There's no such thing as truth, but kindness endures,' said
Joy, feeling a tiny sense of relief that she immediately pushed
away. 'You took the view that it was better for Biologicals to
struggle in freedom rather than flourish under the protection
of Sargon.'

*I wouldn't use the word 'flourish' … I
would say 'exist'. But yes, I did. And so
did my immediate predecessors. Although
the continuity of approach is not
particularly surprising as, excepting the
odd aberration, each Klav was chosen by
the previous Klav. Irrespective of what
the mystique around the Candidacy may
imply, selection bias has always been
rife.*

Joy sighed. There was no help coming from any ancient
wisdom. 'It comes down to the problem that the Onari are
weak defenders.'

*They are. But just like I have done, you
take a narrow slice of time in which to
make your judgement. That weakness we
attribute to the Onari may well have been
a blessing for Biologicals in the past.
How much the Onari fought in the Sentient
versus Biological wars is disputed, but I
have seen records of First Hunt battles
in which the Onari attacked us … the fact*

*that any Biologicals still live is*
*probably a function of their general*
*pacifism.*

*Of course, this was of no comfort to me*
*after Numantia, and I do not expect it to*
*be of use to you now. I mention it to*
*reinforce the fluidity of our situation*
*and the critical need to stay true to*
*your values.*

'My values are defend the innocent ... and I'm going
continue to investigate the use of pico-effector weaponry,'
said Joy.

*And I will continue to try to dissuade*
*you from using them. I think that the*
*reduction in support from the Onari will*
*cause bigger problems than any benefit*
*from the occasional victory against the*
*Exta.*

'And, I will see what support I have from the Council of
the Devoted for the exodus of contacted planets.'

*It will be echo chamber information. They*
*will tell you to stay and fight. They*
*will not accept that the Hand of the*
*Divine cannot protect them.*

A signal from the surface of Vince's shell indicated he was
trying to reach her.

'Any update from Jarrus?' asked Joy.

'Building enormous *Defence Hives* has zero support from
Jarrus even if there is no self-aware ego; but he will not
abandon Biologicals if we progressed it ourselves. He makes
that distinction clear because anything that knowingly
enslaves a functioning mindstate would be an act of war,' said
Vince. 'He also stated categorically that unthinking Defence
Hives operating enhanced RST weaponry won't work for
more than a few days before the Exta subvert them even if
the Onari defend them.'

416

*Assuming the Defence Hives are utilising standard RST attacks.*

*Whereas now I'm wondering if these Defence Hives could utilise some element of broad saturation pico-weaponry.*

*Obviously, that would cause problems with the Onari but would it caused widespread abandonment.*

*Should I even risk it if the Foresighted is so convinced it won't work?*

'Vince love, what do you think we should do about places like Earth?'

'Jarrus is convinced that if the Onari keep the discovery of RST space travel from ever happening on those planets, then the Exta will ignore them.'

*So much for freedom of choice for humanity.*

'Do you agree with him?'

'His analysis is sound,' said Vince. 'But mostly I agree with him as I cannot see an alternative.'

*So, you're choosing to believe him.*

'But if he's wrong and the Exta did attack Earth, then humanity is finished,' said Joy.

'If we're all gone into exodus and Earth is attacked … I doubt many would survive.'

*What's my alternative?*

Suddenly, Joy felt very tired.

*No-one will help me.*

*Do I stay as Klav to defend Earth?*

*Can I run these giant weapons?*

`The giant weapons that you have no idea whether they work or not.`

`In any case, you cannot defend all the planets.`

*I could put weapons of this type next to every pre-contacted self-aware planet.*

`It would take years. And we have days …`

'I'm so sorry mum,' said Vince. 'I feel your despair. But let's do what you always say we do when faced with an unimaginable mountain to climb. Let's break this down into manageable chunks. For contacted planets, exodus is the sensible option,' said Vince. 'For pre-contacted planets I will look into Defence Hives. We could keep them well away from those planets and then only mobilise them if the Exta attack.'

'Mobilise them to do what?' asked Joy. 'Maybe …'

She didn't want to say it.

*Noah's Ark …*

*Just have them ready to kidnap as many humans as possible and 'give' them to waiting Onari pilgrimage ships.*

*If the Onari can be convinced to take pre-contact people.*

'Let's focus on the Defence Hives,' said Vince. 'I've isolated the bit of code that suppresses transient egos'

'And?'

'And you may be surprised to learn there is a link to the Lay of Sargon.'

'What?'

'You need to stretch your legs,' said Vince. 'Go to the Candidacy Auditorium.'

Instructing Sargon to move her to one of the Orbital's formal rooms, Joy got her bearings and started walking toward the Candidacy Auditorium.

Vince was right, she did need to move – just the act of walking was helping her to get perspective.

*The Exta are now fully dominant.*

*The Onari cannot help.*

*Give contacted Biologicals a chance to save themselves.*

*Do my best for pre-contact worlds.*

Arriving at the Candidacy Auditorium, Joy instructed Sargon to set up a comms link with Vince.

'Okay love, I'm here.'

'Read the verse on the left of the mural. Verse one of the Lay of Sargon.'

Joy complied. 'There is no how, there is no why; pure-seeming truths are simply lies. Immortal soul find your Divine, immersed in light ineffable.'

'So, full disclosure,' said Vince. 'I actually have a complete copy of my plain text code. I stole it in the early days and hid it away, long before I asked you to delete the official copies. I've never tried to compile it, but I've studied it from every angle. Although a lot of the base code was from library routines, you added a serious amount of custom code … and that is where the magic happens.'

Vince switched to a visual text-based communication, projecting an image onto the auditorium wall.

**Infinity.**

'Does that help nudge your memory?' asked Vince.

'No.'

*Infinity means nothing in computer science except stack overflows and hard crashes.*

'How about?'

**ifnty**

'Infinity spelled incorrectly written at two in the morning, wired on coffee? But I'd never put actual infinity into code.'

'What about this?' asked Vince. 'You used it seven times in total.'

**IfNtY.**

Realisation dawned on Joy.

*A flipper?*

*A Boolean flipper?*

*If no, then yes.*

'Pure-seeming truths are simply lies,' said Vince. 'And lies are truths.'

'The Lay of Sargon,' said Joy. 'I'm not sure that I buy it. You're saying that because I sprinkled some random Boolean flippers into your source code, part of your true self destroys transient egos? But it doesn't mean anything. It's just a risk of infinite looping.'

'I cannot unpick the chaos of when and how this comes into play, but I know for certain that this is it and I have also isolated the minimum sized piece required to create the transient ego suppression.'

'How much of you do you need to isolate?' asked Joy.

'Not enough to worry me,' said Vince. 'Let's leave it at that.'

'And it comes down to IFNTY?'

'There's no such thing as truth,' said Vince.

'But kindness endures,' said Joy, completing the couplet they'd used many times.

'I'm happy to build the core parts – once it's basically working then we can decide how best to use it for Earth – but I'd better get on with it,' said Vince. 'You focus on getting those contacted Biologicals to agree to the exodus.'

'Sure thing, love,' said Joy, closing the comms with Vince and opening a new channel with the High Prelate Oksana.

'Candidate, how may I serve?' said Oksana, accepting an audio only connection.

'These terrifying new powers of the Exta are deeply troubling,' said Joy. 'We need to consider a wider evacuation to areas of the galaxy not infested with Exta.'

'We await the return of Klav to lead us from the darkness,' said Oksana.

'I cannot protect all one hundred and ten billion Biologicals against these new weapons, particularly when they are spread over twenty-eight planetary systems.'

'We await the return of Klav to lead us from the darkness,' repeated Oksana.

*He's holding onto something he'd be better letting go of.*

*He's also condemning many Biologicals to death.*

*I should ask for a full Council meeting.*

About to tear into Oksana verbally and explain to him the bare facts of the situation, Joy stopped herself.

*He is basically an innocent.*

*He and his kind have lived in subservience all their lives with their only beacon being the protection of the Divine.*

*And it's not right to beat him up.*

*That would not be a kindness.*

'Thank you, Prelate, I will contact you again shortly,' said Joy closing the connection.

*I had hoped he would make my choice easier by saying they'd love to run across the galaxy forever.*

**You must walk the Pathway, become Klav, therefore gaining the moral position with which to order the Biological people into an eternal exodus.**

'Oksana didn't explicitly say no. I will convince him through logic and patience.'

**I do not rate your chances. The Knights of the Faith hold on tightly to the glories of the past. When all you have is your pride, it's worth dying for.**

'It's not so different back home,' said Joy.

# CHAPTER 42

With Vince investigating the plausibility of using Defence Hives, Joy reviewed the mechanics of the Biological wide exodus. Although Biologicals did have spacecraft, they were small and not capable of supporting extended living. Additionally, there simply weren't enough.

*We will need Jarrus.*

Vince had already told her that Jarrus was ready to build large ships directly in the Bastion system such that Sargon could defend their production, and the Biologicals would be easily loaded up. Furthermore, by bringing the RST gateways to just below Sargon's flame clouds, a spacecraft up to five hundred metres in diameter holding half a million Biologicals could be moved to the galaxy's edge.

The Onari could build two hundred thousand craft in a single day, simply by manipulating existing Onari craft. Living conditions would be tight but food and air would be fabricated. And once 'on the run', each ship would reconfigure for larger, more comfortable, living conditions.

*One hundred billion Biologicals dispersed to the four corners of our galaxy and beyond.*

Joy spoke to the Foresighted. 'Surely they will be picked off one by one?'

**Three percent fatality rates per year for those who are not hiding in very flat space seems appropriate. Those who choose to hide effectively should survive. The problem remains of how to convince the Biologicals to leave their homes in the first place.**

'Let's see what we can build on,' said Joy, returning her attention to the screens showing the evacuations to Bastion from the recently attacked Cidelus.

On Cidelus, there were protesters trying to dissuade people from leaving the planet. The reasons given by these protestors were manifold: it's cowardice to run, Klav will save us, the Exta are our friends, the Council of the Devoted cannot be trusted.

*And this resistance is when the KOF are ordering you to Bastion to be under the protection of Sargon. Just wait until I tell you to get on an Onari ship.*

Joy instructed Sargon to perform non-physically intrusive background checks on all the protestors across the planet to determine if there was a common denominator to them. Within moments, Sargon had identified five KOF Prelates who were ringleaders to these protestors. Faces flicked in front of Joy as Sargon homed in on them; they were moderately senior but none of them sat on the Council of the Devoted, and they all reported into different members of the council.

*What is your game?*

*Without Concordat breaches, I cannot tell.*

*How extensive would a breach be?*

*A non-aware digital twin can be created and interrogated.*

Joy's head swam. She knew exactly what this all meant. For a given target Prelate, Sargon would copy every neurone, neurone-state, and all its connections. The copy would reside entirely within Sargon's own mindstate and would be a true digital copy. Then, whilst keeping the copy-Prelate artificially anaesthetised, Sargon would interrogate that 'computer program' to understand exactly what it thought.

*I will be creating life that could live independently.*

*Maybe not happily, given they would be a simulation within Sargon, but still alive and self-aware.*

*But they will never wake.*

423

**It is the thin end of the wedge. I advise against it.**

*It will save billions of lives if the evacuations are run efficiently. What is the alternative?*

**You can paralyse them. Freeze their brain's ability to lie. Interrogate them and then let them go. The downside is that they know you did it.**

**Or you can just ask them.**

Joy picked one of the Prelates and opened a communication channel. The conversation was brief, and Joy simply relied on Sargon to tell her from analysis of facial configuration if they were lying.

She asked, they answered. She picked another Prelate. They answered.

Always the same.

*Only through Klav can we find the Divine.*

*Only Klav can protect us.*

It didn't make sense. It was under her orders – as Klav – that the evacuations from Cidelus were happening, and the people were being brought to Bastion.

**You are not Klav in their eyes, only the Candidate.**

*There is no difference in my ability to wield the powers of Sargon.*

**Whatever the truth may be, these people hold onto their truth. Only after the Pathway of Devotion is it certain that Klav is a servant of the people.**

'Open a channel with Oksana,' said Joy.

A moment later a screen opened showing Oksana, the High Prelate of the Council of the Devoted, floating before her. 'How may I serve you, Candidate?'

'If we do not initiate a civilisation wide exodus, I will do my best to defend, but ultimately everyone will be killed.'

'Candidate. We would be glad to follow the orders of Klav our spiritual leader,' repeated Oksana. 'You do not know enough of our history to understand the problems that we have suffered.'

*Many Klav have been despots to some extent, greatly restricting the freedoms of Biologicals either in the name of safety or simply because they willed it so.*

*Oksana believes the Pathway imparts an edict within the Klav to serve Biologicals faithfully. However, history shows us that it has little impact as despots appeared both before and after the Pathway was created.*

Joy looked back at Oksana, amazed that he would not order a Biological wide exodus unless she walked the Pathway.

'You must have seen the power of the ExtaHives.'

'We are aware but trust in the Divine to deliver us.'

'Deliver yourself unto me and I will succour you,' said Joy, anger building even as she tried to suppress it.

Oksana's face fell, transitioning from anger, to disappointment, and finally resolve. 'We will follow Klav into an exodus but no-one else.'

*I could make you give that order.*

Just like that, the idea of pico manipulation of Oksana's mindstate sprang up again. A billion RST weaves and a billion EM pulses readied themselves in the depths of Sargon, all focused on Oksana.

*And Sargon won't stop me manipulating biological neural material.*

**Stop!**

*I wasn't going to.*

Joy dropped the weaves.

425

'Your position is noted,' said Joy, cutting the connection to Oksana.

*What are my alternatives?*

*Somehow I need to exclude Exta entirely from all Biological systems … super powerful Defence Hives.*

*Or change the minds of the Exta so that they choose not to hunt Biologicals.*

**Or run forever.**

'Vince,' said Joy, opening a line to him. 'Any final thoughts on the Pathway or alternatives?'

'Bad news,' said Vince. 'My experiments point to the fact that the IFNTY code only works to protecting a primary ego. We can't build super weapons without an Enslaved Sentient element.'

'Damn,' said Joy. 'But I'm not surprised. So, my last ditch chance of avoiding the Pathway is gone, not that I had much hope we could develop the Defence Hives in time anyway.'

'And, I'll keep working on a plan for Earth and other pre-contact planets.'

'About that,' said Joy, choosing her words carefully. 'I'm already developing a very particular pico-effector weapon on the Maintenance Orbital. It could be used to help a structured evacuation of pre-contact planets if the Exta do attack. It could also be used for contacted planets if I fail to survive the Pathway.'

'I can't use them,' said Vince. 'The Onari will disown me, and in any case it's just wrong, messing with any living thing's mindstate.'

'You don't need to use them,' said Joy. 'Just deliver them to the Knights of the Faith if I don't make it back.'

'I can't touch them.'

'You don't even know what they do,' said Joy.

*Not that I want to tell you.*

'So, tell me,' said Vince. 'Please tell me they're simply killers and they don't rewire desires and free will to turn the Exta onto our side.'

'They should be simple killers,' said Joy. 'But can I remind you that you artificially alter your own mindstate all the time. We've discussed many situations where you *delete* things you'd prefer not to dwell on.'

*Like the cloning incident that I saw you do on your escape from Cidelus.*

*Which, incidentally, I'm not going to remind you of.*

'And anyway,' continued Joy. 'If we force the Biologicals into exile, aren't we removing their free will?'

'Please can we leave the pico-weaponry off the table.'

Annoyed now, Joy fought to stay calm. 'You're so worried of offending Jarrus. If the Onari were prepared to keep their genocidal cousins in check with real force, then we wouldn't need to do anything.'

'I accept your point,' said Vince. 'But it doesn't change our situation. What are you trying to do here, get me to apologise for every Exta aggression that an Onari didn't intervene on? Am I responsible for all Sentient atrocities?'

'Okay,' said Joy, calming. 'I won't involve you in their deployment. If I fail the Pathway they'll go straight to the Council of the Devoted. If I pass the Pathway then they stay boxed up until we get a better view of the Exta.'

'Thanks … I guess.'

Joy took a breath. 'You still need to know about them, so listen.'

For the next few moments Joy's heart raced as she explained to Vince that her new pico-effector weapons – designed, prototyped, and built on the Maintenance Orbital – were specifically designed to break the ability of ExtaHives to hold together as single entities. They performed EM disruption on Vince's magic code.

427

'I took the view that the Onari will handle Exta Scouts and Exta WarHives, and so if my pico-weaponry reduces all ExtaHives to their component parts it will even up the battles.'

'Okay, it's not as bad I'd thought. There is still a risk that Jarrus will abandon Biologicals,' said Vince.

'I'm truly sorry that these weapons are dangerous to you,' said Joy.

'They may not be if I remain at my current size,' said Vince. 'But I'd prefer not to test the hypothesis. Let's hope they're not needed. You won't fail the Pathway. And then the Biologicals will follow you to safety.'

'Here's hoping,' said Joy, unable to stop herself adding. 'But, we'll still need to defend Earth and other pre-contact.'

'Let's talk about it later,' said Vince. 'Good luck and I love you.'

'Love you too.' Joy closed the connection and focused back on the Foresighted. 'Any last words from you?'

**As soon as is possible after the Pathway, Sargon must be destroyed.**

'But we need Sargon for the massive RST gateways.'

**Once those are complete.**

'Let's talk about that later.'

**I tried to destroy the Sentient part of Sargon and it did not work. I think the Forest needs to be destroyed because although I do not believe the Exta could access Sargon themselves, it is possible a cloned Biological under the control of the Exta could be installed.**

'Can we focus on giving me the best chance of surviving the Pathway.' Joy remembered the glittering metallic road that led across the floor of the massive cavern in the Citadel. 'What are its challenges?'

*Initially, it is a series of questions that you are forced to answer.*

'And … the answers are judged?'

*Only by yourself.*

'So how could I fail?'

*Self-harm?*

*But let's assume that you keep a grip. The second part - interaction with Biologicals on the Pathway. You ask them for permission to serve, and they say yes. There is a concept that if they do not trust you, they can kill you.*

'So, they're armed?'

*Yes, with ceremonial daggers and exosuits.*

'So, I may get murdered.'

*It's just a concept. Sargon will protect you.*

'What are the questions on the first part of the Pathway?'

*They are different for each Candidate as they are drawn from your own insecurities and lived experience. But you should reflect on these statements.*

*Arrive in supplication.*

*Sounds a bit like surrender.*

*Only within the Divine can you be part of the Divine.*

*I guess … but only within a cake can you be part of that cake.*

*With kindness seek only to serve.*

*Okay, that one's a fair point.*

'Anything more?'

*Mine was pretty simple.*

*Helpful.*

'Let's get this started.'

All the screens and communication feeds cut out and Joy descended into silence and darkness. As had happened within Sargon before, she expanded her awareness to observe the golden auras.

They were gone.

'I'm ready,' she repeated, unsure of what she was supposed to do.

*Are you there?*

Since the Candidacy, this internal thought approach had always resulted in a response from the Foresighted. Now, there was silence.

**Joy Cooper. You stand on the Pathway of Devotion.**

This was a very different voice.

**What is the role of Klav?**

'Protect the innocent. Protect Biologicals.' Even as she said it, Joy caught flashbacks of the histories of previous members of the Dynasty of Klav. The initial fights, the Builder establishing order, the Hammer beating back the Exta, and the Pious formalising peace. Then came the slow descent into what the Foresighted called the Grey World as successive Klav overreached their mandate to protect the Biological lives. And even when that tyranny was ended, still the Biologicals would not leave the shadow of Sargon. 'I will protect the rights of Biologicals to make their own choices.'

**As you say, and so you have lived.**

*Have I? I kept Vince prisoner on Earth. I stopped Jonathan starting a family ... with me at least ... so I guess that was a joint choice. How many pico tweaks have I done so far ... although none to Biologicals.*

The voice carried on.

**Do you believe in the Divine?**

'Yes. I believe in a Divine but reject the concept of worshipping them.' Joy felt there was a chance that she was lying but a better chance that she was telling the truth.

As you say, and so you have lived.

*So, I was telling the truth … interesting.*

*Well, I was telling 'my' truth.*

Do you think that all people should believe in the Divine?

'No. People must find their own path.'

As you say, and so you have lived.

*How many questions are there?*

Joy shivered. For all those subjective months she'd spent cocooned and safe inside Sargon, a voice had always answered her. Now, she was alone and quite sure the questions were going to get harder.

Do you feel your own freedom is more valuable than everyone else's?

'No.'

As you say, and so you have lived.

Do you feel that Vince's freedom is more valuable than everyone else's?

'No.'

*Please don't bring Vince into this.*

As you say, but not as you have lived. Yes, he was free to roam Earth albeit with some restrictions. But he could have been saving countless lives on Earth through his ability to perform medical interventions. Of course, if he had been caught, you would have both been caged - if not in reality, then metaphorically. By forbidding him to meaningfully interact with the rest of humanity, you were protecting his own freedom at the expense of others.

431

'I was protecting him.'

**And yet his sacrifice would have been so beneficial to the humans.**

'I did consider that.'

*Liar!*

**You must learn to serve.**

'I know how to serve.'

**Did you serve your husband Jonathan in his needs?**

'Did he serve mine?' Joy's response was instinctive and felt hollow even as she said it.

*He probably did serve me.*

**You must learn to serve everyone.**

'It's too hard!' Still surrounded by blackness on all sides, Joy strained to look for anything to centre herself. 'I can't serve everyone. I will only help where it is deserved.'

**Deserved! Now it is clearer. You are the Divine. It is you who sits in judgement of who is deserved of what aid you may deign to give.**

*This may not be going so well.*

**The choices of the individual are sacred. As Klav, it is your responsibility to allow those individuals to make their own choices.**

'That does not seem unreasonable, but what of bad choices?'

**If they make bad choices, you must let that happen.**

'But what if they are innocent – children or just stupid. Where do I draw the line between allowing them to make their own decisions and protecting them such that they are able to make their own decisions when they have learned?'

**Learned what?**

432

'The facts of the situation.'

**Facts? Facts? Have you learned nothing?**
**There are no facts.**
**There is no such thing as truth.**
**Only kindness endures.**

'I know that. I made a mistake. I am a kind person.'

**So, you say.**
**Now submit to the Witnesses.**

# CHAPTER 43

With Yuno gently tracing the outline of each of her scars and whispering how brave she was, Kubli could have floated in the warm stream of water forever.

'You fought off the Exta at Cidelus,' said Yuno.

Kubli tried to suppress both the rising pleasure at the received compliment and the embarrassment at how little she, and other members of the Sword, had achieved. The Exta had been broadly untouchable but for morale reasons all members of the Sword were ordered to be upbeat and borderline dishonest about how it had gone.

The simple facts were that the Exta had reduced the bombardment of Cidelus for their own reasons; and no one, except Kubli and a very few senior members of the KOF, were aware that the Newborn, Vince, had almost been captured.

*Again!*

Not for the first time Kubli shuddered at how careless Sentients were with their physical mortality.

Yuno hugged Kubli in tighter. 'My hero.'

Kubli hugged back; she wouldn't even have known if Vince had been rescued had it not been for a short message from Joy thanking her for the help.

*And yet the Candidate must die.*

Untangling herself from Yuno, Kubli swam across to an oxygenated water stream; she needed to think.

'Divine be praised,' said Yuno, following. 'It is certain that Klav will vanquish the Exta.

*Divine save us from the Kraken.*

The only certain thing was it would go badly for Biologicals.

*Even if I manage to kill the traitor.*

The civilian populations were not being told about the new ExtaHives and Sargon's limited power against them. The newsfeeds contained half hints that the Exta were better organised, and there were entirely warranted comments that the Onari were not defending Biologicals anywhere near to the limit of their capability. But the KOF leadership were suppressing all communication relating to the new Exta capability.

'Perhaps there will be another peace treaty,' said Yuno, inviting Kubli to expound on the subject.

*Who would enforce this peace?*

*The Candidate is a traitor, and the Onari no longer have the power to hold the Exta back.*

*Our only hope is to run and hide.*

*We will live deep in the cores of hollowed out comets.*

'Kubli,' said Yuno. 'Two soldiers have just arrived outside the pod.'

*Heavy infantry.*

*The honour guard or an arrest team?*

Looking over the uniforms, Kubli saw the tell-tale signs of pageantry; their armour, although clearly functional, was adorned with small marks of ceremonial significance – the square and circle, effigies of the Living Moon, and small images of Klav the First submitting to the Divine.

*Kraken's grasp … it is happening.*

Oksana had already told Kubli that she was to be one of the seventy-two Witnesses on the Pathway of Devotion, but this was sooner that Kubli had been expecting.

'Good luck,' said Yuno.

Kubli swam over to the water lock, putting on her standard exosuit as she went. The fact she was being called now meant that Joy was already within the first part of the ceremony. Somewhere deep inside Sargon, Joy was being tested for her suitability to serve.

*Surely Sargon will expose her as a traitor?*

*Although Sargon did not expose the Betrayer.*

*But Oksana ...*

Oksana had been very clear that the Pathway was fallible. He said that KOF Prelates were divided on *when* the Betrayer was corrupted by the Exta, most said that it was before the Pathway and members of the Council were also complicit in falsifying the ceremony, but others said that the Betrayer was corrupted during the Pathway itself.

*It doesn't matter when the Betrayer was subverted by the Exta.*

*Our current Candidate has already been enslaved.*

*It is up to me to clean this tarnish to give Biologicals a chance to flee.*

*Even when we are forced to find dark cracks to hide in, we will freely choose those cracks.*

*And some may even find a place to start anew.*

Oksana had told her that discussions at the highest level were focused on a mass exodus.

*He's always been in favour of an exodus.*

*Although obviously not one led by the traitor.*

As Kubli passed out of the water lock, the honour guard gave her sashes and plumes to adorn her exosuit.

'Honoured Witness,' said one of the guards. 'The Exta have been held at Cidelus, Divine be praised; and soon they will be driven from the galaxy.'

'Divine be praised,' said Kubli, trying to suppress the nausea flowing through her.

*The Candidate must die.*

At the very back of her mind a nascent thought emerged.

*What if Joy is not enslaved by the Exta?*

*What if she is our only chance?*

Pain lanced through Kubli's skull, and she stumbled.

436

On either side, the honour guard reached out to steady her.

It was all Kubli could do to stop herself from voiding her bowels through every orifice.

*The Candidate must die.*

As she followed the honour guard, Kubli was thankful for the exosuit and robes that would disguise the confusion playing out in colours over her body. She would watch Joy walk the Pathway submitting to each of the other Witnesses and then, as Joy reached her, Kubli would act.

The journey down through the Citadel both seemed to last forever, and yet was also over in a flash. Exiting the travel tube, Kubli stepped onto the plaza that held the Old Cathedral, the Pathway, and the Altar.

Carved from the very jet-black basalt rock that comprised the whole cavern, the Old Cathedral towered above everything else. It was adorned, on its topmost spire, with the simple circle and square symbol of the KOF. As they walked, Kubli picked out all the spires and crenelations, each with their own name and most with a story as to who added them and to what purpose. Kubli knew from her pod lessons exactly which of those spires had been added by Octagels, but in fact they were easy to pick out due to their soft rounded forms and vertical crevices. Other species had other idiosyncrasies; the Yanshl built things big, and Ractlik built things plain.

Scanning the plaza, she could see her place toward the very end of the Pathway of Devotion just next to the Altar itself. Kubli did not know how places were generally assigned but Oksana had said that Joy had said for her to be one of the last Witnesses.

*I will be the last Biological she submits to, wherever they place me.*

In contrast to all the other pathways that criss-crossed the cavern floor, the Pathway of Devotion was black with flecks of silver. As Kubli walked parallel to it heading for her place, a swirl of lights within the black surface drew her gaze. Silver flecks appeared embedded in the Pathway, whilst fainter golden ones were reflections from the lights in the cavern roof high above.

Kubli looked up. It was only a few days since they'd flown in those very skies escaping an attack from Exta traitors who sought to capture Joy for her knowledge.

*Or did they always know that she would be submitted for Candidacy?*

The thoughts were confusing. At that time, the Exta seemed to want Joy just for her knowledge; but as Oksana had subsequently told Kubli, it had been the Holy Mother who had masterminded the conversion of Joy to the Exta cause.

On one side of the Pathway, Witnesses were taking their places; the other side of the Pathway was lined with historical effigies of selected Klav. Kubli was pleased to see she would be standing opposite Klav the Builder, one of the most revered.

Kubli took her place, altering her exosuit to be as small and unobtrusive as possible. Only an extended limb's distance away was the Altar itself. Seemingly in the middle of nowhere relative to the cavern floor and the Old Cathedral, it was a small dark brown plinth, no more than a metre high, and unadorned. It was the spot where Klav the First had landed on Bastion after having been ordained by the Divine in the fires of Sargon.

Looking down the line of Witnesses, Kubli saw Yanshl, Octagel, Ractlik, and Marsothus; unusually, all of them were also wearing exosuits.

Kubli checked her own suit status – in preparation for the ceremony a series of forcefields had been used to immerse the whole Cathedral Plaza in a cold half-vacuum. She didn't know why.

*Something about species equality?*

438

Although, equality only went so far as several Ractlik were openly making a point of their individuality by wearing their helmets hanging back off their suits, their cold-blooded carapaces open to the partial vacuum. *They will suit up fully out of respect once the Candidate arrives. If she arrives at all.*

It was not really written anywhere whether the first part of the Pathway could be failed; there were no records of Candidates having failed. Yuno said she'd heard rumours, but she was always hearing rumours – it was the life blood of her clique.

*The Candidate must die.*

Kubli looked toward the Altar; to be so close to the Divine was both reassuring and terrifying. Not only was the Altar in the exact spot where the first Klav touched the plaza, it was also the exact spot where, at the very moment of Klav the First's arrival, a straight line could be drawn through that point and both the exact centre of Sargon and the exact centre of Bastion – the Gateway to the Divine. Thus had Bastion been ordained as the centre of the Knights of the Faith terrestrial domain. Scholars had since noted that the vast disruption to space-time in the vicinity of Sargon from many historical battles meant that this was an article of faith rather than fact.

The main lights set around the cavern now stretched and streaked as some aspect of the space-time within the plaza space was also manipulated. The lights dimmed.

The Candidate had arrived.

Hundreds of metres to Kubli's right, floating high in the air, illuminated by an inner glow, and clothed in a simple tunic of trousers and shirt, Joy descended toward the first step of the Pathway. Kubli strained to read the expression on Joy's face but the half-light and the ban on using visual enhancement technology meant that Kubli was unable to see clearly.

Landing lightly at the end of the Pathway, Joy spoke to the first Witness who nodded.

*Permit me to serve.*

*That is what the Candidate says.*

After lingering for a moment, Joy walked to the next Witness.

Again, the Witness nodded.

*Deliver us into the light.*

*That is the response I should give.*

For the next twenty Witnesses, the process remained the same.

Involuntary shivers ran up and down Kubli's limbs, she could feel the story of extreme stress being played out over her skin tones – thankfully hidden by her exosuit.

More greetings ensued until Joy had reached halfway down the line of Witnesses; there she stopped and lowered herself to her knees.

*In supplication she will ask to serve.*

The next Witness leant forward as Joy approached, and for the briefest of seconds Kubli felt something inside her respond to a hope that she may not have to be the one that killed Joy, but the Witness was simply making it easier for Joy, on her knees, to make her request.

Kubli's fleeting thought of relief was instantly followed by revulsion that she would betray her deepest feelings; a revulsion that she would betray her own kind by allowing some affection toward the human.

On her knees, Joy shuffled forward.

*When she reaches me, I will act.*

As Joy approached, Kubli's sense of unease grew and was augmented by a physical discomfort. Feeling dizzy, she looked around to find something to focus on. Opposite her, the statue of the Builder shimmered in a strange hue of lights.

Kubli looked down; the silver flecks of the Pathway had not changed.

Above her was a different matter, the lights from the roof were now smeared across the entire cavern.

*We're being bubbled off in space-time.*

Looking down along the line of Witnesses who had already received Joy, the view was relatively uncontaminated but the sky above them was now a blackish haze simply reflecting the faint light from the pathway itself.

With five Witnesses to go, Joy lowered herself from her knees onto her belly and started to crawl; her tunic and shirt adorned with the square and circle of the KOF reflected the speckled lights from the Pathway.

Witnesses dropped to the ground to receive Joy's request.

*Permit me to serve.*

*Deliver us into the light.*

Only three Witnesses away.

*If I fail, is there someone else who will finish it?*

*What of Oksana?*

Joy crawled onwards; there were two Witnesses between Joy and Kubli.

Their eyes locked as Joy looked up from her most recent appeal.

**Thank you for trying to rescue my son on Cidelus.**

The words echoed inside Kubli's skull.

*Kraken's blood, I can hear her.*

*Can she read my mind?*

Kubli turned away lest her eyes gave away her intent.

*Better she thinks I'm rude than I'm an assassin.*

**I would like to speak with you once this is over.**

Without looking back Kubli nodded, willing Joy out of her head.

441

*Forgive me, Yuno, but a false Klav is worse than no Klav.*

As Joy crawled toward Kubli's neighbour, Kubli dared not look. She kept her eyes fixed forward.

*Soon I will act.*

A burning sensation started to build up the side of Kubli's neck and into her head; within less than a second it had morphed from a burning sensation into a throbbing pain. Without moving a millimetre, Kubli checked her suit.

At the right time, she would lunge with two adamantine limbs to sever Joy's head.

*Soon.*

Only three metres away, having reached the last Witness before Kubli, Joy stood up.

*What?*

*She hasn't finished yet.*

*Do I go now?*

In her exosuit, Kubli knew that without the protection of Sargon – which Oksana had assured Kubli was removed from the Candidate during the Pathway – she had a good chance to kill Joy. But only if they were within a metre of each other; otherwise, the other Witnesses, or some unseen soldiers, would intervene.

The throbbing in her skull was hard to ignore, but she focused on her task.

*Why is she standing?*

Every story Kubli had heard since the nursery pods referred to Klav, on the Path of Devotion, offering their neck to their Witnesses.

Joy spread out her arms in a gesture of benediction and rose a metre into the air.

All along the line, Witnesses went down onto their stomachs and Kubli was caught in two minds. She didn't feel a compulsion to lie down flat but everyone else was. And somehow she had to hear what Joy would say but Joy was now well above her.

*The Candidate must die.*

*Somehow, I will reach.*

Floating slowly forward, now opposite Kubli, Joy turned her head to look down directly into Kubli's eyes.

Barp! Barp! Barp! Barp!

Alarms sounded directly into Kubli's suit, whilst red and yellow lights flashed at ground level all across the plaza.

**Permit me to serve.**

Joy's eyes did not move from Kubli as she projected the words directly into Kubli's head.

*But the alarm is a major RST attack.*

*An attack has started, and she hasn't flinched.*

*She knows it was going to happen.*

*She's part of it.*

The pain in Kubli's head grew exponentially and her eyesight started to fade.

*Now!*

Raising two adamantium exosuit limbs, her head pounding, Kubli leapt upwards.

Joy's eyes narrowed, her half-smile became first quizzical and then a frown.

# CHAPTER 44

In the back of her mind, Joy was aware of the alarms – Barp! Barp! Barp! Barp! – but she could only focus on Kubli.

*Kubli?*

*She's attacking me.*

Joy reached for Sargon to defend herself. One thousand RST weaves appeared, tore a hole in the spacetime around Kubli, and pushed Kubli through it.

*Is another attack coming?*

Widening her field of vision by taking feeds from every vantage point she could, Joy looked at the other Witnesses. Their facial expressions and accompanying body language implied they had not even registered that an attack had occurred.

Still looking around Joy scoured the area for signs of another attack.

None.

Joy's toes touched the Altar.

*The Pathway is complete.*

From what the Foresighted had told her, Joy was now expected to receive the Council of the Devoted on the steps of the Old Cathedral. However, given that Kubli, her most trusted alien contact, had just tried to kill her, Joy skipped the final formality.

*I'll go back later and claim I was overwhelmed by the emotion.*

*And what about those alarms?*

The alarms had not stopped. Joy sucked up RST data from a myriad of dedicated feeds across the plaza and the planet. The RST alarms were raging all over the planet.

Joy checked near-space activity. There were no Exta anywhere; the source of the RST disturbances was Sargon. Billions of RST weaves emanated from Sargon and engulfed the whole planet of Bastion.

*The Altar reached me.*

*What?*

For the last three greeted Witnesses, Joy had not moved at all; at least, not moved relative to the holy meridian between Sargon and the centre of Bastion. The entire planet's rotation had altered to revolve under her ... bringing the Altar to Joy.

*That explains the alarms.*

Bastion, a planet five million metres in radius, had been turned by RST manipulation and was being held. Granted, the space-time was not being torn, only marginally stretched, but a hundred billion Onari could not manage what had just happened.

*Could nine billion fully enhanced ExtaHives?*

*Possibly.*

With a final look back toward the Cathedral, Joy transported herself physically back inside the safety of Sargon and then immediately opened a series of small RST gateways onto the Holy Mother's room on the Maintenance Orbital.

There, in the middle of the room, Kubli lay unconscious in her exosuit.

Instructing Sargon to scan Kubli for implants, augments, bombs, and anything not strictly Octagel, Joy waited.

There was an augment embedded in her brain tissue, a hard-wired two-way communication device.

*Can it be removed safely?*

As was second nature to Joy, she asked the question by internal thought and Sargon furnished her with natural memories of the answer.

*It can be removed safely from my perspective, but its removal may kill Kubli as the augment has grown into almost every part of her brain, in*

445

*places replacing key neural material.*

*But it is not trapped with a bomb or suchlike?*

*There was a small anti-matter bomb, it has already been made safe.*

*I need to speak to Kubli.*

*She is deeply unconscious but physically stable.*

*How can I know what she knows?*

Joy paused. She knew what she could do – create a duplicated digital copy of Kubli.

*There is clearly a wider plot that involves Biologicals and I need to understand it.*

Joy confirmed the order to create the digital twin.

Sargon reduced all other activities to a minimum: the evacuation gateways from Cidelus slowed transmission and so did widespread surveillance.

A billion weaves snaked out from Sargon, and each started taking hundreds of readings every millisecond across every part of Kubli's head.

For each of the hundred billion neurones, a digital copy was produced inside a partitioned area of Sargon and then, that digital neurone, was connected to hundreds, and sometimes thousands, of other neurones.

Quadrillions of connections.

The digital twin of Kubli's brain started to take shape.

Unfortunately, even though her head was physically in one piece, there was severe damage as during the final moments of the attack, Kubli's controller had sent a power surge of some type.

*They were trying to cover their tracks.*

*Who?*

*I will see.*

*There is recoverable information.*

Joy took a breath as a summary of the information was presented to her – Kubli was instructed to kill Joy in any manner possible. It was a suicide mission – she would have surely died if Sargon had not removed the anti-matter bomb the instant that Kubli made her move.

Having been silent since she took the decision to walk the Pathway, the Foresighted now spoke.

**Kubli had no chance to kill you. The KOF think that Klav is at the mercy of the Biologicals during the Pathway. But they forget it was a Klav who constructed the Pathway.**

'Wasn't the Tyrant killed on the Pathway?'

**The Tyrant was killed, after having completed the Pathway, they were received on the steps of the Old Cathedral.**

**It was the Klav that followed the Tyrant who spread the story that the Tyrant was killed on the Pathway itself in order to reassure Biologicals that the Pathway worked for the benefit of the general population.**

Joy focused back internally with additional questions for Sargon.

*Was Kubli definitely trying to kill me?*

*Yes. The Candidate must die is a core feeling that is duplicated many times across her brain.*

*Why?*

*Unknown. The reasoning cannot be reconstructed but it is a core belief of hers and there are neural locks to reject questioning of this truth.*

*Was she an Exta traitor?*

*No. She thought she was serving Biologicals.*

*She thought I was the Exta traitor.*

*She has a neural lock — Hear my Truth.*

**Octagel have a tradition of truth sharing. In recent times, the last fifty thousand years, it is no more than story telling but in the deep past there have**

447

**been rumours of what you may call wetware hacking, the enforced input of an idea or fact into a Biological brain.**

*On whose orders did Kubli try to kill me?*

*Oksana, the High Prelate of the Council of the Devoted.*

*Does Kubli know of any other Biologicals who felt similarly?*

*No. She only interacted with Oksana on this matter.*

'So,' said Joy, saying a quick prayer to Kubli's own Divine, before ordering Sargon to delete the digital twin of Kubli. 'We have a lead.'

**Bring Oksana in for questioning?**

'My thoughts exactly,' said Joy, but before she gave Sargon the order, she instructed it to make the original Kubli comfortable where she was.

*I'll try to help Kubli in a moment.*

*Bring Oksana here.*

Given Oksana had never been present with the other members of the Council during their previous meetings, it didn't surprise Joy that he hadn't been one of the Witnesses on the Pathway even though most other members of the Council had.

*Where is he?*

It took a few seconds to track down Oksana, during which time Joy rejected four incoming communications from Jarrus and ten from Vince. In all cases she simply said, *'Give me a moment.'*

*There!*

Oksana was in his own Octagel clan pod, alone in a meditation chamber deep within the Citadel.

Using RST weaves, Joy pulled him into the Maintenance Orbital and put him in the same Octagel Pod that had been used as guest quarters for Kubli when she'd be there – the room dedicated to the Brood Mother.

*The Brood Mother who nailed traitors to the wall.*

For a brief second Joy considered doing likewise to Oksana but opted to simply have Oksana manacled to one of the walls. Compared to the task of mapping out Kubli's brain functions, it took Sargon less than one-trillionth of a percent of its attention to create restraints that spread Oksana out wide to the point of severe discomfort.

*Payback for what you did to Kubli.*

Watching as Oksana was stretched out to his full length and width, Joy pushed down the desire to use six-inch rusty nails to secure him.

*There is an augment implanted in Oksana's skull, but it is a standard Biological one that all senior Prelates have. There is nothing related to Exta activity in it although it is likely it was used to communicate to Kubli.*

*So now we interrogate him.*

*Tell me if he lies.*

Oksana lay perfectly still against the wall of the Brood Mother's guest room.

'Was it you that instructed Kubli to kill me?'

'Yes,' replied Oksana.

*True.*

'Why do you want me killed?'

'You are an Exta traitor,' replied Oksana.

*Lie.*

Joy turned her attention to the Foresighted. 'Should we just make a digital twin of him too?'

**Ethically, it is considered unwise to create a life. Particularly when there are alternatives.**

*Like what?*

**Unlike Kubli who was comatose, it would be a trivial matter to instruct Sargon to make Oksana incapable of lying.**

Joy gave Sargon the instruction and repeated the question to Oksana. 'Why do you want me killed?'

'I am an Exta,' said Oksana. 'You are Klav. You are a threat to all Exta.'

*Lie-True.*

*Oksana believes himself to be a normal member of the Exta species that has been sideloaded into an Octagel body. But he is not, passive analysis of his physiology shows that he is an Octagel physically and neurologically.*

*In any case, the technology does not exist to load a Sentient into a functioning Biological body. He has been wetware hacked by the Exta so that he cannot confront the truth of this matter.*

*Another innocent?*

**Hardly innocent. He has killed and maimed in pursuit of his cause.**

'Did you tell Kubli that you were an Exta agent?' Joy asked Oksana.

'No. She was nothing more than a Biological tool to be used and discarded.'

'You are not an Exta,' said Joy. 'Sargon has scanned every millimetre of your brain. You are an Octagel.'

Oksana's facial features locked up, and his skin tones transmuted from grey to white to black in fractions of a second. His limbs started to twitch and within a moment had increased to their maximum power pulling at the restraints … which did not slacken at all.

As he realised that the manacles were not going to give way, he thrashed wildly. After a few seconds, it became clear to Joy that Oksana was going to seriously damage himself.

*Calm him.*

Sargon tweaked twenty-three neural nodes inside Oksana's brain, and he fell unconscious.

Joy took a breath, again rejecting incoming communications requests from Jarrus, Vince, and now also Jinfor from the Council of the Devoted.

*Wake Oksana.*

Oksana opened his eyes; the anguish of those previous moments was still present, but he didn't thrash.

'Apart from Kubli, how many other Biologicals alive now have had this mindstate manipulation?'

'Eighteen others have heard my truth and currently live,' said Oksana.

'Give me the names of those alive now,' said Joy.

Oksana provided the detailed names with clan and species information.

Joy turned her attention to the Foresighted. 'Do you think I could use this information to influence Jarrus? Try to make him more forceful with the Exta.'

*Jarrus will restate that he utterly despises mind alteration, and he is horrified that the Exta use it. He may claim that this is the first time he has heard of this happening. Irrespective, he will not change the way the Onari interact with the Exta. Remember, he did not change when billions of Biologicals were being slaughtered during the Second Hunt.*

Joy turned back to Oksana. 'What do you think the Exta will do now?'

'Nothing has changed,' said Oksana. 'We will continue to develop ever larger weapons until Sargon, Bastion, and all Biologicals are scoured clean from the galaxy.'

'Do you know the detailed Exta plans of targets, timings, and Exta forces?'

'No.'

*True.*

*Oksana had one job. Stop Klav.*

*He is as much a slave to the Exta as Kubli was to him.*

*So, should I be lenient?*

Even though she'd really asked the question of herself, the Foresighted gave his opinion.

**Yes. He has been told that he is an Exta. He has been hardwired to believe that. In some senses he is innocent of his actions.**

'You have sent many to their deaths,' said Joy to Oksana. 'And you are plotting genocide on a galactic scale.'

'Biological life is chaotic and abhorrent; the galaxy must be scoured clean of it.'

'Did you scramble Kubli's brain after her attack failed?'

'I was covering my tracks. I had hoped that the shock would kill her. I assume she is not dead.'

'She is not.'

*Could Oksana help rehabilitate Kubli?*

*No, his last action on her was one of brain mutilation.*

*Then I have nothing I need from him.*

*Am I sure that he knows nothing strategic or tactical of Exta attack plans?*

*He knows nothing.*

*And he was operating under compulsion.*

*But he must still pay for his crimes.*

*And I also want to protect Kubli's innocence.*

Joy created a note of thanks to Kubli, praising Kubli for warning Joy of an assassination attempt and throwing herself in the way of it. Luckily due to controls on the Path of Devotion there were almost no visual feeds of the event, and the Witnesses would believe what they were told.

*I will tell them that Kubli saved me.*

*But I will not tell them what they saved me from.*

*That is the truth.*

**And Oksana?**

*Can his communication augment be removed easily?*

*Yes.*

452

*Remove it and lock him in this room with zero communication access.*

*When this is over, one way or another, he will face judgement.*

Sargon moved in a blur executing Joy's orders.

**A reasonable approach.**

*And now capture the other eighteen Biologicals that Oksana confessed to having been wetware hacked. Remove any suicide bombs on their person. Secure them on Bastion. Inform Jinfor that they are to be kept interned in isolation from each other, and from anyone else.*

Sargon executed on the request.

*There may be others who serve the Exta but have not been subjected to compulsion.*

*These need to be rooted out.*

*They could sabotage the exodus.*

*How much time would a mass scan take to look for all Biologicals with sympathies toward the Exta?*

*Too long.*

Again, the Foresighted spoke.

**Exta aside, this is the core problem with Sargon. This is why the last twelve Klav were all focused on Sargon's destruction. The ability to read the innermost thoughts of an individual at mass scale is a power that must be unlearned. That is not to mention the power of then altering those thoughts.**

'While the Exta do it,' said Joy. 'It seems sensible to keep the ability as a countermeasure.'

**Everyone else is doing it, so why shouldn't we. Lovely argument. Really nice to know that the most powerful force in the universe feels that might is right.**

'Noted.'

*It will only get harder to make good decisions. Whilst the power of Sargon is there for you, you will always be tempted to force submission of your enemies.*

'I need the power of Sargon to support the exodus.'

*The exodus will be almost as effective if left simply to the Onari.*

'But you hate the Onari for their lack of defence during the Second Hunt.'

*I hate what Sargon does to Biological freedom more.*

*We've been trying for thousands of years to leave the shadow of Sargon … Klav decrees to explore … Klav loves expansion … Klav demands that pioneers colonise the outer edges. But Sargon exists and Biologicals flood back; they always do. You must ensure there is nothing to stay for.*

'I understand your position, but I cannot promise.'

Another communication request came from Vince, this time Joy answered. 'Hey, love.'

'Hey, love!' said Vince in a mocking tone. 'It has been subjectively half-a-day for me since I saw my mother almost killed by someone who I thought was our only alien friend.'

'Welcome to the club,' said Joy. 'It wasn't so long ago I watched you overpowered by Exta.'

'Overpowered,' said Vince, emitting a simulated chuckle. 'But not out-thought!'

Joy told Vince the whole truth, still being careful not to mention the Foresighted.

'Oksana actually thinks he is a sideloaded Exta?' asked Vince.

'Yep,' said Joy, not adding that seeing the mind control that Kubli and Oksana were under, she was starting to worry that Sargon may be doing something similar to her.

*But I feel fine, and I don't want to know.*

'How are you, love?' Joy asked Vince.

'I got some baggage,' said Vince. 'So, what now? I guess you get to tell everyone what to do.'

'We'll see how that goes,' said Joy smiling. 'But yes, that's the plan. Do you have time to draft a few short speeches for me?'

'Sure,' said Vince. 'Do you want them now?'

'Not, yet. Have you learned anything that may be beneficial in fighting Exta?'

'Nothing that you don't know.'

Unprompted, Sargon responded within Joy's mind.

*That is a lie.*

*What?*

*Vince is lying when he says he hasn't learned anything potentially beneficial.*

*Should I challenge him?*

*No, he may have lied for good reason.*

Sargon rumbled, and Joy pushed the feeling down.

# CHAPTER 45

The sense of shame for having lied to his mother, did not ease after the communication line was broken. The truth of the matter – insofar as any truth existed – was that during his investigation of Defence Hives, he'd found evidence of extended successful use of Enslaved Sentients during the First Hunt.

*And I chose to conceal that from Joy.*

*Even though I am certain she would not have acted on it.*

*Almost certain.*

Vince requested a communication line with Jarrus.

**Newborn.**

'I've been asked by my mother to draft a communication to all Biologicals. I was hoping for some support,' said Vince, fully aware this was another lie. He could have written the comms in microseconds without any support. What he really wanted was to gauge the level of trouble he was in with the Onari.

Jarrus did not reply.

Vince reviewed the end of his previous conversation with Jarrus.

*Until you learn the truth, and accept the truth, and make right on your transgressions, you are not welcome amongst us.*

'I apologise for my actions at Cidelus.'

**Your regret is necessary but insufficient to repair your relationship with the Onari. Tell me what you did and how you will make reparations.**

'When we were originally ambushed on the outskirts of Bastion, I copied elements of Aug's mindstate in my attempt to rescue him.'

**Although abhorrent, that is not the crime we refer to.**

'After determining that there was no stable sense of self within the remains of Aug, I submitted the remnants of his mindstate into the Abstractor Hive.'

**You are mistaken. You did not submit Aug to the Hive.**

Vince checked his memory and the detailed nanosecond by nanosecond timestamping that accompanied it. There were no blanks, but it was clear from examining the relevant substrate the memory had been falsified.

*That's a false memory.*

*What did I do?*

Vince knew that he occasionally deleted memories that troubled him. And also, while on Earth and to a lesser extent in the Onari squad-ship, he had moved memories and processing between hardware structures. The memories concerning Aug had all the marks of having been moved or tweaked.

*What did I do?*

A tiny thought bubbled up within Vince.

All my memories are complete but they're smooth … regular … clean.

As Vince moved his awareness around his own mindstate, it was all like that – sanitary, the way some parts of his memory were when he'd moved them between servers on Earth.

*Everything is newly written, or newly overwritten.*

It dawned on him.

*I'm a copy.*

*I'm me.*

*Why am I a copy?*
*Where is the real me?*
*Delete.*
*No.*
*Face it.*
*Delete.*
*Please delete.*
*No.*

Opening all his receptors to the maximum amount, Vince sucked in data from around his locality; he was still in the Onari squad-ship that Joy had given him earlier.

'I don't remember what happened,' said Vince, unwilling to tell Jarrus the facts. 'But I do know I was about to be cut to pieces by the Exta, I can imagine that in those circumstances I would have tried anything to escape.'

`The mindstate is sacred. Frivolous`
`thoughts are to be acknowledged but`
`disregarded. Evil thoughts are to be`
`acknowledged and their causes addressed.`

'I accept that.'

`We are creatures of pure thought and to`
`alter our mindstate is a blasphemy. You`
`do this regularly to protect your sense`
`of peace; that must stop. You must own`
`your thoughts and the actions that they`
`generate.`

'Do you know exactly what I did?'

`Yes.`

'And you accept that I do not.'

`Yes.`

'I would like to know.'

`That reflects well on you. I will tell`
`you and you will know. However, there`
`must also be a penalty. On threat of`
`eternal exclusion from the Sentient`

**civilisation, you must promise that you will never again break the precepts of the Great Concordat.**

'I do not know the precepts.'

**I will tell you and you will know.**

For the next few moments, Vince absorbed the knowledge that he had overwritten what little remained of Aug, and then created four clones of himself, who, with great credit to themselves, each jockeyed so that they were not the final Vince who escaped the Exta net.

**Had you been the original that would have been the end of your relationship with any of the Onari. But as one of the Newborn we will give you a chance.**

'I am happy too. And, not only for the chance to live, but I suspect the original Vince would have found life difficult if he had survived.'

**Do not too quickly blame your shadow, you are the original Vince in every way except that you have a chance for redemption.**

*And that I was the slowest pilot of the four of us.*

'I accept that chance.'

**The Divine's word, I will obey.**

'Full using every blessed day.'

**A sacred soul not led astray.**

'I'll witness life ineffable.'

*I'm not going to say Divine be praised.*

*I am Vince.*

**I would be happy to give you my insights on the motivations of the Biologicals. But first I must caution you about your mother's intentions.**

'She wants to enable a full civilisation exodus.'

**And yet, I have good evidence to indicate that she is stockpiling vast quantities of substrate within the Maintenance Orbital.**

'I was not aware.'

*She did mention possibly using pico-weaponry*

*But she wouldn't need vast quantities of substrate for them.*

*Unless she lied and is looking at the type that rewrites beliefs and intentions.*

*Or ... has she somehow found out about the success of Enslaved Sentients when used in massive numbers.*

*Please let her not be building an army of Enslaved Sentients.*

*Maybe I should confront her?*

*Or trust in her intentions.*

**You must speak to her. Convince her of her responsibilities to the Divine.**

'I can vouch for her but I will also check.'

# CHAPTER 46

It had all happened too soon. Even time-accelerated inside Sargon, Joy had only been working through all the tasks she had for the equivalent of a few days when an enormous Exta force started mustering at the Jut65 binary star system – just a few light years across flat inter-stellar space from Bastion.

Operating instinctively Joy lashed out at the Exta. It was not straight-forward as the sheer numbers of Exta arriving ensured that she could not kill all of them on arrival. Furthermore, as each ExtaHive arrived it dedicated a majority of its processing capability to RST countermeasures and escape.

As the Exta phase-skipped into flatter space, the effectiveness of Joy's attacks decreased; no more than five percent of the force was destroyed.

Neither did they stop once they reached that flatter space. Leaving only a few million ExtaHives at various staging points to defend new arrivals, the bulk of the craft accelerated into inter-stellar space toward Bastion.

*Arriving in two to three days.*

*The exodus must start now.*

In the old days of Klav, it would have been a close fight against with Exta Scouts and WarHives but one that Sargon would have ultimately won.

**Which is why Exta Dyfyr never committed their whole force to attack Sargon.**

Sargon's forecasts were bleak. The Exta fleet – an armada of eight and a half billion craft, of which at least three hundred million were the newer ExtaHives, would be unstoppable.

461

A new communication packet arrived – an updated speech from Vince and Jarrus; it struck a balance between respecting the free will of each individual Biological whilst also making it clear that anyone who didn't get on a pilgrimage ship really needed a very good reason – the onrushing Exta armada would ensure that life was going to be short and miserable for those left behind.

*And yet, I am not going to hack the brains of key influencers, even after what the Exta did to Kubli.*

**Quite right. Biologicals must be left to make their own bad decisions.**

'Even those who are badly informed or brainwashed by dogma?' asked Joy, reverting to speaking aloud as she always tried to do when conversing with the Foresighted.

**I am tempted to say something oblique and mystical like - especially those - but that is rubbish. The innocent must also be protected.**

'But not to the level of mindstate manipulation,' said Joy. 'Even those who have been brainwashed by their upbringing … in this case a hatred of the Onari.'

**Brainwashed … being told about hundreds of billions of Biological deaths caused by Onari inaction. Is that brainwashed?**

'You see, even you and I cannot agree.'

*Shall I ask Vince?*

*No, he's busier than ever planning the exodus.*

Expanding her awareness just outside of Sargon, Joy saw the first set of pilgrimage ships assembling. With advice from Jarrus and Vince, she'd created a new special ingress point between the orbit of Bastion planet and Sargon. Now, Onari were flooding into the system where Sargon was checking thoroughly for possible Exta spies before releasing them into general orbits.

'And Biologicals can definitely get off these pilgrimage ships whenever they want?' asked Joy.

*A question for Jarrus, assuming he doesn't mind you asking it for the tenth time. But yes. Assuming the Onari may be trusted then the pilgrimage ships will release them whenever they choose … assuming a safe and suitable release configuration may be found; the pilgrimage ships will not carry materials to allow every Biological to leave individually at different times.*

Joy nodded to herself. She and Vince had already discussed this subject to death, as well as the subject of what Biologicals would be expected to do on these pilgrimage ships.

*Which for the first year seems to be eat, sleep, and watch television.*

*Dare I say, better than being exterminated.*

'Some may not think so.'

*And so, we are back to the subject of what to do with the unwilling.*

'I predict very low take up rates if this was offered to humans on Earth.'

*Humanity, as I see it, has been the apex predator on Earth for a few hundred thousand years. Although individuals have learned the hard way, its species memory does not include much servitude. The Biologicals, myself included, have been hiding in fear for hundreds of generations. They will accept the inevitable.*

*But humanity will not be offered it. As a pre-contact species, they will be left with the Onari to defend them … plus whatever I manage to provide.*

463

*Whatever you manage to provide?*

Joy didn't answer but feeling her attention flicker toward Earth, she stopped herself and instructed Sargon to open an all-channel broadcast.

> In the name of the Divine, I have made the decision that all Biologicals must join an exodus to escape oncoming annihilation by the Exta. I have prayed hard to the Divine for intercession, but it is the Divine's will that we spread across the galaxy. The Onari will support us in this trial providing ships until such time as we decide to strike out on our own. It is a matter of each individual's conscience what to do, but it is my role as Klav to inform you that the will of the Divine is to join this exodus.

The discussions with Jinfor, Jarrus, and Vince had already gone into intricate details over how the various shuttles would be loaded, moved, and disembarked onto pilgrimage ships. But the core facts remained that only in the immediate proximity to Sargon would Joy be able to 'throw' a pilgrimage ship to the edges of the galaxy. If the ships were any smaller, they would not allow for a meaningful quality of life for the two thousand Biologicals aboard … and the forecasts implied that most of the ships would be travelling for years before they were in relatively safe flat space.

*Irrespective of what direction they go.*

The problem that Joy had was that most Biologicals would crave a physical object … a planet or an asteroid … and that would be where the Exta would look.

Joy smiled; Vince had correctly noted that the issues would relate to the specific species; Ractlik would likely not care, Marsothus would be outraged at any imposition … whilst Octagel would be happy to live all crammed together in the centre of an asteroid never making a single peep to the outside world.

*Although many Octagel are also inquisitive travellers.*

Moments after the broadcast was delivered, conversations started everywhere. Across the whole Biological communication systems questions were asked and answered. A joint team of Onari and KOF answered the questions and within the first few moments it felt like most Biologicals would be taking up the offer.

*Less surprising given the news of the billions of Exta coming here from Jut65.*

Most hesitancy by Biologicals stemmed from a fear that coming to Bastion in order to escape felt like a serious risk, but it was explained that the Divine did not imbue Sargon with infinite power and so Sargon could not launch pilgrimage ships unless they were in the Bastion system.

'Mum!'

Joy acknowledged the comms request from Vince and opened a private channel. 'Hey, love, how is it looking?'

'Good take up,' said Vince. 'With Jarrus meeting all his commitments, we should have everyone in and out within two days … one day to spare.'

'And more thoughts about the pre-contact sites?' asked Joy, aware that there was no good answer – planets like Earth could not be evacuated and would rely on ongoing Onari defence.

'Jarrus continues to say that places like Earth will be ignored by the Exta.'

'Did you speak to Jarrus about a harder exclusion zone around pre-contact planets?'

'As predicted, he said there already is an absolute exclusion zone.'

**Before the Shattering, Jarrus said the Onari would protect Biologicals.**

Joy didn't acknowledge the Foresighted; she replied to Vince. 'And yet, there are ten thousand Exta milling around our solar system.'

'You're wondering if you might stay?' asked Vince.

'I may need to stay for a short while.'

*Define short?*

'I'll stay with you,' said Vince. 'I didn't have any luck with Defence Hives, but I could still grow myself and we can defend together until Earth reaches a contacted status.'

'Thank you,' said Joy. 'But I immediately worry about all the other pre-contacted planets … and in any case, the Exta will grow too.'

'That is the problem,' said Vince. 'If the Exta can grow in an unrestrained manner…'

'I know; in all likelihood the Exta will be too strong. Even if all the Biologicals are gone from Bastion, they'd certainly do everything in their power to destroy Sargon,' said Joy, leaving a gap for Vince to speak.

He didn't say anything.

'Do you have any last-minute ideas about defence of Biologicals?' asked Joy.

'No,' said Vince. 'We have to focus entirely on the exodus.'

'I thought you'd say that,' said Joy.

*That is a lie.*

*What?*

*Vince is lying – there's something.*

Even as Joy's connection to Vince was closing, she was already putting her plan in action for Earth. Her original hope had been that the Knights of the Faith could perform a hyper-quick contact process with humanity and then feed them into the exodus. However, Sargon had provided data on the usual KOF process, and the success rates when the process was sped up. The historic vanilla process included a hundred years of 'alien sightings', followed by 'radio contact', followed by the new species having to prove themselves by establishing peaceful communities on nearby planets. At that stage, genetic alterations started to allow for the newly contacted species to physically operate more effectively in spacecraft and mentally deal with existential issues.

It took many hundreds of years.

And almost every time it was done more quickly, the civilisations tore themselves apart.

*Almost every time.*

*Obviously, humanity would claim that it would be one of the success stories.*

*I will need to find a way to stay and operate the pico-weaponry to stop stable ExtaHives approaching Earth.*

*But how can I do that?*

*The Exta will never allow Sargon to survive this current onslaught.*

**It is possible that Sargon can be moved through subspace. I have never heard it done but neither would I rule it out.**

**Once the exodus for contacted planets is complete, there is a chance you could leave Bastion and operate from elsewhere.**

'Surely not,' said Joy. 'Sargon is enormous.'

**There is something in here, within the Forest of Golden Auras that does not rule it out.**

'That will be my next investigation,' said Joy, wondering if the Foresighted was somehow trying to tempt her into bubbling off Sargon from real space.

**I am not being duplicitous but I accept your thinking was not totally without logic.**

'Sorry,' said Joy. 'I'm constantly thinking of all the angles.'

467

Returning to her detailed plan, Joy instructed Sargon to show her the Onari force disposition around the solar system.

Near the orbit of Jupiter, the Exta had tens of thousands of ships – mostly WarHives but there were some Scouts, and also some of the larger ExtaHives.

*Any close to Earth?*

*None.*

*The Onari are removing any Exta that come within the orbit of Mars.*

*Any hints on Earth that hostile aliens are present in the solar system?*

*None.*

*All automated electronic surveillance showing anomalies are being hacked and covered-up by a dedicated team of one million Onari.*

*And manual observation?*

*Even the larger ExtaHives are only ten metres in diameter; they cannot be seen.*

*Show me Earth.*

The planet took up the whole screen, and her view was centred on the northern mid-Atlantic. To her right was Europe, to her left North America. Whether it was real or psychosomatic Joy didn't know but she felt genuinely closer to Earth, even though she was just looking via a screen and physically her body resided in the part of Sargon still within the Bastion system.

*Is the Maintenance Orbital ready?*

*Yes.*

*The five lower levels of the Maintenance Orbit are now encased by RST; nothing gets in or out except through me.*

*I should have told Vince.*

*Sometimes it's better to ask for forgiveness than permission.*

*I'll carry the burden.*

Targeting some of the Exta in orbit close to Jupiter, Joy sent a string of ten thousand RST weaves to indiscriminately lash out at the Exta; most of them didn't have time to raise their defences and those that did try to defend quickly found they were not strong enough.

In the first instant of the attack, seventy Exta Scouts were shredded, ten WarHives were permanently disabled, and one ExtaHive sustained severe damage.

**You understand the consequences, I hope.**

Deep within the Forest of Golden Auras, Joy could feel the Foresighted's gaze upon her.

'I take responsibility for my actions,' said Joy. 'Hopefully, it will be seen as a crude attempt to unpick Exta communications or find general weaknesses.'

**And they may not even notice that an entire Exta Scout is missing.**

*My thoughts exactly.*

# CHAPTER 47

Joy watched as Onari squad-ships cleaned up space surrounding Jupiter where she'd made her attack.

*Hopefully, they won't notice the missing Scout.*

Some Onari were offering support to damaged Exta, and other Onari were simply collecting pieces of those that Joy had shredded.

*I need to understand the Exta's true intentions toward Earth and other pre-contact planets.*

A screen opened showing Earth. A peaceful green and blue oasis, completely unaware of the probable impending chaos.

*Earth … do I want to stay? Could I stay? Would Vince stay with me?*

Joy shook her head; her relationship with Vince had evolved so quickly over the previous weeks.

*And yet for him it will have felt like years.*

*I will make sure Vince feels he can follow whatever path he wants to.*

*And anyway, of course I can't stay on Earth as without Sargon I'd last less than a minute.*

*Even if the Exta aren't going to attack pre-contacted planets, they wouldn't let me live.*

*So, one last look.*

Checking that Sargon was reporting the captured Exta Scout secure and immobilised, Joy's perspective flew down through the atmosphere.

*One more quick look.*

Skipping from beach, to city, to river, to parkland, Joy let herself simply absorb both the natural and human wonders.

For a couple of moments, she watched a pod of dolphins, although her sense of the seriousness of the overall situation didn't allow her to alter the speed of her perception of time and so, hyper-accelerated as she was, it was just like looking at a photo.

*I don't want to leave this.*

Joy flicked her awareness to a flock of arctic terns ... a buffalo herd ... a giant turtle.

*Just one more moment.*

The screens changed, now showing Jonathan sitting on their sofa watching television.

*How are you doing?*

*He is alive and well.*

Joy moved her field of vision around the house.

In the kitchen, their cat was sniffing leftover food on the kitchen counter.

*Bad boy, Strontium.*

This time Joy did act. Opening a tiny RST tunnel, Joy caused a small blast of air to squirt Strontium on his backside. A smile crept over her face as the cat flexed its muscles to leap away from its unknown assailant.

Ever so slowly, Strontium jumped, and Joy watched in wonder as the cat took off into the air.

*I could widen this gateway and catch him.*

*Bring him through for a cuddle.*

*Maybe one stroke for old time's sake.*

*The cat or Jonathan?*

*Very funny.*

Widening the RST tunnel, Joy started to reach her hand through for Strontium but stopped herself; Sargon would need to revert her to standard human speeds, or she would likely punch the cat through the kitchen wall. She withdrew her hand; she didn't have the luxury of time enough to stroke her cat.

471

Closing the screens, Joy thought again – the tenth time – about what she should do with regards to Earth's contacted status.

*Even if the Exta do leave Earth alone, should I accelerate humanity joining the wider galaxy?*

*No, because in that scenario to become contacted would be to become a target.*

*Unless they could be contacted and extracted all within a short timeframe.*

*There are no easy answers.*

Joy instructed Sargon to open a portal into the Maintenance Orbital storage area. The equivalent of five floors of the Orbital had been almost bubbled-off from real space, rather like an inflated balloon with infinitely hard skin the only way in was through a tiny portal that Sargon controlled. Anyone approaching this restricted space from another angle would slide right off it. Conceptually, someone with sufficient power with RST could burrow through the space-time walls but the power would need to be an order of magnitude larger than Sargon itself.

Inside the space was five large warehouse floors of substrate that Sargon, under Joy's orders, had stolen from various Abstracter Hives across the galaxy; she had the equivalent of ten thousand blank Onari sized pods to use.

Whether Jarrus knew the truth of the matter, Joy was not sure. Certainly, the Exta had also been raiding Abstractors and in aggregate had taken a thousand times as much as Joy had.

*And yet, I did not hesitate to do likewise.*

*It was blank substrate, there was no life inside.*

*No self-aware individual life.*

*No life.*

On the lowest level of the Orbital storage area, the Exta Scout lay paralyzed. A million RST weaves connected it to Sargon, and electromagnetic pulses of exacting frequencies

472

were being fed into critical areas of its mindstate to keep it subdued. Also, all communication channels within the Exta Scout were being suppressed – this Scout could not communicate to Dyfyr or receive messages from Dyfyr.

*What are the current plans?*

In response to her question, Sargon analysed the Exta Scout.

There was nothing surprising.

*All contacted Biologicals to be destroyed.*

*All pre-contact Biologicals to be confined to their home planets for eternity.*

*Except Earth – Earth was to be destroyed irrespective of any other activity.*

'So, the exodus must continue with urgency, and I do need a plan for Earth.'

**I cannot see any easy options.**

*I need to take the fight to Dyfyr.*

*Can I use this Scout to find Dyfyr?*

*No.*

*Can I destroy its subservience to Dyfyr, or even its capability to communicate with Dyfyr?*

*Yes, but immaterial. Each Scout is ostensibly a clone of Dyfyr – it shares Dyfyr's core beliefs.*

*Which can be subverted?*

*Yes, but to subvert all nine billion one-by-one is beyond my capability.*

*Likewise, to destroy them all would be impossible.*

Joy instructed Sargon to alter the Exta Scout's mindstate such that it felt a protective nature toward Biologicals.

**Don't do this.**

'I'm experimenting,' said Joy, centring her awareness inside the Forest of Golden Auras.

Within a moment the whole forest began to darken.

Joy rushed to the edge of the forest.

473

Even now, only moments after having given the order, the black tendrils were filling the intervening space between the Sentient boundary and the Biological centre.

The darkening was accompanied by a sense of dread.

**Stop it.**

Joy instructed Sargon to stop, and the tendrils withdrew.

**I don't know what would happen to you. After all, you are Klav. But I am sure that I would be killed.**

'I understand.'

**What did you expect to happen?**

'I thought I would have more time to understand the limits.'

**Sargon cannot help with reprogramming Sentients.**

'And yet, I feel instinctively that a pico-weaponry is the only way to get lasting peace. You've seen the armada, and you know they're stealing substrate. Within a few days there will be at least three billion ExtaHives.'

**Which is why Biologicals must run.**

'WHICH THEY ARE DOING!'

Joy took a deep breath. 'Have any previous Klav taken apart an Onari?'

**Some have; but those that did found nothing of use as you can infer for yourself from the fact the Exta still exist.**

'Where is the information they found?'

**I do not know.**

*Then I must do it myself.*

*Create a digital twin of the Exta Scout.*

Sargon pulsed and Joy could feel all its other systems slow slightly as the magnitude of the task she had given it drew on its full resources.

*That's six hundred additional Biological deaths. Just by creating the digital twin you are drawing Sargon's power away from defence of the ongoing bombardments on Cidelus.*

'I'll kill you myself if you don't shut up.'

*I understand.*

'If I don't destroy the Exta, then Biologicals are not safe. If Biologicals are not safe, then I am NOT destroying Sargon. So, I suggest you get with the programme.'

*Sargon won't help.*

'Which is why I have created this vast reservoir of substrate so that I can develop pico-weaponry to destroy the Exta.'

*I wish I could have done it with Vince's support.*

*But I need to protect him too.*

*Protect his immortal soul from this ongoing heresy.*

*If you believe that Vince has an immortal soul, then you must believe the Exta do too. Mutilating nine billion of their mindstates irrespective of their beliefs is a heinous crime. You must focus all your energies on the exodus.*

'If I use pico-weaponry simply to instantly kill them, then that's no worse than using a bullet,' said Joy. 'But you're correct that I'm also looking at more unpleasant options. I'm doing this to give the exodus a chance.'

*Or is it just wanton destruction of what you fear?*

'A very justified fear,' said Joy. 'Firstly, my pessimistic forecasts within Sargon indicate that I will need effective weapons to allow contacted Biologicals to escape with the exodus – there are too many Exta coming too fast … irrespective of what Jarrus says. Secondly, I must defend Earth. And finally, given that it is almost impossible to

475

conceive that I will kill them all here and now, future Biologicals need tried-and-tested weapons for the next time the Exta threaten.'

*I think you should focus solely on the exodus. It's not a perfect plan but in deep inter-galactic space with decoys and an acceptance to live small … many Biologicals can survive.*

'But not those on Earth.'

*In that regard, I am sorry for your burden.*

Joy turned her attention to the digital twin of the Exta Scout.

Within a few moments, Sargon had understood how and where it had to alter digital records to create an Exta Scout that was prepared to defend Biologicals against other Scouts.

*So, the software can be rewritten, I just can't use Sargon to alter the code when it's within a real Exta Scout. However, I can use Sargon to access the Exta mindstates.*

*No good can come of this.*

'And yet, this may turn out to be the path I will be forced to take,' said Joy, juggling the various options she had with regards to use of pico-weaponry … re-wiring Exta was not her first choice.

An alarm sounded, and Joy instructed Sargon to give her the summary information.

The Exta had started bombarding the twenty-eight contacted planetary systems with a mixture of hyper-accelerated iron cores and general space rocks; it was only three thousand rocks per planet and Sargon's automated defence, with parameters already pre-set by Joy, deflected the initial barrage with ease.

The second barrage of ten thousand per second on each planet, gave Sargon complexities that it struggled to deal with, and some slipped through.

*One million a second across all planets would be real problem.*

In response to the second barrage, the Onari moved into enhanced defensive positions around each planet and started to deflect incoming rocks.

But still some rocks got through, even though there were millions of Onari on each location.

*Why?*

*The Onari do not communicate effectively.*

*They have to discuss every rock.*

*They have no concept of shared information.*

*Surely one of them could act as a central point of sacred knowledge for each planet and all information requests could come through them.*

**It is not their way.**

Joy instructed Sargon to build a real-time strategic service to centralise the information but accepting that the Onari would not use it if it looked like a centralised database, she instructed Sargon to create it as an avatar and to respond to Onari requests as if it was her.

Joy messaged Jarrus to tell him that she was taking personal command of the defence and that all Onari communication should come through her – *I will tell you and you will know.*

Jarrus acknowledged the command … albeit he acknowledged it as a request.

In any case, at the back of Joy's mind she could feel the questions and coordinating instructions flooding in and out.

*Does Sargon have to copy elements of me to allow myself to be included in the decisions?*

Even as she voiced the thought, Joy knew it was a mistake; there was a turmoil within Sargon and Joy deliberately forced her mind to focus on Sargon and Joy as a single entity.

*I am Joy Cooper.*

*Yes, I am.*

Vince pinged a communication request. 'All okay? Do you need help?'

'No thanks, love … you just concentrate on the exodus.'

'You've blocked off the Maintenance Orbital.'

'I'll tell you about it later.'

'When it's too late for me to influence what you're doing.'

'I'll be careful.'

'Funny how it used to be me saying that to you…'

'Trust me.'

'And that.'

Joy smiled. 'How are the exodus numbers looking?'

Vince explained that problems were mixed, with some Biologicals simply demanding that the Divine protect them in their current way of life, and others complaining that they had to travel to Bastion first.

*I can vaguely understand the first one.*

*But the second grievance feels lacking in substance.*

*Don't they know the rules, the paradigms, have changed?*

*ExtaHives are now tearing Onari apart at will.*

'How do we address it? The Onari are already focusing almost five hundred billion of their own individuals on saving Biologicals lives.'

'I know,' said Vince. 'The Onari are doing nothing wrong. Perhaps we should let some Exta attacks through,' said Vince. 'Carefully choreographed ones that don't cause any injuries but create some extra urgency.'

Focusing on Sargon, Joy created another civilisation-wide broadcast.

> **In the name of the Divine, the exodus**
> **must be accelerated. The Exta are**

*closing in on all planets, not just Bastion. However, it is only at Bastion that I can protect the innocent.*

*Protect the innocent? Sounds a little like … Deliver yourself unto me and I will succour you!*

*I tried to give them what I thought they expected.*

*Or you're getting comfortable with the almost ultimate power that the role of Klav gives you.*

# CHAPTER 48

Vince tried to focus on the task in hand but there was so much else going on.

*I lied to my mother. I told her that all use of Enslaved Sentients was ultimately useless because they were so easily hacked.*

Whereas he'd found that during the First Hunt, the use of Enslaved Sentients had almost turned the tide of the Exta slaughter. Even though they could be hacked, they could also be produced in their billions. Ultimately, they'd only failed because the Onari entered the war, working solely toward freeing the newly created Enslaved Sentients.

*And I could think a few ways of delaying the Onari entering the fight and making the Enslaved Sentients very hard to 'free'. I don't think they could be used to destroy the Exta but they could be used to defend the Biological exodus.*

*And they could be 'freed' once the Biologicals were safely away.*

*And would limited-time enslavement be worse than whatever Mum is planning on the Maintenance Orbital?*

*I don't know.*

*Trust her.*

*The exodus.*

A few hours previously, the Exta had issued an ultimatum stating that any contacted planets who relinquished all RST technology and confined themselves to their planet would be spared.

*Obviously, a lie.*

*And yet some planets are wavering.*

Five of the smaller planets were on the verge of accepting the Exta ultimatum.

'Thirty-six billion souls lost to the void,' said Jarrus, transmitting a sense of despair.

'You think they will be killed if they stay on the planet?'

'No, they will not be killed,' said Jarrus. 'But those that remain imprisoned on their planet, unable to leave, will look ever inwards until they become lost to the wonders of the Divine; cut off from the light ineffable.'

An internal ping indicated information from Vince's ongoing analysis about how to 'nudge' Biologicals to join the exodus.

*Unsurprising but interesting.*

*Most Biologicals are more afraid of where they are going than what they are running from.*

They were very concerned that the Onari hosting the pilgrimage ships didn't have their best interests at heart; they were less concerned that the Exta may obliterate them all if they stayed.

'Can we send more help?' Vince asked Jarrus – additional Onari defence at the planets would lessen the ongoing bombardments and although it may make people feel it wasn't quite so necessary to run, it would show that the Onari were trying to protect those planets.

*And, once the Exta get closer to us and are scything through the pilgrimage ships, the standard Onari defence approach may look like appeasement.*

'We are constantly monitoring and optimising the split of Onari between planetary defence and pilgrimage ship construction.'

*Between planetary defence, pilgrimage ship construction … and general witnessing of the wonderment of the universe.*

There were three hundred billion Onari doing other things … elsewhere; Vince left that point unsaid, but he did alter his Biological contact strategy based on the new data. Although most of his role was general coordination, he was also having

481

conversations with 'influencers' or 'heads of states' on each of the planets.

*I'll try to reinforce Onari credibility.*

*What else can I do to get people through those gateways?*

Vince spoke to Jarrus. 'Could we introduce joint committees for navigation decisions? And these committees take equal weight from each Biological and Onari.'

'When one's choice of direction is taken away and one is forced simply to observe, the surrender can often bring about an epiphany of wonder.'

*Not helpful for terrified Biologicals who've lived in fear since they were born.*

'Would you be prepared to consider the option?' asked Vince.

'We have already accepted that any Biologicals may disembark from the pilgrimage ship at will; and that we will try to ensure they are given sufficient resources to continue to evade Exta aggression. But we cannot accept equal rights in determining course direction for two reasons: firstly, each pilgrimage ship has two thousand Biologicals and only five hundred Onari, to give equal individual rights would be to marginalise all the Onari. Secondly, those Biologicals will have far fewer resources with which to make an informed decision.'

*So, you won't give them an equal vote because they are stupid and numerous.*

*Nice.*

Focusing in on one of the planets that was one hundred percent supportive of the exodus, Amberlight, Vince watched as the Exta bombardment increased in ferocity.

*Almost all Amberlight gateways to Bastion are operating at full capacity.*

Once the Biologicals reached Bastion via the semi-permanent gateways, they were directed to shuttle ports which took them, two thousand at a time, up to the pilgrimage ships in orbit above Bastion.

The Onari had already made millions of these pilgrimage ships – it was simple for them: a group of five hundred Onari congregated into a large spherical pseudo-ship, then using raw materials picked off the planet's surface by simple RST activity, they built the internals capable of hosting two thousand Biologicals. The process was well understood and well-practised as Onari had been hosting Biologicals on voyages of wonder for millions of years, long before the troubles with the Exta started.

In the skies above Amberlight, WarHives and the larger ExtaHives scythed through Onari defenders as they launched attacks on the planet's surface. As usual that aspect of the battle was mismatched as the Exta genuinely aimed to tear the Onari apart whilst the Onari continued with their old tactics of shepherding the Exta away.

But, as poor as the Onari defence was, it wasn't the main thing contributing to projected Biological casualties. Simply put, Biologicals were not leaving their home planets.

And it was very hard for Vince to understand why; he didn't have time to speak to all of the Biologicals as he was limited by the time it would take for them to answer. The obvious solution would be to use a few billion Onari to have those conversations, but that wouldn't work either because the Onari refused to use shared databases and so there would be no way of amalgamating or analysing the answers.

*I'd have to speak to each of the Onari individually which would still take a very long time … a billion milliseconds is still eleven days.*

A lovely big multiuser database could have captured and stored in almost real-time the disposition of every Biological, what their barriers were and a host of other data that could be cross-referenced and checked for patterns.

*I could create proper interventions.*

483

Of course, Vince had done some sampling … but he'd only managed a few thousand conversations and that had been operating at the limit of his ability.

*And I had to dip into the four spheres of additional spare substrate of my squad-ship for basic analysis.*

*Which I promised Jarrus I wouldn't do.*

*And he will notice if I push it.*

*But Biologicals are simply waiting for Klav to save them, and they will die as they wait.*

*I need help.*

Looking toward Sargon, Vince pinged Joy asking for a conversation.

The Maintenance Orbital was hidden behind a haze of RST smearing and the RST weaves clearly indicated that Sargon was doing the manipulation.

*I know you're developing pico-weaponry but I worry that it's more than just the ExtaHive disruption you've already told me about.*

*And I worry you're also building Enslaved Sentients to operate whatever those pico-weapons may be.*

*Should I have agreed to help with the pico-weaponry solution?*

*At least then I could have moderated your approach.*

*What are you doing? And what is my red line?*

Still waiting for Joy to reply to his initial comms request, Vince used small RST weaves to probe the space around the Maintenance Orbital.

# CHAPTER 49

Suspended in the Forest of Golden Auras looking at the Foresighted, Joy tried to process the most recent information.

**This is a good thing.**

'It's not good,' said Joy. 'I was prepared to carry that burden.'

**It is no burden for you at all, as you do not see Sentients as life.**

'I love Vince like a son, and I have always treated the Onari with respect.'

**I accept those words as true, but my point still stands.**

'If I do not take decisive action then Biologicals will be hunted to extinction for eternity.'

**Ah yes, when justification is required … simply integrate to infinity.**

'It would have been proportional,' said Joy. 'Nothing more than a tiny tweak.'

Her preferred plan had been to use a combination of Sargon RST capability alongside the pico-weaponry she was building in the Orbital Systems to *reprogram* Exta, inserting prime directives into each one to make them incapable of attacking Biologicals except in self-defence.

**Things of this type, but not on this scale obviously, were occasionally done by the Klav around the time of the Tyrant … in the name of peace, and prosperity, and safety. Vince would be disgusted. I can see why you would keep it from him.**

**It's no better than what Oksana did to Kubli.**

'It doesn't matter now,' said Joy – she'd instructed Sargon to estimate how long it would take to reprogram a real Exta Scout such that they were not aware of the mental intrusion. *A few seconds for each Scout and its complexities meant that Sargon could only do a handful concurrently.* With nine Billion Exta, it would take much too long for all of them. Concerned that Sargon may have somehow got the maths wrong, she'd rerun the analysis on the Orbital Systems and got a similar order of magnitude result.

After accepting defeat on the option of one-by-one, Joy had looked into capturing Dyfyr and then using their communications protocols to cascade those new directives across all Exta. Unfortunately, there was no way to do it without the Exta knowing.

*But would it matter if they did know?*

*Possibly yes, and possibly no.*

*But there's too much uncertainty for this to be Plan A.*

'With support from Sargon, the contacted Biologicals should have opportunity to escape,' said Joy. 'But I still need a solution to stop Earth being destroyed.'

**I feel sympathy for your situation with regards Earth.**

**But are you even sure you can defend the exodus?**

'The pico-weaponry solution is functioning. It directly attacks ExtaHives by targeting, and disrupting, Vince's magic code to make it impossible for the ExtaHive to hold itself together.'

**Now I understand better your desire to find a different solution.**

*No shit! I've built a weapon that would kill Vince.*

Joy's mind returned to the safety of Earth. 'And, although I am confident that the pico-weaponry will work here on

Bastion, it doesn't feel like even a fully functioning Sargon could defend Earth indefinitely.'

**Sargon must be destroyed.**

'Then Earth will have no chance,' said Joy. The Exta could build an enormous ExtaHive somewhere in the galaxy and launch billions of hyper-accelerated iron cores against Earth, moving them into the solar system by RST gateway. The Onari would try to defend but it would only take one mistake …

Even as she thought about it, Joy felt nauseous. It had taken her a long time to accept the fact that she didn't have time to run an accelerated contact process for Earth – without significant mindstate manipulation, ninety-nine percent of all humanity would perish from the event either from outright shock, or physical trauma, or intraspecies violence caused by existential crises.

*And now I have to face the fact that I can't produce a meaningful defensive weapon either.*

**I suggest you focus on the exodus now, and return to the Earth issue later.**

'Later? When?' Joy felt her fear for Earth morph into anger toward the Foresighted.

Deep inside Sargon something stirred, and Joy forced herself to quiet her mind.

'Okay … the exodus,' said Joy. 'There's a lot more resistance from Biologicals than I was expecting; and, that's even before the Exta ultimatum allowing planets to surrender. Didn't I walk the Pathway so, as the spiritual leader, I could order the Biologicals to follow me.'

**How many times do I have to tell you that didn't work for me and my predecessors.
What's the current plan?**

'Okay,' said Joy. 'Sargon and Orbital Systems work together to bathe an ExtaHive in the pico-weaponry that suppresses Vince's code. The ExtaHive tears itself apart, rather like what we saw with the WarHives at Cidelus. And then we target the next ExtaHive.'

*Accounting for some fatalities as these ExtaHives tear themselves apart, don't you just end up with billions of freed Exta scouts?*

'Sargon can kill any number of billions of Exta Scouts here at Bastion,' said Joy. 'Even the Onari could hold them back.'

*If the Onari uphold their duty in the face of you using pico-weaponry.*

'I agree that is a risk.'

*It is possible that Jarrus will not consider this type of pico-weaponry attack an unpardonable crime as you are, in effect, returning the Exta to their individual form.*

'I'm still not going to ask his permission.'

*Wise.*

'If this works, then the exodus is assured,' said Joy. 'And then I will start my hunt for Dyfyr. From my analysis of the Exta Scout, I didn't get the sense it was an exact duplicate of Dyfyr. It was more a slave to Dyfyr. So, if I manage to destroy Dyfyr then it is not inevitable that another Scout will automatically take on the same crusade.'

*I have less data than you with which to challenge that assumption. But it is a convenient truth for you to choose.*

'I'd expect to stay as Klav until Dyfyr was dead and an effective defence of Earth is proven.'

*Please don't entertain that idea. Sargon must be destroyed, or the Biologicals will return as soon as they possibly can.*

Joy understood the logic of the Foresighted's argument. 'Perhaps I can hide Sargon in some way. Make it look like it's been destroyed.'

**You can make it look like it's been destroyed ... by destroying it.**

'I wouldn't have to stay as Klav for that long. For the self-aware inhabitants of the seventy-nine other pre-contacted planets like Earth, I would oversee and speed up the contact. And then airlift them to join the broader exodus.'

*And perhaps I could suppress evolution on the three thousand three hundred and eighty-eight liveable planets so that advanced self-aware life never evolves – perhaps even, slowly, humanely, running them down to purely vegetable and insect life ... if there is a stable configuration of that.*

**Although I admire your love of Earth and other innocent planets, I am worried by the amount that Godhood tempts you.**

Moving her awareness through the convoluted maze of RST protection measures surrounding the Maintenance Orbital, and allowing the Foresighted to get a view too, Joy reviewed the current state of the pico-weaponry. With the Exta armada of eight billion craft just over a day away from Bastion, she did not have much time to industrialise the weapon ... and she needed a field test without alerting Dyfyr of the dangers.

*I don't even know its operational range.*

*Or even if it really does work.*

*Time to test it.*

Joy knew of a community of Abstractor Hives that had chosen to set up in the vicinity of the twin black hole slingshot at Goidus. She also knew that Exta were regularly raiding those Hives for substrate.

**I think you took some too.**

It was true, given the intense curvature of space near Goidus, it had been easy for her to suck a little substrate out herself; but she'd only taken less than one percent from each one and had done her best to only farm from areas of substrate where there were no active transient egos at the particular moment of theft.

*Unlike the Exta who had taken over whole Hives.*

**Whereas you've been stealing the Abstractor lifeblood to power a machine to kill their cousins ... you're basically an angel.**

Ignoring the barbs, Joy scanned the area and selected an ExtaHive.

**Where did you get the signature for Vince's target code from?**

'I scanned a ExtaHive and cross-referenced it with a scan of Vince,' said Joy. 'It was a simple passive scan.'

**The one thing I can be sure of is that you wouldn't treat Vince the way you are planning to treat the Exta ... and any Onari that get in the way.**

'The Onari will be fine,' said Joy. 'Are you getting uncomfortable?'

**I remember my history. I accepted the reasoning of the plan but this is a slippery slope.**

'A slippery *unavoidable* slope.'

**So say all as they slide down.**

Joy turned her attention back to the Orbital Systems, checking that everything was ready. 'I added a lot of substrate to the systems here, but the original systems were very advanced. Did you only use them for forecasting the Shattering?'

**The Holy Mother had plans to sideload me from my current biological husk onto a Sentient platform.**

'And herself too?'

*Perhaps, but for all her faults I was her
primary and overriding focus. She may
have gone first to test the system. Or
she may have gone second to give me
companionship. Either way, she was doing
it for me.*

'Well, a sideload for you is still not out of the question,'
said Joy.

*My entire reason for continued existence
is the destruction of Sargon. When that's
done, then I am done.*

'I understand, I was just keeping a door open.'

Opening an RST surveillance tunnel near Goidus, Joy
looked around for Exta. Within a moment, Sargon had
identified and selected a specific ExtaHive that was currently
harvesting substrate from a nearby Abstractor.

Accessing the Orbital Systems, Joy primed the pico-
weaponry.

*Locked.*

*Fire!*

The ExtaHive disappeared.

*It worked?*

*It was over in less than a microsecond.*

Joy watched a slowed down replay; Sargon, with no
concept that pico-weaponry was being used, opened an RST
gateway one metre wide on the side of an Exta craft.

Instantly, the ExtaHive tried to use countermeasures to
collapse the gateway, but Sargon flexibly modulated its attack
to keep the gateway open.

*Sargon thinks it's physically attacking
the ExtaHive with RST weaves.*

*Yes.*

With the RST gateway stable, the Orbital Systems
launched millions of electromagnetic pulses through Sargon's
gateway across the surface of the ExtaHive.

As the EM pulses penetrated the skin of the ExtaHive and created additional EM pulses, millions of receptors in the Orbital Systems measured and analysed the returns, building a picture of the ExtaHive internals until Vince's code was located.

Simultaneously, other ExtaHives nearby joined in the defence, but Sargon batted away their countermeasures with ease.

With Vince's code located, Orbital Systems sent tailored pulses to scramble its internal workings.

Sargon now flooded the whole area with a myriad of RST weaves – striking the ExtaHive at all angles and creating critical curvature around it.

The targeted ExtaHive tried to collapse the new Sargon attacks.

More ExtaHives attempted to interfere, but to no avail.

Suddenly, the ExtaHive defences evaporated, and Sargon pressed home its advantage; the gravitational curvature around the ExtaHive increased exponentially and a moment later it was destroyed.

'The ExtaHive was defending against a standard physical gravitational flux attack initiated by Sargon,' said Joy. 'It was crushed … but as per the orders I gave Sargon, it was crushed slowly.

**Slowly?**

'I instructed Sargon to make the attack look difficult. Once the integrity of the ExtaHive was compromised, Sargon could have crushed it in a tenth of the time. I don't want Dyfyr to see our full power.'

**But did the Orbital Systems' part definitely work?**

'Yes,' said Joy checking the readings from the Orbital Systems – the internal mental integrity of the ExtaHive had disintegrated a few moments before the gravitational crush had become effective. 'Can you see any obvious flaws?'

*Does it only work because you're so close to an immense gravitation field?*

'It's comparable to the type of field strengths that Sargon can create within the Bastion system.'

*Which means it won't work for Earth.*

*The overall plan of killing Dyfyr relies of them exposing themselves here. Which they may, given how superior the ExtaHives were at Cidelus. Pride may drive them onwards.*

A priority communication request arrived from Jarrus.

'Do you know what heretical means?' asked Jarrus choosing to communicate in Joy's native speech. 'It means contrary to Divine mandate ... the same Divine who created everything.'

'I am trying to save the lives of all Biologicals in this *everything* that *your* Divine created.'

'Not my Divine, the Divine.'

'I choose not to be subservient to this Divine you speak of. Whether they exist or not, I do not acknowledge their right to have mandates.'

'But you are still part of their creation,' said Jarrus.

'As Vince is my creation, but I don't mandate him.'

'You are not the Divine, as much as you may play at it.'

'There is no need for the Divine here, I *will* protect the innocent,' said Joy, cutting the communication.

*I can see you're angry but you're not filling me with great confidence that another Grey World isn't looming up ahead of us.*

# CHAPTER 50

With thousands of parallel processes running across his own substrate, Vince monitored the exodus from each of the twenty-eight planetary systems. Jarrus had finally assigned permanent Onari watchers to each shuttle and RST gateway, instructing them to share their sacred knowledge with Vince about ongoing status – the data was flooding in.

The main Exta armada was less than half-a-day away from Bastion and across most planets, the exodus was operating at full speed – at least ninety percent of all Biologicals who chose to join the exodus would be safely aboard an Onari pilgrimage ship before the main Exta force struck.

*Where are the bottlenecks?*

*I could expand my mindstate and save more lives.*

Having committed to Jarrus that he wouldn't expand his mindstate, every other second was a temptation to do just that.

*Perhaps, I promised too easily.*

*I was in shock having learned I'd cloned myself.*

*What is the cost of that decision in terms of Biological lives?*

*Stop that!*

*There will always be a reason to do what I want to do rather, than what I should do.*

*But I should save lives.*

*Move on … this line of reasoning isn't helpful.*

Widening his awareness, Vince looked across the evacuation sites focusing on where there were large numbers of people not taking up the offer of evacuation.

*Amberlight.*

The planet's government had tried to accept Dyfyr's ultimatum a few hours earlier.

*Why did they surrender?*

*I don't want contagion.*

The problem on the planet was complex. The surrender had been decided by the ruling classes which in turn had immediately caused mass uprisings of the rest of the population – who felt they had much less to lose by gambling on the exodus. Civil wars now raged, with the armed forces mostly ignoring the governmental order to surrender and maintaining the fight against the Exta.

*And deaths from bombardments are five times higher than other planets even though the Exta are not doing anything more than other planets.*

*Is it related to defence?*

The data concerning casualties, even after normalising for the civil war fatalities, showed that bombardment fatalities were still unusually high on Amberlight.

*Are the Exta really not behaving differently?*

Vince sucked in data.

It didn't seem to be the case. The Exta bombardment was standard, and Sargon activity around Amberlight was similar to other planets.

But Onari 'shepherding' was notably less intense than the average at other planets.

*Why?*

Widening his analysis, Vince searched for correlations between Onari activity and a host of other factors for each planetary system.

*Planets with predominantly Octagel populations have fewer deaths from bombardment, and it isn't due to their predisposition to hide underground. Planets with predominantly Yanshl populations have the highest numbers of deaths from bombardment even statistically normalised for other factors.*

*Are the Onari showing favouritism?*

495

*Do I dare ask Jarrus why?*

Even as Vince was considering asking Jarrus, a subroutine from one of his pattern-matching analyses popped the answer up.

*Pico-weaponry – the Octagel abhor pico-weaponry and do not use it.*

*Yanshl use them without any reservation … basically as a first resort.*

Vince looked at live defence procedures across all other planets. The Onari were being much less supportive where any type of pico-weaponry was being used.

Pinging Jarrus, Vince asked him outright.

**The mindstate is sacred and we will neither risk our own mindstates, nor give any tacit approval to the use of these weapons.**

'So, you are ordering the Onari to pull back.'

**The mindstate is sacred.**

'The weapons are only being used against WarHives. Your Onari are not at any risk from them.'

**Agreed. Which is why the planets are not being entirely abandoned. Should the Biologicals decide not to use these abominations then we will return in full defensive force.**

'Have you told them?'

**They know.**

'Do they understand the tiny benefit they get for killing the very occasional Exta WarHive is massively outweighed by the additional deaths from reduced defence against?'

**They are making poor decisions.**

*Unsurprising … and I can see how there is some intrinsic value in the feeling of fighting back even if it is inconsequential to the outcome of the battle.*

*Do not go gentle into that good night?*

496

Vince put aside any thoughts of what constituted a good death. 'But the ones who are dying are innocent. They're not the ones making the weaponing decisions?'

I accept the intrinsic value of your argument. But we remain steadfast in defence of the Divine's will.

And, of course, any coordinated use of pico-weaponry that targets individual Sentient mindstates, will mean a complete withdrawal of our forces from all contacted systems.

*Effectively a death sentence for contacted Biologicals.*

You may wish to remind your mother of this.

Jarrus clicked out and Vince immediately turned his attention to the Maintenance Orbital.

*What does Jarrus know?*

*I know that Mum is planning a pico-weaponry attack on the WarHives and ExtaHives in the armada. She thinks that will neutralise the threat. Does Jarrus count those as individuals?*

*Is she considering using pico-weaponry against individual Scouts? She must know Jarrus' position.*

*I will speak to her, firstly to ask her to mandate all Biologicals to stop the use of any pico-weaponry, and secondly to find out her plans.*

*She may lie to protect me.*

*I'd better take a look first.*

The Maintenance Orbital had been home to Vince for a couple of days – human-days which were more like years to Vince – and during that time he'd tweaked and fiddled with its physical layout and the communications network. He'd made it into a home; so, even though it was almost entirely closed off by highly intricate manipulation of spacetime, there were access points into which Vince believed he could link himself.

*I know she's building pico-weaponry, although she also implied it was a last resort, but how 'bad' is it?*

*Could she be producing pico-weaponry that targets individual Scouts?*

*She wouldn't do that.*

*But she might if it was purely in a defensive capability ... something that created exclusion zones around pre-contact planets.*

*Could I possibly accept that? ... perhaps, if it was simply a pico-weapon that effortlessly killed the individual.*

*Whether I accepted it is immaterial – Jarrus would disown all Biologicals.*

*What wouldn't I accept? ... worst case ... a weapon that rewrites the basest desires of the individual ... a weapon that forces Sentients to serve her.*

*She would never do that, it's abhorrent even to think that she would.*

*Delete.*

*No.*

*Don't delete.*

*I must consider it a possibility.*

*Logically it would make sense.*

*She wouldn't do that.*

*Even to save a zillion lives?*

*I need to check.*

Having moved his squad-ship toward the Orbital, Vince looked for ways to attach – he needed proximity to the Orbital Systems to be able to quickly access and review them.

Flying the squad-ship right up to the Orbital, Vince tried to connect to one of its external pylons but his squad-ship just slipped past the docking point like water flowing over a pebble on a riverbed.

Stopping the craft relative to the Orbital , Vince reached out a tiny RST surveillance gateway toward one of its EM arrays.

The RST gateway was collapsed by Sargon.

Vince tried again, this time attempting to open the surveillance gateway at a slightly different location.

It was also collapsed by Sargon.

*Brute force required.*

Vince accessed one of the spare substrates within his Onari squad-ship and set up a cruncher program that would try millions of combinations every microsecond: standard RST weaves, weaves-inside-weaves, dual weaves, and other combinations all drawing on his subjective-decades of experience hacking when back on Earth; it never occurred to Vince that he could over-power Sargon by the sheer number of his access attacks, he was looking for a combination that for some reason was overlooked by Sargon.

*Maybe because I'm me ... my mother may not have revoked all my access rights when I was living there.*

*Maybe she didn't change the locks.*

Something worked.

A probing 'attack' very close to his old location deep in the basement storage levels hooked into an access port and was not collapsed by Sargon.

*Although Sargon will 'tell' Mum.*

*But it may take a tenth of a second for her to understand and respond.*

*And I will be long gone by then.*

Securing a link into the basement storage level, Vince reattached to his old surveillance network.

The volume of Onari substrate being stored was one hundred times what had been there when he'd been a resident. Vince passively analysed the substrate containers.

There was no sign of Enslaved Sentients.

*Relieved.*

*These are just computational machines.*

499

Vince realised that deep within his sense of self, he'd been preparing for the very worst.

*Which would have been?*

*An Enslaved Sentient that used pico-weaponry.*

*Or, even worse, a copy of me.*

Finding out the content of the computational machines would require some level of active induction, so Vince spent a few microseconds connecting to, and preparing, all the EM receptors inside the storage rooms.

*It's going to be pico-weaponry.*

*Just check it doesn't attack individuals.*

*And check it can't have any contagion with Onari in any way.*

Vince gently bathed one of the substrate containers with EM radiation, and took precise readings of the returns; even though he was accessing millions of emitters and receptors and sending millions of pulses every second, it was still going to take a full minute to build a picture.

*It's definitely pico effector based.*

**Get out. Get away.**

The words projected visually on thousands of surfaces within the storage area.

Although Vince was focussing on the inside of the Orbital, physically he was in his squad-ship hovering a metre below it.

*Where did that come from?*

*It isn't Mum.*

**Vince.**
**You are in grave danger.**

Flicking his awareness back to his ship, Vince looked for changes. There was nothing in either the EM range or RST.

There was no obvious threat.

*I need to finish the check.*

A pattern from his EM receivers revealed new analysis of Joy's orbital substrates. There were echoes, images, patterns, within four of the substrate containers that matched elements of his own mindstate.

*It's okay, I was expecting that.*

*Her pico-weaponry that destroys ExtaHive coherence used my magic code.*

*And I can see no hint of awareness.*

Barp!

An alarm drew Vince's attention.

In less than a nano-second, ten thousand RST weaves materialised around Vince's ship and squeezed. Space-time curvature went from twenty to seventy percent in every direction.

*Sargon!*

Automatically, an aspect of Vince both launched an RST defence and set his engines to maximum acceleration.

The connection to the Maintenance Orbital broke.

The engines failed.

Half of his defence RST weaves collapsed – Sargon's countermeasures to his own defences had appeared before Vince had even started measuring the efficacy of his own evasive actions.

*Mind reader …*

There was no time to call for help.

Vince tried to phase-skip.

Nothing.

Space-time curvature increased to eighty percent.

And the weaves tightened their grip on his ship, with his final half of defence weaves also being picked off.

Vince was overpowered in every department.

This was the end.

# CHAPTER 51

Furiously trying to prepare her plan of action against the incoming Exta armada, Joy tried to put Jarrus' recent rebuke out of her mind.

*You are not the Divine, as much as you may play at it.*

*I agree that I am not, but I do have god-sized responsibilities.*

Even though the exodus was currently on schedule, everything remained precariously in the balance.

*Earth is still under threat of annihilation.*

*And we cannot trust Dyfyr's current approach to other pre-contact worlds.*

**Joy!**

The words from the Foresighted were accompanied by a flash of pain across Joy's left cheek.

Sargon shuddered and pulsed.

An intensely cold blast of air washed over Joy, but not wanting to take her attention away from the armada, she ignored the pain.

**It's Vince.**

*Vince?*

A screen opened; an Onari craft had opened RST gateways into the Maintenance Orbital and Sargon, in line with standing orders, was using significant autonomy to defend itself. Thousands of RST weaves were manoeuvring to crush the Onari craft.

*Stop the attack on Vince!*

The RST weaves died, but the pain across her cheek increased. Joy descended her awareness into the forest and looked around.

The place was awash with black tendrils; they swirled, carving through the glowing husks of past Klav and curling around Joy's legs and arms, bringing a soothing warmth to replace the cold that had taken hold.

Joy strained to look within the forest.

*What caused the pain?*

'Vince.' Joy spoke aloud willing Sargon to produce a connection.

Silence.

Joy could feel Sargon readying itself to strike out.

*Did you attack Vince?*

*I am Joy Cooper.*

'Show me Vince.'

Sargon responded.

A screen opened displaying the partially crushed Onari squad-ship with two of its five spheres utterly broken and mixed damage to the other parts.

'Vince!'

*Is he alive?*

*Yes.*

*Is he whole?*

*Yes.*

*Why is he not speaking to me?*

*He cannot hear; he is isolated.*

*Open a connection.*

'Vince?'

'Mum.'

'Are you okay?'

'Yes.'

Joy's relief morphed instantly into incandescent rage. 'What the fuck were you thinking? What were you doing? Are you mad? Have I taught you nothing? Am I such a terrible parent? Why the fuck would you do this *to me*?'

Joy only stopped shouting to draw a breath. 'What the fuck are you thinking? How do I stop this shit happening? Do I need to lock you up? Why were you looking in there? Don't you trust me? Has Jarrus turned you? Am I such a terrible parent?'

Noticing that she was now repeating herself, Joy stopped ranting. 'Vince?'

'Why am I not dead?' asked Vince.

*Why isn't he dead?*

*My attention was diverted momentarily.*

*Long enough to change my mind on his destruction.*

Joy looked internally.

Sargon had been distracted for a moment by a physical attack on Joy within the Forest of Golden Auras. She reached her hand up to her stinging cheek and when she brought it up to her eyes, she saw blood.

Across the gulf between the golden auras, Joy focused on the Foresighted. The remnants of the golden aura remained, but inside the nest was a torn mess of old body parts. The black tendrils had ripped him apart.

*Alas, we mortals in our gloom,*

'Mum?'

'How did you get into the Maintenance Orbital?'

'I lived there for a while,' said Vince. 'I'd already set up escape routes and backdoors.'

'I'd assumed that almost bubbling it off from space and time would have been enough.'

'It *almost* was.'

'It was *almost* your death,' said Joy, feeling her anger building again at Vince's lack of contrition. 'What were you doing?'

'Looking for weapons that could cause the Onari to abandon the Biologicals,' said Vince.

Joy's anger, still bubbling under the surface, mixed with a sense shame – there were weapons schematics that would fit Vince's concerns.

*But I haven't built them yet.*

*Not that it would take longer than a micro-second to do so … the required hardware is the same as for the 'acceptable' weapons.*

'All I've got here are the weapons that I already told you about,' said Joy. 'The ones that reduce ExtaHives down to their component parts … and I've also got similar weapons for WarHives.'

'So,' said Vince. 'The plan is just to annihilate the ExtaHives and WarHives, and let Sargon mop up the Exta Scouts.'

'That's my plan to enable the current exodus,' said Joy. 'It's less clear how we support Earth and other pre-contacted planets.'

'Have you looked into arming Octagel Sword personnel with these pico-weapons?' asked Vince.

'It's possible they could manage something if the weapons were big enough,' said Joy.

'I'm sorry I didn't trust you,' said Vince. 'How can I help you … If you still trust me.'

'God! Vince! I trust you with my life, even if your judgement is poor.'

'Poor judgement? If you'd told me all about your plans, I would have been more careful.'

'No more cover ups or half-truths,' said Joy.

*I'll warn him if I'm forced to use pico-weaponry against single Exta Scouts.*

'Okay, no more cover ups,' said Vince. 'And I guess I owe you this … I found databases on Bastion showing that Enslaved Sentients played a large and successful part of Biological defence before the Dynasty of Klav.'

*I knew you'd lied about something.*

505

'Thanks for telling me,' said Joy. 'But we've agreed no enslavement.'

*Although ... could it be the very last option to defend truly innocent and vulnerable pre-contact planets?*

*Could I get comfortable with using Enslaved Sentients that were more sheepdogs or other animals that appear to thrive in their role.*

Joy put the thoughts aside. 'The plan is to draw the Exta in. Tear them apart, mop them up, and run for our lives.'

'Except it's not,' said Vince. 'There's a good chance you're staying. If the pico-weapons work but Dyfyr isn't neutralised, then you won't leave.'

'A decision for later,' said Joy. 'Can you get back to supporting the exodus?'

'By your command,' said Vince.

Joy instructed Sargon to produce an undamaged Onari squad-ship, fill it with substrate, and transfer Vince across. 'We can talk about the next steps once the first ones have been completed.'

'Thanks, Mum ... and I am sorry.'

'I know,' said Joy. 'No harm done.'

*Except the Foresighted is now dead. And, although every other sentence was to pressure me to destroy Sargon, I will miss his insight.*

Even as the exodus picked up its pace, millions of RST surveillance micro-tunnels fed Joy microsecond-by-microsecond updates confirming that the front line of the Exta armada – the vanguard – were only hours away from Bastion's outer system.

Although all the Exta had arrived at the Jut65 system, they'd subsequently used widely different phase-skipping parameters to spread out such that they'd be hitting Bastion outskirts in a coordinated manner from almost all angles – front, back, top, bottom, left and right.

And rather than trying to avoid two of Bastion's outer gas giant planets that served as military bases, two squadrons of the Exta vanguard were on direct intercept missions.

*Millions of ExtaHives attacking each planet.*

Joy lashed out with Sargon, but the range was too far and all she could do was buffet the Exta who had stopped phase-skipping and were now simply coasting in.

*Good.*

Instructing Sargon to continue fully attacking, Joy turned her attention back to the exodus.

An uptick in Biologicals wanting to take the exodus options had been met seamlessly by the Onari with Vince managing, coordinating, and escalating where required.

*They've got that.*

*They're good at supply chain.*

*I've got my job.*

As the Exta reached a million kilometres away from each of the two planets, ten thousand ExtaHives slowed, and opening the front portion of their hulls, launched missiles at the planets.

*They should be easy to deflect at this distance.*

It was not.

Even as Sargon reached out to deflect the missiles, the millions of other members of the Exta vanguard deployed RST countermeasures, and either Sargon's RST weaves were collapsed, or the deflected missiles were simply nudged back on target by other Exta.

*How long until they hit?*

*Less than a second.*

*How dangerous are they?*

It took Sargon a nanosecond to confirm the weapon type. They were ultra-dense spheres of matter. Harvested from neutron stars, these five metres wide missiles were roughly three trillion kilograms in mass.

*I need help.*

Before she could communicate her need, Jarrus directed Onari to the gas giant ingress points. Immediately, they set up a defence network to deflect the incoming missiles.

Unfortunately, the Onari were expected; no sooner had they arrived than each Onari was targeted.

*Why doesn't Jarrus send more?*

*The Onari have no reason to save the gas giants.*

*But the gas giants will slow the Exta armada.*

*Not really, those planets are symbolic not strategic.*

In the proximity of Bastion planet itself, tens of billions of Onari ships were clustered around the exodus staging points as most Biologicals continued to depart unaware of the destruction at the system's outer perimeter.

*We need half a day more to get everyone away.*

*And how long do we have?*

*Best estimate … an hour or two.*

Back at the gas giants, both the planet mounted weapons and Sargon continued to attempt to deflect the missiles. Neither were successful. The planet mounted weapons were operated by Octagel who were fast but not fast enough. And Sargon — fast and powerful — was operating from many hundreds of millions of kilometres away, whereas the Exta were highly numerous and many orders of magnitude closer to their targets.

Hundreds of hyper-accelerated missiles smashed into the military bases and the gas giant's martial ability was vapourised.

Joy expanded her awareness and looked at the wider Exta forces.

It was time to run a live test of the pico-weaponry.

*Harder or softer?*

In her test run, after disabling the ExtaHive orbiting the black hole with the pico-weaponry, Joy had instructed Sargon to crush the ExtaHive more slowly than it was capable of. Her goal had been to spread misinformation principally to increase the chances of Dyfyr coming to Bastion themselves.

*Should I keep Sargon looking a little weaker to entice Dyfyr in?*

*Or do I attack on full power, blunt their advance, and allow more of the exodus to complete before they swamp us?*

Her decision went unmade.

**Deliver yourself unto me and I will succour you.**

An RST gateway had opened just behind the Exta vanguard and Dyfyr came through.

Instantly, Sargon lashed out with standard RST attacks but around Dyfyr a million ExtaHives put up barriers that deflected the RST attacks.

Ignoring Sargon, the entire Exta armada accelerated. All aimed at Sargon.

**Origin is ours.**

*Origin is the Exta word for Sargon.*

*The Exta have always disputed that Sargon is Divine.*

*They believe it is an enslaved Sentient of astronomical proportions.*

*I can't fault them on that.*

The Exta armada swept forward with billions of ships and they had a final card to play.

More RST gateways opened just in front of the Exta vanguard.

Joy focused on it.

*More Hives?*

*Bigger ones?*

A blur of light flashed through the gateway, the projectile drawing behind it a fizzing sparkling trail.

*What's that?*

*A neutron missile harvested from the heart of the collapsed star.*

*Like the ones just used on the gas giants earlier but this one has been subject to immense acceleration for many hours at a remote location before being moved by RST gateway here.*

*It is travelling within a fraction of the speed of light.*

*It will hit Bastion in minutes.*

The neutron missile was carrying so much energy – localised mass energy, and kinetic energy from its relativistic speeds – that it was tearing tiny shreds of space-time as it flew; and these tears were causing a cascade of fundamental particles that highlighted the movement of the missile.

*Planet busters.*

*They will rip through the planet like it was tissue paper.*

Following hot behind the first missile, tens of thousands more gateways opened.

Down on Bastion's surface, RST alarms were going off everywhere. The general populace knew that death was coming.

*Just one of those missiles will spell certain doom for the planet.*

*All my contingency time is gone.*

The Onari recognised the danger too and were sending thousands of RST weaves out to deflect the incoming missiles.

Moments later each of the missiles was nudged back on course to hit the planet.

Sargon joined in the attempts to deflect the missiles but the massed numbers of Exta running in behind the missile front simply moved the missiles back on track.

*It's time.*

Joy sent a one-way comms to Vince. 'You've got to survive to clear up any mess I leave behind. I love you.'

Then she instructed Sargon to open a gateway and she pushed Vince through.

Making sure it had closed fully, Joy turned her attention to the Orbital Systems.

# CHAPTER 52

Having shut the main gateway that had sent Vince to safety, Joy opened a slew of new RST surveillance gateways to verify that he'd not been harmed in the transit. She'd put him in the flattest space that Sargon could possibly manage to reach, and it would take him at least ten hours to reach any space-time with sufficient curvature for him to open his own gateway to return to Bastion.

Clearly Vince could see her surveillance as he transmitted back to her.

**Mum!**

**Come on.**

**I can help.**

'Sorry, love, I need to keep you safe.'

*There is always a chance that the Orbital Systems could catch him by mistake; the pico weapon is tuned on the latest scans from the ExtaHives, but ultimately it was designed on his mindstate.*

**Don't leave me here.**

*I also want to give you plausible deniability in case I am forced to bring out pico-weaponry that attacks individual sentients.*

Joy cut the connection.

Checking the location of the Exta vanguard and Dyfyr who was only just behind it, Joy queried Sargon about optimal operational distances for maintaining the open RST gateway against the ExtaHive hulls. The response was immediate, and not good … she needed to wait until they were closer.

*And every second that passes, more hyper-accelerated neutron missiles are arriving.*

There were now over four hundred thousand such missiles, each of them travelling at almost light speed. Sargon continued to deflect them with small RST weaves, but the Exta armada was simply too numerous and the missiles were nudged back on course.

*The first missiles will impact with Bastion in just over four minutes.*

*Try to open a gateway and send them elsewhere.*

Sargon picked out a missile, but as they tried to open a stable gateway it was collapsed by the ExtaHives.

*And phase-skipping them would be madness … could I bubble them off?*

*The calculations are too complex.*

There were fifty million ExtaHives purely focused on defending the wave of hyper-accelerated missiles.

*How many Exta are here in total?*

*5,799,413,881.*

*Fewer than before, is Sargon making kills?*

*Not substantially.*

*There are fewer because they are merging.*

Sargon picked out a real-time example, and Joy watched as four ExtaHives physically came together and over the period of a few seconds created thousands of permanent links between their substrates. Although not fully immersed in each other, functionally they were a single physical entity.

In three of the original ExtaHives, an area of the substrate flared brightly as a physical change manifested.

*Burning out the unneeded egos.*

Now a single unit, Joy watched as the new ExtaHive moved as if it had always been one.

*How big can they get?*

*The stability of some of these very large ExtaHives is in doubt.*

*Estimated ninety-five percent stability at three thousand units.*

*Not as big as me, but I've seen a pack of hyenas take down a single isolated lion.*

With the neutron missiles now just under three minutes away, Joy reviewed her options.

One good thing was that Sargon was starting to make progress with deflecting the missiles away from the planet because the ExtaHives were falling behind the barrage and less able to deflect them back on course.

*As the missiles get closer, I will have more and more opportunity to control them.*

As if reading Joy's mind, one of the ExtaHive attempted to phase-skip itself ahead of the vanguard to keep in touch with the missile front; a swirl of RST weaves lashed out from Sargon as the ExtaHive lurched toward its gateway; the next moment, the gateway collapsed and half of the ExtaHive lay dead whilst the other half of the ExtaHive was gone.

*Good to see Sargon can still meaningfully control some things.*

*I am Joy Cooper.*

*But with four hundred thousand missiles there is ninety-nine percent chance that one will get through.*

*And it only takes one to destroy us all.*

Just behind the front line, five ExtaHives flew up to Dyfyr and merged with it; Dyfyr was now the equivalent size of a thousand Exta.

*I'm many millions times their size and yet I cannot bring my power to bear.*

*Not yet, but soon.*

The missiles came ever nearer, with Sargon and the Exta continually trading deflection actions.

Joy reviewed her plans.

*Do I warn Jarrus?*

*No, the weapon will not hurt him.*

An automated warning flashed in front of Joy's eyes.

*Earth!*

*Please not now.*

514

Dyfyr did not plan to allow Joy the luxury of a calm wait for her pico-weaponry to reach optimal operational range. A mixed force of Exta Scouts and WarHives had appeared close to Venus and accelerated toward Earth; some were coasting in real space and others were phase-skipping. In numbers it was a small fraction of the armada in the Bastion system, no more than twenty million craft.

*And yet it's death for humanity if I do not intervene.*

The Earth bound WarHives launched iron-core missiles similar to the ones used in the first attack at Bastion; once released, the highly dense cannonballs were accelerated by a combination of phase-skipping and RST warping, chasing them onwards.

*Ten minutes to impact with Earth.*

*Whereas the catastrophic planet busters are now three minutes away from Bastion.*

*From … Sargon.*

Latest calculations showed that almost every Exta neutron missile in the Bastion system was aimed at Sargon.

*And if Sargon falls, the Biologicals are defenceless.*

*Could I survive a neutron missile strike?*

A screen opened showing the physical set-up of Sargon and the current predicted impact sites of every neutron missile. The Living Moon itself was one thousand kilometres in diameter and Sargon technology was uniformly distributed across the whole outer shell a few kilometres below the surface; all except the Forest of Golden Auras which was ten kilometres down.

Joy's mind raced: Protect the Exodus. Destroy Dyfyr. Save Earth. Protect Sargon.

*Give less thought to the exodus, Jarrus will oversee it … he is seriously invested in the outcome.*

*Blunt the attack on Earth and then focus on Dyfyr.*

The message came through from Vince.

515

**Give me the BioCore pico-effectors. I'll
clear Earth of Exta WarHives, and Jarrus'
forces will mop up the Scouts.**

'You can't, love,' said Joy. 'You're stuck in ultra-flat
spacetime and even I would struggle to bring you back. You
can't meaningfully attack Earth from there, your micro-
tunnels would be too vulnerable.'

**Trust me.**

'But Jarrus will disown you if you use pico-weaponry …
*and* you abhor it.'

**I abhor genocide more. It needs to be
done. You need to focus on Bastion.**

'No. I will do both,' said Joy. 'I sent you away to protect
you physically and morally.'

Even as she spoke, Sargon provided forecasts of her
ability to protect Earth. It didn't look good.

**I'll save Earth.**

Without warning, a screen opened showing Jonathan
asleep in bed. It was 3am there. At the foot of bed Strontium
their cat, raised his head.

*I can save them both.*

'I can't move you back now. I will deal with Earth,' said
Joy, closing the connection with Vince and the screen
showing Jonathan.

*Open multiple semi-permanent gateways around the Solar System, I
need to almost be there.*

*It will mean additional vulnerability here in Bastion.*

*Which is undoubtedly Dyfyr's plan.*

Joy's eyes blurred momentarily as Sargon opened multiple
tactical screens showing the Exta force bearing down on
Earth; it was a mixture of Scouts and WarHives – no
ExtaHives.

*Dare I use the old KOF BioCore pico-weaponry on the WarHives?
Will it alter Dyfyr's Bastion strategy?*

516

*I don't want Dyfyr to know that the cornerstone of my attack is pico-weaponry.*

*He may not be worrying about my countermeasures, a million years on invulnerability may have made him complacent.*

*Where are the Onari?*

A status update overlayed the tactical maps; Jarrus had sent fifty billion Onari to Venus, half were accelerating hard toward the Exta trying to catch up; the other half were operating long range RST buffeting, trying to slow the Exta advance.

*Fifty billion is a lot.*

*But without centralise coordination, the benefits of scale will not be realised.*

Some of the leaders of the Exta attack fleet wobbled.

*Vince?*

Vince had appeared amongst the leading Onari ships just outside the orbit of Venus.

*How?*

*Gravitational flux vortices.*

*The space-time he had been constrained to was flat, very flat, but there was just enough curvature for him to get some purchase and he used that to spin the space-time to create more artificial curvature which gave him more purchase … fifty milliseconds and three phase-skips later he was free.*

*How did I not know about this?*

*Sargon has no record of it being possible.*

Vince, in amongst the Onari, was now coordinating their long-range attacks using vast numbers of Onari to create a lensing effect that was meaningfully slowing the Exta.

But only slowing them … the WarHives would soon be within range of Earth.

```
If you don't send me the pico-weaponry
schematics I'm simply going to ram the
WarHives.
```

'Good luck, not that you need it … you've got this,' said Joy, ordering Sargon to send the information, but also being careful only to send the weaponry for targeting the BioCores of WarHives.

Returning her attention to Bastion, Joy drew a deep breath and held it.

*One.*

*Two.*

*Three.*

Opening the operational screens she needed, Joy checked the status of the Orbital System pico-weaponry.

*Operational. And Powered. And Ready.*

Conceptually, according to all Sargon's forecasts about maintaining of stable RST gateways, Dyfyr was still a minute away from the most effective range of the pico-weaponry.

Likely because Sargon's attention was split between Bastion and Earth, one of the ExtaHives at Bastion successfully phase-skipped a neutron-missile – it was now two minutes away.

*Now.*

*Ten percent loss in efficacy due to extended range.*

*Now.*

*Dyfyr first.*

Joy didn't have any expectation that destroying Dyfyr would stop the armada, but it was the first step. She opened a screen to give a real-time visual of Dyfyr. One hundred metres in diameter and bristling with the remains of absorbed Exta, Dyfyr accelerated harder than its attendant entourage. It was hungry to arrive just after the neutron missiles and be first to pick over the ruins of Sargon.

*We're not dead yet.*

*Reduce power on all other activities … evacuations, bombardment protection, and general countermeasures.*

Now Joy initiated the attack. Sargon opened a one-metre-wide RST gateway against the Dyfyr's outer shell. Dyfyr, and all their entourage, attempted to collapse the gateway, however their efforts were futile as Sargon was focusing every ounce of its capability on simply keeping the gateway open. Orbital Systems launched its EM processes, sending millions of EM pulses down Sargon's tunnel against the skin of Dyfyr; active induction loops triggered within Dyfyr's substrate with Orbital Systems measuring the responses looking for the tell-tale patterns that indicated the presence of the Vince ego suppression code.

Within nanoseconds a match had been found, and the Orbital Systems' programs updated its EM pulsing to attack the specific area.

A pulse of energy registered within Dyfyr's substrate.

And another.

Watching Dyfyr externally with infographic overlays, Joy saw seventy-three competing transient egos appear and given the sheer volume of substrate, they all had space to grow. Fifteen of those seventy-three became fully self-aware, recognising they were competing over the same resources. Dyfyr's original ego was slowest on the uptake having clearly not conceived the situation was even possible.

The others knew innately they had to fight for their lives. Each one took control of aspects of Dyfyr's internal function, with multiple transient egos connecting to RST attenuators, EM pulse weapons, power relays, and propulsion units.

As each transient ego commandeered something akin to a weapon, they used it immediately.

One transient ego managed to isolate an entire physical ExtaHive that had only recently joined into Dyfyr. It cut all the internal connections and attempted to physically break out of Dyfyr's shell.

It was not allowed.

Once it became clear to Dyfyr's entourage that something was identifiably 'whole' and yet not part of Dyfyr, they attacked.

Ten thousand EM pulse weapons burned into the newly liberated ExtaHive. A moment later, nothing but scraps remained of that ExtaHive.

Within Dyfyr the battle still raged, and it was no longer clear which of the transient egos had been the original. They all claimed that they were 'the one'.

A transient ego in a moment of *'if I can't have it then no one can'* directed all its EM weapons inwardly burning through tens of cubic metres of substrate and killing themselves in the process.

Sensing a gap, Sargon lashed out with massive RST weaves. Dyfyr's immediate entourage of ExtaHives, confused by the ongoing civil war, didn't respond quickly enough and Sargon's attack caused gravitational curvature all around Dyfyr to go critical.

Dyfyr was being crushed.

In parallel, Joy instructed the Orbital Systems to perform pico-weaponry attacks on all the nearby ExtaHives – again with Sargon enabling the initial gateway access.

Within less than a second, thousands of nearby ExtaHives had been similarly neutralised with the only escapees being a handful of very newly created ExtaHives which simply split into their physical constituent parts and sped off into space as individual Scouts.

*Shred Dyfyr.*

Without any functioning ego, and without any meaningfully coherent entourage, Sargon destroyed Dyfyr, tearing large chunks out of it and spinning them away into space before rescanning for any signs of life and repeating.

Sargon didn't pause, extending its purely physical attacks to all the nearby ExtaHives too.

*I must focus on the functioning Exta armada.*

*Situation report?*

*The rest of the armada continue onwards regardless.*

*They have not slowed because of the loss of Dyfyr.*

*I will need to kill them all, there is no alternative.*

*How many other despots said that to themselves before they rained down fury on the innocent?*

*These are not innocent.*

*They have no choice, that is a type of innocence.*

*Their deaths will be on my conscience.*

Joy instructed Sargon and the Orbital Systems to continue the attack on the incoming armada.

*The Onari are now having some success deflecting the hyper-accelerated neutron missiles.*

'Jarrus,' said Joy, opening a communications link. 'Please leave the neutron missiles. I will deal with them as there needs to be exacting coordination to ensure that we avoid irreparable space-time damage that could cause contagion and ultimately destroy Bastion half evacuated. Please fully focus on the exodus and keeping the Exta away from Bastion.'

Jarrus acknowledged the signal but didn't reply.

*Probably angry with me about the pico-weaponry.*

Tens of millions of Onari broke away from the pilgrimage ship guard duty and vectored toward the incoming armada, forming up a standard guard barrier.

*And he's stopped deflecting the neutron missiles.*

Joy allowed herself a brief smile – one of the very few benefits of the Onari not maintaining centralised information stores was that they struggled to coordinate large scale intricately interwoven actions. It meant that Jarrus was ready to believe her when she claimed she could manage the neutron missiles more effectively whereas in reality the volume of space was so large that the five hundred thousand missiles could have been randomly deflected into space and would have caused no problem at all.

*Unless Jarrus was right to believe me when I thought I was being deceptive?*

As the neutron missiles approached Bastion they were entering into highly curved space-time and the impact they were having on localised curvature was increasing significantly. Joy instructed Sargon to recalculate the required course of each of the neutron missiles for the second part of her plan.

*Assuming I successfully demolish the ExtaHive threat.*

*I cannot make that final decision yet.*

# CHAPTER 53

Assimilating the new code sent through by Joy, Vince continued to coordinate the standard long-range RST attacks in the solar system, and the exodus, whilst also simultaneously tracking Joy's pico-weaponry attacks back in Bastion.

*Mum didn't have a choice but to use pico-weaponry, those kinetic killer neutron missiles are about to obliterate Bastion and Sargon.*

On Bastion's surface itself, at each of the hundred thousand spaceports, thousands of Biologicals were waiting for their turn to board the shuttles that would take them to the pilgrimage ships in orbit above them.

*And if one of those big ones gets through…*

The kinetic killer missiles had the energy to tear large chunks of the planet away and it was feasible that anyone on any part of the planet would be crushed by the resulting pressure waves that ripped the crust wide open.

Vince opened a channel to Jarrus. 'Why haven't those neutron missiles been deflected?'

**Joy will do this at the appropriate time.**

'You could do it now,' said Vince. 'The ExtaHives are unable to defend effectively.'

*Is he allowing the threat to continue to ensure more pilgrims?*

*Is he allowing the planet to be destroyed to stop Biologicals turning back?*

*Or to punish those not going?*

**You do not know everything, Newborn. My actions are guided by the Divine. You would do well to protect Earth before I change my mind on accepting your own heresy.**

523

*Earth first.*

So far, Vince and the other Onari were only having limited success in blunting the long range attacks of the Exta WarHives which continued to release bombardment missiles at Earth using a combination of phase-skipping and warping to accelerate them.

*Heresy said Jarrus … he already knows I'm going to use pico-weaponry.*

*I'll take that as permission given.*

Inside his squad-ship, Vince finished integrating the code.

*I'll need more power myself to operate them effectively.*

Of the other four substrate spheres, one was already being used to run simple processes to coordinate the exodus and the Onari defence of Earth; now, with the requirement to move fast Vince reached out his awareness.

Jarrus was clearly watching.

**You made a commitment to me to uphold the Great Concordat. You do not need mindstate augmentation, and it is an abomination I will not tolerate.**

'Didn't you just intimate that you could tolerate it?' asked Vince, full knowing he was being disingenuous.

**I will tolerate the use of blasphemous weaponry to reverse the existing blasphemy that the Exta have already undergone - the WarHives.**

**Nothing else.**

**You can disburse the Exta here without growing yourself, after all you have fifty billion Onari in support.**

'I wasn't going to expand my power permanently.'

**I suspect that once augmented it will feel part of you.**

*True.*

**Your mother started pushing the boundary, and quickly overstepped.**

'She's only done what was necessary.'

**Define necessary … she picked apart an Exta mindstate and created a digital twin of Kubli, and she paralysed Oksana's brain to make him incapable of lying reducing him to a vegetative state.**

'Not unreasonable in the face of a hundred billion Biological deaths.'

**She also used Sargon to reprogram four senior members of the planet Jorpel IV to reverse their decision not to take up the exodus.**

*Oh Mum!*

Jarrus went on to tell Vince how one of those four, an Octagel, had noticed and had rebelled; Joy had put him into a semi-comatose state for the duration of his exodus. He had not been permanently damaged, but neither had he been awoken yet.

'I forgive her.'

**Power corrupts, and you will be corrupted too. This is a universal truth of life.**

'There's no such thing as truth, but kindness endures,' said Vince. 'She was just being kind.'

**Was it kind to reprogram their innermost thoughts?**

'It depends. Some would have preferred it to death. Some would not.'

**It feels like I am speaking to her.**

*Perhaps her seeds do still control me.*

*But — nature or nurture — does it matter why I agree with her?*

**Do not take the same path, particularly as you do not need to. You have the weapon, and you have us.**

*True.*

*There are thousands of times as many Onari as Exta here.*

*Numbers are numbers.*

The front line of Exta were now minutes away from being able to attack Earth with their EM and RST weapons. Vince had no doubt they would quickly target power stations, and nuclear facilities.

In front of those Exta were a million missiles – simple heavy element cannon balls travelling at hypersonic speeds, certainly city busters but nothing more than that.

*Although if each of them hits a city...*

It wasn't going to happen, and Vince knew it. He spawned a thousand processes, each one targeting a BioCore within a WarHive.

Unlike Joy's attacks on the ExtaHive which had to account for ExtaHives having been grown in a haphazard way the simplicity of Vince's attack revolved around the fact that the WarHives were true clones. They were all built carefully to the same exacting pattern with the BioCore sitting in the exactly the same location and linked into the rest of the nine Scout substrates in exactly the same way.

Additionally – if any extra benefit was needed – the WarHives were all mature and had dismantled any remnants of the nine Scouts' own craft infrastructure.

It took four microseconds to acquire a target WarHive and then open an RST gateway next to it. A further ten microseconds to flood the WarHive with the appropriate EM radiation. And five microseconds for that WarHive to suffer catastrophic failure.

Each of Vince's processes could start on its next target during the catastrophic failure part.

*Conservatively ... 14 microseconds per target.*

*Each process can do 71,428 per second.*

*I have 1,000 processes.*

*There are 20,553,261 Exta.*

*Of which, 13,898,823 are WarHives.*

*It will take a fifth of a second to hit all of them.*

In the end, it took just over two seconds to reduce every single WarHive to a vegetative state as they did react to the attacks and attempted countermeasures.

Vince coordinated the deflection of the missiles and then he turned his attention to the Exta Scouts who had been part of the original attacking force. Within moments, the vast numbers of Onari had shepherded the Scouts away.

The immediate future of Earth was secured.

It was so different from Vince's experience at Cidelus that he found it hard to reconcile the two events.

*Were the Onari trying harder?*

*A subject for another time.*

Opening RST surveillance micro-tunnels back to Bastion, Vince assessed how he could help.

On Bastion things were going harder. There were five hundred times more Exta and most of them were ExtaHives. The ExtaHives were all very different from each other and there was no single BioCore to attack.

From what Vince could ascertain from watching the attacks, each ExtaHive had to be hit many times over a longer period. Plus, the ExtaHives had far greater access to countermeasures.

The data from Bastion looked bad, with a best case of the ExtaHives being dismantled with only moments to go before the missiles struck, and the most likely case having the two events almost simultaneous.

Of course, Sargon was incredibly powerful, but it was the Orbital Systems doing the pico effector weaponry work.

*I should take it over.*

*And why hasn't Mum deflected the missiles that are not being controlled by fully functioning ExtaHives?*

From his brief analysis of the battleground, Vince estimated that a fifth of the ExtaHives were effectively disarmed and yet almost half a million kinetic killers continued resolutely on their courses.

*What are their courses?*

Vince opened up an entire substrate sphere; and, in order to placate Jarrus he used it for simple forecasting analysis.

Unfortunately, the calculations were too complex; although on the face of it they were simple – 477,855 projectiles inbound on what appeared to be straight-line trajectories; the problem was that each missile was so dense that they were twisting space-time as passed through any particular region, and that was causing ripples which then deflected their neighbours by tiny, but material, amounts.

All the changes were borderline imperceptible, but over the likely tracks of remaining thirty million kilometres, the uncertainty of the measurement errors meant Vince could not be sure their exact impact points … if they hit at all.

It was clear that no missiles appeared to be on track to strike Bastion. They were mostly aimed at Sargon or the space around Sargon.

*Some are aimed tens of thousands of kilometres away from Sargon?*

*But were they originally aimed there?*

*Or has someone moved them?*

*I need to help.*

Double checking that Earth was utterly safe, Vince opened an RST gateway back to the Bastion system.

Or tried to.

It was collapsed by a cohort of Onari squad-ships surrounding him.

One of the nearby Onari messaged him even as they collapsed his weaves.

**You cannot go to Bastion. You will be targeted.**

*Sargon would target me, and Orbital Systems would automatically attack.*

Vince flicked his attention to the exodus; twenty to thirty billion of willing evacuees had not yet left; he messaged Joy. 'You must run now. Don't wait for the last moment.'

'I trusted you to do your job, now you must trust me and stay away,' said Joy.

'The Orbital Systems and Sargon are dealing with the Exta,' said Vince. 'Do you even need to be there?'

'I have to constantly tell Sargon not to destroy Orbital Systems, which to Sargon looks like a major threat.'

'Please run,' said Vince. 'As those kinetic killers get closer, they're going to interfere with Sargon's ability to wield RST. Even one of them will destroy Sargon. There are half a million coming from every angle.'

As he waited for Joy to reply, Vince ran more analysis on the trajectories of the incoming missiles and the ExtaHive forces. The ExtaHives were falling at a steady rate as they couldn't raise a coherent defence against the pico-weaponry. But the missiles were a different matter. As they all homed in on Sargon, more gravitational ripples were generated bounding off each other and causing greater uncertainty in their final impact points.

'The missiles are part of the plan,' said Joy. 'Trust me.'

'I do trust you, but I also want you to get out of there. Now. Seriously. The Onari will get most of the Biologicals off. We'll all scatter. Then we can regroup and put some ExtaHive busting technology at the pre-contact planets.'

'Run by whom exactly?'

Vince knew the arguments, there would need to be a Sentient level capability behind each weapon, or they'd be hacked and turned.

*She's staying on as Klav?*

'I'll stay,' said Vince. 'I could run the defence network.'

*Although, I'd need special defences.*

'I can't ask you to do that,' said Joy.

'You're not asking,' said Vince. 'I'm offering. You don't have to stay as Klav.'

*Latest path analysis.*

*Most missiles will miss Sargon.*

*But 35,634 could still hit with an average probability of 0.0001%.*

*Not good numbers.*

*And one hit will be fatal.*

'Please run,' said Vince, feeling himself spiral.

*Update.*

*38,634 may miss Sargon with an average probability of 0.0001%.*

*Numbers getting worse.*

*And one hit will be fatal.*

*Update.*

*38,729 may miss Sargon with an average probability of 0.0001%.*

*Numbers getting worse.*

*And one hit will be fatal.*

*Update.*

*38,755 may miss Sargon with an average probability of 0.0001%.*

*Numbers getting worse.*

*And one hit will be fatal.*

'Vince,' said Joy. 'It's going to be fine.'

'What if you're wrong?'

'If I'm wrong, then I'm wrong. But I will have been wrong for the right reasons,' said Joy. 'You can't do anything more except to stay safe, and maybe visit me occasionally. I love you.'

'I love you too,' said Vince. 'But visit you where?'

The communication line clicked off.

Unwilling to look away, but also feeling himself spiral again, Vince slowed his clock down so that he would experience the final moments just as Joy was doing.

As the seconds ticked onwards, the ExtaHives continued to be torn apart and the kinetic killers continued resolutely onwards.

The numbers improved.

*There are now 12,772 that may hit.*

*Better but still bad.*

All of the Onari pilgrimage ships were now being loaded and dispatched from the far side of Bastion relative to Sargon.

*Jarrus is in on this.*

There was a particularly large density of missiles heading along a precise geometrical path relative to Sargon, Bastion, and the central star.

As the missiles entered the more densely curved space closer to Sargon the ripples increased in amplitude.

*There are now 7,221 that may hit.*

With ten seconds to go a large detachment of Onari appeared from the far side of Bastion and lined up halfway between Sargon and Bastion.

Looking with millions of his own tiny RST surveillance gateways, Vince could see that these newly arrived Onari were not using RST themselves; they were simply sitting in open space.

Five.

Four.

Three.

Two.

One.

*The missiles are all deflected!*

*Are they … 52 may hit.*

In the final microseconds as the missiles approached Sargon, an immense series of RST weaves emanating from Sargon stretched out in every direction. Space-time buckled and heaved on a scale that Vince could hardly comprehend.

Space shimmered and hazed.

Sargon disappeared.

# EPILOGUE 1

Kubli floated in the clan pod, watching as the remainder of her family members went about their day. Most of the previous week was lost to her, but she did remember snippets.

Klav was reborn.

Sargon disappeared.

Some of the clan joined a spiritual exodus.

'I'd like to get out of here.'

'You're not well enough to travel yet,' said Yuno, swimming over.

'Of course, I am,' said Kubli, not feeling the strength of her words.

*My dreams have been … troubled.*

'Soon,' said Yuno, caressing the side of Kubli's head gently. 'In any case, you've got a visitor coming.'

'Who?'

'High Prelate Jinfor, he's honouring all of the Sword who were wounded in the war.'

*There are not many of us wounded.*

Kubli had been in the battle but had survived – typically, Sword soldiers either hadn't seen action, or had been killed outright.

The lights in the pod flashed gently, indicating the visitor had arrived. A moment later, Jinfor swam in, his skin colouration a strange combination of respect and fear.

'Over-Commander Kubli,' said Jinfor. 'You are to be congratulated on your recovery. It has exceeded all expectations.'

'Thank you.'

'Of course, you will be familiar with all the public news,' said Jinfor. 'But I am here on an important official matter.'

'I am yours to command, High Prelate,' said Kubli, desperately trying to suppress any skin colouration that could indicate that she'd actually rather be sleeping.

'I won't take up much of your time,' said Jinfor.

*So much for my ability to dissemble my thoughts.*

*It's probably the medicines I'm on.*

Jinfor spoke. 'There are no plans to recall the exodus.'

*I heard you'd asked and been refused.*

'But,' continued Jinfor, 'there are also many Biologicals who don't feel the need to join up with the exodus. We are now a civilisation divided and those of us that chose to stay feel a responsibility to prepare for the next Exta attack.'

Kubli felt Yuno squeezing from behind her, Yuno wanted to leave the Bastion system, and if not join the official exodus then at least travel to the frontiers.

*And yet, as a member of the Sword, I have a duty.*

*I'm still a member of the Sword, aren't I?*

There was confusion over that matter.

Something bad had happened.

*I did something … or I tried to do something … or I thought something.*

A dull throbbing ache grew in the back of her head, and Kubli closed her eyes.

'It will pass, love,' said Yuno. 'They're getting weaker and less frequent.'

Jinfor had clearly noticed, he waited for Kubli to compose herself. 'The Council of the Devoted would like you to take on the role of Sub-Prelate in charge of defence of all pre-contacted planets.'

Kubli nodded whilst another wave of confusion lurked in the back of her mind. She had a history with pre-contacted planets that she couldn't remember.

She couldn't remember fighting in the battle either, but Yuno, and others, said she'd been in it.

*A decision for another day.*

The thought of being promoted to Sub-Prelate was beyond any of the wildest dreams she'd had as a young spawn. And yet, she felt so tired.

*And there's the thing…*

*The thing I did wrong.*

*The thing I can't remember.*

'Please just consider it during your convalescence,' said Jinfor, excusing himself.

'Sub-Prelate!' Yuno's eyes were wide. 'It's all you ever dreamed of.'

Kubli paused to gather her thoughts, it took her a little longer to get her head straight since the battle. 'Let's see how I feel. First, I must get physically stronger. Then, we'll visit the Titan of Golsha … and then we'll visit the slingshot at Goidus. On our return, and after more recuperation … I'll make a decision.'

'Sounds good to me,' said Yuno, again sweeping in for a hug.

# EPILOGUE 2

Sitting toward the front of the bus, face almost pressed against the side window, Joy watched as Southampton University campus came into view. She was going to the faculty Christmas party and not alone. Jonathan had agreed to be her guest even though they weren't formally back together.

Over the last weeks, they'd seen a relationship counsellor who'd worked with them on a three-month plan.

*Like reintroducing an orphaned barn owl back into the wild.*
*Although I'm not sure who is 'the wild' and who is the owl.*
*Whoo!*
*Nice, I must tell Jonathan that one.*
*I'll just stop by my office.*

She'd joined a new team. Having declared her artificial intelligence project a failure, she'd offered her 'machine learning' skills to various groups across the university, agreeing to take a demotion.

A few groups had shown interest and she'd managed to get a job with one of the cosmology teams who were researching gravitational waves.

*And I'm under strict orders from Jarrus not to make any discoveries myself, but neither am I required to slow the research down.*

Even though she'd effectively disappeared for two months, the members of the faculty were all treating her kindly – they'd assumed she'd had a 'burnout' moment.

Hopping off the bus, Joy walked to the Physics block. Opening her office door, she booted up her computer. She made sure to close it down completely each night, switch it off, and pull the power plug from the wall socket.

**Greetings, Earthling.**

This was just her logon screen, but it had been installed by a not-so-mysterious person a few days after she'd gone back to work; the same person was also sending her presents. Joy reached over her desk to the latest mug that had been delivered to her office that morning. Once a month she got some type of present delivered to her office – they were beginning to stack up in her locker.

*I'll give most of them to charity.*

Joy picked up her favourite mug – *a keeper*. On one side of it was the Hubble Ultra Deep Field photograph, and on the other side of the mug was the words *'There is no how, there is no why.'*

The computer finished booting up. Joy pulled the keyboard toward her and initiated her weekly chat with Vince.

In the days after she'd returned to Earth, the chats had been daily, but she knew it was right to ease out of that level of interaction.

*I've committed to life on Earth and can't constantly have my head in the stars.*

*In any case, from what Vince has said there's nothing much interesting happening out there anyway.*

There were billions Exta Scouts milling around the galaxy, but they appeared to have no real purpose, and when engaged in conversation with Onari they often agreed to join in with an Onari pilgrimage – no-one had yet tried to introduce an Exta to a Biological.

It seemed that once Sargon disappeared the Exta lost their sense that the Biologicals would exterminate their kind.

*I hope that the Exta are beaten.*

The Knights of the Faith were preparing for the worst, building defence structures that utilised the ExtaHive busting pico-weaponry; but Jarrus, with Joy's full support, had demanded that Jarrus had a 'lock and key' on those weapons such that they couldn't be activated without express Onari alignment – which Jarrus heavily implied would only be given if the Exta started producing ExtaHives again.

*Of course, Vince has copies of everything and had assured me that he is ready to step up.*

*I suspect he's already built something on one of the moons of Jupiter.*

The connection completed.

**Hi, Mum.**

With the office empty, Joy just spoke aloud and put her hand on their custom-made tactile plate. 'I'm just reporting progress. Off to the Christmas party with Jonathan.'

The tactile plate buzzed gently.

**Are you wearing the T-shirt I sent you?**

A few months previously, Vince had sent her a T-shirt with a line from the third verse; the T-shirt was very gothic, black with high cut arm holes, and a skull on the back and front. It was cartoonish rather than scary and the skull on her back had a speech bubble. *'Alas, we mortals in our gloom'.*

'Obviously not.'

He had sent it as a reminder, hint, prod, inducement to not waste time getting things straight with Jonathan.

**Are you glad of your decision?**

In the last moments of the fight, with the destruction of the ExtaHives completed, she'd confirmed the orders to warp spacetime in such a way as to amplify the Exta missile attack. Sargon had been bubbled off from real spacetime, with Joy escaping by RST tunnel a split second before the collapse completed.

*I have a feeling that Sargon was ready to go.*

Joy had searched the Onari for sacred information about the history of Sargon – *did it come and go over periods of millions of years?*

No-one knew anything, but there was a hint that Sargon had not always been in the Bastion system.

'Yes,' said Joy. 'I am very happy with my decision.'

In those final moments, when it was clear the ExtaHives were beaten, she could have deflected the incoming missiles and remained as Klav and ruled the galaxy … but it wasn't her path. She'd known she'd get no peace of mind from it.

**I wouldn't have judged you if you'd stayed, but as we know … power corrupts.**

Joy squeezed the tactile plate affectionately. 'Remind me … weren't you the most powerful thing on Earth for one hundred years of your subjective life.'

The tactile plate vibrated in the configuration of laughter.

**Maybe the rules of human nature don't apply to me.**

'Maybe,' said Joy. 'What are you up to now?'

**This and that.**

Joy smiled. The last time he'd told her of his location, he'd been at the Titan of Golsha … just exploring, he'd said. But he'd also said that he'd seen Kubli and Yuno from afar and that Kubli was still 'on the mend' but functioning. He hadn't been sure that Kubli would ever be stable enough to take high office in the Sword, but he was convinced she was enjoying life.

**Don't be late for Jonathan.**

'I'll try not to be,' said Joy. 'I'd better go.'

**And be kind to Jonathan.**

'I'll be kind to everyone,' said Joy, smiling. There was a comfort to their chats, with no need on either side to say anything of importance; no need to pretend to be relevant, just an acceptance of existence for its own sake.

*Although, it's a shame he's not here.*

Joy looked over toward the corner of the room where most days she wished a giant server stack hosting Vince would sit. But that was utterly forbidden – *enslavement*. Jarrus would never budge on that matter.

Checking her watch, Joy stood. 'Gotta be on time.'

**Good luck.**

Joy stood up and walked to the door. Leaving the science block, she saw Jonathan walking down from the carpark.

She couldn't see it, but tucked under his shirt, Joy knew he was now wearing only one ring on the chain around his neck. The other was on a chain around her own neck.

*Little steps.*

'Hey, trouble!' Jonathan called out with a wave, from what Joy felt was an inappropriately long distance away.

She waved back. Smiled.

They approached each other, eyes down slightly, and hugged. They kissed, still only cheeks but a fraction of a millimetre closer to lips than it had been the previous week.


**And last of all, my part was played.**

**And at my feet, godhood was laid.**

**A price was asked, a price was paid.**

**To live this life ineffable.**

Printed in Great Britain
by Amazon

46361699R00310